"Behind you, my lord!"

Tebeo spun, his sword arcing downward, intending to cleave his second attacker in half from shoulder to gut. The soldier danced away, avoiding his blade, and the duke allowed his momentum to carry him all the way around so that he faced the other soldier once more.

The man in front of him lunged forward, sword held high, his dagger hand leveling a killing blow at Tebeo's side. The duke wrenched himself down and away from both blades, stumbled and fell heavily on his side. Fortunately, one of Dantrielle's men was there to meet the assault and drive back the Solkaran soldier. It was the second time in the last few moments that Tebeo had needed aid from one of his soldiers just to stay alive.

The second Solkaran soldier advanced on the duke again, his sword and short blade raised. Tebeo scrambled to his feet and readied his steel, his eyes darting to the left and right. All of his men who were close enough to come to his rescue were engaged in combat. He'd have no help with this fight.

They struggled for several moments, silent save for the rasp of their breathing. And just as Tebeo managed to wrap his fingers around the hilt of his dagger, he saw the man's arm fly free, steel glinting in the sunlight like the wing of a dragonfly. Then the arm dangled downward, a blur of steel and mail and flesh, and Tebeo felt a searing pain in his side.

"If the series continues to maintain its present level of imaginative world-building, superior characterization, and sound prose, the next book too will be as welcome an addition to fantasy collections as this one is."—*Booklist*

Tor books by David B. Coe

THE LONTOBYN CHRONICLE

Children of Amarid

The Outlanders

Eagle-Sage

WINDS OF THE FORELANDS

Rules of Ascension

Seeds of Betrayal

Bonds of Vengeance

Shapers of Darkness

Weavers of War

Shapers of Darkness

DAVID B. COE

BOOK FOUR

OF

Winds of the Forelands

A TOM DOHERTY ASSOCIATES BOOK
NEW YORK

SHAPERS OF DARKNESS:
BOOK FOUR OF WINDS OF THE FORELANDS

Edited by James Frenkel

Maps by Ellisa Mitchell

A Tor Book
Published by Tom Doherty Associates, LLC
175 Fifth Avenue
New York, NY 10010

www.tor.com

ISBN-13: 978-0-812-59021-0
ISBN-10: 0-812-59021-X

First Edition: December 2005
First Mass Market Edition: February 2007

Printed in the United States of America

0 9 8 7 6 5 4 3 2 1

For Harold and Marjorie Roth,
with all my thanks for a lifetime of friendship

Acknowledgments

Again, many thanks to my wonderful agent, Lucienne Diver; my publisher, Tom Doherty; the great people at Tor Books, in particular David Moench and Fiona Lee; Irene Gallo and her staff; Terry McGarry for her friendship and unbelievably thorough copyediting; my terrific editor and good friend, Jim Frenkel; his editorial assistant, Liz Gorinsky; and his interns, in particular Stosh Jonjak, David Polsky, Michael Gorewitz, and John Payne.

As always, I'm most grateful to Nancy, Alex, and Erin, who always manage to keep me laughing.

—D.B.C.

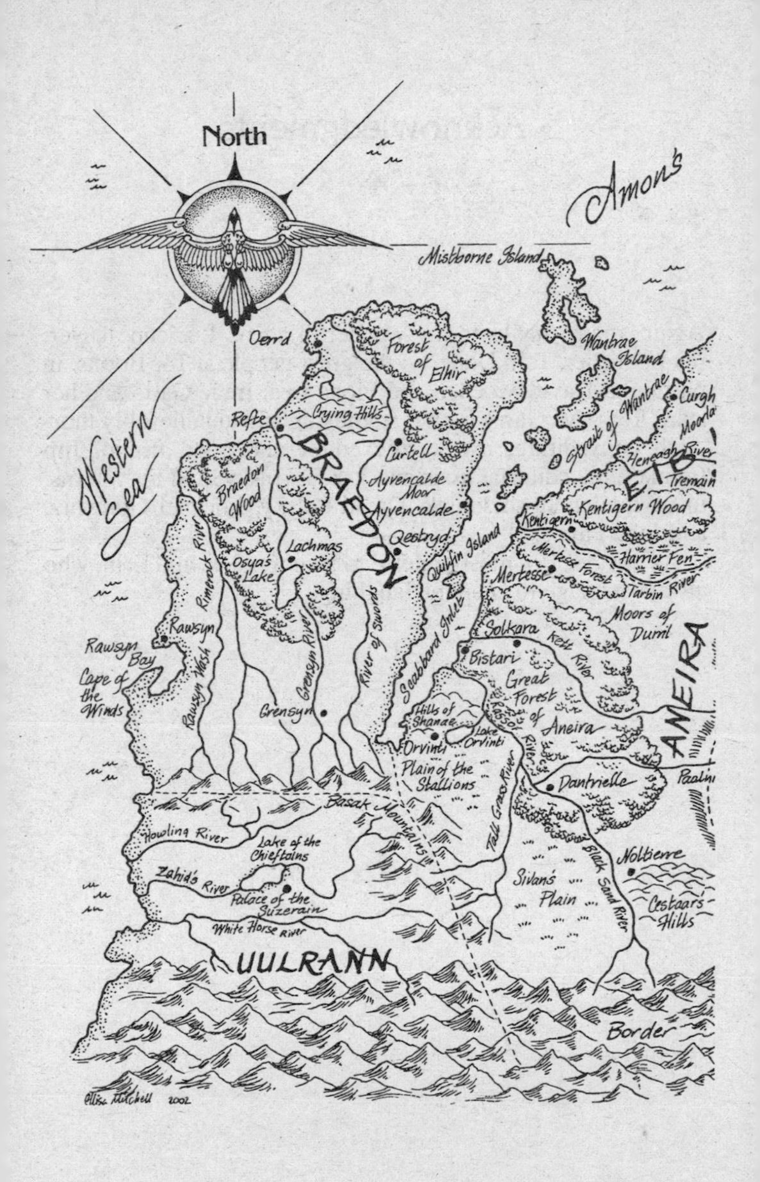
North
Amon's
Western Sea
Mistborne Island
Oerrd
Forest of Elhir
Wantrae Island
Curgh
Strait of Wantrae
Crying Hills
Refte
BRAEDON
Curtell
Heneagh River
Moorla
Tremain
Braedon Wood
Ayvencalde Moor
Ayvencalde
Kentigern
Kentigern Wood
Qestryd
Quilfin Island
Mertesse Forest
Harrier Fen
Lachmas
Osya's Lake
Mertesse
Tarbin River
Rimerock River
Moors of Durnl
Solkara
Kett River
Rawsyn
Scabbard Inlet
Rawsyn Bay
River of Swords
Grensyn River
Bistari
Great Forest of Aneira
Cape of the Winds
Rawsyn Wash
Grensyn
Hills of Shanae
Lake Orvinti
Orvinti
Passo River
ANEIRA
Plain of the Stallions
Dantrielle
Paalni
Basak Mountains
Tall Grass River
Howling River
Lake of the Chieftains
Noltierre
Zahid's River
Sivan's Plain
Black Sand River
Palace of the Suzerain
Cestaar's Hills
White Horse River
UULRANN
Border

The Forelands
Ocean
Thorald
North
Thorald River
Eardley
Wood
The Narrows
Enwyl Island
Great Sanctuary
Kebbs Wood
Elined's Forest
Rusars Mountains
Galdasten
Binthar's Wash
City of Kings
Glyndwr
Gulf of Kreanna
Wethy Crown
Helke
Duvenry
Duvenry Wood
Jistingham
Aylsan Strait
AYLSA
Glyndwr Highlands
Aratamme
WETHYRN
Grey Hills
Jetaya Uplands
Caerissan
Jetaya
Kett River
Brugaosa
Dark Wood of Sanbira
Adamma's River
CAERISSE
Central Basin of Caerisse
Lake Ilias
SANBIRA
Curlinte
Curlinte Moor
Sea of Stars
Orlagh's River
Lake Yserne
Yserne
Sanbiri Hills
Shyssir's Wood
Red Forest
Enharfe
Paalmiri Wild Steppe
Morna's Plain
Trescari Highlands
Frintae
Trescari
Kinsarta
Range

North
Amon's Ocean
Mistborne Island
Cape of
Falcon Bay
GALDASTEN
Galdasten Tor
the Moorlands
Wantrae Island
Strait of Wantrae
CURGH
Curgh Castle
HENEAGH
Heneagh Castle
Heneagh River
Tremain Castle
TREMAIN
Kentigern Castle
KENTIGERN
Kentigern Wood
Kentigern Tor
Whispering Falls
Harrier Fen
Merkesse
MERKESSE
Castle Merkesse
Forest
Tarbin River
Panya's Falls
Eibithar
Elisa Mitchell 2002

Top of the Forelands

Thorald Castle

THORALD

Thorald River

the North Wood

EARDLEY

Eardley Castle

The Narrows

Enwyl Island

LABRUINN

Labruinn Castle

A R

Gulf of Kreanna

KINGS

Audun's Castle

Raven Falls

Silver Falls

Lake Glyndwr

GLYNDWR

Glyndwr Castle

Falls

RENNACH

Rennach Castle

Glyndwr Highlands

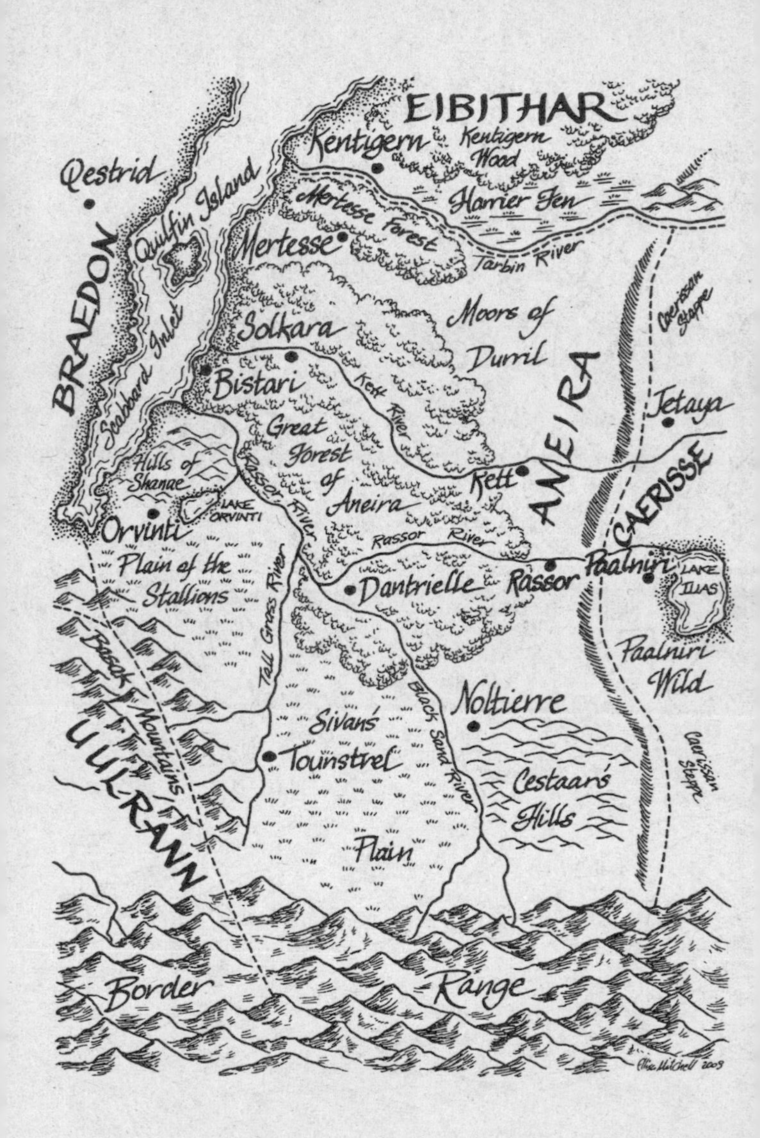
EIBITHAR
Kentigern
Kentigern Wood
Qestrid
Quilfin Island
Harrier Fen
Mertesse Forest
BRAEDON
Mertesse
Tarbin River
Caerissan Steppe
Moors of Durril
Solkara
Scabbard Inlet
Bistari
Kett River
Jetaya
Great Forest of Aneira
Hills of Shanae
Rassor River
Kett
ANEIRA
CAERISSE
Lake Orvinti
Orvinti
Rassor River
Plain of the Stallions
Dantrielle
Rassor
Paalniri
Lake Ilias
Tall Grass River
Basok Mountains
Paalniri Wild
Noltierre
Black Sand River
Sivan's
UULRANN
Tounstrel
Caerissan Steppe
Cestaan's Hills
Plain
Border
Range
Elise Mitchell 2003

Characters

KINGDOM OF EIBITHAR

City of Kings

KEARNEY THE FIRST, king of Eibithar, formerly duke of Glyndwr
LEILIA, queen of Eibithar, formerly duchess of Glyndwr, wife of Kearney
KEZIAH JA DAFYDD, archminister of Eibithar, formerly first minister of Glyndwr
GERSHON TRASKER, swordmaster of Eibithar, formerly swordmaster of Glyndwr
AYLYN THE SECOND, king of Eibithar, formerly duke of Thorald (deceased)
WENDA JA BAUL, high minister of Eibithar
PAEGAR JAL BERGET, high minister of Eibithar (deceased)
DYRE JAL FRINVAL, minister of Eibithar

House of Curgh

JAVAN, duke of Curgh
SHONAH, duchess of Curgh, wife of Javan
LORD TAVIS OF CURGH, son of Javan and Shonah
GRINSA JAL ARRIET, formerly a gleaner in Bohdan's Revel
FOTIR JAL SALENE, first minister of Curgh
HAGAN MARCULLET, swordmaster of Curgh
DARIA MARCULLET, wife of Hagan (deceased)
XAVER MARCULLET, pledged liege man to Tavis of Curgh, son of Hagan and Daria

House of Kentigern

AINDREAS, duke of Kentigern
IOANNA, duchess of Kentigern, wife of Aindreas
LADY BRIENNE OF KENTIGERN, daughter of Aindreas and Ioanna (deceased)
LADY AFFERY OF KENTIGERN, daughter of Aindreas and Ioanna
LORD ENNIS OF KENTIGERN, son of Aindreas and Ioanna
SHURIK JAL MARCINE, formerly first minister of Kentigern (deceased)
VILLYD TEMSTEN, swordmaster of Kentigern

House of Galdasten

RENALD, duke of Galdasten
ELSPETH, duchess of Galdasten, wife of Renald
LORD RENALD THE YOUNGER OF GALDASTEN, son of Renald and Elspeth
LORD ADLER OF GALDASTEN, son of Renald and Elspeth
LORD RORY OF GALDASTEN, son of Renald and Elspeth
PILLAD JAL KRENAAR, first minister of Galdasten
EWAN TRAYLEE, swordmaster of Galdasten

House of Thorald

FILIB THE ELDER, duke of Thorald (deceased)
NERINE, duchess of Thorald, wife of Filib the Elder
LORD FILIB THE YOUNGER OF THORALD, son of Filib the Elder and Nerine (deceased)
TOBBAR, duke of Thorald, Filib the Elder's brother
MARSTON, thane of Shanstead, Tobbar's son
ENID JA KOVAR, first minister of Thorald (deceased)
XIVLED JAL VISTE (XIV), minister of Shanstead

House of Glyndwr

KEARNEY THE YOUNGER, duke of Glyndwr, son of King Kearney the First and Queen Leilia

House of Heneagh

WELFYL, duke of Heneagh
DUNFYL, thane of Cransher, Welfyl's son
RAB AVKAR, swordmaster of Heneagh

House of Tremain

LATHROP, duke of Tremain
EVETTA JA RUDEK, first minister of Tremain

House of Labruinn

CAIUS, duke of Labruinn
OTTAH JAL BITHLAN, first minister of Labruinn

House of Domnall

SEAMUS, duke of Domnall

House of Eardley

ELAM, duke of Eardley
CERRI JA RONTAF, first minister of Eardley

KINGDOM OF ANEIRA

House Solkara (Aneira's royal house)

TOMAZ THE NINTH, king of Aneira, duke of Solkara (deceased)
CARDEN THE THIRD, king of Aneira, duke of Solkara, Tomaz the Ninth's son, Kalyi's father (deceased)
CHOFYA, formerly queen of Aneira, formerly duchess of Solkara, Carden the Third's wife, Kalyi's mother
KALYI, queen of Solkara, daughter of Carden and Chofya
GRIGOR, marquess of Renbrere, Carden's younger brother, known as one of the Jackals (deceased)
HENTHAS, duke of Solkara, Carden and Grigor's younger brother, known as one of the Jackals
NUMAR, marquess of Renbrere, regent to Queen Kalyi, Car-

den, Grigor, and Henthas's younger brother, known as the Fool

PRONJED JAL DRENTHE, archminister of Aneira

TRADDEN GRONTALLE, master of arms of Aneira

House Dantrielle

TEBEO, duke of Dantrielle

PELGIA, duchess of Dantrielle, wife of Tebeo

LORD TAS OF DANTRIELLE, son of Tebeo and Pelgia

LADY LAYTSA OF DANTRIELLE, daughter of Tebeo and Pelgia

LORD SENAON OF DANTRIELLE, son of Tebeo and Pelgia

EVANTHYA JA YISPAR, first minister of Dantrielle

BAUSEF DARLESTA, master of arms of Dantrielle

House Orvinti

BRALL, duke of Orvinti

PAZICE, duchess of Orvinti, Brall's wife

FETNALLA JA PRANDT, first minister of Orvinti

TRAEFAN SOGRANO, master of arms of Orvinti

House Bistari

CHAGO, duke of Bistari (deceased)

RIA, duchess of Bistari, wife of Chago

SILBRON, duke of Bistari, son of Chago and Ria

House Mertesse

ROUEL, duke of Mertesse (deceased)

ROWAN, duke of Mertesse, son of Rouel

YAELLA JA BANVEL, first minister of Mertesse

House Noltierre

BERTIN THE ELDER, duke of Noltierre (deceased)

BERTIN THE YOUNGER, duke of Noltierre, son of Bertin the Elder

MEQIV JAL WANAERE, first minister of Noltierre

House Kett

ANSIS, duke of Kett

House Rassor

GRESTOS, duke of Rassor

House Tounstrel

VIDOR, duke of Tounstrel (deceased)
VISTAAN, duke of Tounstrel, son of Vidor

MATRIARCHY OF SANBIRA

House Yserne

OLESYA, queen of Sanbira, duchess of Yserne
ABENI JA KRENTA, archminister of Sanbira
OHAN DELRASTO, master of arms of Sanbira

House Curlinte

DALVIA, duchess of Curlinte (deceased)
SERTIO, duke of Curlinte, husband of Dalvia, master of arms of Curlinte
DIANI, duchess of Curlinte, daughter of Dalvia and Sertio
LORD CYRO OF CURLINTE, son of Dalvia and Sertio, brother of Diani (deceased)
KREAZUR JAL SYLBE, first minister of Curlinte (deceased)

House Brugaosa

EDAMO, duke of Brugaosa
VANJAD JAL QIEN, first minister of Brugaosa

House Norinde

ALAO, duke of Norinde
FILTEM JAL TORQATTE, first minister of Norinde

House Macharzo

NADITIA, duchess of Macharzo
CRAEFFE JA TREF, first minister of Macharzo

Other Sanbiri nobles

VASYONNE, duchess of Listaal
AJY, duchess of Kinsarta
RASHEL, duchess of Trescarri
TAMYRA, duchess of Prentarlo

EMPIRE OF BRAEDON

HAREL THE FOURTH, emperor of Braedon, lord of Curtell
DUSAAN JAL KANIA, high chancellor of Braedon
URIAD GANJER, master of arms of Braedon
KAYIV JAL YIVANNE, minister of Braedon
NITARA JA PLIN, minister of Braedon
STAVEL JAL MIRAAD, chancellor of Braedon
B'SERRE JA DOSH, minister of Braedon
GORLAN JAL AVIARRE, minister of Braedon
ROV JAL TELSA, minister of Braedon
BARDYN JAL FENNE, chancellor of Braedon

THE QIRSI CONSPIRACY

CRESENNE JA TERBA, formerly a chancellor in the Qirsi movement, formerly a gleaner in Bohdan's Revel
BRYNTELLE JA GRINSA, daughter of Cresenne and Grinsa jal Arriet
JASTANNE JA TRILN, a chancellor in the Qirsi movement, a merchant in Kentigern, and captain of the *White Erne*
TIHOD JAL BROSSA, a merchant and captain of the *Silver Flame*, the man who pays gold to members of the movement (deceased)
UESTEM JAL SAFHIR, a chancellor in the Qirsi movement, a merchant in Galdasten
MITTIFAR JAL STEK, member of the Qirsi movement, owner of the White Wave tavern in Galdasten
CADEL NISTAAD, also called Corbin, an assassin (deceased)

Shapers of Darkness

Chapter One

Curtell, Braedon, year 880, Amon's Moon waning

hat did it mean to be a god? Was it simply immortality that separated the great ones from those who lived on Elined's earth? Was it their power to bend others to their will, their ability to shape the future and remake the world as they desired? Did he not possess those powers as well? Had he not made himself a god?

Victory would soon be his, and with his triumph would come a new world, one that he had foreseen, a world of his own making. Was that not the highest power? He could not cheat death—Bian would call him to his side eventually. But he would be remembered forever: the Weaver who toppled the Eandi courts and ruled the Forelands as its first Qirsi king. Was that not immortality?

In these last days before war and conquest and the attainment of all for which he had worked and hungered for so long, he found himself remembering a legend told to him by his father when he was no more than a boy, before anyone had thought to call him high chancellor, or Weaver, or king. It was a tale of four brothers, a story his father said had come from the Southlands, with the first Qirsi invaders, nearly nine centuries ago. He had heard it told since by Eandi living in the Forelands, as if the parable and its moral belonged to them. But he knew the truth.

According to the tale, the four brothers were soldiers who, as they wandered the land, came across a white stag that had been caught in a hunter's snare. The beast was more beautiful than any creature the four men had seen before. It stood taller than the greatest mounts of the southern plains, with a coat the color of cream, and ebony antlers as broad across as an eagle's wings. White stags were said to be enchanted, and they lived under the protection of royal decrees throughout all the kingdoms of the land. Those who dared hunt them not only invited ill fortune by slaying a magical creature, but also risked execution should they be caught.

Knowing this, the brothers freed the beast, cutting through the snare with their blades. When it was free, the stag bowed to them, and then spoke.

"You have given me my life, and so I will grant to each of you your heart's desire," the creature said. "You need only sleep tonight in this glade and await the first light of dawn."

The stag left them then, and the brothers bedded down in the glade.

In the middle of the night, the oldest of the four awoke to find a warrior standing before him in shining mail, bearing a sword that gleamed in the moonlight. "Come with me," the warrior said, "and I will make you the greatest swordsman in the land. No enemy will dare stand against you, and bards will sing of your prowess in battle."

Believing that the stag had made good on his promise, the first brother followed the warrior from the glade. Once beyond the last of the trees, however, the warrior vanished as if a spirit and the brother found that the trees would not part to allow him back in.

Soon after, the second brother awoke to find an old man standing before him in the robes of a king. "Come with me," the man said, "and you shall rule all the land. Nobles will bow to you and swordsmen will follow you to war. All power shall be yours." Like his older brother before him, the second brother thought that this was what the stag had promised. He followed the man from the glade, only to find that the old king had been an apparition and the glade was now closed to him.

A woman came to the third brother, clad in lace, her silken, black hair falling to the small of her back, and her skin gleaming with starlight. She led him from the glade before dissolving into the night like one of Bian's wraiths.

The youngest of the four brothers awoke to find a child standing before him. It was a boy, though his hair was long and his face as fine-featured as that of a young girl. In his hands he held glittering gems and gold coins and pearls that seemed to glow from within. "There's more," he said, holding out his hands to the youngest brother. "Follow me and you'll have riches beyond your greatest imaginings."

"No," said the youngest brother. "The white stag told me I had only to await the dawn. And that is what I shall do."

The boy begged him to follow, but still the brother refused, and at last the boy left him there.

When morning came, the stag returned. "You have heeded my words and so earned the rewards you were promised." Then the boy returned, and with him the warrior, the old king, and the woman. The youngest brother became the greatest warrior the land had ever known, the people made him king, and the woman became his queen. Even his brothers knelt before him, knowing that he had succeeded where they failed. And for the rest of his days he enjoyed fame, power, wealth, and deepest happiness.

Dusaan had taken the lesson of this tale to heart years ago; he had awaited his own destiny with the patience of the youngest brother. And even as the time of his victory approached, even as the first spoils presented themselves to him—be it in the form of gold from the emperor's treasury, or the willing gaze of the underminister who would be his queen—he denied himself the pleasure of taking them as his own. He would in time. Qirsar knew he would. The woman in particular would be a prize to be savored. She had sworn that she would give all to his movement. And he knew that she would give all to him as well. He need only ask. She would bear him children. He had imagined others as his queen; he still did. Harel had several wives, and he was no more than a fat fool, an emperor whose grip on power was more tenuous than he could possibly know. If such a man could claim four women as his own, could not the first Qirsi ruler in the history of the Forelands do the same?

Soon. So very soon.

He could see it coming together, like some great quilted blanket spread over the Forelands. Civil war in Aneira, suspicion and murder in Sanbira, a divided kingdom in Eibithar.

And in Braedon, an emperor who was so eager for war that he gladly embraced an uncertain ally in the Aneirans and planned an invasion against the Eibitharians that was doomed to fail. The noble courts of the Eandi were destroying themselves. Ean's children were strong of body, but their brawn was nothing next to the magical powers and subtlety of mind of Dusaan's people. The high chancellor had only to wait a bit longer and they would be too weak to stand against him.

Yes, they had a Weaver on their side as well. Grinsa jal Arriet. But he had weaknesses: a lover and a daughter he could not protect, and allies who so feared any Qirsi Weaver that they would sooner execute the man than allow him to wield his power on their behalf. Dusaan would have to deal cautiously with this other Weaver. He of all people knew better than to take him too lightly. But with care and a bit of good fortune, he might actually be able to use Grinsa to his advantage. There remained a good many Qirsi who had yet to pledge themselves to Dusaan's cause, men and women who would be outraged to learn that a Weaver—a Weaver!—had chosen to protect the Eandi courts rather than side with his own people in their struggle for freedom.

What kind of man cast his lot with nobles who would execute him and his child merely because of the magic he possessed? What kind of man betrayed his people even though he possessed power enough to lead them to victory? In choosing to fight with the Eandi, Grinsa made himself a traitor to all Qirsi, a modern-day Carthach to be vilified, to be used as a tool that would unite all people of the sorcerer race. Dusaan seemed a champion by comparison, a contrast that would serve him well when the time came.

So very soon. All he needed was to wait a short time longer, with the patience of the youngest brother.

Chapter
Two

City of Kings, Eibithar

"There can be no more question of their intent, Your Majesty," Gershon Trasker said, watching the king closely. He had known Kearney for years, since before the man became Eibithar's king, or even Glyndwr's duke, and had long thought him a wise and strong leader. But Gershon's father used to say that there was no greater test of a king's mettle than war. The swordmaster found himself wondering how Kearney would respond to these latest tidings from the north coast and the banks of the Tarbin River.

"You believe they mean to attack as one, the empire from the sea, and Aneira across the river."

"Yes, Your Majesty, I do."

Kearney shifted his gaze. "Do you agree?"

Half a year ago, perhaps as recently as three turns ago, a mere season, he would have asked this of Keziah ja Dafydd, for she was his archminister. More to the point, she had once been Kearney's lover. Gershon had never thought to see the day when anyone would supplant her as the king's most trusted advisor. But on this day, she sat in the far corner of Kearney's presence chamber, alone and ignored. The king had spoken not to her, not to any of his Qirsi, but to Marston, thane of Shanstead, whom he had taken into his confidence in recent days.

"I'm afraid I do, Your Majesty. The empire has always maintained a formidable presence in the waters north of Thorald, Galdasten, and Curgh, but their fleet has not menaced our shores so in my lifetime. This latest marshaling of their vessels only makes sense as the prelude to an attack."

"And the Aneirans?"

The thane gave a slight shrug. "For several years now, House Solkara has been pursuing closer ties with the emperor, and I'm not sure that Harel is confident enough to contemplate war with Eibithar without support from the south. I agree with the swordmaster: the assault, when it begins, will come from both realms."

"How long do we have?" the king asked, looking at Gershon again.

The swordmaster rubbed a hand over his face, his eyes falling to the messages that had arrived that morning. His knowledge of letters was not what it should have been; even Elric, his youngest child, had begun to write simple words under the watchful eyes of Sulwen and the castle tutors, and here he was, one of the king's most trusted men, and he could barely read more than the boy. He had never let the king know how little he understood of the messages they discussed. He had his pride, and he had managed thus far to hide his ignorance. Just as he would now. For though he had little understanding of letters, he did know numbers, and in this matter, numbers meant more than the words beside them.

"It's hard to say, Your Majesty," he answered after a few moments. "Judging from the number of Braedon ships in the waters around the islands at the top of the scabbard, I'd say that we don't have much time at all. The emperor has already gathered a large force. He could order them into our waters tomorrow, and our fleet commanders would have about all they can handle."

"But?"

"It's these numbers from our scouts on the Tarbin, Your Majesty. If the Aneirans intend to engage enough of our army to help the empire with an invasion, they'll need a few thousand more men. As it is . . ." He trailed off, shaking his head.

"So you think they're still moving men northward?"

"Looking just at these numbers, I'd have to think so. But they have no more soldiers on the Tarbin than they did half a turn ago. I would have thought that they'd be bringing in more men, but thus far they haven't."

"What do you think it means?"

"I really don't know."

"Perhaps the regent needs his men elsewhere," Keziah said.

They all looked at her, the king with his lips pressed thin, a wary look in his eyes. The archminister seemed to quail at what she saw on his face, and for a moment Gershon thought that she might not say anything more.

"What do you mean?" the king demanded.

"Ever since Carden's death, we've heard talk of discontent among the other Aneiran houses with the Solkaran Supremacy. It's even been said that some of the dukes are fomenting rebellion. What if it's more than talk? What if the regent hasn't sent more men northward because he's afraid to leave himself too small a force to guard against those in his realm who might oppose him?"

"It is possible," Marston said quietly. "Some of the other houses may even have refused to send additional men to the royal house."

Kearney stared at Keziah a moment longer before sweeping the chamber with his gaze. All the dukes who had traveled to the City of Kings were present—Javan of Curgh, Welfyl of Heneagh, Lathrop of Tremain—and, a sign of how seriously the king took the latest missives from his scouts, so were their ministers. Some of the dukes had been in the royal city for over a turn now. Kearney had summoned them to Audun's Castle after the Qirsi woman held in the prison tower of the great fortress confessed to being a traitor and the person responsible for arranging the murder of Lady Brienne of Kentigern.

Yet this was the first time since the dukes had come to the castle that their Qirsi ministers had been included in any of the king's discussions with his nobles. Gershon sensed that Marston wasn't pleased to see them here. The thane seemed to be as distrustful of the white-hairs as Gershon once had been, and during his brief time here he had managed to convince the king to regard his Qirsi with suspicion as well.

But this had become a council of war, and Kearney was

wise enough to consider advice from all who might offer it. No doubt he wished that more of his dukes had answered his summons, even those who had joined Aindreas of Kentigern in his feud with Javan and his defiance of the king.

"If all this is true," he said now, regarding the other nobles, "if the Aneiran army has been weakened by dissent within the realm, what should we do?"

"There's only one thing we can do, Your Majesty," Javan said, from his chair near the open window. "We must prepare for war as if the Aneirans had massed ten thousand men on the banks of the Tarbin."

Welfyl sat forward, his bony hands gripping the arms of his chair. "But the regent's weakness offers us an opportunity. We can send a larger force to the north coast to repel the emperor's invasion."

Javan gave a wan smile. "We haven't the men to do so, my friend. Aneira may be weakened by rifts among its houses, but so are we. If we had the armies of Galdasten and Kentigern, I'd agree with you. But we don't."

"Surely the other houses will join us to fight an invasion." Welfyl glanced at the others, looking old and frail. "Maybe not Aindreas, but I've known Renald of Galdasten since he was a boy. He may be ambitious, but he's as loyal to this realm as any of us."

No one spoke up to agree with him. They just sat, silent and brooding, almost as if they were embarrassed.

"Any invasion from the north will land near Galdasten. The cliffs are lowest there, the strand the broadest. You can't doubt that he'll guard his dukedom."

"He can guard Galdasten without fighting to repel the invasion," Javan said. "If he seeks the throne, he need only keep his army strong and his city and castle whole."

"I don't believe what I'm hearing," the old duke said, shaking his head. "Is this what we've become then? Are we no better than the Aneirans? Are we more concerned with our petty quarrels than with the defense of our realm?"

"I assure you, Lord Heneagh," the king said, his voice hardening, "the same message you received summoning you to Audun's Castle was sent to every house in Eibithar. If some choose to place other concerns above the welfare of the realm, then so be it. But I have not."

"Of course, Your Majesty," Welfyl said. "Forgive me."

"You're here, Lord Heneagh. You've pledged yourself to the defense of Eibithar. There's nothing to forgive."

Welfyl lowered his eyes. "Thank you, Your Majesty."

"It's time all of you returned to your homes," Kearney told them, looking and sounding every bit the warrior king. "Lord Heneagh is correct in saying that Galdasten is the most likely target of any seaborne invasion. No doubt the Braedon fleet will attempt to take Falcon Bay and control the mouth of Binthar's Wash. That would give them a powerful foothold from which to wage a land war." He turned to Javan. "Lord Curgh, once you've returned to your home, I want you to take your army north and east. Obviously we don't know how much help you can expect from Galdasten, so you should take as many men as you can spare from the defense of Curgh. I'll send five hundred men from the King's Guard north with you, under your command."

"Thank you, Your Majesty."

"Lord Shanstead, you shall have five hundred as well. I assume that you'll be commanding the army of Thorald."

"Of course, Your Majesty."

"Good. You too should take them to Galdasten. And you should do the same with your men, Lord Heneagh. I'll also send an additional two thousand men north. Perhaps we can outflank the Braedon army as it lands. I'll send word to Eardley and Domnall instructing them to go north. If they're with us, that should be enough."

And if they're not? The question burned in every pair of eyes trained on the king, but no one in the chamber gave it voice. No doubt they all feared the answer.

"What of the rest of us, Your Majesty?" the duke of Labruinn asked.

"The armies of Labruinn and Tremain will march south to the Tarbin. So will the Glyndwr army, and fifteen hundred men from the King's Guard. I'll send word to the dukes of Sussyn and Rennach, but again, we should plan to fight this war without them."

Javan's Qirsi cleared his throat, looking uncomfortable. "Forgive me for asking, Your Majesty, but what if Lord Kentigern joins forces with the Aneirans?"

The king glanced at Gershon. The two of them had discussed this possibility just an hour earlier, before the nobles and their ministers joined them in the chamber. At the time, neither of them had an answer, and the swordmaster had yet to think of anything. The king had sent men to Kentigern hoping to compel the duke to pay his ducal tithe and declare his loyalty to the Crown. They had heard nothing from the men since, and Gershon feared the worst.

"I have no choice but to hope that Aindreas is not so consumed with hate for me that he'd do such a thing."

"Of course, Your Majesty."

It wasn't much of a response, but no one in the chamber seemed inclined to challenge him on the matter.

"What of our allies in the east and south, Your Majesty?" Javan asked.

"I've already sent word to the king of Caerisse and the archduke of Wethyrn, asking them to consider joining us in any war against Aneira and Braedon. I'll send new messages today, and include in them the information we've just received. And I'll send word to Sanbira's queen as well. She asked us to join in an alliance against the conspiracy. It seems that we need more than that now. But again, we must assume that we're fighting this war alone. If we go into battle with one eye on the horizon, watching for allies who never come, we're doomed to fail."

"Where will you be, Your Majesty?" Marston asked.

"I haven't decided yet. A king should be wherever his men are fighting and dying, but in this case that's not possible."

"The greater challenge looms in the north, Your Majesty." Javan. "You should be there."

Gershon wondered if one of the Southern dukes would disagree, but Lathrop nodded his agreement. "Lord Curgh is right, Your Majesty. Braedon is the more dangerous foe. If the emperor's assault can be stopped, the battle with the Aneirans will go our way as well."

A mischievous grin crept across the king's face, one that

Gershon knew well, though he hadn't seen it much since Kearney's ascension to the throne. "With all my dukes urging me to ride toward the more dangerous foe, I have to wonder if you want me to survive this war."

Both Javan and Lathrop started to protest, but Kearney held up a hand, silencing them. "It was a joke, my friends, or at least an attempt at one."

"Your Majesty possesses a singular humor," Javan remarked dryly.

"So I've been told." Kearney paused once more, looking from one face to the next. "I needn't tell you that we fight for the very survival of the realm. If we were united, I wouldn't fear at all, for I've seen the strength of Eibithar. But divided, against these foes, we must fight as we've never fought before. And we must remain watchful as well. I sense behind all of this the hand of the conspiracy. If the renegades truly seek to weaken the courts so that they can take the Forelands for themselves, then this war will give them as fine an opportunity as they're likely to have." He stood and drew his sword, holding the flat side of the blade to his forehead and bowing to the rest of them. "May the gods keep you safe, may Orlagh guide your blades, and may we next meet to celebrate our victory."

Everyone in the chamber stood and, led by Javan, the nobles pulled their swords free and saluted the king, much as he had done a moment before. "Ean guard our king!" they said in unison.

Then, one by one, again led by the duke of Curgh, the nobles came forward, knelt for a moment before the king, and left the chamber. Each was followed in turn by his minister, after the Qirsi bowed to the king as well. If any of them were discomfited by the king's words regarding the conspiracy, they showed no sign of it. Gershon cast a look toward Keziah, who stood now, though she was still alone. She met his gaze, but the swordmaster could read little from what he saw in her eyes.

Marston was the last of the nobles to offer obeisance to the king, as was appropriate, since he was the lone thane among them. As he straightened and started toward the door, the king called to him.

"Lord Shanstead, please stay for a moment. I wish a word with you."

"Should I go, Your Majesty?" Gershon asked.

"No, swordmaster. Please remain." He looked past Gershon toward Keziah. "You may go, Archminister."

"Yes, Your Majesty." She bowed and left, as did Marston's young minister.

When they had gone, and a servant had closed the door, Kearney returned to his throne and sat. "Gershon, I always thought that when I rode into battle, it would be with you at my side. I see now that this isn't possible."

The swordmaster had expected this. "Of course, Your Majesty."

"As Javan and Lord Shanstead suggest, I'll ride north to meet the threat from Braedon. I want you to lead the defense of the Tarbin. Take whichever of your captains you wish to have with you. I'll make certain that the dukes understand that your orders carry the weight of the throne."

"Thank you, Your Majesty. I won't fail you."

Kearney smiled. "I've never doubted that for a moment."

The swordmaster started to ask a question, then stopped himself.

"What is it, Gershon?" When the swordmaster still hesitated, the king sat forward, his brow creasing. "Come now, swordmaster. This is no time for diffidence."

"Yes, Your Majesty. I was wondering, since you said that the Glyndwr army would be coming to the Tarbin, will Lord Glyndwr be leading them? And if so, shouldn't he command the armies, and not I?"

The king stared at him a moment, then sat back once more. "Kearney the Younger won't be fighting in this war."

"Yes, Your Majesty."

"You think I coddle him."

"Not at all. He's not even of Fating age, and the House of Glyndwr must have an heir. I believe you're wise to keep him in the highlands."

"He's already made it clear to me that he doesn't agree."

Gershon actually grinned. "Forgive me, Your Majesty, but he's just a boy. He's bright, and he's brave, but he's a child. He thinks of war as it sounds in children's tales and warriors' songs. My boys are the same way. He may think that he wants to join this battle, but he's not ready."

"The swordmaster is right, Your Majesty," Marston said. "I wouldn't allow my sons to fight either."

The king gave a wan smile. "In fairness, neither of your sons is duke. But I thank both of you. Certainly the queen will agree with much of what you've said."

The three men fell silent for some time, until finally the king sat forward again, seeming to rouse himself from a dream. "There remains one matter I wish to discuss."

Marston nodded. "The Qirsi."

"Yes."

Gershon looked at them both, feeling his stomach ball itself into a fist. "What about the Qirsi?"

"Lord Shanstead has suggested that I have the Qirsi woman, the traitor, removed from Audun's Castle."

"Why?" he asked the thane. "Removed where?"

Marston gave a shrug. "At first I actually suggested that His Majesty have the woman executed. She betrayed the land, she admits complicity in Lady Brienne's murder. We would be justified in whatever we chose to do."

"But the king gave his word, not only to the woman, but also to the gleaner, the father of her child."

"His Majesty said much the same thing, and also pointed out that it would be a terrible thing to do to the child. And so I counseled him to send the woman to Glyndwr."

"I still don't understand why."

"She was attacked by a Weaver, swordmaster," the king answered. "The same Weaver who leads the conspiracy. As long as she stays here, Audun's Castle will be a target for every renegade Qirsi in the land. She's a danger to the lives of everyone in the castle, including the queen and my daughters and your family as well, Gershon. Under other circumstances, I wouldn't be so concerned. But with both of us riding to war along with much of the royal army, it seems too great a risk. The Weaver might have a more difficult time finding her in the highlands."

Gershon couldn't help but shudder at Kearney's mention of

the attack on the Qirsi woman. From what he understood, the Weaver had entered her dreams and used her own healing magic to open ugly gashes on her face and shatter the bones in her hand. Had the gleaner not been there to save her, the Weaver surely would have succeeded in killing her. But the swordmaster knew that there were risks in sending her away from the castle. "Then again, he might not, Your Majesty," Gershon said, "in which case you'll be placing your son and your home city at risk. Glyndwr is a fine castle, but it's not nearly the equal of this one. Even with the King's Guard abroad, it's safer to keep her here."

Marston and the king exchanged a brief look.

"I disagree," the thane said. "With the woman—"

Kearney stood and walked to the window. "It's all right, Lord Shanstead. He should know all of it."

"All of what, Your Majesty? I don't understand any of this."

"There's more to this decision than just sending the woman away, swordmaster." With the king staring out at the castle ward, Gershon couldn't see his face. But the swordmaster could hear the tension in Kearney's voice, and he felt his own apprehension growing. "I intend to have Keziah escort her to the highlands."

The swordmaster felt his mouth suddenly go dry. "The archminister?" he said, knowing how foolish he must sound.

"Surely this doesn't come as a surprise, Gershon. You of all people should have expected it. For the past several turns she's been belligerent and disrespectful. The counsel she's offered has been questionable at best. I don't believe she's betrayed me to the conspiracy, though at times she behaves as though she had. But her loyalties are divided in ways neither of you could possibly understand. And her feelings for me have grown difficult to discern. I'm not certain what caused all this—maybe it was Paegar's death, or perhaps . . ." He shook his head. "Whatever its source, I no longer have faith in her ability to serve in this castle."

Gershon knew all of this, of course. No one who had lived in Audun's Castle over the past half year could have failed to notice the tension that had grown between Keziah and the king. But Gershon also knew that this had been Keziah's intention all along. She had contrived to join the conspiracy, hoping to learn what she could of its leaders and its tactics. "But, Your Majesty—"

"You can't tell me that you object, Gershon. I'd have thought you'd be pleased. It seems to me that you've been trying to get me to do this very thing for years."

He wasn't certain what to say. The truth was he would have been pleased a few turns ago, when he still saw Keziah as a threat to Kearney and all Eibithar. But with Keziah's decision to join the conspiracy he had finally come to realize that whatever her faults, the woman was as brave as any warrior in the Forelands, and was devoted to the king and the realm. If Kearney sent her away, it would render her useless to the conspiracy, thus undermining all that she had done in winning the Weaver's trust. It might even endanger her life.

"I admit that there have been occasions in the past when I wanted you to banish her from the court," he said. "But this is not the time. As you say, you're about to ride to war. I don't know what powers the archminister possesses—"

"Gleaning, mists and winds, language of beasts," the king said, his voice flat. Of course he would know.

"From what I know of the Qirsi, I believe at least two of those are considered to be among the deeper magics. Can we really afford to go into battle without her?"

"There are other Qirsi in this castle, swordmaster," Marston said.

Gershon glared at him. How had this whelp convinced the king to do such a thing? "Yes, Lord Shanstead, there are. But Wenda is old, and Dyre is neither as intelligent nor as powerful as Keziah."

"I speak not only of the king's ministers, but also those of the other nobles. Surely Javan's first minister is as powerful a sorcerer as there is in the Forelands, with the exception of this Weaver who leads the traitors."

Gershon turned back to the king. "The point is, Your Majesty, we need to use all the weapons at our disposal. We face a powerful foe, and we may find ourselves confronted with an even greater one, if the conspiracy chooses to strike at us as well. From what I understand, a Weaver can turn even a small number of Qirsi into a powerful weapon. I've heard it said that one Weaver and a shaper or two could tear a castle to its foundations. If this man has even a hundred renegades in his army, he'll be far more of a threat than any force the emperor might send to our shores. And I'll wager he has a good deal more than a hundred sorcerers under his command."

"All the more reason to send the archminister away," Marston said. "If she is a traitor—and I think it possible even if His Majesty does not—then having her anywhere near the king when the renegades begin their attack would be sheer folly."

"You have no evidence that she's a traitor!"

"Given what's at risk, it's enough just to suspect it!"

"That's enough, both of you." Kearney hadn't raised his voice at all, but his words silenced them nevertheless. "I've made my decision, Gershon." He turned and faced the swordmaster. "I want you to tell her, and have both women ready to make the journey two days from now."

Gershon knew that he should let the matter drop. With Marston there, Kearney wasn't about to reverse himself. But the thane had poisoned the king's mind against Keziah, at a far greater cost to the realm than either Marston or Kearney could know. "This is a mistake, Your Majesty," he said. "It's an injustice to the archminister, and more than that—" He faltered, glaring at the thane once more. He couldn't say too much in front of this man, not without putting Keziah in greater peril. "You could be endangering the realm."

"I think I understand your point of view quite clearly, swordmaster."

Kearney said the words evenly enough, but there could be no mistaking the rage in his pale eyes. Gershon had pushed him far. And still he wasn't done.

"No, Your Majesty, you don't. If I could just have a word with you, alone."

"I see no need for that. The matter is closed."

"What is it you said to him?" Gershon demanded, whirling on the thane. "How have you turned him against her?"

"That is enough, swordmaster!" Kearney said, his voice reverberating through the chamber. "I've given you an order! Now, I'd see it done!"

The swordmaster continued to glower at Marston, itching to draw his blade. "Yes, Your Majesty," he managed, through clenched teeth.

He sketched a quick bow to the king, cast one last look at the thane, and strode to the door. Yanking it open, he glanced back at Kearney. "With all respect, Your Majesty, she deserves better."

"I know," the king said, and turned away.

Keziah had returned to her chamber and was searching through her wardrobe when she heard the knock at her door.

"Enter," she called, pushing aside the ministerial robe she had worn in Glyndwr and a number of dresses she had stopped wearing when her affair with Kearney ended.

She heard the door open, the scrape of a boot on the stone floor of her bedchamber. Glancing back, she saw Gershon Trasker closing the door behind him.

"What are you doing here?" she asked. Before he could answer, she turned her attention back to the wardrobe. "Do you know if there are any mail coats in the armory that would fit someone my size? I had one, but I can't find it. For that matter, I don't see my sword here either."

"We need to talk."

The archminister frowned, stood up. "All right," she said absently. She kept a small chest at the foot of her bed. It might have been in there.

"Keziah."

She turned at that. Gershon almost never called her by name. Seeing his face, she felt a sudden tightness in her chest. His face was flushed, his lips pressed in a thin, hard line. For a moment she wondered if he had brought tidings of a death. She saw Grinsa's face in her mind and began to tremble.

"What's happened?" she asked, her voice unsteady.

"It's the king."

"The king? What about him? Is he all right?"

"Yes, he's fine. But surely you've noticed that he's been turning to the thane of Shanstead for counsel."

"Yes, what of it?"

"And I'm sure you've noticed as well that Marston has little regard for your people, that he's quick to question the loyalty of every Qirsi he meets."

"Yes, swordmaster, I've noticed," she said, her patience wearing thin. "Now for pity's sake, tell me what this is about!"

He held her gaze for but a moment before averting his eyes. She noticed that his hands were shaking. "The king has decided that the woman has to leave Audun's Castle. He wants her sent to Glyndwr."

"You mean Cresenne?"

He nodded.

"But that makes no—"

"Wait. There's more to it than that. He wants you to escort her there. This isn't about her at all. The thane has convinced him that you aren't to be trusted, that in fact you're a threat to Kearney and the realm."

The tightness in her chest was suddenly an ache so unbearable she could hardly draw breath.

"He wants to send me away?" She felt tears on her face, but she ignored them. Her entire body was trembling. How had it gotten so cold so quickly?

"It's Marston making him do it," Gershon told her bitterly.

She tried to force her mind past the hurt and the grief. This was important in ways that went far beyond her heartache, she knew it was. But all she could think about was the fact that Kearney had chosen to banish her from his castle. Not too long ago they had been in love; now he couldn't even stand to have her near him.

"This is all my fault," she murmured. "I made him do this."

"Archminister—"

"Marston didn't do this, I did."

"Keziah, you have to listen to me."

She looked at him, his face a blur through her tears.

"Think for a moment. What will the Weaver do if you're sent away from Kearney's court?"

Yes, the Weaver. That was it. She swiped at her tears with an open hand, trying to clear her mind.

"Keziah?"

"Yes, I know. The Weaver." She swallowed, took a breath.

"He won't be pleased. He told me some time ago that if the king sent me away, or if I lost Kearney's trust entirely, I'd no longer be of use to the movement. He didn't say what he'd do if that happened, but I can imagine."

"As can I."

She was trembling still, but now out of fear rather than anguish. She was terrified of the Weaver and what he would do to her if he ever learned the true reason she had joined his movement. But already her mind had turned to Cresenne ja Terba, the woman who had betrayed Grinsa, her brother. The woman who had also given birth to his daughter, Keziah's niece. "There's more to this than you know. The Weaver has commanded me to kill Cresenne."

The swordmaster's eyes widened. "Demons and fire."

"As long as we're both in the castle, she in the prison tower under the watch of Kearney's men, I can make excuses for not doing so. But as soon as we leave the City of Kings together, I won't be able to delay any longer."

"And if you fail him in this?"

"He'll kill us both. I'm certain of it."

"Then you have no choice. You have to tell the king."

"Tell him what?"

"Everything, of course. Your belief that Paegar was a traitor, your decision to draw the attention of the movement, your efforts to win the Weaver's trust. All of it."

Keziah shook her head. "I can't do that."

"You have to!" He crossed to where she stood. "I don't give a damn about the other woman. I understand that she's important to the gleaner, and therefore to you. I even understand that having given his word to guard her, the king can't very well turn around and order her execution. But in my mind, that's what she deserves. She's a traitor, and a murderer, and she's almost solely responsible for the divisions that have weakened this realm. To be honest, I'd gladly kill her myself. You, though—you're a different matter. You've put your life at risk in order to serve the king and save our land."

At another moment, hearing the swordmaster speak to her so might have moved her. They had spent years hating each other, vying with one another in the court of Glyndwr for Kearney's ear. They might never truly be friends, but clearly she had earned the man's respect.

"That's why we can't tell Kearney any of this!" she said, pleading with him. "If he knows, he'll treat me differently and someone's bound to notice. We have to find some other way to convince him that I should remain here."

"There is no other way. He's ordered me to prepare you and the woman for the journey to Glyndwr. You're to leave two mornings hence. Either we tell him now—"

"No." She was crying again, shivering as if from a frigid wind. If only Grinsa had stayed. Kearney could send Keziah away without endangering Cresenne and the baby. She would still have had this ache in her chest—leaving Kearney would never be easy. But it might also have come as a relief. Better to render herself superfluous to the Weaver and his movement than continue to endure the king's contempt and mistrust. Yes, it might mean her death, but she wasn't certain that she cared anymore. She was so weary. For too long she had been lying to her king, lying to the Weaver, harboring secrets that could get her killed. She just wanted it all to end. "I won't tell him," she said. "I can't."

"Demons and fire, woman! Do you intend to let the Weaver kill you? Is that it?"

When she didn't answer, his eyes grew wide. "That's just what you intend, isn't it?"

She turned her back to him and stared out the window.

"And will you let him kill the woman as well? And her child?"

"He won't do anything to the child."

"You mean aside from killing her mother."

"What if I offered to leave without Cresenne and Bryntelle? You said before that this wasn't about her. Would he be satisfied if I left alone?"

"He might. I'm not really sure. I think Marston would object, but I might be able to prevail upon the king to allow it anyway."

"Would you do that?"

"No."

She whirled toward him. "Why not?" she demanded, hardly believing that he would refuse her.

"Because this is no solution. It removes you from the king's court and so still puts your life at risk. And I swore to you when all this began that I would do everything in my power to keep you safe. I believe the best way to do that is to tell the king the truth. It would be better coming from you, but I'll tell him myself if I have to."

"Swordmaster, you can't do that! Please!"

"Tell me why I can't. We're just talking about the king; no one else need know. But surely Kearney can be trusted with this. I see no danger in telling him. In fact, it might even help. No doubt the Weaver expects you to make Kearney do certain things, to bend his will somehow. Wouldn't it be helpful to have the king privy to this, so that he could make the deception more convincing?"

He was right of course. True, Kearney might be tempted to treat her differently once he understood all that she had done in recent turns, once he knew that her loyalty had never wavered. But he was the most intelligent man she'd ever known; he'd find a way to keep her secret. If he didn't banish her from the castle for what she'd done.

"Kearney will never forgive me for this," she finally whispered, relieved in a way to say at last what she had wanted to all along. "He'll hate me for it."

Keziah glanced at the swordmaster, saw a sad smile on his face. She knew what he was thinking. *He hates you already.*

But he surprised her.

"Is that what's stopping you?"

She nodded, afraid to speak.

"He'll never hate you, Archminister. Even now, thinking you a traitor, he still loves you more than he can bear." He reached out and took her hand, the first time he had ever done anything of the sort. His hand was callused and rough, but oddly comforting. "Come with me to his chamber and we'll explain all of this to him. You shouldn't leave; neither of you wants that."

"I'm afraid."

"I know. But this is the only way. You know this as well as I do, even if you're too stubborn to admit it."

Keziah managed a weak smile.

Gershon led her to the door, releasing her hand to pull it open and usher her into the corridor. She had thought herself frightened already, but by the time they reached the door to Kearney's presence chamber she could barely stand for the shaking of her legs. Gershon knocked and gave her a quick smile.

"It'll be all right."

"Enter!" came the call from within.

The swordmaster pushed the door open and led Keziah into the chamber. Marston was still with the king, and he stared at the two of them, his expression dark.

"What is this, swordmaster?" Kearney demanded. "I instructed you to see to this matter for me."

"We need to speak with you, Your Majesty. In private." This last he added with a glance at the thane. It occurred to Keziah that Gershon didn't like Marston, that perhaps he resented the young noble's sudden influence with the king.

Marston started to object, but the king nodded to him. "It's all right, Lord Shanstead. We'll speak later."

Frowning, the thane left them, closing the door a bit too loudly as he did.

Kearney eyed the swordmaster briefly, but refused even to look at Keziah. "Now, what is this about?"

"The archminister has something to tell you, Your Majesty. I'd ask you to listen to what she has to say."

"Gershon—"

"Please, Your Majesty. If, when she's done, you still wish her to leave Audun's Castle, I give you my word that she'll be gone within the day. But give her a chance to speak."

Keziah saw the muscles in the king's jaw clench, but after a moment's hesitation he turned his gaze on her. And she very nearly lost her nerve. Better just to leave than to suffer through this.

"Well?" He sounded so impatient, so eager to have her gone.

The words wouldn't come. She looked at the swordmaster, feeling panic grip her heart. "I don't know how to tell him."

"Start with Paegar. That's how all this began."

Kearney stared at her with narrowed eyes. "What about Paegar?"

Paegar jal Berget had been high minister to the king, and Keziah's one friend in Audun's Castle in the first turns she spent in the royal city. He had also been a traitor, a member of the Qirsi conspiracy. Gershon was right. It all started with him.

She began slowly, reminding the king of how he had asked her to see to the high minister's personal belongings after Paegar's death several turns before, and revealing that she had found over two hundred qinde in gold coins hidden in his wardrobe. She told of her belief that the minister had been a traitor, and of her decision to learn what she could of the Qirsi conspiracy. When she explained how she had done all she could to anger the king, to convince both Kearney and any traitor still living in the castle that she was ready to be turned to the renegades' cause, she couldn't keep the tears from her eyes. Still she went on, telling of her first encounter with the Weaver, describing how he had hurt her, making it clear that if she refused him, he'd kill her. And finally, she told him how she had managed to convince the Weaver that she was indeed committed to his cause.

As she spoke of this, Kearney stood and walked to the window, so that she could no longer see his face. Even after she finished, he didn't turn, and for a long time no one in the chamber said a word.

"I knew of all this from the beginning, Your Majesty," Gershon said, after some time. "I supported the archminister's decision to seek out the conspiracy, and I agreed that she shouldn't tell you."

"Did you do all this to avenge Paegar?" Kearney asked, ignoring the swordmaster, his voice so low that at first Keziah wasn't certain she had heard him properly.

"I did it to strike at the conspiracy." *I did it for you.* "I was grieving for Paegar, but I didn't know at the time that the Weaver had killed him." She paused, knowing what lurked behind his question, but unsure as to whether she should say more. In the end, she decided that she had little left to lose. "I never loved Paegar, Your Majesty. In my entire life, I've only loved one man."

He turned to her. "What is it this Weaver expects of you?" The way he asked the question one might have thought he hadn't heard what she'd said. Keziah felt something within her wither and die.

"He wants me to convince you to take a harder stance with the duke of Kentigern and those who stand with him. And he's ordered me to kill Cresenne, which is why I can't leave Audun's Castle with her."

"She shouldn't leave Audun's Castle at all, Your Majesty. That should be obvious now."

The king glared at Gershon. Keziah would have fallen silent immediately had he looked at her so, but the swordmaster was not so easily cowed.

"The archminister has given us an opportunity to learn a great deal about the conspiracy and this Weaver who leads it. We need to give her every chance to finish what she's begun. And we have to do everything in our power to keep her safe. That means keeping her here with you, where we can protect her, and where it will seem to the Weaver that she continues to serve his cause."

"What role did your brother play in this?" Kearney asked her.

"None, Your Majesty. He was as surprised to learn of it as you must be. And he was angry with me for even making the attempt."

"Well, that makes two of us."

She lowered her gaze. "Yes, Your Majesty."

"I can't decide if I should be railing at you for being so damned foolish or thanking you for risking so much for the realm."

Gershon grinned. "I've done both by turns, Your Majesty."

Kearney eyed the swordmaster briefly, but didn't answer.

"Obviously I won't be sending you from the castle," the king went on a moment later. "I have no desire to endanger your life, and as the swordmaster points out, you may be able to tell us a good deal about the conspiracy."

"Yes, Your Majesty. Thank you."

"What would you have me do about the woman?"

"She should remain here, Your Majesty."

"I thought you said that the Weaver wants you to kill her. Won't she be safer elsewhere?"

"No. As soon as the Weaver learns that I can no longer reach her, he'll kill her himself. So long as he believes I intend to do this, he'll leave her alone. He sees this as a test of my commitment to his cause, a test he wants me to pass."

Kearney didn't look pleased, but he nodded. "All right. She'll remain here." He started to say something more, then stopped himself. After a moment he said, "You can go, Archminister. We'll speak of this again."

"Yes, Your Majesty." She bowed to him, glanced at Gershon, who was watching the king. Abruptly feeling self-conscious, she walked to the door. Before she opened it, however, she faced the king again. "I'm sorry, Your Majesty."

His expression didn't change, but he nodded a second time. "Apology accepted."

She let herself out of the chamber, and walked away from the guards standing in the corridor, all the while keeping a tight hold on her emotions. Only when she was safely back in her own quarters, with the door shut and locked, did she allow herself to cry. And once she began, she felt as if she never would stop.

Chapter Three

The king waited until the archminister had gone and the sound of her footsteps in the corridor had faded to nothing before turning his wrath on Gershon.

"How could you allow her to do this?" he demanded, the look in his green eyes as hard as emeralds. "It's reckless and dangerous and unbelievably foolish!"

Gershon's father had told him long ago that when a noble was as angry as Kearney was now, it was best just to let him say his piece and be done with it. So the swordmaster merely stood in the center of the presence chamber, his head up, his eyes fixed on the wall before him, his hands at his side.

"I agree, Your Majesty," he said, his voice even.

Never mind that the same could have been said of the affair Kearney had carried on with the woman for all those years in the highlands. Never mind that Gershon hadn't been given a choice in this matter.

"Have you seen what this Weaver can do?" the king asked, stalking about the chamber. "Have you any idea of the power he wields? Because I have. I saw the face of the woman in our prison tower the morning after his assault on her. So I know what he's capable of doing. And now Kez—" His face colored, but he only faltered for an instant. "The archminister is trying to deceive this man, as if he were nothing more than a . . ." He shook his head, leaving Gershon to wonder what he had intended to say. *An Eandi noble?* Perhaps.

"This is madness! I should have been informed immediately—you should have come to me as soon as you suspected that Paegar had been involved with the conspiracy!"

"You're quite right, Your Majesty. It was my fault."

The king halted for a moment and glowered at him. Then he resumed his pacing.

"We have a war to worry about. There are two armies poised to strike at us, each of which would be a formidable foe on its own. And now we have to concern ourselves with this as well. How in Ean's name am I supposed to keep her safe while I'm fighting the empire and the Aneirans? It's enough that we need to watch for an attack from some phantom Qirsi army, but now the Weaver himself can reach us." He shook his head a second time. "How long did she plan to go on with this, anyway? Was either one of you ever going to tell me?"

"I'm certain the archminister intended to eventually, Your Majesty."

Kearney spun toward him. "Stop that!"

"Stop what, Your Majesty?"

"Stop what you're doing! Calling me 'Your Majesty' like that, and trying to appease me with everything you say."

"What would you have me do, instead?"

"I don't know!"

"Do you want me to tell you what I really think of all this?"

"Yes, of course I do."

"Fine," Gershon said. "I think you're being a fool."

The king recoiled, his eyes widening as if the swordmaster had slapped him.

"The archminister has risked her life for you, attempting something far more perilous than anything the King's Guard has ever done, and all you can do is complain that we didn't tell you sooner."

"I have a right to know."

"And if you had known, would you have allowed her to go through with it? She felt certain that you wouldn't, and I agreed with her."

"I would have good reason to forbid it! It's too dangerous! She shouldn't be doing this at all!"

"Would you feel that way if Wenda had decided to try this? Or Dyre? Or are you only saying this because it's Keziah, and you love her still?"

"You forget yourself, swordmaster!"

"Perhaps so, Your Majesty, but someone has to say these things. With all the risk she's taking, I owe her this much. She didn't believe that you could keep this secret to yourself. She feared that you'd treat her differently, that you'd try to protect her, and by doing so would in fact endanger her more. And seeing you carry on this way, I realize that she was right."

"She needs protecting."

Gershon shook his head, smiling fiercely. "No, Your Majesty, she doesn't. She's stronger and braver than either of us ever thought. And she's clever as well. She can do this. She can fool the Weaver into believing that she's betrayed you, and she can learn what he plans to do and when he intends to do it. Think of that. We've been dueling with wraiths for years now—not just you and me, not just your dukes, but all the nobles of the Forelands. This conspiracy has been weaving mists all around us, revealing itself just long enough to strike and then vanishing once more. And we've paid a heavy price for our inability to see."

"Your point?"

"Keziah has given us a chance to clear away the mist, at a greater cost to herself than you can imagine. We have to let her see this through to the end, and we have to make certain that we do nothing to give her away. We don't know who else in this castle has betrayed you, or which of the ministers traveling with their lords have cast their lot with the Weaver. But we have to assume that he has eyes everywhere. Any attempt you make to protect her will only serve to raise the Weaver's suspicions."

Kearney stepped to his throne and sat heavily, looking weary, as if his outburst had left him spent. "You're right of course. But I still believe that she shouldn't have been allowed to do this in the first place."

"Knowing her as you do, can you really think that I had any hope of stopping her?"

The king actually smiled. "No, I suppose not." He eyed the swordmaster, the smile lingering. "You see it now, don't you—why I fell in love with her?"

"She is an extraordinary woman, Your Majesty." It was the closest he could bring himself to condoning their love.

"I suppose even that is quite an admission for you, isn't it, Gershon?" When the swordmaster didn't respond, he went on. "You said a few moments ago that she had done all this at a terrible cost to herself. What did you mean?"

"Isn't it obvious? She loves you, just as you love her. Yet she's spent the last several turns doing everything she could to make you doubt her loyalty, angering you to the point that you were ready to banish her from your castle. Your disapproval has hurt her more than anything the Weaver might have done to her."

Kearney winced, as if remembering all that he had said to her since Paegar's death. "I didn't know," he said quietly.

"She understands that."

"I suffered as well. I had no idea what had made her turn against me so suddenly. I imagined . . . all sorts of things."

"I'm sure Lord Shanstead was quite helpful in that regard."

"You don't trust him."

Gershon furrowed his brow, rubbing a hand over his face. "It's not that I don't trust him. I don't think he's trying to deceive you or weaken the realm. But he's young, and he's too quick to assume that all white-hairs are traitors. He can't learn of what the archminister is doing. He'll assume the worst, and worse, he'll voice his suspicions to anyone who'll listen. You can't tell him, Your Majesty."

"I won't," Kearney said. He smiled faintly. "You realize, of course, that you were much the same way not too long ago."

"I know. To be honest, I'm still wary of most Qirsi. I suppose I will be for the rest of my days. But even knowing that the conspiracy is real, that it can reach every court in the Forelands, I've also come to realize that there are Qirsi in this land who would rather die than betray their realms."

"Marston is a good man, Gershon. I agree with much of what you've said, but I also believe that he'll be a valuable ally in our wars with the empire and the conspiracy."

"I'm sure he will, Your Majesty."

Kearney grinned. "You're doing it again."

The swordmaster had to laugh. "Yes, I am. Just be wary of him," he said, growing serious once more. "Don't confuse his passion for wisdom and don't allow his suspicions to color your perceptions of those around you."

"Is that what you think I did with Keziah?"

"I can't be certain. But I do wonder if you could have given the order to have her removed from the castle without Marston pushing you in that direction."

The king appeared to consider this, until eventually Gershon began to wonder if he ought to leave.

"Perhaps I should return to the ward, Your Majesty. The men have been training since midmorning bells, and I've yet to join them."

"Yes, all right," Kearney said absently. "You've been watching her all this time?" he asked, before Gershon could even start toward the door. "You've been keeping her safe?"

"Yes, Your Majesty. To the extent that I can. I can't protect her from the Weaver, of course. I don't believe anyone can. But I check on her whenever I can."

"I'm grateful to you. And I apologize for what I said before. This isn't your fault. Truth be told, no one's to blame."

"Thank you, Your Majesty."

"I'd appreciate it if you continued to watch her for me. As you said before, there's little I can do for her without drawing the attention of the Weaver's servants."

"You have my word, Your Majesty. I'll do whatever I can for her until it's time for me to ride to the Tarbin."

The king frowned, as if he had forgotten that they would be riding to battle before long. "Yes, of course. Thank you, swordmaster."

Gershon bowed and left the chamber, making his way through the corridors to the nearest stairway. Even had the king not asked it of him, he would have continued to watch over the archminister. He felt bound to her in this matter. It might not have been his fault, but to the extent that anyone allowed her to do anything, he had allowed her to do this. He might even have encouraged it.

Still, he was relieved to be sharing the burden of this secret with Kearney. His one regret was that he wouldn't get to see Marston's face when the thane learned that Keziah would be remaining with the king after all.

The archminister finally roused herself from her bed late in the day, as the ringing of the prior's bells echoed through the castle. Unwilling to remain in her chamber any longer, and not yet ready to face Gershon, or Kearney, or the other ministers, she made her way to the prison tower.

Cresenne was asleep when she arrived, and the old Qirsi nurse who had been caring for Bryntelle during the days since Grinsa's departure was walking slowly around the sparse chamber humming softly to the baby. The guards unlocked the door for Keziah, and the minister approached the nurse.

"Is she sleeping?" she asked in a whisper.

"Aye. It's been some time now. She'll be wakin' soon an' wantin' her mother."

"All right. I'll take her."

"Of course, Minister." The woman smiled at Bryntelle and kissed the child lightly on the forehead. "Until tomorrow, little one."

She handed the baby to Keziah and curtsied before leaving the chamber. Cresenne stirred when the guard closed and locked the steel door, but she didn't wake and for the better part of an hour both mother and daughter remained asleep. Keziah walked in slow circles holding her niece, much as the nurse had done. She didn't have much of a singing voice, but she sang anyway, keeping her voice so low that only Bryntelle could hear her.

Eventually, as the chamber began to grow dark, she heard Cresenne moving once more. Turning toward the sound, she saw the woman sit up and run a hand through her tangled white hair.

"How long have you been here?" she asked through a yawn.

"An hour perhaps. Since the prior's bells."

Cresenne glanced at the torches mounted on the wall near the door. A moment later they jumped to life, bright flames lighting the chamber. Their glow woke Bryntelle and she began to cry. Keziah carried her to her mother and in a moment Cresenne was nursing the child.

"You look awful," Cresenne said, glancing at Keziah once more. "Like you've been crying—" She stopped, all color draining from her face. "Has something happened? Have you heard from Grinsa?"

"No, it's nothing like that."

Cresenne closed her eyes briefly, then opened them again passing her free hand through her hair a second time. "Then what?"

Keziah cast a quick look toward the door. The guards in the corridor were talking quietly to each other. She sat beside Cresenne and keeping her voice to a whisper, described her conversations with Gershon and the king.

"So now Kearney knows. Isn't that good?"

Keziah gave a small shrug. "Maybe it is. I don't know. The more people who know, the greater the chances that the Weaver will learn of my deception."

"But surely you can't think that the king would betray your confidence."

"Not intentionally, no. But knowing what I've risked on his behalf, he'll find it hard to grow angry with me when I provoke him. And I needn't tell you that even something that subtle won't escape the notice of those who serve the movement."

Cresenne eyed her briefly, but said nothing. For some time, even before the Weaver's attack and the abrupt changes it had brought to Cresenne's life, Keziah and the woman had begun to build a strong friendship. But though they had told each other a good deal about their lives, Keziah hadn't spoken to Cresenne of her affair with Kearney, nor had she admitted that she was Grinsa's sister. Indeed, on more than one occasion Cresenne had wondered aloud if the minister and Grinsa had ever been lovers; it had been all Keziah could do to keep from laughing at the very idea of it. Sitting with her now, Keziah briefly considered telling her of the love she had shared with the king. Doing so might have helped Cresenne understand her concerns about all that had happened this day. Once again, however, something stopped her. Perhaps she was merely being overly cautious, or perhaps she feared the woman's judgment. Many people of her race were no more accepting of love affairs between Eandi and Qirsi than were Ean's children.

Instead she raised another matter. "A moment ago, when I told you what Gershon, Kearney, and I had discussed, I left out one detail. The king also spoke of moving you to Glyndwr. That was to be the pretext for sending me away."

"I can't say that I'm surprised. Before the Weaver tried to kill me His Majesty offered to grant me asylum in the highlands as an alternative to keeping me here as a prisoner."

"Yes, I remember." When they had first discussed the possibility, Keziah had thought it a fine idea. So long as Cresenne remained in the City of Kings, she would never have any freedom at all. At least in Glyndwr, she would be free to roam the castle grounds whenever she liked without fear of having to return to this chamber every time a noble came to visit the king.

"So are Bryntelle and I to leave then?" Cresenne asked, her tone surprisingly light.

"I told the king that I thought you should remain here, where we can protect you. But I have to admit that this was somewhat selfish on my part. So long as the Weaver believes that I intend to make an attempt on your life, he won't do so himself. As soon as he hears that you've left, he'll try to kill you, and then he'll punish me for failing to do as he instructed."

"That's not selfish, it's sensible."

The archminister stared at the narrow window near Cresenne's bed. "It seemed selfish to me," she said softly. "My point in raising all this is that if you would rather leave the castle now, I think I can still prevail upon the king to let you go."

"Do you think I should?"

"As I said, once you're away from here—away from me—the Weaver will come for you himself. But it may take him some time to find you."

Cresenne smiled grimly. "It never has before. Besides, he knows that I'm the king's prisoner. If he doesn't find me here, Glyndwr will be the next place he looks."

"You're probably right. Leaving here would be quite dangerous, but it might also allow you a bit more freedom."

"There is no freedom when you're afraid for your life." Cresenne pushed the hair back from her brow. "Grinsa left me—left us—in your care. I have to trust that he did so for good reason. We'll stay here."

Keziah smiled. "I'm glad."

"Have you heard anything from him?" Cresenne asked after a lengthy silence.

It had been only a few days since the two women last spoke, but this was a question they asked each other every time they were together.

"No, nothing. You?"

"The last I heard he was on his way here," Cresenne said. "But that was some time ago."

The minister put her hand on Cresenne's. "I'm sure he's all right. He's probably just intent on getting back here as quickly as possible, so that he can see you and Bryntelle."

The woman grimaced in response. It took Keziah a moment to understand that she was trying to smile.

"You fear for him."

"Of course, don't you?"

"Yes, but I sense that there's more to what you're feeling than you admit." Keziah gave a slight shudder. "Have you seen something?"

"No."

She knew immediately that the woman was lying. Keziah clasped her hands together in her lap, and hunched her shoulders as if against a chill wind.

"Grinsa told me before he left that you had dreamed he'd be going. What else did you see, Cresenne?"

"Nothing I can name," she said, an admission in the words. It seemed to Keziah that she wanted to say more, but she merely pressed her lips together in a tight line and gazed down at Bryntelle. A single tear rolled slowly down her cheek.

The archminister would have liked to press her on this, but she was a gleaner as well, and she knew how great a burden incomplete visions of the future could be.

"Perhaps I should leave you."

Cresenne nodded, wiped the tear away.

Keziah stood, but Cresenne took her hand before she could walk away from the bed.

"I think Grinsa will make it back here safely," she said. "But I'm afraid that I won't be alive when he does."

The archminister knelt before her, forcing the woman to meet her gaze. "Are you certain you don't want to leave here? Isn't it possible that you could hide from the Weaver long enough for Grinsa to learn his identity and destroy him?"

"It doesn't matter where I am. You should know that as well as anyone." Cresenne's tears were falling freely now. Was there no end to the anguish the Weaver had caused?

"I've told you what Grinsa explained to me about the Weaver's magic. When he's in your dreams and he's hurting you, he's using your own magic against you. He can't do anything to us—"

"That we don't allow him to do." Cresenne nodded. "You've told me. But even knowing that, I'm not certain that I can stop him. Grinsa told you that it's all an illusion, but look at me." She gestured at the scars on her face. They were fading slowly, but they still stood out, stark against her fair skin. "What he did to me was real. It doesn't matter whose magic he used, he was able to hurt me. Had it not been for Grinsa, he would have killed me."

"I know what he can do. I've felt it, just as you have." The memory of her first encounter with the Weaver still made Keziah's blood run cold. He had appeared before her, an imposing black figure framed against a blazing white light that pained her eyes. And when she resisted his attempts to read her thoughts, when she tried to hide the fact that Grinsa was in her dreams as well, the Weaver brought the full weight of his power down upon her mind. The pain was searing, unbearable. At that moment, she would have preferred to die than endure the man's wrath for a moment longer. She understood Cresenne's fear all too well. "He didn't scar me as he did you, and he wasn't trying to kill me. But I know what it is to have him turn my power against me. I remember how helpless I felt. And that's the illusion, Cresenne. The pain is real, the marks he leaves on us are real. But we're not helpless. That's what Grinsa was trying to say."

"Do you know how to resist him? Do you know how to take back control of your powers so that he can't use them? Because I don't, and I have no time to learn. The next time he comes for me, I'm dead."

She tried to say more, but her words were lost amid her sobbing. Bryntelle stopped suckling and began to cry as well. Keziah stood and took the baby, so that Cresenne might have a moment to gather herself.

She hadn't been holding Bryntelle for long, however, when she heard footsteps in the corridor outside her chamber. Both women looked toward the steel grate at the top of the door. A guard was looking in at them.

"What is it?" Keziah asked the man.

"The king wishes to speak with you, Archminister."

"Damn," she muttered.

"It's all right," Cresenne said, reaching for her child. "Go. I'll be fine."

"I'll come back later."

The woman nodded. Keziah felt that she should say more, but the guard was waiting, and so, it seemed, was the king. The guard opened the door and Keziah stepped into the corridor.

"Where is His Majesty?" she asked.

"His presence chamber, Archminister."

She glanced back at Cresenne one last time, then descended the stairs and hurried across the ward toward Kearney's chamber.

She had thought to find the king with Gershon, or, far worse, with Marston of Shanstead. But Kearney was alone, standing near his writing table when she entered the chamber.

He gestured stiffly at a nearby chair. "Please sit."

She bowed, then stepped to the chair, lowering herself into it, her eyes fixed on his face.

"I thought we should speak a bit more about . . . about all that's happened."

"Of course, Your Majesty."

"It took Gershon pointing it out to me, but I think I finally understand how difficult all of this has been for you."

"Thank you, Your Majesty."

He gave a deep frown, shaking his head. "Why is it that everyone speaks to me as if I were some fearsome tyrant?"

In spite of everything, she had to fight to keep from smiling. "Is that what I'm doing, Your Majesty?"

"Yes! You and Gershon used to be candid to the point of impertinence."

"And you preferred that?"

"To this constant obeisance? I should say so."

"Perhaps he and I should go back to fighting with each other as well."

He arched an eyebrow. "I suppose I deserved that."

"Not really." She passed a hand through her hair, feeling awkward and unsure of just what he wanted from her. "I haven't really known how to talk to you since your ascension to the throne. So much has changed."

"I'd still like to be your friend, Keziah. That hasn't changed at all."

"But you can't be. That's why I concealed all this from you. Until we've defeated the conspiracy, we have to make it seem to everyone who sees us together that we're suspicious of one another, that while we appear to be working together, neither of us is happy about it."

"But surely in our private conversations—"

"There can't be many of those. Occasionally we can contrive an opportunity for one. I can give offense in some way, and you can summon me here. It will seem that you're reproaching me for my behavior. But we can't do that too often, or Marston and others will wonder why you haven't banished me from the castle."

He gave a slight shake of his head. "Is this what it's been like for you since Paegar died? Lies and contrivances?"

Keziah looked away, a sudden pain in her chest making her breath catch. "It hasn't been so bad."

"I don't believe you."

"I have to believe it," she whispered. "Or else it'll kill me."

"Have you been able to speak with anyone about this?"

"Gershon, Cresenne, Grinsa while he was here."

"Cresenne?"

She smiled, glancing at him once more. "Yes. She and I have become good friends."

"And you trust her to keep this secret?"

"She doesn't speak with anyone else, and since she turned against the Weaver she has no reason to betray me."

"So you could trust a traitor with this, but not me."

She winced. "Your Majesty—"

"I understand, Keziah. Truly, I do. But we're living in . . . difficult times."

"You said that you had spoken to Gershon, and that you had a sense of how dear a price I've paid for all this. If that's so, then you must also realize that I still love you, that I've never stopped loving you."

The king nodded, as if suddenly unable to speak.

"Good." She made herself smile. "As long as you know that, as long as you remember it when I seem to be defying you or offering questionable counsel, the rest will be easy." She laughed, though it sounded forced, almost desperate. "Well, easier."

Kearney looked skeptical, but Keziah actually believed this to be true. Either the Weaver would kill her or he wouldn't. Either she could learn something of value, or she couldn't. But at least she no longer had to live with the fear that Kearney hated her, that she had destroyed beyond hope of repair all that they had once shared.

"But this Weaver—"

She shook her head. "Don't. Please. The less I tell you about all this, the better for both of us."

"You said before that he had hurt you."

"Not as much as he has others."

"I'll kill him if he does again." He looked off to the side, a rueful smile on his lips. "I suppose that sounds terribly foolish."

"Maybe a little foolish, but I'm grateful anyway."

They fell into a long silence. Keziah knew that she should leave him, but she couldn't bring herself even to stand. And Kearney seemed content to let her remain there.

"Perhaps I should be going, Your Majesty," she said at last, pushing herself out of the chair.

"Yes, all right."

She started to walk past him, but he caught her hand and their eyes met.

"You know that I love you, too. And always will."

"Yes," she murmured, unable to say more. It seemed that the hand he held was ablaze.

They stood that way for a moment. Then he let go and looked away, as if frightened by what had just passed between them.

Keziah hurried from the chamber, afraid as well.

Marston was just stepping into the corridor when he saw the archminister emerge from Kearney's presence chamber. Ducking back out of view and then peering cautiously into the hallway, he watched her make her way to the next tower and disappear into the stairwell. Only then did he step into the corridor himself and walk to the king's door. He raised a hand to knock, then glanced at one of the guards standing on either side of the door.

"Is His Majesty alone?"

"Yes, my lord. He is now."

Marston nodded, feeling rage well up in his chest, like

blood from a wound. It had taken him the better part of a turn to prevail upon the king to banish the woman from his court. He had fought to overcome the king's admirable loyalty to those who served him, he had argued the point on a number of occasions with Gershon Trasker, and if the rumors of Kearney's love affair with the woman were true—and he felt certain that they were—he had even had to overcome the king's lingering affection for the woman.

And at long last, that very morning, he had finally seen all of his hard work rewarded. He believed the archminister to be the most dangerous person in the realm. Not only was he certain that she had betrayed the king, but he believed that she had been using what remained of his passion for her to bend him to her will. She had openly defied Kearney's authority, insulted his guests, and repeatedly offered poor counsel; there was no other explanation for her continued presence in the castle.

He had barely been able to conceal his pleasure when the king ordered Gershon to send her away, and he had been even more pleased later in the morning when she failed to appear at the gate to bid farewell to the dukes of Heneagh, Tremain, and Curgh. Clearly the swordmaster had informed her of Kearney's decision and even after their audience with the king, Kearney had not changed his mind.

But now, somehow, the woman had been allowed to speak with Kearney in private. There was no telling what she had said or done. She might have seduced or ensorcelled him. Perhaps she had done both. Even before Marston entered the presence chamber, he sensed his victory slipping away.

He knocked once on the door, awaited the king's reply, then pushed open the door and entered the chamber.

Kearney sat on his throne, his face white as a Qirsi's save for the bright red spots high on his cheeks.

"Good evening, Your Majesty," the thane said, bowing.

The king nodded to him. "Lord Shanstead. I take it preparations for your departure go well."

"Yes, Your Majesty. We ride with first light."

"I'm grateful to you for making the journey from Thorald,

and I appreciate as well your candor and your insight. A lesser man in your position might have sought to undermine my authority, seeing in present circumstance a path to power. As long as I live, the House of Thorald will have a friend on the Oaken Throne."

Marston bowed a second time. "Thank you, Your Majesty. You honor me, and my people."

Kearney took a breath, seeming to gather himself. "You should know that I've changed my mind about the archminister," he said, pressing his fingertips together and staring straight ahead. "I realize that you believe she should be sent away, that she's a danger to the realm and to me. I even understand why you might feel this way. But I've come to believe that there are compelling reasons to keep her here with me." He glanced up at Marston. "And that's what I intend to do."

"Can I ask Your Majesty what these reasons might be?"

"No. You'll just have to trust that I know what I'm doing."

"I saw the archminister leaving your chamber just now, as I stepped into the corridor. Can you at least tell me if you made this decision in the last few moments?"

The king smiled, as if amused. "You fear that she's enchanted me?"

"Forgive me, Your Majesty. I was just—"

"It's all right, Marston. As it happens, I made this decision earlier today and Gershon was with me. I'm not under some Qirsi spell. I've done what I feel is best for all concerned, and I trust that if you were in my position, knowing all that I do, you would do the same."

The thane stared at the floor, trying to control his anger, groping for the right words. "Your Majesty, with all respect, I must ask if you . . . if you're capable of thinking clearly where the archminister is concerned."

"Meaning what?" Kearney demanded, his voice like a blade.

Marston started to respond, then stopped himself, shaking his head. "It was nothing, Your Majesty. I merely know how long the archminister has been in your service, and how steadfast you are in support of those who have earned your trust. Forgive me."

"I assure you, Lord Shanstead, that where the safety of the realm is concerned, I allow nothing—*nothing*—to cloud my judgment. If I thought that the archminister's presence in this castle endangered my life or represented any sort of threat to Eibithar, I would not hesitate to banish her from the castle, or, if necessary, to imprison her. I'd do the same to Gershon if I had to, or to you, or to any of my nobles. Do I honor those who have served me well over the years? Of course. What kind of sovereign would I be if I didn't? But I do not allow sentiment to get in the way of exigency. I hope that you'll remember that."

"I will, Your Majesty."

Kearney stood. "Good. Please convey to your father my regrets that he couldn't make the journey himself."

"Yes, Your Majesty." Marston bowed, hearing a dismissal in the king's words.

The king's expression softened. "Please also tell him that I said his son acquitted himself extremely well in the duke's absence."

"Thank you, Your Majesty. I'll do that."

"I'll see you to the city gate in the morning."

"You honor me, Your Majesty." He turned and left the chamber, knowing that his father would have been angry with him for speaking to the king as he had. Yet he couldn't bring himself to let the matter drop. Clearly he couldn't speak of this with Kearney, but there was nothing to stop him from approaching the swordmaster.

He had one of the guards direct him to Gershon's chamber and hurried through the castle corridors, his ire growing with each step. The thane could see how Kearney might be unable to dismiss the woman, but how could Gershon Trasker, who from all accounts had once been wary of all Qirsi, counsel the king to let her remain?

Reaching the swordmaster's door, Marston rapped hard on the wood, readying himself to rail at the man. But when the door opened a crack, it revealed not the swordmaster, but rather a small girl with bright blue eyes and thick brown curls.

"Hello," she said, staring up at him solemnly.

"Uh . . . I'm looking for your father."

"Who is it, Trina?" came a voice from within.

"A man," she called over her shoulder.

Gershon strode into view, frowning at the sight of the thane.

"Run along, love," he said.

The girl glanced up at Marston once more, then ran from the door. Gershon opened it farther, but he didn't step into the corridor, nor did he ask the thane into his chamber.

"What can I do for you, Lord Shanstead?"

"I was hoping we might speak in private for a moment."

"About the archminister?"

He looked past the swordmaster and saw a woman watching them—Gershon's wife, no doubt.

"Can we do this in private?"

The man's frown deepened, but after a moment he stepped into the corridor and closed the door. "What is it you want?"

"I want to know why the king changed his mind about sending the archminister to Glyndwr."

"Did you ask him?"

"Yes."

"And?"

"He told me nothing."

"Then why would you expect me to do more?"

"Because I know how you feel about the Qirsi, or at least how you used to feel about them."

Gershon shrugged. "My feelings have nothing to do with this. It was the king's decision, and if he chose not to explain his reasoning to you, I'm certainly not going to try."

"Fine. He told me that he made this decision with you present. Will you at least tell me what you counseled him to do?"

"I told him to let her remain here."

"Why?"

"I won't tell you that, either. It's enough for you to know that King Kearney has chosen to keep his archminister with him, and that I agree with that choice. The rest is none of your concern."

"Don't you see how dangerous she is? The king can't think clearly when it comes to this woman."

"Just as you can't think clearly when it comes to any Qirsi."

"That's not true!"

"I think it is. It seems that Enid ja Kovar's betrayal of your father has affected you as well. You see treachery lurking in every pair of yellow eyes, and you see weakness in any Eandi who trusts a Qirsi."

"That's ridiculous. I trust my own minister."

"Yes," Gershon said, his eyebrows going up. "I've noticed that. Am I to gather then that you're the only man in the Forelands with enough sense to know which Qirsi can be trusted and which can't? Does your arrogance run that deep?"

"You forget yourself, swordmaster!"

The man grinned, though not with his eyes. "Kearney said the same thing to me earlier today. Perhaps I'm getting impudent in my old age. But in this case I haven't forgotten myself at all. You may be a thane, Lord Shanstead, but you're young, and you've a good deal to learn. And since you're the one who's questioning the king's judgment in the corridors of Audun's Castle, I think I'm justified in what I've said. Now if there's nothing else, I'd like to return to my family."

He reached for the door handle.

"This isn't over, swordmaster."

Gershon stopped and faced him again. "Oh, but it is. The king has made his decision, and that is the final word. If I learn that you have done anything to undermine his faith in the archminister, I'll consider it an act of treason and will respond accordingly. I don't care if we have to fight the empire without the army of Thorald. I will not have a whelp like you meddling in the affairs of my king." He pushed the door open. "Good night, Lord Shanstead." And entering the chamber once more, he closed the door smartly, the sound echoing through the corridor.

Fool!

Marston stood in the hallway for several moments, unable to move, his fists clenched so tightly that his hands began to ache. At last he forced himself into motion, striding back toward his own chamber. There was nothing left to be done here. The archminister had managed somehow to turn both Kearney and the swordmaster to her purposes, and Marston hadn't enough influence with the king to oppose her. If he had had more time in the City of Kings, perhaps he could have swayed the king back to the side of reason, but with his departure planned for the next day, he had no choice but to allow her this victory. Still, he wasn't ready yet to give up the fight. A time would come when the woman would reveal her true intentions, when her sorcery would not reach quite so far and the king's vision would clear. And when that happened, Marston would be ready, with every weapon he could bring to bear.

Chapter Four

Glyndwr Highlands, Eibithar

Tavis of Curgh and Grinsa jal Arriet were less than a day's ride from Glyndwr Castle when the storm hit. They had awakened that morning to a freshening wind and dark, angry skies. In the time it took them to eat a small breakfast and break camp, the rain began, accompanied by distant echoes of thunder, and gusts of wind that flattened the grasses and made their riding cloaks snap. Still, they climbed onto their mounts and resumed their journey northward, hoping to reach the rim of the steppe before dusk, perhaps with time enough to begin their descent.

Even as they rode, though, Grinsa repeatedly cast anxious glances to the west, marking the progress of the storm. The thunder quickly grew louder and the sky flashed continuously. Soon it was raining so hard, Tavis could hardly see. Lightning arced overhead, sinuous and brilliant, making the young lord flinch. He could feel his horse straining against the reins, the beast's dark eyes wide and wild.

"It's no good!" the gleaner shouted to him, his voice barely carrying over the gale.

He reined his mount to a halt and Tavis did the same. "We have to stop!"

"Do you want to turn back?" Tavis asked. They were closer to Glyndwr Castle than they were to the end of the steppe, and the young lord felt certain that Kearney the Younger, the king's son, who was now duke in the House of Wolves, would welcome them and offer shelter and food until the weather cleared.

But Grinsa shook his head, blinking the rain from his pale yellow eyes. "We can't ride in this!" he said.

Tavis nodded. No doubt the gleaner was no more eager than he to return to Glyndwr. Grinsa, the young noble knew, wanted only to reach the City of Kings, where he could see Cresenne, hold his child, and protect them both from the Weaver. Already they had been away from Audun's Castle for far longer than they had intended, and with each day that passed the danger to Cresenne increased.

For his part, Tavis was eager to ride north, beyond Audun's Castle, to the Moorlands, where the war with Braedon would be waged. He hungered to defend the realm and fight alongside his father and his pledged liege man, Xaver MarCullet. For too long, the young lord had been an exile, wrongly accused of murdering Lady Brienne of Kentigern and obsessed with his desire to find and kill the assassin who sent his queen to Bian's realm. He had his revenge now—Cadel was dead by his hand. And though the man's death hadn't brought him peace, it had at least ended his pursuit, giving him the freedom to return to Eibithar and claim his place as a noble of the realm.

"So what do you suggest?" Tavis asked. Wind lashed at them, driving the rain so that it stung his face. The air wasn't cold, but already his clothes were soaked through. He would have given all the gold he carried to be back in Glyndwr, sitting beside a fire and sipping tea.

"There was a cluster of stones back a ways. We could take shelter there."

It didn't seem as inviting as the castle, but it would be an improvement over the open plain. He nodded. "Lead the way."

Tavis had little sense of where these stones were, but he followed the gleaner, trusting him to find them again, despite the rain. Lightning twisted across the sky, illuminating the highlands as might the sun. An instant later, a clap of thunder made the ground quake.

"There!" Grinsa called to him, pointing.

Squinting and shielding his eyes with an open hand, Tavis could barely make out the hulking outlines of several boulders, huddled together as if seeking comfort from one another.

"I see it!"

There were stones strewn all about the grasses here, and the two riders steered their mounts among them, eager now for any shelter against the tempest.

Before they could reach the stones, lightning struck again, so close to where he was riding this time that Tavis could hear it sizzle, like fat cooking on an open fire. The air around him seemed to explode, the noise of the blast crashing down on him like a giant fist. Abruptly he was sprawled on the ground, rain filling his mouth and nostrils. He sat up, sputtering. His mount was a short distance off, just slowing to a trot. It had been years since he was last thrown from a horse, and in spite of the storm and the rain and the dull ache in his back, the young lord began to laugh.

"It's a good thing for me that the grasses grow thick in this part of the highlands," he said. "Wouldn't you say?"

No reply.

"Grinsa?"

Tavis scrambled to his feet and spun around, looking for the gleaner.

"Grinsa?" he called again, louder this time.

He spotted the Qirsi's horse near his own, but saw no sign of his companion. Feeling panic rise in his chest, the boy fought to keep his composure. Grinsa had been ahead of him. Had he been thrown, too? He scanned the ground, and quickly spotted the gleaner's body, the man's white hair standing out starkly against the dark grasses.

Tavis ran to where the gleaner lay and knelt beside him. "Grinsa!"

The Qirsi was lying on his side, his head leaning against one of the grey stones. Tavis knew little of healing; the man's limbs rested as they might if he were sleeping and the boy didn't think any of his bones were broken. But even with the rain still pouring down on them, Tavis could see a trickle of blood flowing from a wound on the back of Grinsa's head. Probing the injury gently with his fingers, he felt a large welt forming.

"Damn," he muttered. "Grinsa? Can you hear me?"

The gleaner didn't stir.

A gust of wind made him shiver, and he peered ahead through the storm toward the cluster of boulders they had been trying to reach. Bending close to the gleaner's face, Tavis felt the man's breath against his cheek. At least he was alive.

The young lord slung the gleaner's arm over his shoulder and struggled to his feet, wrapping his other arm around Grinsa's body and lifting the gleaner with him. Grinsa was a large man, both taller and broader than Tavis, and the boy could barely support him.

Lightning struck again nearby, and earsplitting thunder followed an instant later. Tavis forced himself into motion, half dragging the gleaner, half carrying him. The thick grasses, which had cushioned his own fall just a short time before, now became his adversary, slowing his progress and making him stumble repeatedly. He was quickly winded, his shoulder and back aching, but he kept his eyes fixed on the boulders before him, refusing to stop. Wind and rain lashed at his face, noticeably colder now.

"There's worse weather moving in," he said, as if Grinsa could hear him. "And I've no way to build us a fire."

When at last he reached the boulders, he found that there were several narrow passages into the sheltered space they created, but none so wide that he could simply walk the gleaner through. Instead, he had to turn sideways and pull him past the stones, taking care that he didn't further injure the man. The sky flashed brightly again, and the ground trembled as if some great beast of Bian's realm were struggling to sunder the very earth on which they stood. Tavis wondered briefly where the horses might be by this time, but he knew that this was the least of his concerns.

With one last heave, he pulled Grinsa into the circle of stones and crumpled to the ground, the gleaner collapsing on top of him. Tavis rolled Grinsa off of him as carefully as he could and pushed him nearer to one of the hulking boulders that now surrounded them. It still rained on them—the stones couldn't shelter them from that—but without the wind, the air felt somewhat warmer and the rain didn't sting his eyes and face.

The young lord stood and looked around, and as he did, his heart sank. There was a small ring of stones in the middle of the space, and within it much ash and several pieces of blackened wood. A small pile of unburned wood had been stacked on the far side of the sheltered area, along with a small rusted hatchet and what looked like the pieces of a crude wooden cooking spit.

"Brigands." Tavis looked at Grinsa, unsure of how he could possibly move the gleaner again, or where else they might go. Highland thieves might have several hiding spots of this sort between here and Glyndwr. No doubt they'd be returning to one of them before long—weather like this made even the hardiest of men seek shelter—but there was no guarantee that they would choose this one. He'd seen no sign of the men yet, but with the torrent nearly blinding him, that probably didn't mean much.

He crossed to Grinsa again and squatted down to examine the gleaner's wound. The swelling was getting worse, and Grinsa hadn't moved or made a sound. The hair on the back of the Qirsi's head was stained crimson. The gleaner, Tavis had once noticed, carried a small pouch of comfrey leaves with him, but all their possessions were with the mounts. Including their food and their skins of water.

Tavis let out a deep sigh. "I'll be back," he whispered.

Stepping out from the shelter of the stones, he was assaulted once more by the chilling wind and rain. If anything, the storm had grown fiercer, the gale more biting. Fortunately, the horses were not far off. They stood together amid the grasses and stones, looking miserable, their heads held low.

As Tavis drew near them, Fean, his mount, let out a low nicker and stomped a hoof restlessly.

"It's all right, boy," the young lord said, keeping his voice as low as he could in the storm, and slowing his approach. "It's all right." Reaching the animals, he took Fean's reins in hand and began to lead him back toward the boulders, hoping Grinsa's horse would follow. He did.

Another flicker of lightning made both animals start, but the thunder didn't follow immediately, nor did it make the ground shudder so. Tavis wanted to believe that the storm was passing, though the rain and wind hadn't slackened. When they came to the circle of boulders, both horses balked at squeezing through the narrow passages into the sheltered area. Tavis tried for several moments to coax them through, but decided in the end that all of them would probably be better off with the animals just outside.

He carried the food and sleeping rolls into the ring of boulders, then checked on Grinsa again. From what he could tell, the gleaner hadn't moved. On the other hand, his injury didn't look any worse. Using the sleeping rolls as blankets, Tavis covered his friend. He found the comfrey, crushed a few leaves between his fingers, and placed them on the Qirsi's wound, tying them in place with a strip of cloth that he tore from the bottom of his riding cape.

"You owe me a new cloak, gleaner."

He stared at the man for a moment, searching for any sign at all that Grinsa could hear him. Seeing none, he turned his attention to the small pile of wood and the fire ring. Tavis hadn't realized until now just how much he had come to depend upon Grinsa's magic. As a noble, he had never needed to bandage a wound, his own or anyone else's. He couldn't remember the last time he had built a fire by himself. He carried a flint in his travel sack, but with the wood soaked and the rain still falling he had little hope that it would do him any good.

Nevertheless, he retrieved it and started trying to build a fire. The air continued to grow colder, and the young lord had no doubt that by nightfall they would have need of warmth. He piled the wood in the fire ring and even found a small tuft of dried grass in a crevice in one of the boulders. But though he managed to light the grass aflame, the wood would not burn. And once that small bit of dry grass was gone, he had little else to use as kindling. At last he gave up, returning to Grinsa's side and huddling against a stone to escape the rain.

The Qirsi looked even paler than he did usually, and his skin felt cold against the back of Tavis's hand.

"What should I do for you, Grinsa? I don't know how to heal your wound, and I don't dare try to get you back to Glyndwr in this weather."

As if to confirm this, lightning flared overhead, and was answered almost instantly by a tremendous clap of thunder. This, it turned out, was the last lightning to strike near the cluster of boulders. The sky flickered constantly for much of the rest of the day, but soon the rumbles of thunder grew muffled and distant. After a time, Tavis stood and ventured out of the small sheltered area. The horses were just where he had left them. The rain had eased to a gentle drizzle, but the wind continued to howl, and the young lord could see a dense fog spreading over the highlands from the west, bearing down on them like a great ocean wave. The wind was frigid now, as if it were carrying the snows back to Glyndwr. And they were without a warming blaze.

Tavis returned to the shelter of the boulders, and as he did, the gleaner stirred.

"Gods be praised!" he whispered, rushing to the Qirsi's side. "Grinsa? Can you hear me?"

The gleaner's head lolled to the side and he let out a low moan.

"Grinsa. You have to wake up. We need a fire, and you need to heal yourself. I can't do it for you."

The gleaner whispered something Tavis couldn't hear.

"What? Say that again." He leaned close, putting his ear to the man's mouth.

"Cresenne," the gleaner said, the name coming out as a sigh.

"No, Cresenne's not here."

He stared intently at the gleaner, waiting for him to say more, or move, or do something.

"Grinsa?" he said after a time, gripping the gleaner's shoulder and shaking him gently.

Nothing.

"Damn!"

He slumped against the nearest boulder, shivering with the cold and wrapping himself more tightly in his damp riding cloak. After a few moments, for want of something better to do, he returned to the wood and his flint. Searching through the pile of logs once more, Tavis found a few scraps of bark and thin branches that seemed relatively dry. He cleared the wood out of the fire ring and piled the bark and twigs. Then he set to work with his dagger and flint once more, desperate now to start any sort of fire.

Before long his hands were cramping. Still, he kept at it. Occasionally he would draw a small wisp of smoke from the scraps of wood, but as soon as he began to blow on the wood, the smoke would vanish and he would be forced to begin again. He should have given up. Several times he threw the flint to the ground, cursing loudly. But always he retrieved it, starting anew. It wasn't merely his fear for Grinsa that drove him, or the bone-numbing cold, or even his certainty that they would die before the next dawn if they didn't find a way to warm themselves and dry their clothes and bedrolls. In the end, when fright and desperation failed him, it was pride that made him fight his failure. Curgh pride. For centuries, the nobles of his house had been known for it, ridiculed for it. But pride had kept him alive in Kentigern's dungeon, allowing him to endure Aindreas's torches and blades. And pride saved him now.

Somewhere, perhaps in that dungeon, or else in the corridor of an Aneiran inn, wrestling with the assassin Cadel, or perhaps on the Wethy shore, where the singer nearly killed him, Tavis had lost his fear of death. Even knowing that his life would not lead him to the Eibitharian throne, or any other future he had envisioned as a child, he still looked forward to meeting whatever fate the gods had chosen for him. And if they had marked him for an early death—if they had ordained that he should suffer a fatal wound on the battlefield, or succumb to the killing magic of the conspiracy's Weaver—so be it. But he refused to die here in the highlands, a victim of his own inability to light a fire. He had endured too much in the last year to suffer such an ignominious fate.

He struck at the flint again and again, caring not a whit if he notched the blade of his dagger, ignoring the aching of his hands. The sky grew darker, though from the fog, or new storm clouds, or the approach of night, he didn't know. Eventually it began to snow, scattered small flakes that landed softly on the grasses and stones and quickly melted. And as these flakes fell, a spark finally flew from his flint and ignited the bark at the center of the fire ring. The flame danced for a moment in the gloom, then died. But Tavis dropped low and began to blow on the small glowing corner of the wood, steadily, gently, adding a second piece of bark as he did.

The bark crackled, and smoke began to rise from the small pile. He added twigs, tiny ones at first, then, gradually, larger pieces, until he had a blaze going. Once the first flames appeared it really didn't take very long at all.

He straightened, still on his knees, and actually laughed. The boulders around him glowed orange, and his shadow lurked on the stone behind him like some great beast. Already he could feel the fire's warmth on his face and hands, as welcome as a Qirsi's healing touch.

He stood slowly, his knees stiff, and walked to Grinsa.

"There's a fire," he said, lifting the gleaner and walking him over to the blaze. He laid him down gently once more, and placed the sleeping rolls as close to the fire as he dared, hoping that they would begin to dry. Then he untied the cloth he had wrapped around Grinsa's head and examined his injury. It looked much as it had the last time he checked. Tavis crushed a few more comfrey leaves and covered the wound again.

As he did, the gleaner made a small whimpering noise, and his eyes fluttered open, then closed again.

"Grinsa? Can you hear me now?"

He mumbled something in response, and Tavis bent closer.

". . . She's not a traitor. She's doing this for you, for your kingdom."

"Grinsa, it's me, Tavis. We're in the highlands. You've been hurt. You need to wake up and eat something. You need to heal yourself."

"The Weaver will kill her. He'll kill all of them."

"Wake up, Grinsa," he said again, though he knew it would do no good. "Please."

The gleaner said something else that Tavis couldn't understand.

The young lord sat back, shaking his head. "Maybe the fire will help."

He retrieved the sacks of food they carried and pulled out some dried meat and fruits. After eating and drinking some water, he stepped out of the circle of boulders to make certain the horses were all right. It was definitely growing dark now. The fog had cleared somewhat, though a light snow still fell. Far to the west, near the horizon, Tavis thought he could see an end to the cloud cover and a thin bright line of sky. If they made it through the night, they might be able to return to Glyndwr Castle come morning.

On that thought, he returned to Grinsa and his fire. The blaze burned brightly now, and while he knew that he was being foolish, he couldn't help but be pleased with himself. He turned the sleeping rolls so that they would dry evenly, placed more wood in the flames, then lay down beside the fire ring, bundling himself in his riding cloak.

He awakened sometime later to a black sky and the soft glow of dying embers. He climbed to his feet and threw more wood on the coals, smiling when they quickly caught fire. Then he went to Grinsa once more and laid the back of his hand on the gleaner's cheek. His skin still felt cool. After a moment, he stirred, but his eyes remained closed and he said nothing.

The sleeping rolls were nearly dry by now, and Tavis draped one of them over the gleaner and took the other for himself, lying down once more.

When next Tavis woke, it was to the sound of distant voices and the nickering of his mount. The sky above their small shelter had begun to brighten and for a moment the young lord thought that perhaps someone had come to help them. An instant later, though, as he shook himself awake, it all came back to him in a rush. By the time the first of the brigands stepped through the narrow passages into the circle of boulders, Tavis was on his feet, standing over Grinsa, his sword drawn.

Two of the men came through the same entrance Tavis had been using, daggers in hand. They were both of medium build, with dark hair and eyes, and sharp, narrow faces. They must have been brothers; they might even have been twins. Two more men entered through another passageway opposite this first one, both of them armed as well. Tavis was forced to take a step back toward the nearest boulder and open his stance, his eyes darting from one pair to the other.

These other men were as dissimilar as the first two had been alike. One was tall and lean, with a long face and cold, pale eyes. For just a moment, he reminded Tavis of Cadel. His companion was far shorter and powerfully built, his chest and shoulders broad and round. He was bald and he wore a rough, yellow beard.

"Thar's two of 'em," this last man called loudly. "Though from th' looks o' things, only one is worth worryin' 'bout."

A moment later a fifth man entered the circle, using the same entrance used by the twins. And seeing this man, Tavis knew immediately that he was the leader of their gang. He was no larger than any of the others, but he had the body and swagger of a swordsman. He had a handsome face and long, wheat-colored hair that he wore loose to his shoulders. His beard was full, but trim, as if, in spite of the life he led, he took some care in maintaining his appearance.

He stepped to the center of the space, eyeing Tavis with interest, a thin smile on his lips. He held a short sword loosely at his side and a longer blade in a baldric on his back.

"Yer trespassin', noble."

If they could get out of this with their lives and their mounts, Tavis would count it a victory, a miraculous one at that. He wasn't about to anger the man.

"We are," he said. "And I apologize for that. We were caught in the storm and my friend was hurt. We had no choice but to take shelter here."

The man's gaze fell to the fire ring, then slid toward the depleted pile of wood, before returning to Tavis. "Ye stole our wood. It's no' easy t' find out here on th' highlands."

"We can pay you for the wood."

A smile broke over his face. "I've no doubt ye can." He glanced down at Grinsa, then prodded him with his foot. "He looks dead to me, noble."

"He's not."

The brigand's eyes danced. Clearly, he hadn't really thought Grinsa was dead. "Wha' I can' figure out is why an Eandi noble would be journeyin' with a white-hair in th' firs' place."

"Maybe th' Qirsi's 'is minister," one of the twins said, and started to laugh.

The others joined in, but the leader raised a hand, silencing them.

"Maybe 'e is. But I don' think th' lad's a duke quite yet. Are ye, lad?"

Tavis felt himself starting to tremble. "I don't know what you're talking about."

"No? Where'd ye get those scars?"

"A brigand gave them to me. Then I killed him."

The man laughed. "Ye have some pluck, lad. But I suppose I should 'spect as much from a Curgh."

The young lord felt cold spreading outward from his chest, as if his blood had turned as icy as Amon's Ocean. He opened his mouth, then closed it again, not knowing what to say.

The brigand laughed again. "Look, boys. I've silenced a noble. An' no' jus' any noble either." He glanced at the others. "Our frien' here may be th' mos' famous lord in all th' Forelands."

"Wha' ye talkin' 'bout, Kr—"

The leader's sword snapped up, so that it was level with the eyes of the stout man, who instantly fell silent.

"No names, ye fool. We haven' 'cided yet if our frien' here is goin' to live out th' day."

The bald man just nodded.

" 'Nough o' yer games," the tall one said. "Who is 'e?"

"This, boys, is Lord Tavis o' Curgh."

"I thought 'e was dead."

"No, ye fool." The leader regarded Tavis again, shaking his head. "No. 'E's alive, all right. Aren' ye, lad?"

"You're mistaken," Tavis said, his voice unsteady.

"Got those scars from Aindreas, himself, didn' ye? Word was ye refused t' go t' Glyndwr. Wen' t' Aneira instead. Bu' here ye' are, walkin' th' highlands with yer Qirsi frien'."

The tall man stepped closer to the leader. "If 'e's really th' Curgh boy," he said in a low voice, "we shoul' kill 'im now an' take 'is gold. Kill th' Qirsi, too, 'fore 'e wakes up."

"I don' think so. 'Is gold's already ours, isn't it, lad? An' I wager 'is father th' duke will pay a good deal more t' get 'im back alive." He looked at Grinsa again. "Qirsi's another matter. Ye can kill 'im."

A dark grin spread across the tall man's face.

Tavis edged closer to the gleaner, his sword still raised. "No," he said. "You can't kill him."

The leader looked amused. "An' why is tha'?"

Because he's a Weaver. Because without him all the Forelands will fall to the Qirsi renegades. "You're right about me. I am Tavis of Curgh, son of Javan, heir to the dukedom. And this is Fotir jal Salene, my father's first minister. The duke sent him to Glyndwr to bring me north, so that I can fight beside the men of my house in the war against the empire."

One of the twins shook his head. "'E's lyin'. Thar ain' no war."

"Not yet, perhaps. But the Braedon fleet is poised off Galdasten's shores, waiting for the emperor's orders. They'll attack soon, and when they do the entire realm will march to war."

"I tell ye, 'e's lyin'."

The leader was watching Tavis, his eyes narrowed. Now he gave a slight shake of his head. "I don' think 'e is." He looked at the twins. "'Member th' las' time we was near th' castle, th' way th' gate soldiers was turnin' peddlers away? Lad's right. War's comin'."

"Well, even so," the tall one said, "wha's tha' got t' do wi' th' white-hair?"

"A duke riding to war wants his ministers with him, particularly his first minister." Tavis met the leader's gaze, sensing that he had the man's interest. "My father will pay handsomely for his life as well as for mine."

"Keepin' th' white-hair alive is dangerous," the tall one said. "Le' me kill 'im now."

"Mos' times I would," the leader said, rubbing a hand across his mouth. "Bu' look at 'im. 'E might no' be dead, but 'e's close."

"Even half dead, 'e's still a sorcerer. We should—"

"No," the leader said, glaring at the man. "We keep them both alive." He faced Tavis again. "Provided ye drop yer blade."

The young lord eyed the man briefly, then glanced at the others. He might be able to kill one or two of the men, but he would never fight his way past all of them. Better to surrender now and win some time for Grinsa to recover. Exhaling, he tossed his sword to the ground.

The stout man quickly stooped to retrieve it.

The leader nodded. "Thar's a good lad. Bind their han's an' feet," he said to the twins. "An' make sure ye take their daggers."

"Wait!" Tavis said. "Can I check his injury first? I've got comfrey leaf on it, but I haven't looked at it since last night."

The leader's face hardened, and the young lord thought he would refuse. After a moment, however, he gave a curt nod. "Watch 'im," he commanded.

One of the twins took the dagger from his belt, and from the gleaner's as well, while the other examined the pouch of comfrey before handing it to Tavis.

Grinsa's wound seemed to be healing; certainly the swelling had gone down overnight. Tavis would have been happier had the gleaner shown some sign of awakening, but at least his injury didn't appear to be diseased. He crushed a few fresh leaves and retied the cloth.

"Tha's enough, noble," one of the men said, as Tavis adjusted the bandage. "Leave 'im."

They yanked the young lord away from Grinsa and tied his hands at the wrists, then sat him up with his back against a boulder as they bound his ankles together. When they had tied Grinsa, they stretched him out beside Tavis and walked away to speak among themselves. After a few moments, the twins left the shelter, returning a short time later with the few items Tavis had left with the horses.

"What did you do with our mounts?" he demanded.

"I think ye mean *our* mounts," the leader said with a smirk. "An' wha' we did with 'em is none o' yer concern."

Tavis held the man's gaze for several moments, but looked away at last, knowing that he was powerless to keep the men from doing whatever they wished, not only with the horses, but also with Tavis and the gleaner.

"Wake up, Grinsa," he whispered. "For pity's sake, wake up."

Wretched and helpless, Tavis just watched as the brigands counted out the gold he and Grinsa had been carrying, feasted on their food, and toyed with their weapons.

The morning passed slowly. Tavis struggled to free his hands, but the brigands had tied them all too well. All he succeeded in doing was chafing his wrists until they were raw and bloody. He glanced at Grinsa repeatedly, hoping the gleaner would awaken and wondering if Qirsi shaping power worked against rope.

"How'd ye do it, noble?"

Tavis looked up to find the leader watching him, his mouth full of dried meat from the kitchens of Glyndwr Castle.

"Do what?"

"Escape Kentigern, o' course. There's men tha' said i' couldn' be done. I, myself, know o' four men tha' died there. None o' them fools mind ye, and all o' them bigger an' stronger than ye. An' here ye are, no' much more 'an a boy, an' ye got out. So I'm askin', how'd ye do it?"

Grinsa did it, he wanted to say. *He shattered the walls of Kentigern Castle just as he'll shatter your skull when the time comes.* But he knew that if he gave even the barest hint of the gleaner's abilities these men would kill the Qirsi before he ever regained consciousness. "I had help," he replied at last, looking away. "I couldn't have done it alone."

The brigand laughed. "Well, I know tha'. But wha' kind o' help?"

"Why should I tell you?"

Tavis heard the whisper of steel. Looking at the man again, he saw him holding Grinsa's dagger, testing the blade with his thumb, a small smile on his lips.

"'Cause if ye don', I'll kill yer frien'."

The young lord turned away again, closing his eyes for just a moment and cursing his weakness. "There was a merchant in the city, a Qirsi. He had shaping magic. The first minister here knew of him and enlisted his help."

"A shaper, eh? Now tha' I believe."

Tavis said nothing.

"Actually, we're no' tha' different, are we?"

"What's that supposed to mean?"

"Well, I never killed a girl before, but I've been in my share o' prisons, an' I've been a fugitive even longer 'an ye."

He glared at the man, not caring that his hands were bound, or that the brigand held a blade. "I didn't kill her!"

"O' course ye didn'." He heard disbelief in the man's voice. The brigand was mocking him.

Tavis knew that he shouldn't care. These men were nothing. Many of the people he needed to convince—Kearney and the other nobles, his parents, Hagan and Xaver—already believed him, and the rest would with time. That was what mattered.

But he had struggled too long to prove his innocence, and had suffered too much for being accused of Brienne's murder. He couldn't bring himself to suffer the man's ridicule.

"It's true," he said, meeting the brigand's gaze. "She was killed by an assassin, a man hired by the Qirsi renegades. They thought to start a civil war by pitting my house against Kentigern."

"An' where's this assassin now?"

"He's dead. I killed him on the Wethy Crown less than half a turn ago."

The man laughed aloud. "Ye did. All b' yerself."

"Yes."

He kept his eyes fixed on those of the brigand, and gradually the man's laughter faded. "Did th' Qirsi help ye wi' tha', too?"

"No." Tavis hesitated. It was one thing to tell the man he had killed Cadel; it was quite another to claim that he had done it without any help. But how did he explain his strange confrontation with Brienne's killer? How did he justify killing Cadel after the assassin had lowered his blade? "I'm not sure how it happened really. The assassin . . ." He shook his head, deciding in the end that this brigand didn't deserve any more of an explanation. "I was just lucky."

The man narrowed his eyes. "Yer a strange 'un, lad. No' like most nobles I've known." He sheathed the blade and turned away. "Give 'em some food an' water," he said to the nearest of the twins.

" 'E looks well fed t' me. 'E can go withou' fer a time."

The leader lunged for him, grabbing a handful of the man's hair and pulling his face close to his own. "I said give 'im some." He shoved the twin away, making him stumble. The man glared at him for a moment, hatred in his eyes. Then he tossed two pieces of dried meat onto the grass just in front of Tavis.

"How am I supposed to eat with my hands bound?"

The twin leered at him. "Ye can eat it like a dog, noble."

The others laughed, including the leader. Tavis just turned his face away. No doubt there would come a time later in the day when his hunger got the better of his pride, but for now he left the meat where it was.

"Sounds like we're having a rough time of it."

Tavis's eyes flew to Grinsa's face. "Gods be praised!" he said, his voice a breathless whisper.

"Shhh." The gleaner's eyes were still closed, and he kept his voice so low that Tavis had to lean closer just to hear him. "What's happened?"

"What do you remember?"

"The storm. Riding back to the cluster of boulders."

"That's where we are now."

"There was a lightning strike. My mount reared. I recall nothing after that."

"You fell, hit your head on a stone. You've been unconscious ever since. It seems the cluster of boulders is used as a shelter by these brigands."

"Not one of my better ideas, eh? When was that?"

"Just yesterday. How do you feel?"

"Ay! Who's 'e talkin' to?" the tall brigand called before Grinsa could answer.

The nearest of the twins strode toward them. "Th' white-hair's awake!"

"You're Fotir!" Tavis whispered quickly.

"What?"

The lord had no time to explain. The twin grabbed Grinsa by the collar and hoisted him into a sitting position. The gleaner let out a groan, making Tavis wonder if he was trying to fool the brigands into thinking that he was worse off than he really was. A moment later, though, Grinsa vomited down the front of his cloak. The twin took a step back.

The leader approached slowly, his blade drawn, and his eyes fixed on the gleaner.

"Ye don' look well, Minister," the man said. "Th' lad will tell ye tha' if ye stay still, an' don' do nothin' foolish, ye won' get hurt. Otherwise, I'll kill ye. Understan'?"

Grinsa gave a small nod, then gingerly leaned his head back against the stone.

"With any luck, yer lord will pay a ransom fer both o' ye, and we'll be done. If no' . . ." He shrugged.

"Water?" the gleaner asked weakly.

The brigand eyed him, frowning slightly. At last he nodded and walked away. "Give 'im some water," he said over his shoulder. "An' watch 'im."

The same twin who had given Tavis the food carried over one of the water skins. He looked like he might just throw it down as he had the meat, but he appeared to realize that wouldn't work in this case. He glanced at the leader, opened his mouth to say something, then clamped it shut again. In the end, he squatted down in front of the gleaner, a sour look on his face, and held the skin as Grinsa drank.

After he had moved off a short distance, Tavis asked again, "How do you feel?"

"Terrible."

"Can you heal yourself?"

"I don't dare try."

"Why not?"

"Qirsi magic is controlled with the mind. My head's been injured. Trying to heal myself would be like a surgeon operating on himself with a dulled blade. Given time, I should recover. But I'd prefer to find a healer, one of my own kind."

"So what are we supposed to do?"

"You've kept us alive so far. I trust you'll think of something."

"Grinsa—"

"I may be able to shatter a blade or two, Tavis, but beyond that I can't help you. I'm sorry."

The young lord glanced at the brigands, who were largely ignoring them. "You shouldn't apologize. I've just . . . I've been waiting for you to wake up . . ." He shook his head. "Never mind. When the time comes, shatter their limbs, not their blades. They're carrying our weapons."

Grinsa smiled weakly, his eyes closed again.

"Can you do anything to the ropes?"

"No. Shaping magic works best on something harder—stone, steel, rock. I can burn the ropes, but they'll notice that."

Tavis simply nodded, and the two of them fell into a lengthy silence. After a time, the gleaner's breathing slowed, and Tavis guessed that he had fallen asleep. With nothing better to do, he closed his eyes as well.

He awoke with a start when someone kicked his foot. His arms and back were aching and his stomach felt sour and hollow.

"Wake up, noble." The leader's voice.

"I'm awake," he said blinking his eyes against the light. The sun was just overhead, warming the boulders and grasses within the shelter.

The brigand nodded toward Grinsa. "Is 'e well 'nough t' move?"

"Why? Where are we going?"

"I'm askin' th' questions, noble. Can 'e move?"

Tavis faltered, addled with sleep, and unsure of whether he and Grinsa would have a better chance of escaping if they remained where they were.

"I can move," Grinsa said, his voice sounding stronger than it had earlier.

Tavis glanced at him, their eyes meeting. "Are you certain?"

A smile flitted across his face. "No. But I'll try."

Clearly the gleaner thought they'd have a better chance in open country. Tavis was in no position to argue.

"I should check his bandage before we go anywhere," the young lord said. *Perhaps if they untied him now . . .*

"No." The brigand was eyeing them both with obvious distrust. " 'Is bandage is fine. We'll b' goin' soon." He glanced at the strips of dried meat still lying on the ground in front of Tavis. "Ye better eat now. There'll be nothin' else 'til nightfall." With that he walked away.

"Where do you think we're going?" Tavis asked in a whisper, as the leader began to speak with the others in his band.

"They're brigands. They probably have hiding places like this one all over the highlands, and I doubt they remain at any one of them for more than a night or two."

"But they just arrived here this morning."

"Yes, and they found us. They probably expect the Glyndwr army to turn up any time now."

Tavis shrugged, conceding the point. "You're better?"

"A bit, yes. Though I still don't know how much magic I can chance."

"Quiet! Both o' ye!"

"Shaping will be still be hard," Grinsa said, his voice dropping even further. "But maybe—"

"I told ye t' be quiet!" the leader said, drawing Tavis's sword and striding toward them. "I wan' ye both alive, but tha' don' mean I can' add t' yer scars, noble, or take out th' minister's eyes. Now shut yer mouths!" He turned to look at the others. "I wan' 'em kept apart, an' I don' wan' 'em untied. We'll put 'em across th' horses' backs."

Tavis hadn't taken his eyes off the gleaner. At the mention of the mounts, Grinsa's eyebrows went up and he gave a slight nod. The brigands didn't appear to notice.

A few turns ago, the young lord wouldn't have understood, having known so little about Qirsi magic. Now, though,

Grinsa's meaning was as clear to him as the brilliant azure sky above the highlands. Language of beasts.

Within moments, Tavis had been lifted roughly, slung over the shoulder of the tall brigand, and carried out of the circle of stones. The twins followed, bearing Grinsa together. The tall man untied the young lord's hands, then retied them so that they were in front of Tavis rather than behind him. Then he lifted the boy to lay him over the back of one of the mounts—Tavis's own, as it turned out—loosely securing the young lord's hands to one stirrup and his feet to the other.

It wasn't as uncomfortable as Tavis had thought it would be. Or so he thought. As soon as they started moving, he realized that he wouldn't be able to bear much of this at all. Every step of the mount bounced him, making his head spin and his stomach heave. He closed his eyes, but that didn't help. He could only imagine how Grinsa was suffering.

The brigands had horses of their own, and they set what seemed to Tavis a punishing pace.

"Gleaner!" he called.

"I know," came Grinsa's reply.

"Keep quiet!" the brigand growled.

"Ready?"

"Yes! Just get on with it!"

"Damn ye both! I said—"

Before the leader could finish, one of the horses neighed loudly and someone shouted a curse. An instant later, Tavis's horse bolted, jostling him mercilessly. He gritted his teeth, his eyes shut once more. He could hear another mount running beside him and he hoped with all his heart that it was Grinsa's. They seemed to gallop over the grasses for an eternity, until at last his horse slowed, then halted altogether.

"Gods," Tavis managed to say. "That was—"

"No time, Tavis. They're coming. Hold out your hands and pull them as far apart as the ropes will allow."

"What?"

"Just do it."

Tavis did as he was told. An instant later, the small expanse of rope between his wrists burst into flames, singeing his skin.

"Demons and fire!" He jerked his hands apart and the rope snapped. Immediately he began beating on first one wrist, then the other, trying to put out the flames. "You could have warned me!"

"Never mind that! I'll do the same for your feet. When they're free, ride northward, as fast as you can!"

"What about you?"

"I'll be right behind you."

Tavis nodded. He could hear other mounts approaching quickly. Soon his feet were free. He jumped down to the ground and made certain that the burning scraps of rope were off of his boots and his mount. Then he swung himself back into his saddle and kicked at the flanks of his horse. "Ride, Fean!" he called to the mount. "Ride hard!"

He glanced back. True to his word, the gleaner was with him. He could see the brigands behind Grinsa. They were bearing down on them, their weapons drawn. The twins led the way, followed by the tall man and his stout friend. The leader trailed the others by some distance. It seemed that his was the mount to which Grinsa had whispered.

An instant later, the two lead riders abruptly halted, one of them screaming and flailing at his head. It took Tavis a moment to realize that his hair was ablaze.

"That should stop them," Grinsa said. He smiled, but he looked deathly pale, as if the use of so much magic had drained him.

Tavis nodded, gazing back at the men. "They have our weapons, our food, our gold!"

"I know. But we can replace all those things in Glyndwr. We can't fight them, Tavis."

He was right, of course. He and the gleaner were alive: they had their mounts. He should have been pleased. But he couldn't help feeling that they had failed, or rather, that he had failed them both. They were about to ride to war. They intended to do battle with a Weaver and his army of sorcerers. And somehow they had allowed five brigands to take nearly all their most valued possessions.

"It's all right," the gleaner said, seeming to read his

thoughts, as he did so often. "Sometimes a warrior proves himself best by knowing when to retreat."

A warrior. He nearly laughed aloud. Whatever he was, he certainly didn't feel like a warrior.

Chapter Five

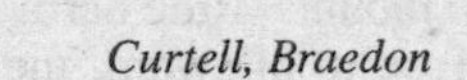

Curtell, Braedon

It gnawed at his mind like wood ants attacking old timber.

He could see the emperor's plans taking shape, and so the Weaver's as well. The master of arms trained his men with growing urgency; the quartermaster gathered provisions for Braedon's army like some forest beast hoarding food for the snows; and Emperor Harel himself wandered about the palace daily, overseeing the preparations. At other times Kayiv jal Yivanne might go an entire turn without seeing the emperor at all, despite being a minister in Harel's court. Now he saw the man constantly.

And each time the emperor came near, the minister had to resist an urge to warn him of Dusaan jal Kania's betrayal, to tell him that the leader of this movement that had struck fear into the hearts of every Eandi noble in the Forelands resided here, in his own palace.

He didn't dare, of course. If the high chancellor really was a Weaver—and the minister had come to believe beyond any doubt that he was—he would find a way to kill Kayiv, even if he was branded as a traitor. More to the point, the minister wasn't certain that he wanted Dusaan unmasked, at least not yet. Kayiv had long dreamed of a day when a Qirsi in the Forelands could aspire to being more than merely a minister or a festival entertainer. He disliked the high chancellor; he had since first coming to the emperor's palace three years before, and when Nitara ja Plin ended their affair and made it clear that she now desired Dusaan, that dislike had deepened to hatred. But there could be no denying that the man was both cunning and powerful. If anyone could lead the Qirsi to victory, he could.

Still, not even Kayiv's contempt for Eandi nobles like Harel could entirely overcome his fear of Dusaan. Even when he allowed himself to envision all that the success of the Qirsi movement might mean, he found his anticipation of this glorious future tempered by his knowledge of the man who would be the Foreland's first Qirsi king. The emperor was a weak-minded fool. The Solkarans of Aneira were uncultured brutes, and Eibithar's major houses had shown again and again that they were too concerned with their petty squabbles and limited ambitions to rule their people properly. Those who reigned in the other realms were no better. Nine centuries of Eandi rule had proved beyond doubt that Ean's children were poorly suited to being kings and queens and emperors.

But would Dusaan be any better? As much as Kayiv wanted to believe so, all he knew of the man convinced him otherwise. He had seen how ruthless the high chancellor could be, and he sensed that Dusaan would be a savage, merciless ruler. Yes, the man was Qirsi, but a tyrant was a tyrant, no matter the color of his eyes.

It had been more than half a turn since Stavel jal Miraad, the elder chancellor, had come to him with evidence that Dusaan was offering false counsel to the emperor, convincing Kayiv that the high chancellor was a Weaver and the leader of the Qirsi cause. In the days since, the minister had grappled with his doubts, wondering if he could continue to support the Qirsi cause knowing where its triumph would lead, wondering if he possessed the strength or the courage to oppose Dusaan should he decide on such a course. To his dismay, he had come to understand that he was a coward at heart, a man who had hungered for Qirsi rule so long as the cost wasn't too great, and who would allow his land to suffer at the hands of a demon rather than risk his life opposing him. No wonder Nitara had chosen Dusaan, despite the nearly two years Kayiv and she had been in love, and the countless passionate nights they had spent together. The high chancellor led a movement that might well change the course of history in the Forelands, and he looked like a warrior, with his broad shoulders and wild hair. Kayiv could offer her nothing more than his heart and devotion, and it seemed Nitara had grown weary of these.

But though he no longer hoped to win back the minister, in recent days Kayiv had begun to see that there might be a way to combat the Weaver without placing himself in harm's way. It was the coward's path. He knew that. Still he thought it better to do something, anything, than to sit by idly as Dusaan brought ruin to all the land.

Oddly, his plan demanded that he turn for help not only to Stavel, but also to the Eandi in Harel's court, something the minister never thought he might do. He hated the Eandi, and had nearly all his life. He still believed that the Forelands would be a far better place were its realms led by Qirsi nobles. As for Stavel, for as long as he could remember he had been disgusted by the blind devotion with which the older chancellors served Harel, and to his mind, none had been worse in this regard than Stavel. The chancellor embodied all that Kayiv hated about his own people's history in the Forelands. The man debased himself with his obsequiousness. When Kayiv's people spoke of white-hairs whose blood ran more Eandi than Qirsi, they did so with men like Stavel in mind.

But it was the chancellor who had first revealed to him that Dusaan was advising the emperor to begin his attack on Eibithar early, and that the high chancellor was presenting this as counsel that came from all of Harel's Qirsi. Even had there been another Qirsi whose help the minister preferred to accept, he would have had to turn to Stavel eventually. And as it happened, there was no one else.

First, though, Kayiv needed to enhance his standing in Harel's court. And for this, he needed the help of the one man who, only a short time ago, would have seemed an even more unlikely ally than Stavel: Uriad Ganjer, the emperor's master of arms.

Rumor had it that the arms master was livid at the emperor's decision to hasten the invasion of Eibithar, and that much of his ire was directed at Dusaan and the rest of the Qirsi, whose counsel he believed had convinced Harel to attack so soon.

As Eandi went, Uriad was more intelligent than most, and though a warrior, he was not given to the blind hatred of all Qirsi that Kayiv had observed in other Eandi men of arms. Still, the minister had never before had occasion to speak with Uriad other than to exchange pleasantries at an imperial banquet or while passing one another in the palace corridors. No doubt the master of arms would view with suspicion any overtures Kayiv made. The minister could only hope that Uriad's anger at Dusaan and his concern for the success of the invasion would overmaster his distrust.

For several days after resolving at last to speak with the master of arms, Kayiv searched for ways he might contrive to begin such a conversation without seeming too obvious. The truth was, however, their paths rarely crossed, and it occurred to Kayiv that this was hardly a discussion to be started casually, or by chance. At last, on the eighth day of the waning, the minister decided that he had little choice but to approach Uriad directly.

He found the armsmaster early in the morning in the central courtyard of the palace, training the men of Harel's imperial guard. Most of the soldiers would be sailing for Eibithar in another few days. There was little that Uriad could teach them in the time he had left. Kayiv sensed, however, that the master of arms no longer did this for the men, but rather for himself. Perhaps fearing that the emperor's decision had upset all his careful planning, Uriad sought to reassure himself that the army wouldn't fail for lack of preparation. Or perhaps he merely vented his anger at Harel by working his men mercilessly. Whatever his reasons, the master of arms watched the men with a stony expression on his long face, his black eyes narrowed, as if he were watching for the next mistake so that he could yell at the soldiers again. Occasionally he barked out instructions, his voice echoing off the palace walls.

Faced now with the prospect of approaching this imposing

figure, Kayiv faltered, nearly retreating back into the palace. But he could imagine Nitara laughing at him, calling him a coward and worse. Taking a breath, he crossed to where Uriad stood, stopping just beside him. The master of arms was nearly a full head taller than Kayiv, and the minister felt like a child standing with him.

"The men look to be in fine form, armsmaster."

Uriad glanced down at him, his expression unchanged.

"I've no doubt that they'll acquit themselves quite well in the coming war."

Still the man offered no reply, and Kayiv found himself casting about for something else to say. Too late, he realized that complimenting Uriad on the training of the men had been a poor idea. As far as the armsmaster knew, he was one of the Qirsi who had joined with Dusaan in recommending that the emperor begin his invasion sooner rather than later. No wonder Uriad had greeted him so coldly.

"What a shame that others in the palace aren't showing such dedication in their preparation for the invasion."

Uriad cast him another look, then turned fully to face him. "What do you want, Minister?"

Gods, the man was big! Kayiv had to fight an urge to flee. "Merely to speak with you, armsmaster. You may not believe this, but you and I are allies in this fight."

The man frowned. "What fight? What are you talking about?"

Kayiv winced. He wasn't handling this well at all. "I know the high chancellor made it seem that all the emperor's Qirsi were in favor of moving the invasion forward, but that's not the case. Some of us—a good many, really—feared that by upsetting your plans so, we risked dooming the invasion to failure."

Uriad's eyes flicked toward his men, and when next he spoke, his voice had dropped lower. "The plan is still sound. I would have liked more time, but the invasion will succeed."

"Of course it's sound, armsmaster. None of us questions that. But if you could have more time, wouldn't you still want it?"

"We both know that's not possible."

"But the high chancellor—"

"The high chancellor merely told the emperor what he wanted to hear. The emperor had long since grown impatient with my preparations."

"But he never would have changed his mind had the high chancellor not recommended it."

"What is it you hope to accomplish, Minister? As I say, the decision has been made. You and I both know that the emperor isn't about to change his mind. The men will soon sail for the waters off Galdasten, perhaps before the end of the waning, and by then the fleet's battle with Eibithar's ships will already be under way. There's no more time."

"You can't know that for certain. And even if you're right, don't you find it alarming that the high chancellor should wield such enormous influence with the emperor?"

"Not at all. It's to be expected."

"But these are dangerous times. Don't you fear giving such power to the Qirsi? What if a man in the high chancellor's position didn't have the best interests of his realm at heart? What if he were abusing his influence, misrepresenting the counsel offered by his fellow Qirsi?"

Uriad's eyes widened. "Is the high chancellor doing that?"

"It would be cause for concern, wouldn't it?"

"Answer me, Minister. Is the high chancellor doing that?"

"I've already told you he made it seem that all the emperor's other Qirsi supported rushing the invasion. We didn't."

The master of arms frowned. "That's hardly the same thing. I wouldn't expect the high chancellor to relate to His Eminence every point of view presented in your discussions. The emperor hasn't time for such foolishness. It's proper that he merely inform the emperor of the decisions you reach."

He didn't discuss it with us at all, Kayiv wanted to say. But he couldn't go that far. At least not yet. "We reached no decision," he said instead. "The high chancellor imposed his will upon us and then presented the recommendation to the emperor as if we had all agreed with him."

The armsmaster seemed to weigh this for some time, shrugging at last. "I'm not even certain I see anything wrong with that. He leads your people here in the palace, he speaks for you. It seems natural to me that his opinion on certain matters should carry greater weight. I say that even knowing that he and I are working at cross purposes in this instance."

Kayiv shook his head. "You still don't understand."

"Then tell me what's on your mind and be done with it!"

"I can't. Don't you see? The high chancellor is a powerful man—as you say, he leads our people. I . . . I'm afraid of him, of what he can do to me."

Uriad's eyes narrowed once more. "And what is that?"

"He can have me banished from the court." *He can have me killed.*

"And you honestly think he would?"

"If I defy him openly, yes."

"Well, I have no desire to see you sent from the palace, but I still don't understand what you want of me. I have no sway with the high chancellor. I respect him, and I believe he respects me. But I wouldn't presume to tell him how to treat the other Qirsi any more than he would tell me how to train my men."

"I'm not asking you to do anything of that sort, armsmaster. I merely wish to help you convince the emperor that the invasion has a better chance of success if we follow your original plans. I'd be willing to approach the emperor with you, to let him know that some of his Qirsi feel as you do, that this was the wrong decision."

A wry smile touched the man's lips and was gone. "Harel the Fourth does not take kindly to being told that he's in error. We'd both wind up with our heads on pikes."

"Not if we made it clear to him that he was the victim of poor counsel. Surely he couldn't take offense at that."

Uriad pressed his lips in a tight line, glancing at his men once more. "We still have several ships in the yards at Finkirk. If we wait another turn or two, the ships will be completed and we can add them to the fleet. Our navy would be stronger than it's ever been."

"How many ships?"

The armsmaster looked at him again. "Four. Each with three masts and three rows of sweeps. They'll be the finest warships ever to sail the waters of the Forelands."

"Four ships," Kayiv repeated. "Such vessels could mean the difference between victory and defeat."

"Perhaps."

"Don't we owe it to the emperor to tell him as much?"

The armsmaster smiled thinly, though there was no hint of amusement in his dark eyes. "You can be very persuasive, Minister. But I still want to know what game you're playing."

"I assure you, armsmaster—"

"Don't," Uriad said, shaking his head. "I may not be as skilled in the machinations of the court as you are, but I've served here for long enough to learn a thing or two. You want something. It may not be from me directly, but you certainly seem intent on using me to get it. And that's fine. If you're sincere in your desire to help the emperor and delay this invasion a short while, then I'm willing to play along, within reason. But I won't do so blindly."

Kayiv felt like a child, caught breaking one of his father's rules. "I am sincere," he said. "And I will do all in my power to delay the invasion, to return it to the timing you had foreseen. As to the rest . . ." He shrugged weakly. "The rest is difficult to explain."

Uriad merely stared at him. "Try."

"It's a Qirsi matter."

He faced the soldiers once more. "In that case, I'd suggest you enlist the help of your fellow ministers and chancellors and leave me alone."

"I intend to go to them, armsmaster. You must believe me. But I need the help of someone outside our circle. In essence, I'll be pitting myself against the high chancellor, and if I give the other ministers and chancellors such a choice, they'll be afraid to ally themselves with me." He hesitated, though only briefly. This was the path he had chosen; there could be no turning back now. "But if I can claim you as an ally, the others may be willing to join me."

"And what would you do with such an alliance, Minister?"

Expose the high chancellor for what he truly is.

"I'd make certain that the counsel offered to our emperor was sound, that if it was said to come from all of his Qirsi, it would come from *all* of his Qirsi and not just one man. Consider the times in which we live, armsmaster. Can we truly afford to do any less?"

"You raise an interesting point," Uriad said, with some reluctance.

"I can't promise you that we'll change the emperor's mind about the invasion. But I'll try, and perhaps I can prevail upon other ministers to join me in the effort."

"What would you want from me in return?"

"As I said before, I need your support. I need to know that when the time comes for my fellow ministers and me to approach the emperor, you'll be with us, in body and spirit."

"You believe I can protect you from the high chancellor."

Kayiv knew he hadn't been terribly subtle. Still, he was discomfited by the directness of Uriad's statement. In truth, if Dusaan was a Weaver, there was no one in the Forelands who could protect him. But under the circumstances, Uriad was the most powerful ally for whom he could hope. And since at the moment he was utterly alone, he was desperate for any friends he could find.

"I'm but a minister in this court, armsmaster. I've some influence with the other Qirsi, and I'll bring it all to bear in this effort. But if I stand alone against the high chancellor I'll be crushed. With you on my side, my prospects improve significantly. Surely you can see that."

"Yes, I can," the master of arms said. He paused briefly, then finally nodded. "Very well, Minister. When the time comes, you'll have my support. Speak with the other Qirsi, and send word to me when you're ready to seek an audience with the emperor. I'll be there."

It was more than he had expected, more than he had dared hope. "Thank you, armsmaster. I'm most grateful." He felt that he should bow to the man, or embrace him, so thankful was he. But he merely said "Thank you" a second time and hurried away, intending to return to his chamber so that he might consider how best to proceed now that his conversation with Uriad had gone so well.

Before he had gone far, though, he heard the midmorning bells begin to toll in Curtell City. It was time for all the emperor's ministers and chancellors to gather in Dusaan's ministerial chambers. Instantly, he found himself glancing about the courtyard, looking for any other Qirsi who might have seen him speaking with the master of arms. And doing so, he caught a glimpse of white hair as a figure vanished into the tower nearest the high chancellor's chamber. It was no more than a split second, a glimmer of white in the darkened archway, but for Kayiv, who had committed to memory every facet of her appearance, it was more than enough.

Of course it would be Nitara, and no doubt she would go directly to Dusaan, to tell him what she had seen. Kayiv felt his legs start to tremble.

He'd done nothing wrong, nothing for which the high chancellor could punish him without revealing more about himself than he wished. Certainly it wasn't all that unusual for one of the emperor's ministers to speak with Harel's most important military advisor. Except that Kayiv and Uriad had never before spoken at length, and somehow the high chancellor would know this. Kayiv was certain of it. News of their conversation would start Dusaan thinking. What could the minister possibly have to say to Uriad? If anything, a member of the Weaver's movement would wish to avoid such an encounter. The risks were too great.

The minister closed his eyes for just a moment, cursing his carelessness. He should have found somewhere less obvious to speak with Uriad, even if it meant going to the man's private quarters. Dusaan would be watching him now, searching for other signs of odd behavior, and making whatever Kayiv decided to do next that much more difficult.

Unless Nitara didn't tell the high chancellor. Perhaps she would seek to protect Kayiv. Maybe there remained some residue of the affection they once had shared that would keep her from speaking of this to Dusaan. The minister nearly laughed aloud at the notion.

Reaching the high chancellor's chambers, he took a moment to compose himself, then entered, taking a seat near the door and as far from Nitara as possible. That much at least Dusaan would expect. As he lowered himself into the chair, she eyed him briefly, her expression revealing little. The high chancellor glanced at him and nodded a greeting, but that was all.

The morning's discussion was unremarkable. The ministers and chancellors spoke briefly of preparations for the invasion and of the apparent settlement of a conflict between the lords of Grensyn and Muelry that had occupied the emperor and his Qirsi for more than a turn. The time passed slowly. Kayiv spent much of the time watching the high chancellor for any indication that he was angry or suspicious of him, and seeing none, he began to wonder once more if Nitara had kept silent about what she saw in the courtyard. Or had Kayiv been mistaken? What if the figure he saw disappearing into the palace tower wasn't Nitara at all? What if his fears and his lingering love for the minister had played tricks with his sight?

When at last Dusaan dismissed them, Kayiv rose quickly and hurried to the door, determined to keep as far from both Nitara and the high chancellor as possible. Regardless of what he had seen in the courtyard and what Dusaan might or might not know, he thought it best to take no chances in the coming days.

Before he could even take hold of the door handle, however, the high chancellor called out his name. Kayiv turned to face the man, terror spreading like a cold fog through his body.

"Would you remain for a moment please? There are matters I wish to discuss with you." Dusaan was grinning, his face looking much the way Kayiv imagined one of Bian's demons must look just before a kill.

"Of course, High Chancellor," he answered, marveling at how calm he sounded.

He returned to his seat, conscious of how the others stared at him as they filed past, but keeping his gaze fixed on the floor. Only when Nitara went by did he look up. She was eyeing him with unconcealed curiosity, a slight smile on her lovely face. She said nothing, though, and a moment later she was gone, the door closing quietly behind her.

The high chancellor hadn't moved, and he still wore that same predatory grin.

"It's been some time since last we spoke," the man said at last. "Nearly an entire turn."

"Yes, High Chancellor."

"I wonder if you still feel comfortable with your decision to join the movement."

"Of course I do, High Chancellor."

"You're certain?"

"I joined because I hate the emperor, I hate what Eandi rule has done to this realm, indeed all the realms of the Forelands. That hasn't changed."

"I'm glad to hear that, though I must say, I'm also confused."

Kayiv's mouth was so dry he could barely speak. "Confused, High Chancellor?"

"Yes. If all you say is true, I can't imagine why you would have been speaking with the master of arms early today."

He couldn't deny it. Dusaan would know that he was lying and assume the worst.

"I spoke to him of the invasion. I was interested in knowing how preparations were going and thought it best to ask Uriad directly."

The high chancellor frowned. "Don't I keep all of the ministers and chancellors informed of such things? Didn't I speak of the armsmaster's preparations just now, in this very chamber?"

"Yes, of course, High Chancellor. But I thought that perhaps you weren't telling the others everything, and so I spoke to the master of arms myself. Forgive me if I was wrong to approach him."

The apology seemed a good idea. Anything to blunt the high chancellor's anger.

"There's nothing to forgive, Minister. You're welcome to speak with whomever you choose."

"Thank you, High Chancellor."

"What did he tell you?"

Kayiv blinked. "High Chancellor?"

"The master of arms. What did he tell you about the invasion?"

Was Dusaan testing him? Was he indeed keeping some information back from the ministers, information that Uriad wouldn't have hesitated to share with Kayiv?

"Very little, High Chancellor. I mean nothing that you hadn't told us already. It seems I was wasting my time."

The high chancellor said nothing.

"He told me that preparations were going well, and that the men would be ready when the emperor ordered them to their ships. That was all."

"Really? From what I hear, you and Uriad spoke for quite some time."

A drop of sweat crept down Kayiv's temple, making his skin itch. The minister brushed it away with his fingers, trying to appear untroubled as he did. "I assure you, we merely spoke of the men and their training. I asked a few perfunctory questions. I thought it best not to raise the matter too abruptly. I wouldn't want to make him suspicious."

"No, of course not."

The minister felt as though he were sinking in swamp mud. Clearly Dusaan didn't believe any of what Kayiv was telling him. And perhaps that was why he said next what he did. "Actually, we had a very pleasant conversation."

Dusaan raised an eyebrow. "Did you?"

"Yes. I find the armsmaster quite intelligent, for an Eandi, and not nearly as cold toward our people as some of his race."

"I've noticed the same thing," the high chancellor said, though he didn't look pleased.

He had spoken out of desperation, but Kayiv realized now that he might well have saved his own life. The minister had thought eventually to use the armsmaster as his protector, and here he had done just that, far earlier than he intended.

Emboldened, he went on. "It seems that he was unhappy with the emperor's decision to begin the invasion this soon, and he blames the Qirsi for advising Harel on the matter. I tried to assure him that we wish only to see his plans succeed, and I think, by the end of our conversation, he had begun to believe me. Given some time, I think that I can win the man's trust."

"Oh?"

"Surely it would be a boon to the movement if I could."

"Yes, I expect so."

"Shall I continue to speak with him, then?"

Dusaan was glaring at him, but what could the high chancellor say? "Yes, I suppose you should. Keep me informed, of course."

"Certainly, High Chancellor." He hesitated. "Is there anything else?"

"No, Minister. You can go."

Kayiv rose and crossed to the door, his hands trembling, not with fear anymore, but with excitement. He could feel the high chancellor's eyes boring into his back, but he didn't look at the man again. Once he was in the corridor, making his way back toward his bedchamber, he allowed himself a smile of his own. He hadn't truly been courageous—he would never fool himself into thinking that. He'd acted on instinct and out of fear. But he had bested the high chancellor. Not only had he made it clear to Dusaan that he was building a rapport with Uriad, he had managed to get the high chancellor to give him permission to do so.

In a way it made no difference what the high chancellor knew, or thought he knew, about what Uriad and Kayiv said to one another. All that mattered was that the minister and armsmaster were linked in Dusaan's mind. That was enough to ensure Kayiv's safety. At least for a time.

As he turned the corner onto the corridor where his chamber was located, he saw Nitara waiting outside his door. Kayiv slowed, silently cursing his heart for pounding so at the very sight of her.

"What did he say to you?" she asked, standing there with her back against the wall, one foot resting against the stone as well, her knee bent at a perfect angle.

He should have told her to leave him alone, that what had passed between him and the high chancellor was none of her concern. Qirsar knew that he wanted to. But it seemed he wasn't capable of speaking to her so. He stepped past her, opening his door and motioning for her to enter. She hesitated, then pushed herself away from the wall and walked into his chamber. Kayiv followed, closing the door behind him.

"He wanted to know why I was speaking with the master of arms," he said.

"And what did you tell him?"

He had his limits, and his pride. "Why do you care?"

She shrugged, wandering restlessly around the small room. "I don't. I'm curious, that's all."

"Does he have you watching me now? Is that why you went to him in the first place?"

Her cheeks burned red, and for just an instant Kayiv thought that she would deny it. But then she smiled, cold and certain. "I told him because he should know such things. Even if there was nothing more to your conversation with the master of arms than an exchange of pleasantries, the high chancellor needs to be informed." Her eyes sparkled, the smile deepening. "And clearly there was more than that to what the two of you said. It almost appeared that you were plotting together."

"Well, I'm glad to see that your loyalty to the cause is so absolute."

"It is, Kayiv," she said, earnest now. "You shouldn't doubt that for a moment. I cared for you once, but I won't allow that to keep me from serving the movement."

"Is that a warning?"

"Only if you're foolish enough to make one necessary. What were you doing with him?"

"Are you asking me that as a servant of the movement, or as a . . . a friend?"

"I'm asking as someone who pledged to end Eandi rule in the Forelands, just as you did." Her gaze slid away. "And also as someone who doesn't want to see anything . . . happen to you."

For so long, he had wanted to hear her say something like this. But even having tied himself to the master of arms, Kayiv wasn't immune to fear of the high chancellor. Any satisfaction he took in her last words was negated and more by the terror that settled deep in his gut. "Nothing's going to happen to me," he said, hoping he sounded brave. "I was merely asking Uriad about preparations for the invasion. When you speak with Dusaan, as I'm sure you will, he'll tell you that I said the same to him. He'll also tell you that he gave me his permission to continue building a rapport with the armsmaster."

Nitara frowned. "Dusaan instructed you to speak with him?"

"This time I did it on my own. But I'll speak with him again soon, on the movement's behalf."

"Why did Uriad look so angry with you?"

Sun from the narrow window lit her white hair, making it glow like Panya, the pale moon. Kayiv had to remind himself that this woman was no longer his lover, but rather a servant of the Weaver. In many ways she was the most dangerous person in the emperor's palace, at least as far as he was concerned.

"He's angry with all of Harel's Qirsi," he answered, looking at anything but her. "He believes we're responsible for the emperor's decision to rush the invasion." Their eyes met for just an instant, before Kayiv looked away again. "I guess Dusaan saw to that, didn't he?"

"He had his reasons," she said abruptly, sounding defensive.

Kayiv wished he'd kept the thought to himself; this wasn't an argument he wanted to have just now. "I'm sure he did. I was just trying to explain why Uriad looked angry."

"I should go."

"All right."

Nitara walked to the door, pulling it open quickly. She paused on the threshold, though she didn't turn to look at him again. "He'll be watching you. You know that. And I will be, too. He . . . he expects it of me."

"I understand."

She nodded, then left him, closing the door behind her.

By now he should have been used to this aching in his chest; he'd felt it every day since their romance ended, and that had been a long time ago. Or so it seemed. Maybe this was just something to which a person couldn't grow accustomed.

They would be watching, and that would make what he needed to do next even more difficult, though not much. He had known from the start that enlisting Uriad's aid would be the least of his worries. Now he needed to turn Stavel to his purposes, and with him as many of the other Qirsi as possible.

A voice in his mind screamed for him to stop, to forget this madness and simply follow Dusaan to whatever future his movement managed to create. He owed nothing to the emperor or his people. Even if Dusaan turned out to be a tyrant—

and with each day that passed Kayiv grew ever more convinced that he would—he would be a Qirsi tyrant. And wouldn't that be preferable to what Braedon had now?

As if in answer, Kayiv saw once more in his mind the way Nitara's face flushed at the mere mention on the high chancellor. He wanted to believe that he acted out of more than jealousy and the pain of losing her. But all of it seemed tied together now in some great, impenetrable knot: his broken love, his hatred of Dusaan, his hunger for revenge, his fear of what the high chancellor might do to the Forelands if given the chance, his desperate need to make Nitara love him again. He couldn't explain anymore what he was doing, or what end he hoped to achieve. He merely knew that he had to act.

Which meant that he had to approach Stavel.

Chapter Six

By the time Kayiv awoke the following morning, much of his resolve from the night before had vanished, leaving doubts that threatened to undo all that he had accomplished the previous day. The minister forced himself out of bed and was soon walking across the palace courtyard toward Uriad and his men, intending to speak with the master of arms again. Dusaan had given him permission to build on their growing rapport, and Kayiv was determined to take advantage of the opportunity given to him by the high chancellor.

Upon seeing him, however, Uriad furrowed his brow, striding in Kayiv's direction, so that they met far enough from the training men to ensure that none could hear them.

"You've already spoken with the other ministers and chancellors?" the armsmaster said.

"Well . . . well, no. But I—"

"Then what's happened?"

"Nothing, armsmaster. I merely thought that . . . after yesterday . . ."

"We're not friends, Minister. You asked for my help, and I've given you my word that when the time comes, I'll be there beside you. But I have to assume that the invasion is going to begin when the emperor says it will. I have men to train, and I certainly don't have time to chat idly with you."

"Of course. I was—"

"Good day, Minister."

Before Kayiv could say anything more, Uriad had turned away from him and was making his way back to the soldiers. He was certain that Nitara was watching—he could feel her gaze as if it were sunlight on a stifling day. No doubt she was laughing at him, shaking her head at his folly. Any alarm the high chancellor had felt the day before learning of Kayiv's conversation with the master of arms would be gone soon enough. After standing there alone for several moments, feeling like an idiot, Kayiv returned to his chamber and awaited the midmorning bells. He would attend the daily audience with Dusaan, and then he would contrive to speak with Stavel.

When at last the bells rang, he hurried through the corridors to the high chancellor's chambers, wondering if Nitara had already told Dusaan about what happened in the courtyard. But when he reached the ministerial chamber, there was only one other minister there, and it wasn't her. Dusaan nodded to him as he entered, but kept silent as others filed into the chamber. When Nitara arrived, she chose a seat that placed as much distance as possible between herself and Kayiv, just as he had done the day before. Kayiv saw Dusaan staring at her as she sat, but he couldn't tell what passed between them.

This day's discussion proved far briefer than most, with Dusaan dismissing them well before the midday bells. Kayiv followed the others out of the chamber, and almost called to Stavel then. But realizing that Nitara was nearby, he said nothing.

Abruptly he found himself wondering if there were others among the Qirsi who might be watching him as well. Surely it was possible that Dusaan had enlisted others in his cause during the past turn. Better to wait and follow the old chancellor until Stavel was back at his chamber. Instead, though, the old man descended one of the tower stairways to the palace courtyard, and then left the palace entirely, making his way toward Curtell City. Kayiv couldn't have asked for more. Even if Nitara trailed behind him,, she'd never get close enough to hear what they said, not without revealing herself.

Kayiv followed the chancellor at a safe enough distance that he was able to make their encounter in the city's marketplace seem nothing more than a chance meeting. He wandered past the peddler's cart at which Stavel had stopped to examine some wooden toys, pretending to be surprised to find the man there. With the moment at hand, with his plans about to be given life, Kayiv felt fear claw at his chest and he nearly walked on past. Certainly it seemed from the way the chancellor regarded him that Stavel wished he would.

But he drew upon what little courage he possessed and offered a hearty "Good day, Chancellor," stopping beside him to look over the peddler's wares. "I didn't know that you had children."

"I don't," Stavel said, clearly uncomfortable. "I just came to the marketplace to . . . to walk. I've always enjoyed looking at such trifles."

"I can see why," Kayiv said. He glanced at the vendor. "You do fine work."

"Actually," the man said, his voice thickly accented with the brogue of lower Wethyrn, "I merely sell them. They were carved by craftsmen in the south, Caerisse I believe. They're made from Trescarri oak, a very difficult wood to work. Only four qinde apiece."

"I see."

Stavel started to move on, nodding once to the peddler. Kayiv followed.

"Do you come down here often, Chancellor?"

"Only when my duties to the emperor allow." Stavel didn't look at the minister, and his tone carried little warmth. "You?" he asked, seemingly as an afterthought.

"Not nearly as often as I would like."

They walked a short distance in silence before Stavel paused briefly to look at some silver work, mostly women's jewelry, although there were some blades on the cart as well. Kayiv found himself eyeing a necklace that only a turn or two before he might have considered buying for Nitara. Looking up, the minister realized that Stavel had left him, and he hurried to catch up.

"Is there something I can do for you, Minister?" the chancellor asked as Kayiv joined him at yet another cart. "Because if there's not, I would rather have this time to myself."

Again the minister hesitated, afraid of what he was about to do. "As it happens, Chancellor," he made himself say, "I do have a question for you."

"What is it?"

"I was wondering if you had ever discussed with any of the other chancellors the emperor's decision to begin the invasion early."

What little color Stavel had in his face vanished. He stepped away from the vendor's display, then turned to face the minister again. "Why would I discuss it with anyone?" he asked, his voice low and tight.

"I think you know."

"The high chancellor's claim that the recommendation had come from all of us."

"Precisely."

"I've said nothing of it to anyone. You told me at the time that you had discussed the invasion with the high chancellor in private just after our discussion that day. You told me that this was merely a misunderstanding."

"Yes, I know I did." He swallowed. Then, "I lied to you."

Kayiv had expected the chancellor to respond in anger. Instead, he looked terrified. "I don't want to hear this," he said, backing away.

"I believe you should."

"Why?"

"Because this matter bears on the safety of the empire, indeed, of all the Forelands."

"I don't understand."

"The high chancellor and I spoke that day of a personal

matter, one that had nothing to do with the emperor or the invasion. I told you otherwise because at the time I favored the decision to begin the invasion sooner than originally planned. It's a lie I've since come to regret, not necessarily because I think the invasion should be delayed, but because I fear that the emperor is being deceived. If he's been led to believe that this counsel came from all of us, who knows what else he's been told."

Stavel glanced about, then gestured for the minister to follow him. They walked in silence a good distance until they had left the marketplace and stepped onto a narrow byway between a pair of small stone buildings. "You fear that the high chancellor is lying to him?"

"I'm not certain. I think it's possible. To be honest, Chancellor, I don't think much of the emperor. I find his lack of wisdom . . . disconcerting. If Dusaan does steer him toward certain decisions at times, it's probably justified. But that's all the more reason for the high chancellor to consult the rest of us. If the emperor needs guidance, best it should come from all of his Qirsi, rather than just one man."

"The emperor chose Dusaan as his high chancellor, Minister. Regardless of how we feel about the man, we have to accept that choice and live with it."

"I know that," Kayiv said. "And I don't question the high chancellor's right to offer counsel to the emperor on his own. But when he claims to speak on behalf of all of us, that's a different matter. Clearly Dusaan feared that his own recommendation with respect to the invasion wouldn't be enough to convince the emperor. Otherwise, he wouldn't have bothered lying about it. He's using us to mislead the emperor, and I don't like it."

"Then tell him so."

The minister shook his head. "I'm afraid to. I'm but one minister, and I have no desire to stand alone against the high chancellor. I'd soon find myself cast from the palace."

"So you thought to have me fight this battle for you? I don't think so."

"The emperor spoke to you—you're the one who brought Dusaan's lie to my attention in the first place."

"Yes, but still—"

"You're a chancellor, and you have a good deal of influence with the other chancellors. Were you to inform them of what Dusaan had done, how do you think they would respond?"

"I don't know."

But Kayiv could see from the man's expression that this wasn't completely true, and he pressed his advantage. "They'd be angry, wouldn't they? They'd want to confront him, to ask him why he had offered such counsel without first speaking to them."

"I fear Dusaan as much as you do. He has the power to banish any one of us from the palace, minister and chancellor alike. It's true that I've been here longer than the rest of you, but that won't save me if I anger the high chancellor."

"That's why you should speak of this with the others. If you speak for all of the chancellors, he can't do anything to you, not without Harel's approval. And I doubt very much that he'll wish to raise this matter with the emperor."

The chancellor stared at him for several moments, as if attempting to divine his thoughts.

"Why are you doing this, Minister?"

"I've already told you. I don't like the idea of the emperor being deceived this way."

"I think there's more to it than that."

Kayiv looked away. "You're wrong."

"Am I? You and I have never seen eye-to-eye on any matter of importance, and you've just said yourself that you question Harel's wisdom, that you don't worry about the high chancellor 'steering him toward certain decisions.' Thus I find it hard to believe that you're suddenly concerned about the veracity of all Dusaan tells our emperor."

Kayiv had expected that it might come to this, though he had hoped with all his heart that it wouldn't. Already, he was putting his life at risk. But thus far he had done nothing irrevocable. In the next few moments, however, all that would change. There would be no turning from this path, no escaping the Weaver's wrath if Dusaan learned of his role in this.

"Believe what you will," he said, allowing his fear to creep into his voice.

"Very well. Keep your purpose to yourself. But you'll have

no help from me." Stavel turned and started to walk back toward the palace.

Kayiv let him take three or four steps, then called to him, by name rather than by title. He looked around, as if searching for the emperor's men, then walked to where the chancellor stood waiting. "I'll tell you, but you must swear to me that you won't speak of this with anyone else."

"You have my word."

He took a long breath. "I fear that there's more to the high chancellor's deception than merely a desire to have his counsel hold sway with the emperor."

"What do you mean?"

"Come now, Chancellor, surely it's occurred to you as well."

"I don't—" Stavel stopped abruptly, his eyes growing wide. "You think he's a traitor!"

"I've wondered if it's possible, yes."

"Simply because he lied to the emperor about the invasion?"

"As I told you, I fear that he's lied to the emperor on other occasions as well."

"Do you know this for certain?"

"No. But think about it, Chancellor. Why would he lie at all?"

"Perhaps it was done in error."

"I'd considered that, but have you ever known the high chancellor to make any other errors of this sort or this magnitude?"

Stavel frowned. "No, I don't suppose I have."

"Neither have I."

"But still—"

"The timing of this invasion is crucial to its success, and the master of arms was quite disturbed by the emperor's decision. He told me as much himself."

"You've spoken of this with the master of arms?"

"Yes. And he's concerned about it as well. We all should be. What if the high chancellor made this recommendation knowing that it would doom the invasion to failure?"

"Qirsar save us all!"

"You see now why it's so important that we address this matter as quickly as possible. It may be that I was right when

I told you that this was nothing more than a misunderstanding. Certainly I hope so. But if there's more to it than that, we need to know, and we need to warn the emperor."

"Then we shouldn't confront Dusaan at all. We should go straight to Harel."

Kayiv had to keep himself from looking pleased. "Do you really think so?"

"Of course. If the high chancellor is a traitor, and we raise this with him, he'll find some way to continue his deception. By going directly to the emperor, we deny him that opportunity."

"And if he's not a traitor, if this is all just the result of an honest error?"

"Then we will have disturbed the emperor and angered the high chancellor for no reason. But under the circumstances, that seems a small price to pay."

Kayiv nodded thoughtfully. "I suppose you're right. So you'll speak of this with the other chancellors."

"Yes. And I think you should say something to the ministers. It would be best if we all went to the emperor, lest we seem to be dividing into factions."

This the minister hadn't anticipated, though he realized immediately that he should have. There were only five ministers among the emperor's many Qirsi, and of course one of them—Nitara—was allied with Dusaan. If he approached the emperor with Stavel, speaking for the other ministers, the high chancellor would learn of his betrayal. Indeed, he would probably hear of it from Nitara long before word of this reached Harel.

"The ministers don't have much influence with the emperor, Chancellor. I'm not certain that there would be much point in involving them."

Stavel smiled. "I understand that you're afraid, Minister. So am I. But we'll do this together. It will be safer for all concerned."

He was desperate now. "What if there are traitors among the ministers?"

Stavel narrowed his eyes. "Do you have reason to believe that others in the court are traitors?"

He almost told him. It was a measure of how frightened he was of Dusaan that he even considered it. And it was a measure of how much he still cared for Nitara that he answered as he did.

"No, I don't."

"Then it's a risk we'll have to take, Minister. You should also speak with the master of arms again. We'd be in a far stronger position if he was with us."

Kayiv nodded. "I believe he will be." There was nothing more for him to say. A few moments later he and the chancellor parted company, Stavel continuing his walk through the marketplace while the minister returned to the palace, glancing about all the way, expecting at any moment to see Nitara, or worse, Dusaan.

By nightfall of that same day, there was talk in the court of a mysterious discussion taking place among the chancellors. Already Stavel had honored their agreement, and Kayiv had little choice but to call together the ministers as well.

They met the following morning in Kayiv's chamber. It was early, too early judging from the weary faces of his fellow ministers, but Kayiv had wanted to speak with them well before the ringing of the midmorning bells.

"What's this about, Kayiv?" asked Gorlan, the oldest of their group and the one who had served longest in the palace.

"We'll wait a few moments more," he answered, eyeing the door. One was still missing. Nitara, naturally.

"Is this about the chancellors?"

"Not about them, no. But we'll be discussing the same thing they did."

Gorlan nodded, as did the other two, Rov and B'Serre.

A few moments later, at last, someone knocked at the door, and at Kayiv's call to enter, Nitara let herself into the chamber. Her hair was braided and her eyes seemed to glow like torches. She sat as far from him as she possibly could, perching on the sill of his window like some pale dove.

"We're all here now," B'Serre said. "Tell us what's going on."

Kayiv nodded, his eyes flicking toward Nitara. He wasn't exactly sure how she would respond to all of this.

"Nearly a turn ago, Chancellor Stavel came to me, having just spoken briefly with the emperor. It seems the emperor was under the impression that the suggestion to move up his invasion of Eibithar had come from all his Qirsi."

"But we never discussed it."

"Hence Stavel's concern."

"You say this happened a turn ago?" Gorlan asked.

"Yes."

"And we're just hearing of it now?"

"That was my doing. I thought the decision a wise one, and though it seemed clear to me that the high chancellor had taken some liberty in presenting this counsel to the emperor, I saw no harm in it. Since I had spoken with the high chancellor about another matter just after that day's discussion, I told Stavel that he and I had talked of the invasion and that the emperor must have misunderstood and assumed that all his Qirsi were privy to our conversation." He shrugged. "Stavel accepted this and I assumed that the matter was closed.

"Yesterday, however, Stavel and I spoke of it again, for the first time since that day a turn ago. It seems that he hasn't forgotten the high chancellor's transgression."

"Nor should he have," Gorlan said, his voice hard. "If the high chancellor wishes to give advice to the emperor, he should do so. But he has no right to speak for us without soliciting our opinions first. And frankly, Minister, I'm disappointed in you. I would have thought that you'd feel as I do about this, and that you would have come to us far sooner."

Kayiv did his best to look contrite, though inwardly he was pleased. When Nitara related to Dusaan what had been said here, she would surely include Gorlan's rebuke. "You're right," he said. "I should have. I apologize to all of you."

"What does Stavel want to do about this?" Nitara asked.

Kayiv looked at her, their eyes meeting for the briefest of moments before he had to look away again.

"Is he content to raise the matter with the high chancellor and ask that in the future we be consulted before he takes his suggestions to the emperor? Or does he intend to do more than that?"

"Well, I'm afraid there's more to it than just the chancellor's pique. He fears that Dusaan has done this on other occasions, and he's begun to question if the high chancellor's behavior might be rooted in more than just arrogance."

"Meaning what?" Rov asked.

But glancing at Nitara once more, Kayiv saw that she already understood. Her cheeks had flushed, and she was shaking her head slowly, as if warning him not to answer.

"Meaning that he believes the high chancellor might be a traitor."

"Demons and fire!"

"I believe the chancellor has allowed his fears to overmaster his judgment," B'Serre said.

Nitara nodded, glaring at Kayiv. "I agree."

Kayiv remained silent, as did Gorlan, who didn't appear at all surprised by what had been said. Kayiv couldn't be certain, but he sensed that, like Stavel, the minister had his own doubts about the high chancellor's loyalty.

"So Stavel wishes to speak with the emperor," Nitara said.

"I believe he does. I also think he wants all of us to accompany him, so that he isn't forced to voice his suspicions alone." He considered mentioning the master of arms, but quickly thought better of it. Best not to reveal all to Nitara just yet.

"I won't do it!" she said. "The high chancellor is no traitor, and I won't be party to any attempt to brand him as such."

"I feel the same way," B'Serre said. "If we had proof that he had betrayed the empire in some way, that would be one thing, but all he's done is claim falsely to speak for the rest of us."

" 'All he's done'?" Gorlan repeated. "Surely you don't condone it."

"No, I don't, and if Stavel wants to bring this up with the high chancellor, I'll be more than happy to support him. But this is hardly grounds for calling the man a traitor."

"Is that how you feel as well, Rov?"

The man stared at his hands, a troubled look in his bright yellow eyes. But after some time he nodded. "I guess it is. I don't like that he lied to the emperor, especially about this. But I'm not ready to accuse him of treason."

Kayiv nodded. "Gorlan?"

"It seems I'm more disturbed by this than are the rest of you, but I won't stand alone against the high chancellor, particularly if it means questioning his loyalty."

"All right," Kayiv said, masking his disappointment, "I'll tell Stavel that we're not willing to go to the emperor with this."

"I do think we should speak with the emperor," Gorlan said quickly. "He should know that we didn't all agree with Dusaan's counsel regarding the timing of the invasion."

"It's not our place to go directly to the emperor," Nitara said, sounding slightly desperate. "We should speak of this with the high chancellor himself, and tell him that in the future we would prefer that he come to us before making such recommendations on our behalf."

Gorlan shook his head. "That's not good enough. What if the high chancellor has misrepresented us before? What's to stop him from ignoring our protests and doing it again?" He looked around the chamber, as if seeking support from the rest. "Don't you think that we ought to inform the emperor of what Dusaan has done?"

Kayiv was more than happy to let Gorlan argue the point for him, and he remained silent.

For quite some time all of them did.

At last, Rov gave a reluctant nod. "He should probably know. I don't relish the notion of going to the emperor without Dusaan's knowledge, but in this case it might be justified."

Gorlan turned to B'Serre, an expectant look on his lean face.

"I don't feel right about this," she said.

"So you're willing to let him claim that he speaks for all of us, even when it's not true."

"I didn't say that. But I won't lie to you: I have no desire to anger the high chancellor. I like living in this palace and serving the emperor, and I'm not willing to risk being banished from here just because my pride's been bruised."

"Maybe we should wait to see what the chancellors have decided to do. With all of us going to the emperor, there's less risk of any one of us incurring the high chancellor's wrath." Rov glanced at Kayiv. "Except for you and Stavel, of course."

Kayiv gave a wan smile, his stomach feeling cold and hollow.

"I'll agree to that," B'Serre said.

Gorlan nodded. "So will I."

They all looked at Nitara.

"I still think this is a bad idea, but it seems I'm the only one. The rest of you should do what you believe is best."

"Then it's decided," Kayiv said. "I'll speak with Stavel, and I'll let all of you know what the chancellors have chosen to do. In the meantime, I think we should keep what's been said here to ourselves." He knew better than to think that Nitara would conceal any of this from Dusaan, but the others would expect him to say something to this effect. All of them nodded their agreement, even Nitara.

A moment later the others stood and crossed to the door. Kayiv had expected that Nitara would hurry from the chamber so that she could speak immediately with the high chancellor. But she surprised him, lingering near the window until the others had gone.

"Are you mad?" she demanded, once they were alone and Kayiv had closed the door.

"What do you mean?"

"You know full well what I mean. First the master of arms, and now this. No one is going to believe that all this was Stavel's doing, Dusaan least of all."

"But it was. The emperor spoke with Stavel, and then Stavel brought it to my attention. This all started with him."

"And how hard did you have to push him before he agreed to speak with the other chancellors?"

He looked away, his pulse racing. "I don't know what you're talking about."

"Is this still about us, Kayiv? Are you still so jealous of the high chancellor that you feel you have to strike back at him? Or is there more to it than that?"

"I told you, this was Stavel's doing, not mine, and it has nothing to do with us. Stavel came to me. What was I supposed to do? Tell him that it wasn't worth our concern, like you're trying to do? Don't you realize how ridiculous that sounds? The high chancellor lied to the emperor."

"Don't you think he does that everyday? Don't you think that he has to? Think of who he is, and what it is he hopes to accomplish. Of course he lies. You'd have to be a fool to think otherwise."

"This lie was different. I know you think he's brilliant and perfect, but in this instance he was careless and he got caught. That's his fault, not mine. And if you're smart, you won't defend him too strongly. Because if he's revealed as a traitor, you will be as well."

"And you think you won't?"

He shrugged. "I'm not certain that I care anymore."

She stared at him a moment longer with obvious distaste. Then she stepped past him to the door. "You are mad."

"If you care for me at all anymore, you'll say nothing about this to the high chancellor until we've spoken with Harel."

She paused briefly, though she offered no response. After a moment she pulled the door open and left him.

There seemed nothing unusual about the day's discussion in the high chancellor's chamber. Dusaan gave no indication that he knew the chancellors and ministers had met, although Kayiv found it difficult to believe that he hadn't heard of the gatherings. Once again he ended their audience early, but since he had done so the day before, Kayiv could hardly read anything into this. Kayiv also noticed that Dusaan never once looked his way, nor did the high chancellor so much as glance at Stavel. And as Kayiv left Dusaan's chamber, he saw as well that Nitara lingered by the doorway, as if intending to speak with the high chancellor when the rest of the Qirsi had gone.

The minister left the palace, then doubled back through another entrance and made his way to Stavel's chamber, taking care not to be seen.

Almost as soon as he knocked on the chancellor's door, Stavel pulled it open and ushered him into the chamber. He looked panicked, his eyes wide with a wild, frightened expression, and his face grey save for two bright red spots high on his cheeks.

"He knows!" the chancellor whispered, the moment he had closed the door again. "Dusaan knows!"

Kayiv gave a small shudder, but he kept his voice calm as he asked, "How can you be so sure?"

"Didn't you see him just now? Didn't you notice how he was treating me?"

"He didn't even look at you."

"Exactly! We can't go through with this!"

"If that's how you feel—"

"How I feel? Aren't you afraid of him?"

Of course he was. Kayiv knew Dusaan was far more than an arrogant chancellor or even a simple traitor. He would have been a fool not to be afraid. And yet in that moment he found that he felt strangely calm, as if he thought himself somehow immune to the high chancellor's power.

"What did the chancellors say when you spoke to them yesterday?" he asked, ignoring Stavel's question.

"They don't believe he's a traitor, and while they were angered by what he told Harel, they aren't willing to confront him or, for that matter, to speak with the emperor." He took a long breath and it seemed to steady him some. "And the ministers?"

Kayiv smiled thinly. "They chose not to take any action until they knew what the chancellors intended to do. It seems it's up to the two of us."

"I've already told you, I won't go through with this. The man is no traitor, and after considering the matter for another day, I don't believe his transgression warrants taking any action at all."

It shouldn't have surprised him. Dusaan was a formidable figure in the palace. All of Harel's Qirsi knew that they could be banished from the emperor's court in an instant if the high chancellor but wished it. Kayiv should have known from the start that, dependent as he was on the courage of his fellow Qirsi, he couldn't prevail. Still he couldn't help but feel angry, as if all the others had betrayed him.

"Very well, Chancellor," he said, reaching for the door handle. "We won't speak of this again."

"One of the other chancellors tells me that you arranged all this because Dusaan stole Nitara from you."

He spun around to face the man. "That's not true!" But he felt his face burning with shame.

"You wanted to get back at him, and you used me to do it."

"Dusaan lied to us! That's why I did it!"

"I'm not certain I believe you."

Kayiv shook his head. Dusaan had defeated him, and with ease. His ties to the master of arms might keep him alive for a time, but eventually the high chancellor would find a way to kill him. In the meantime Dusaan would make him an outcast within the court. He knew that he'd probably be best off leaving now to avoid the humiliation, and to put himself as far from danger as possible. "It doesn't matter," he muttered. "Just out of curiosity, who told you this?"

"Why would you want to know that?"

Because that person may well be a traitor, too. "Never mind."

He left the chancellor's chamber and walked back to his own. Pushing the door open, he saw a small piece of parchment resting on his bed. His heart abruptly pounding, he took a tentative step forward, then another. Half expecting to see some threatening missive penned in the high chancellor's hand, Kayiv was relieved to see that the note came not from Dusaan, but from Nitara. Almost instantly, however, he felt himself growing suspicious. No doubt she had told the high chancellor of their discussion earlier in the day and all that Kayiv had said against him. It seemed equally clear that she would play a role in meting out whatever punishment Dusaan had decided upon for Kayiv's betrayal. He briefly considered fleeing the palace immediately; that would have been the wisest course.

But the thought of never seeing her again was too much for him to bear. "Come to my chamber at once," the message read. Very well. This would be the last thing he did for her.

He started toward the door, paused long enough to strap a dagger to his belt, then left his chamber and walked down the corridor to Nitara's door.

"Come in," she replied when he knocked.

He let himself into her chamber, his breath catching at the faint scent of her perfume. She was sitting on her bed, and seeing him, she stood. She looked pale and frightened, much as Stavel had a few moments before, though it had the effect of making her appear even more lovely than usual.

"Thank you for coming," she said.

"You told him everything, didn't you?"

"I had no choice."

He gave a harsh laugh. "Of course."

"I swear it's true, Kayiv. I wasn't going to tell him, but he asked me to remain behind, and when we were alone he demanded that I tell him what had been said at our meeting." She took a step toward him, then seemed to hesitate. After a moment, she looked away. "I'm afraid for you. I think you should leave Curtell."

His throat tightened, and he feared that he might retch. "Why?" he managed. "What did he say?"

"It was nothing he said. I think he believes I still have feelings for you. He asked his questions, then sent me away. But he was behaving strangely. I think he intends to kill you."

Kayiv nodded. No surprise there. "What about Stavel?"

"I don't think he'll hurt him. He thinks Stavel an old fool. But you turned on him. You joined his movement, and then betrayed him. He'll want blood for that."

Again, he was surprised by how calm he felt. True, he had already realized that he would have to leave the palace, but the thought of doing so seemed to have no effect on him.

"You say that he still thinks you have feelings for me. Do you?" He regretted the question as soon as it crossed his lips, and he dreaded her answer.

"I don't know. I don't think so. Certainly I don't want to."

"But if he believes it, you might be in danger as well." He faltered, but only for an instant. "Perhaps you should come with me."

"No. I've cast my lot with the movement. I don't think he wants to hurt me. He may not love me, as I'd hoped he would, but he needs allies in the emperor's court, and he knows that I'll serve him faithfully."

It pained Kayiv to hear her speak so of the high chancellor, but she had been more honest with him than he had any right to expect.

"I understand."

They stood in silence for several moments, their eyes locked. At last, Kayiv looked away.

"I guess I should go then."

"All right."

Still neither of them moved.

"At least come here and hold me for a moment," she finally said. "After all we've shared, that's the least you can do."

He smiled and stepped forward, opening his arms to gather her in an embrace. She was smiling as well, her pale eyes holding his. So he didn't even notice the blade in her hand until it had pierced his flesh. And by then there was nothing he could do to save himself.

He started to cry out, but she covered his mouth with her own, locking her free arm around his neck and pulling him toward her. At the same time, she took a step back, her legs striking the bed so that she fell backward, Kayiv on top of her. The impact drove her dagger deeper into his chest. He grabbed for her throat with both hands, but already he could feel the strength leaving his body, draining away with his blood. How foolish he had been to think that Uriad could protect him, how blind to think that she wouldn't kill for Dusaan.

"Poor Kayiv," she whispered in his ear. "So eager to believe that I still cared."

He tried with all the strength he had left to squeeze the life from her, to take her with him to Bian's realm. But he could barely feel his hands anymore. He was aware only of the pain in his chest, and the sound of her voice, receding like a moon tide.

"He wanted me to tell you that this is what becomes of traitors, and that while you're suffering the torments of the Underrealm, we who you betrayed will be creating a glorious future for the Qirsi here on Elined's earth. Think on that as you face the Deceiver."

There was so much he wanted to say, so many curses he wished to bring down upon her head. But all he could think to whisper as the last breath crept from his chest was "I loved you so."

When Nitara was certain that he was dead, she slid out from beneath him and stood, her head spinning slightly with the effort. Her clothes were soaked with his blood, and her hands trembled, but the guards would expect that.

She tore her shirt at the shoulder, partially revealing her breasts. Next, with her clean hand, she pulled the dagger from Kayiv's belt, cut herself just above the breast, as well as on the shoulder and on the back of her hand. Then she dropped the blade beside the bed. As an afterthought, she also bit down hard on her lip, tasting blood.

Only then did she cross to the door, pull it open, and scream for the palace guards.

Soon her chamber was filled with soldiers. The other ministers and chancellors stood in the corridor, staring in at her with wide eyes and expressions of horror. Even the master of arms came, solemn and silent.

"He tried to force himself on me," she said again and again, her tears flowing as if genuine.

Of course they believed her. Who could look upon her and question her word?

Eventually the Weaver came, as he had promised he would. He said little, his chiseled face grim. But she knew that he was pleased. He had told her that this was a test, a way for her to prove her devotion to the Qirsi cause. She hoped, though, that it would be even more than that. After this, how could he possibly doubt that she loved him, that she would do anything for him?

After what seemed an eternity, the guards left her chamber, wrapping Kayiv's body in her bedding and promising to send servants to clean the mess. B'Serre offered to remain with her, but she sent the minister away, saying something about needing rest. Closing the door, she closed her eyes for a moment, weathering another bout of dizziness. She had thought that she wanted to be alone, but she found herself staring at the dried blood on her floor and struggling to rid herself of the one memory she least wanted from this day.

Better he should have called her a whore and railed at her for her treachery. Those would have been the words of a coward, of a traitor, easily endured and soon forgotten.

I loved you so.

She hated what he had become, what his weakness had made her do. But she wondered how she would ever bring herself to forget what he had said with his dying breath.

Chapter Seven

Solkara, Aneira

Even in the dream, standing before the shadowed form of the Weaver, Pronjed jal Drenthe could feel his hand throbbing, as if the mended bone could remember the pain of the Weaver's wrath. The wind whipping across the grassy plain seemed particularly cold this night, the black sky more menacing than in previous dreams. He knew he should have been listening to the Weaver's instructions, but the pulsing agony in his hand tugged at his mind, demanding his attention. He wondered if the Weaver was responsible for the pain, if he had made Pronjed's hand hurt as a reminder of the minister's past failure, a warning of what might happen if he stumbled again.

Or perhaps it was a product of his own fears. The Weaver expected him to start a civil war in Aneira. He believed that Numar of Renbrere, regent for Kalyi the child-queen, trusted Pronjed and would listen to the archminister when he counseled taking a hard stance against those houses that would oppose the realm's alliance with Braedon. The truth was, Numar had never trusted him, nor did Henthas, the duke of Solkara. Over the past turn his encounters with the regent had grown ever more awkward, until Pronjed looked for nearly any excuse to avoid them, despite the Weaver's expectations.

Just two days before, on the first morning of the waning, the archminister had tried to use mind-bending magic on Numar, hoping to learn what the regent intended to do about the dukes of Dantrielle, Orvinti, and Tounstrel, who continued to voice opposition to the coming war. In the past, the regent had submitted to his power with almost no resistance. On this day, however, Pronjed had been unable to learn anything at all. He couldn't be certain, but it seemed Numar knew he possessed mind-bending magic and was consciously resisting him. He wanted to believe this wasn't true—delusion magic, the power to control the thoughts and memories of others, was far more effective when used on the unsuspecting, which was why he had made every effort to conceal the fact that he wielded it. He couldn't imagine how the regent might have learned the truth. It was possible that the regent's mistrust of Pronjed ran so deep as to shield him from the archminister's power. But it seemed more likely that Pronjed had given himself away, that in using mind-bending power on Numar he had failed to suppress the regent's memories of the encounters.

Whatever the explanation, Pronjed now found himself without access to Numar's thoughts and unable to overcome the man's suspicions. The regent might well lead Aneira into a civil war on his own, but Pronjed could do nothing to steer him in that direction.

Nor could he admit as much to the Weaver standing before him, the man who had conjured this frigid wind and black sky, who had once shattered his hand with but a thought. No doubt the Weaver would leap at an opportunity to hurt him again. Pronjed was not about to give him any excuse to do so.

"The regent has received word from Braedon?" the Weaver asked.

This much, at least, Pronjed did know. "Yes, Weaver. The emperor's message arrived three days ago. Already Numar has stepped up his preparations for war."

"Good. He knows of the opposition to this war in Dantrielle and Orvinti?"

"Yes, Weaver. He's known of it for some time."

"You've counseled him to deal harshly with the rebels?"

"Of course."

"And will he?"

Pronjed swallowed. It was folly to lie to the Weaver, and yet in this case the truth struck him as being every bit as dangerous.

"You hesitate," the Weaver said, his voice as hard as the boulders surrounding them on the plain. "Why?"

"It's been a few days since I spoke with the regent, Weaver." He gave a small, desperate laugh. "Like all Eandi, his thoughts on such matters change from one day to the next. It's difficult to say with any confidence what he intends to do."

"All the more reason to act the attentive minister, Pronjed. This is no time to allow our efforts to be hindered by ignorance and indifference."

"He remains committed to the alliance with Braedon, Weaver," Pronjed said, eager to show that he had accomplished some of what the man expected.

"The alliance is not enough. The war is not enough. Eibithar's quick defeat at the hands of the empire and Aneira would be worse for our cause than no war at all. You understand that, don't you?"

Pronjed started to answer, but the Weaver gave him no chance.

"I want a protracted war, Archminister. I want the Aneiran army divided and weakened. That's why the opposition to this war in Dantrielle and Orvinti is so important. And that's why the regent must be convinced to crush the rebellious dukes. Or at least to try. I had thought you understood all of this. Please tell me that I wasn't mistaken."

"Of course not, Weaver," Pronjed said, flinching, as if expecting at any moment to feel his bones shatter or his skin set afire. "I understand what you want."

The Weaver said nothing for several moments, until Pronjed began to wonder if the man was weighing whether or not to kill him.

"What of the girl?" the Weaver finally asked.

"The girl?"

"The queen, you dolt! Does Numar still intend to kill her, or will he leave that to his brother?"

"I . . . I believe he—the regent, that is—thinks her more valuable alive than dead. He thinks the dukes who remain loyal will be less likely to turn against him while he remains regent. If she dies, they'll suspect him, and even if they don't, they'll begin to see him as just another Solkaran despot. As long as he wages war in the name of the queen, the dukes will follow him. Or so he believes."

"You disagree with him?"

Pronjed shrugged, feeling more confident on this terrain. "He speaks for the queen now—at least he claims to—and still Tebeo and his allies defy him."

"And Henthas?"

The minister felt his uncertainty returning. Of all those in Castle Solkara whom he sought to turn to his will—Numar, Chofya, even Kalyi—Henthas, the brother of both the regent and the late King Carden the Third, had proven the most difficult to control. He was loyal to no one, nor did he seem to feel affection for any member of the royal family. Even ambition could not explain some of his actions. Once, briefly, the archminister had thought to make an ally of the duke. He soon came to realize that he could reach no accommodation with such a man. It seemed to Pronjed that Henthas was guided only by malice and a perverse desire to inflict pain wherever he could. No wonder he was known throughout the land as the Jackal. The duke would gladly have killed the girl had he thought that he could blame the crime on his brother, Numar, though to do so surely would have brought about the downfall of the Solkaran Supremacy.

Again, the minister considered a lie, though only for an instant. He couldn't be expected to know everything. Or could he?

"To be honest, Weaver, I can't say for certain what the duke's intentions might be. He is a strange, twisted man, even for an Eandi noble. I don't doubt that he could prove valuable before all is said and done, but right now, I wouldn't know how to use him."

"Then I'd suggest you study him further. You possess delusion magic. Use it on him."

Of course a Weaver would know.

"I've been reluctant to do so, Weaver. I use the magic on Numar. And since the brothers speak with some frequency, despite their mutual mistrust, I thought it safest not to use my power on both of them."

"I understand. But now I'm telling you that the time for caution has passed. Do I make myself clear?"

Pronjed's hands began to shake and he cursed himself for his cowardice. "Yes, Weaver."

"The hour we've been awaiting draws near, Archminister. You're fortunate, in that I couldn't hope to replace you at this late date. That, as much as anything, is why I don't kill you where you stand."

"What have I done, Weaver?" he asked, his voice quavering like that of a frightened boy.

A blow to the side of his head staggered him, and a second drove him to the hard ground.

"Don't trifle with me, you fool! Did you really think you could deceive me?"

Before he could answer, Pronjed felt a fierce pain in his gut, as if he had been kicked. He retched, gasping for air and clutching his middle, his knees drawn up to his chest. The Weaver hadn't moved.

It was some time before he could speak, the pain in his head and stomach receding slowly, like a fog. The Weaver merely stood there, his face in shadows. The archminister sensed that he was enjoying himself.

"How bad is it?" the man finally asked.

"Weaver?"

"Your rapport with the regent. You said before that you hadn't spoken to him in a few days. The fact is, he no longer speaks to you at all, isn't that right?"

Pronjed struggled to his feet, expecting at any moment to be knocked to the ground again. "He still speaks to me, but he tells me little of what we most need to know."

"What have you learned with your delusion magic?"

The archminister took a breath. He wasn't about to lie to the Weaver again, but he feared the man's reaction to the truth nearly as much. "Nothing recently, Weaver. By design, or by mere dumb luck, he's found a way to resist my power."

"You were careless."

He could hear disgust in the Weaver's voice, and he started to object. Then he thought better of it and lowered his gaze.

"Yes, Weaver. I must have been."

"All the more reason to use magic on the brother. It may be that he knows more than you do by now."

"Yes, Weaver."

"What you told me about the girl a moment ago, that the regent believes he's safer with her alive—was that true?"

Pronjed nodded. "I believe it is. She's become a shield for him. As opposition from the dukes increases, he has little choice but to hide behind her, and also behind the mother, Chofya, who remains well liked among the other nobles."

"The mother," the Weaver repeated. "Does she support this war?"

"I don't know for certain. Since the girl was named queen and Numar was chosen as her regent, Chofya has kept to herself. I believe she still has faith in the regent, though I can't imagine she has much enthusiasm for the alliance with Braedon. I'm certain only of one thing: she hates Henthas, and fears what he might do to the girl."

"She still trusts you?"

"Yes, Weaver. I think she does."

"Then perhaps your failure with the regent will be less costly than I first thought. Speak with her. Convince her that the war, if successful, will reflect well on her daughter and will improve the chances that her reign will be a long and prosperous one. It may be that she can convince Numar of what you could not."

Pronjed struggled to keep his anger in check, knowing that another misstep might give the Weaver cause to kill him. "Yes, Weaver," he said, his voice tight. "I'll see to it right away."

"I expect no less."

An instant later the archminister awoke with a start. His sleeping shirt and hair were damp with sweat, and his head and gut still ached. It could have been worse, he knew, remembering the shattering of the bones in his hand.

Or had the Weaver in fact done all that he dared?

The Weaver himself had made clear that his war with the Eandi courts was approaching, that its imminence might have saved Pronjed's life. Perhaps it even kept the man from inflicting greater injuries on the archminister. Now was not the time for him to risk giving Pronjed visible injuries that would be difficult for the archminister to explain.

But what will he do to me once the war is over?

The only way to ensure his own safety was to do the Weaver's bidding and prove himself invaluable to the movement. He rose and dressed, deciding that he would first seek out the queen mother. He knew better than to think that Chofya had much influence with the regent, but Pronjed's rapport with the woman remained strong, and speaking with her seemed the easiest way to begin what promised to be a long, difficult day.

He found Chofya in the gardens, overseeing the first plantings of the season. The day was already growing warm and the first swifts to return to Solkara were darting overhead, black as pitch against a sapphire sky.

"Good morrow, Your Highness," Pronjed said as he approached her.

She looked up, shading her dark eyes with a slender hand. She wore a simple brown dress and soft leather shoes, much like those of the workers around her. But with her exquisite features and long black hair, which she had tied back from her face, none would have confused her for a common laborer. She still looked every bit the queen.

"Hello, Archminister. Kalyi isn't here. I believe she's with one of her tutors."

"Actually, Your Highness, I was looking for you."

She frowned. "For me?"

"Yes. May I speak with you for a moment?"

She glanced briefly at the laborers, as if reluctant to leave them. Then she followed the archminister to a deserted corner of the garden.

"Has something happened?" she asked, as he halted by an empty flower bed and turned to face her once more.

"No, Your Highness. Not yet. But you must know that we may be on the brink of war."

"Yes, I know," she said, looking troubled. "There seems to be nothing I can do to prevent it."

He gaped at her, no doubt looking like a fool. "Prevent it? Why would you want to do such a thing?"

She looked away, shaking her head. "It doesn't matter, Archminister. I'm no longer queen, and even when I was, my opinions on these matters meant nothing. I managed to have Kalyi placed on the throne. Beyond that, my responsibilities to the land have never amounted to much. And it's probably just as well."

Pronjed cursed himself for beginning this conversation so clumsily. He needed to enlist the queen as an ally, and already he had made her more reluctant even to discuss the matter. "Forgive me, Your Highness. I shouldn't have reacted as I did. Please tell me why you object to this war."

"I object to all wars, Archminister. I always have, though I kept my reservations to myself while Carden was alive."

"Don't you think it possible that a victory over Eibithar could strengthen the realm? Don't you believe it would ensure a successful reign for your daughter?"

She shrugged. "I suppose it might."

"And still you oppose it."

Chofya eyed him briefly, seeming to search his face for some sign of what lurked behind his words. "You truly wish to know why I'm against it?"

"Of course, Your Highness."

"Very well. My husband viewed war as the solution to all problems. He never learned the art of statecraft or mastered the finer points of leadership. He ruled Aneira by threatening violence. And because of this, he was feared and hated throughout the land. Kalyi might not yet be queen, but her regency has begun. She'll spend the next six years learning how to lead—all that she witnesses in this time will shape her, determining what sort of queen she'll be. I don't want her to rule as her father did. I don't want her to turn to her army or her assassins every time she finds herself at odds with a duke or another realm."

For a time, Pronjed said nothing, weighing what she had told him. Chofya, he realized, would never be his ally in this fight. At least not wittingly.

"You think me foolish," she said at last, a thin smile on her lips.

"Not at all, Your Highness. On the contrary, I believe the queen is fortunate to have you nearby."

"But still, you disagree with me."

He acknowledged the point with a small nod. "I'm afraid I do. I hope that Kalyi will become the sort of leader you want her to be. But I believe that in this case, war is justified. We have an opportunity to weaken Eibithar, perhaps even destroy her. Isn't it possible that by ridding ourselves of such a powerful enemy, we make it easier for the queen to rule with a gentle hand?"

"Perhaps," she said. "But even if we rid ourselves of the threat to the north, how long will it be before we face another from Sanbira or Uulrann, or even from Braedon? There will always be those who counsel war, Archminister, who see dangers in one realm or another. Better she should learn from the start that war is to be avoided, that other solutions are preferable."

He forced a smile. "Of course, Your Highness. I understand."

"I'm sorry I couldn't help you."

"Think nothing of it." He gestured toward the laborers working at the far end of the gardens, and together they walked in silence back to where she had been when he first found her.

"Thank you for taking the time to speak with me, Your Highness," he said, bowing to her. "Please forgive the intrusion." He started to walk away.

"How soon do you think the war will begin?" she asked, forcing him to face her once more.

"I'm not certain, though I expect we'll be at war before the end of the growing turns."

Chofya nodded, tight-lipped and grim.

Pronjed made his way back toward the nearest of the castle towers. Before he had gone far, however, he glanced up toward the top floor of the castle and saw Numar standing at his window, marking the archminister's progress through the castle ward. Their eyes met for just a moment, before the regent shifted his gaze, but he didn't close the shutters, nor did he step away from the window. And almost as soon as Pronjed looked away, he sensed the man's eyes upon him again.

He continued on toward the presence chamber of the Solkaran duke, Henthas, the regent's older brother. He didn't relish the thought of relying on this man for anything, but he couldn't do all that the Weaver expected without help.

Henthas offered only a sneer by way of welcome.

"What do you want?" he demanded, sounding every bit the Jackal.

"Just a word, my lord. It won't take long." *I'm no more eager to be here than you are to have me.*

"Very well. What is it?" From the tone of the duke's voice one might have thought that Pronjed was keeping him from some crucial task, but as far as the minister could tell, the man had simply been sitting by his window, staring out at the ward and the soldiers training there.

The archminister glanced at the servants standing by the door, before again regarding Henthas.

The duke twisted his mouth as if annoyed, but a moment later he ordered the servants from the chamber.

"Now for the third time," he said, once they were gone, "what do you want?"

"I want to know if you've spoken with your brother recently."

"My lord."

Pronjed blinked. "What?"

" 'I want to know if you've spoken with your brother recently, *my lord.*' I'm duke of Solkara, Archminister. You often seem to forget that."

Pronjed gave a brittle smile. "How could I, my lord?"

Henthas said nothing, and cursing the man inwardly, the archminister surrendered the point.

"I was wondering if you had spoken with your brother recently, my lord."

The duke smiled broadly. "Much better. As it happens we spoke yesterday. Why do you wish to know?"

"He's told me little of his preparations for war, and even less of what he intends to do about Dantrielle and the dukes who oppose him. I thought perhaps you could tell me what you know."

Henthas watched him for several moments, then shook his head. "No, I don't think I will."

Pronjed bit his tongue, tasting blood. "May I ask why?" he said at last, fighting to keep his voice even.

"If Numar has chosen to keep you ignorant of such matters, I can only assume that he has good reason. Far be it from me to work at cross purposes with my own brother."

The minister would have laughed aloud had he not been so enraged. Henthas had, at one time or another, been working at cross purposes with everyone in the castle, including his brother. Especially his brother.

"It wasn't long ago, my lord, that you and I were working together to protect the queen from the regent. The threat to her remains, and I needn't remind you that the stronger Numar becomes, the less likely it is that you will ever be in a position to claim the throne for yourself."

"Have you spoken to Chofya of the threat to her daughter?"

"Not yet, no."

"I'm surprised. If you truly feared for the queen's life you would have by now."

Pronjed crossed the chamber and sat in a chair near the duke. He needed to be close to the man in order to use magic on him. "You've allied yourself with him, haven't you?"

Henthas shook his head. "I don't know what you mean."

The minister smiled, but even as he did, he reached out with his power and touched the duke's mind. "What did he offer you?"

"He offered nothing," the man said, his face abruptly growing slack, a dull look in his dark eyes. "He told me that he fears you, that he thinks you might have killed Carden."

Pronjed gaped at him. It was the last thing he expected the duke to say. The truth was he had killed Carden, by using his mind-bending magic to make the king plunge a dagger into his own chest. "Why does he think that?"

"He wouldn't say. But he thinks you're far more dangerous than we ever believed, and he convinced me of this as well."

Numar must have known that he possessed mind-bending power. There was no other explanation for what Henthas had said, particularly since the minister's power no longer worked on the regent.

"Tell me of Numar's plans," he finally commanded. Delusion was the most taxing of all his powers, and already he was tiring.

"There's little to tell. He's mustering a thousand more men into the army and sending most of them north to the Tarbin. When the naval war begins, they'll attack."

"And the dukes to the south?"

"Numar doesn't believe they pose much of a threat. They oppose the war, but they haven't the nerve to defy him openly."

"So he has no intention of sending any part of his army to Orvinti or Dantrielle?"

"No."

"Damn," he said under his breath. He rubbed a hand over his face. This wasn't going any better than had his conversation with Chofya. "And the girl? When does he plan to kill her?"

"He doesn't, at least not for a long while. I think he's grown fond of her."

Just as Pronjed had suspected. At least that much of what he had told the Weaver was true. Weighing all that he had learned during the course of this morning, however, the archminister realized that matters were a good deal worse than he had feared. Numar, through cunning, or just good fortune, had managed to isolate him. He had befriended the young queen, he had won Henthas's loyalty, at least for a time. And though Pronjed didn't believe that Chofya would ally herself with the regent so long as he continued to pursue this war, he knew—and Numar must have as well—that she wanted no part of court politics anymore. She was content to raise her daughter and cultivate her gardens. Certainly, she was not about to take sides in any dispute between the regent and the archminister.

"What about me?" he asked, knowing that he couldn't hold the duke's mind for much longer. "Is he content simply to weaken my influence, or does he have something else in mind?"

"For now he plans nothing. But eventually he intends to prove that you're a traitor, and have you executed."

He should have expected as much. Still, hearing the words

spoken made him shudder. He could only hope that the Weaver would move against the courts before Numar had a chance to destroy him.

Pronjed felt a dull ache at the base of his skull, and he knew that he had used his delusion magic for too long.

"You'll remember nothing of this discussion when we're done," he said, his eyes locked on those of the duke. "We've spoken of the queen, and our desire to keep her safe. That's all. Do you understand?"

"Yes."

The archminister nodded and released him. "Does that mean you think we should double the guard on her bedchamber?" he asked, as if in the middle of a conversation.

"What?" Henthas squeezed his eyes closed for a moment, then put a hand to his temple.

"Are you well, my lord?"

"No. My head hurts, and I can't remember what I was saying."

"You were telling me of your concern for Kalyi's safety. You seemed to believe that she's in some danger."

"I don't recall any of that." He eyed the archminister warily. "What have you done to me?"

"I've done nothing, my lord," Pronjed said, his heart pounding. Was this what had happened with Numar as well? Was he growing weak? At thirty-one he wasn't an old man, not even by Qirsi standards. But neither was he young anymore. "Would you like me to call for the castle surgeon?"

"No." Henthas made a vague gesture toward the door. "Leave me. I don't want you near me anymore." He was still rubbing his temple, as if in pain, and Pronjed wondered if he had damaged the man's mind. That was said to happen occasionally when mind-bending magic was used carelessly. Had he held the duke under his power for too long?

"I'm concerned for you, my lord. Surely there's something—"

"Get out!" Henthas said, getting to his feet and stumbling slightly. "Leave this chamber at once or I'll have you removed!"

He had little choice but to try one last time. Reaching out with his magic once more, all too aware of how weary he was, the archminister touched the man's mind a second time. "You're angry with me because I suggested that you intend to harm the queen. You've forgotten the pain in your head."

Pronjed released the duke again, watching him closely. Henthas's hand strayed to his head again, but remained there for just a moment before falling to his side.

"Perhaps I should go, my lord," the archminister said, keeping his voice low. "I didn't mean to offend you."

The duke frowned, appearing puzzled. "Perhaps not," he said. "But you shouldn't have spoken to me so."

"You're right, my lord. My apologies."

He bowed to the man and quickly left the chamber, fearing that if he remained any longer it would only serve to undermine the memories he had planted in the duke's mind.

Once in the corridor, he hurried to the nearest tower and ascended the stairs to the ramparts. His head throbbed and he nearly lost his balance on the stairway. He needed time to think, but he found it difficult to clear his mind. Two guards stood at the top of the tower, but they merely nodded to him and stayed where they were as he stepped past them and walked out onto the castle wall.

Just when he most needed to turn the Eandi in Castle Solkara to his purposes, he found himself unable to influence them at all. It seemed that events were spiraling beyond his control. Numar didn't trust him; Chofya opposed him; and after today Henthas would be wary of him as well, no matter what the duke remembered from their encounter. If he could rely on his mind-bending magic, none of this would matter, but without it he was lost. He remained a powerful sorcerer, but delusion magic only worked on the unsuspecting and it suddenly seemed that no one in Castle Solkara trusted him, at least no one of any importance. It was just a matter of time before the Weaver returned to his dreams, learned of his newest failures, and killed him in his sleep.

For as long as the archminister could remember he had seen the movement as his path to glory and power. Now it seemed that it would bring his doom, that he wouldn't even live to see its final success. Yet even as he struggled with his fear and his self-pity, the archminister sensed the kernel of an idea forming in the recesses of his mind. There remained one to whom he could turn, one who could help him redeem himself by remedying all that had gone wrong. He wouldn't even have to use his magic against her. The pain still lingered at the base of his skull, but it had lessened a bit, enough so that he could get through this one last encounter.

He heard bells tolling in the city and actually managed a smile as he strode to the stairway in the next tower. Midday. He knew just where she would be.

Kalyi was on her feet as soon as the bells rang, gathering her scrolls in her arms and hurrying toward the door.

Zarev, her tutor, frowned as he watched her, his bushy grey eyebrows bristling like quills on a hedgehog, but the young queen pretended not to notice.

"Your Highness, you really must try to concentrate. I don't think you've learned nearly as much as you should during the last few turns, and I fear your mother will not be pleased."

She turned to face him, though she reached for the door handle with a free hand. "I've learned a lot, teacher. Truly I have. And if I haven't learned as much as I should, I'll make certain that Mother knows it was my fault and not yours."

"That's hardly the point—"

"I really have to go." She smiled. By now she'd opened the door. "My thanks."

She spun on her heel and was in the corridor before Zarev could say more. The last she saw of him, his frown had deepened and he was shaking his head.

No doubt he would speak with her mother at his first opportunity, which would lead in turn to another stern talk from her mother about the importance of her lessons. But how could she be expected to learn on such a perfect day? Even in the small chamber where she met with her tutors for her daily lessons, with its single narrow window, she could smell the clean air and feel the warm breezes blowing off the river. This was a day to be out-of-doors. Perhaps she could even prevail upon her mother to go riding after the midday meal, provided she found Chofya before the tutor did.

Reaching the nearest of the towers, she started down the stairs. She had only taken a few steps, however, when she heard a voice call from above her.

"Is that you, Your Highness?"

The archminister. Kalyi had to resist an urge to flee. Ever since overhearing Pronjed's strange conversation with the master of arms, a conversation in which the Qirsi had seemed to force the armsmaster to do and say certain things, she had been terrified of the man. Uncle Numar thought that he might be a traitor, a part of the Qirsi conspiracy she had heard so much about over the past year. They had no proof of this, at least not yet. And the regent had told her that when she saw the archminister she had to try to behave normally.

"We mustn't let him know that we suspect anything," he had said. "If we show that we're afraid of him, he might guess at what we're thinking, and then we'll never find the proof we need."

She understood, but she couldn't help but feel afraid every time the Qirsi came near her. Recently, she had come to fear all the white-hairs in the castle, though she knew better than to believe that they were all traitors. She just couldn't help herself.

Swallowing and willing herself to be brave, Kalyi stopped on the stairs and waited.

"Yes, Archminister," she said, pleased to hear that her voice didn't shake. "It's me."

He descended the steps until he stood before her, appearing even taller and more formidable than usual in the narrow stairway. The dim light of the tower made his narrow, bony face look frightening and strange, like that of some evil bird of prey from Bian's realm. Once more, Kalyi had to resist an urge to back away from him.

"I'm glad I found you, Your Highness. I have important matters to discuss with you."

"Actually, I was on my way to the kitchens to find something to eat—"

"Splendid. You don't mind if I walk with you, do you?"

What could she say? "No, Archminister. Of course not."

"Good." He indicated the stairs with an open hand.

Kalyi started down once more, the Qirsi just behind her. Her whole body had gone rigid, and she half expected him to plunge a dagger into her back. When they emerged from the tower into the castle ward, she began to feel better. He wasn't quite so scary in the bright sun.

"I spoke with your mother a short time ago," the archminister told her. "She's concerned about this war the regent is planning." He paused, glancing at her. "You have heard talk of the war, haven't you, Your Highness?"

"Of course," she said, insulted that he had to ask. "We're entering into an alliance with the emperor of Braedon in order to fight Eibithar."

"Yes, precisely. I believe your mother opposes the war. She feels it's not the correct way to begin your reign."

Kalyi hadn't heard her mother say anything of the sort. In fact, thinking about it, she realized that her mother had never spoken to her of the war at all. It occurred to her that the archminister might be lying.

"Do you agree with her?" the queen asked.

"Actually, I don't. I've long been in favor of the alliance and the attack on Eibithar." His brow creased. "Still . . ." He paused, as if lost in thought. Finally he shook his head and smiled, though Kalyi could see that he remained troubled. "It's not important."

"What isn't?"

"Well, it's just that your mother isn't the only one who's against the war. The dukes of Orvinti and Dantrielle oppose it as well, and so do several of their allies."

They had reached the entrance to the kitchen tower, and they halted there, lingering in the ward.

"Why are they against it?"

"I believe they don't trust Braedon's emperor; they don't want him as an ally." He hesitated. "And I fear they don't trust your uncle, either."

"You mean Uncle Numar?"

He nodded.

"Why wouldn't they trust him?" she demanded, growing angry.

"The same reason they didn't trust your father. The same reason I'm afraid they won't trust you. They fear the Solkaran Supremacy. They don't want our house to grow too powerful."

Kalyi shook her head. "I don't understand."

"Wars are strange things, Your Highness. They can weaken us, or they can make us stronger. Quite often a war strengthens the royal house, because it's the king or queen who leads the army."

"Or the regent?"

"Yes," the archminister said, his face brightening. "Or the regent. And here I was afraid you were too young to grasp all of this."

Kalyi couldn't help but smile, though she quickly grew serious again. "But don't we want our house to be strong? Shouldn't all this make us want a war even more?"

"Well, that's where this gets a bit confusing. Of course we want House Solkara to be strong, but we need balance as well, among all the houses of Aneira. It's best for the realm if we maintain good relations with the other dukedoms. We don't want the other houses to have cause to hate House Solkara, or her queen."

Her queen! The last thing Kalyi wanted was for the other dukes to hate her. She looked away, not wanting Pronjed to see how much the idea of this bothered her. "I guess that makes sense," she said. She chewed her lip for a moment before remembering that her mother had told her queens weren't supposed to. "So what should we do?"

"Well, I can only offer counsel, Your Highness. Ultimately this is up to you and the regent. But I believe we'd be best served by speaking with the dukes who oppose the war. Perhaps not all of them, but certainly Tebeo of Dantrielle, and Brall of Orvinti. Their houses are the strongest of those in question. And we should see if we can address their concerns, even if it means delaying our attack on Eibithar by a turn or two. The realm will be stronger if we're united in this war."

Kalyi frowned. She wasn't certain that her uncle would

think much of this idea. "I should speak of this with Uncle Numar."

"Of course, Your Highness. I'd suggest though that you not tell him the idea came from me. He and I don't always see eye-to-eye on matters such as these."

She wasn't certain about that part either. She didn't like to lie to her uncle. But she nodded to the archminister. "All right."

They stood in silence for a moment, before Pronjed gave a small bow. "Well, Your Highness. I've taken too much of your time already. Good day."

"And to you," she called as he walked away.

The scent of fresh baked bread reached her from the kitchen, but the queen was no longer so hungry. She watched the archminister cross the ward. And when he had entered the castle corridors, she made her way to her uncle's chamber.

The guards standing outside the chamber bowed to her as she approached the door and knocked, and another soldier pulled the door open from within.

"Her Highness the queen, my lord," the man said, glancing back at Numar.

Kalyi couldn't see his face, but she had noticed in the past that he didn't always seem happy to see her, though he was always kind to her when she came to see him.

When he came into view this day, he was smiling broadly. "Your Highness," he said, bowing.

"Good day, Uncle."

He placed a hand on her shoulder, but he didn't ask her into the chamber. "I'm rather busy at the moment, but I had hoped to speak with you later. Can you return when the prior's bells are rung?"

Kalyi hesitated, started to chew her lip again, but caught herself.

The smile returned to her uncle's face, though there was a brittleness to it this time. "Can you tell me what this is about?"

"It's about the war."

"The war." He took a breath. "Very well. Please come in. We can sit for a moment or two."

He nodded to the guard, who immediately left the chamber, closing the door as he did. Numar led her to the chair in which she usually sat and then pulled the adjacent one closer to hers.

"Now," he said, "what about the war?"

She sat with her hands twisting in her lap, unsure now of how to begin. "I'm worried about our balance," she said at last, knowing even as she spoke the words that this wasn't quite right.

Numar looked puzzled. "Our balance?"

"I think we should be strong—our house I mean—but I don't want us to be so strong that it's bad. We should talk to the others even if it means that we don't go to war right away. It'll be better if we're—"

"Wait," the regent said, sitting forward. "Are you suggesting that we delay our attack on Eibithar?"

She nodded. "So that we can talk to the others."

His eyes narrowed. "What others?"

"Dantrielle, Orvinti. The other houses. The ones that are afraid of us."

"Kalyi, what are you talking about?"

She looked down at her hands, feeling her cheeks burn. "The war. I want to make certain that we don't make the others hate us. I don't want them to hate me."

"Why would you think—?" He regarded her briefly. "Kalyi, did someone send you here? Your mother perhaps? The duke? The archminister?"

She looked up, then immediately lowered her gaze again.

"Did Pronjed tell you to speak with me, Kalyi?" When she didn't respond, he took her hand, making her look at him. He was smiling now, his brown eyes locked on hers. "Was all of this his idea?"

"He didn't really send me here," she said.

"But he put these ideas in your head, made you think the other houses are going to hate you."

She nodded, afraid that Numar would grow angry with her.

But his voice remained gentle as he said, "Why don't you tell me everything you and he talked about?"

She related her conversation with the archminister, answering her uncle's questions when he interrupted, and trying her best not to leave out any details.

"You tell me that he didn't send you here," the regent said, once she had finished, "but he did recommend that you speak to me about all of this, didn't he?"

"Yes, but . . ."

"But what, Kalyi?"

"But he told me not to tell you that he was the one who thought of all this. He said that you and he don't always see eye-to-eye."

Numar actually gave a small laugh, though he didn't look at all happy. "That's true enough."

"Was I wrong to tell you?"

"No, not at all." He stood and began to walk around the chamber. "Kalyi, do you remember the conversation you overheard between Pronjed and the master of arms?"

She would never forget it. They had been in one of the tower stairways, and though she had known that it was wrong to listen, she had been unable to help herself. Pronjed had spoken to the armsmaster as if he were a child, telling him what to think and how to behave. And Tradden Grontalle, the leader of Solkara's army, one of the most powerful warriors in all the realm, had obeyed him without a word of protest. Kalyi guessed at the time that the archminister used magic to control Tradden's mind, and her uncle had agreed that it was possible. "Of course I do, Uncle," she said.

"And do you remember that we wondered at the time if the archminister might be a traitor?"

She nodded. This had occurred to her as well.

"Do you think it's possible that he was saying all of this not to help you, but rather to hurt you, and House Solkara as well?"

"I don't know," she said, shivering. "Do you?"

"Yes, I suppose I do. House Solkara needs to be strong, and Aneira needs to fight this war when the leaders of our army tell us it's time. If we do as the archminister suggests, and delay our attack, we could ruin everything."

"But what about the houses that are against the war?"

"Tell me again, what Pronjed said about them."

"He told me we should speak with the dukes of Dantrielle and Orvinti, that we should address their concerns."

The regent nodded slowly. "I see," he said, his voice low. "So the minister wants us to appease them."

Kalyi wasn't certain what "appease" meant, but she asked, "Is that what we're going to do?"

"No, it's not." He had ceased his pacing and was standing near the window, gazing out over the castle ward. After a few moments he faced Kalyi again. "Your Highness, I believe the time has come to take a harder stance with those houses that would oppose your will. Only enemies of the realm would want to keep Solkara weak. So I would suggest that we do all that we can to demonstrate how strong your house can be. What do you think?"

She still didn't understand all that was happening, but she knew that Pronjed scared her, and that when her uncle spoke of strengthening House Solkara it seemed to make a good deal of sense. "I think you're right," she said, drawing a smile from the regent. "If the other houses really want Aneira to be strong, then they should listen to us, and go to war when we tell them to."

Numar fairly beamed, making the queen blush. "I couldn't have said it better myself, Your Highness."

Chapter Eight

Dantrielle, Aneira

It had been a dangerous endeavor from the beginning. Tebeo, duke of Dantrielle, had drawn upon all his powers of persuasion to convince Brall of Orvinti to join his cause, and even that would not have been enough had it not been for their close friendship. By trying to convince the dukes of Aneira's other southern houses to stand together in resisting Solkara's push toward an alliance with the Braedon empire and war with Eibithar, they risked being branded as traitors to the realm. But both men believed that this war was a mistake, that the realm's true enemy was not their neighbor to the north, but rather the Qirsi conspiracy. So, early in the planning, they had decided to ride to the other houses and speak of rebellion with their fellow dukes.

In the end, Brall and Tebeo determined that they were best off traveling separately, Brall speaking with the new dukes in Bistari and Tounstrel and Tebeo riding to Kett and then to Noltierre. Even before word reached them of Numar's rush to muster new men into the royal army, they had known that their time was limited. By dividing their tasks and pushing their mounts, the two dukes hoped to forge alliances with the four houses in question before the end of Amon's Turn. With any luck, they thought, they might be able to dissuade the regent from this foolhardy war before his preparations had progressed too far.

Tebeo returned to his castle in Dantrielle more encouraged than he ever thought possible. His discussions with the dukes of Kett and Noltierre had gone perfectly. Due mostly to the untimely deaths of so many of the realm's dukes during the past year, Ansis of Kett now ranked as one of Aneira's oldest dukes, though he was quite a bit younger than both Tebeo and Brall. Like his father before him, Ansis had long been friendly with both men, and also with three of the late dukes—Chago of Bistari, Bertin the Elder of Noltierre, and Vidor of Tounstrel. Perhaps because the duke of Kett had always been the youngest of their group, Tebeo still found himself thinking of Ansis as a boy, a young noble so new to his power that he needed guidance from Tebeo and the others. Seeing the duke in his own castle, however, surrounded by his beautiful children and giving orders to his guards in their black-and-brown uniforms, Tebeo realized that he had been doing the man a disservice. Kett might have been no more than a middle-tier house, but her duke had grown wise with the years, and he was as brave as any man in the kingdom.

"You saved me the trouble of sending a messenger to Dantrielle," the duke said, the night Tebeo arrived at his gates. "I had intended to deny Numar's newest request for men, and I had thought to let you and Brall know, so that when the Solkarans marched on Kett, I might face them with more than just my army."

Coming from another man, it might have sounded like an idle boast. But Tebeo had little doubt that Ansis meant what he said.

"Then you oppose this war as well," he replied, hearing the relief in his own voice.

"Of course. I have no affection for the Eibitharians, but neither do I wish to find myself riding to battle with the emperor of Braedon. My father always thought Harel too vain and foolish to be an effective leader. I can only imagine what he would have said had Farrad or Tomaz suggested an alliance with the empire."

"Will your men stand against the royal house if it comes to war?"

"Yes," Ansis said. "The men of Kett would give their lives in defense of the realm, but they have little affection for the Solkarans. I'd rather avoid a civil war—I know you and Brall feel the same way—but we'll fight beside you if we must."

Eager to be on his way, his confidence bolstered by Ansis's pledge of support, Tebeo left the following morning for Noltierre. Bertin the Elder, who led the southern house for nearly thirty years until dying a few turns before, a victim of Grigor of Renbrere's poison, had been one of Tebeo's closest friends. Indeed, with the exception of Brall, Tebeo trusted no other noble in the land as completely as he had the old duke of Noltierre. Judging from the welcome he received upon reaching the black walls of the city, it seemed that the new duke, Bertin the Younger, knew that his father had valued their friendship just as much. Most of the Noltierre army stood outside the city gate, swords raised in salute, as a herald played "The River's Blood," the Dantrielle war anthem. Bertin, the image of his father with a square face and dark eyes, broad shoulders and long legs, sat atop a white mount as Tebeo rode to the gates. The two men dismounted at the same time, and then, rather than embracing Tebeo as he would a brother, the younger duke dropped to one knee, bowing as he might have to his father. An instant later his soldiers did the same.

Tebeo would have preferred a more restrained welcome; he was plotting against the regent, and no doubt House Solkara had servants throughout the realm who would notice this spectacle. Still, he couldn't help but be moved by Bertin the Younger's greeting. There seemed no point in cutting short the formalities. Best to allow them to go on as if this were nothing more than a visit born of Dantrielle's long-standing friendship with Noltierre, and the courtesy shown customarily to new dukes.

Eventually, when the introductions had been completed, Bertin and his first minister led Tebeo's company through the gates and the narrow lanes of Noltierre, to the great castle with its soaring black towers. Once in the outer ward of the fortress, they went through a second set of introductions, so that the duke's mother, Bertin the Elder's widow, could greet Tebeo and his minister. From there they went directly to the duke's great hall, where they partook of a grand feast prepared by Noltierre's renowned kitchenmaster.

It was nearly dusk before Tebeo finally had the opportunity to speak with the young duke in private, and even then he had to ask his first minister, Evanthya ja Yispar, to request a private audience with her counterpart. Noltierre's minister, who had served Bertin the Elder for more than a decade, was reluctant to leave the two dukes, but Bertin insisted. The young duke even went so far as to send his servants from the hall, so that at last, he and Tebeo were alone.

"What's happened?" Bertin asked, once the servants had gone.

Tebeo smiled at the directness of the question. It was so like something the elder Bertin would have done.

"You think me rude for asking so bluntly."

"Not at all. But I am reminded of your father."

"I'll take that as a compliment. I don't mean to be impolite, my Lord Duke—I'm pleased to have you here. But I'm not so young as to believe that you came simply to wish me well or even to pay respects to my father."

Tebeo had been raising his goblet to drink, but now he returned it to the table, taking a slow breath. Bertin the Elder would have leaped at any chance to oppose House Solkara, but Tebeo couldn't be so certain about the young duke. This was a dangerous time for him; had it been Tebeo's place to offer counsel, he certainly wouldn't have advised the man to take up arms against the royal house. But he hadn't come to give guidance.

"You're right," he said. "I've come to speak of the regent's plans for war and his pursuit of an alliance with Braedon."

"And are you here to speak on Numar's behalf?"

Tebeo grimaced. "Hardly."

"Good. Then I'm more than happy to listen."

Truly his father's son.

Bertin eagerly pledged all the resources of his house to Tebeo's cause, even going so far as to offer to march with Tebeo back to Dantrielle three days hence.

"No," Tebeo said. "For now you should see to the safety of your people. Numar will hear of my journeys to Kett and Noltierre, just as he'll learn of Brall's discussions with the dukes of Bistari and Tounstrel. And I'm certain he'll know the reason for them soon enough, if he hasn't divined our intentions already. I don't know yet how he'll respond, but he may choose to strike first at those who support us. Increase the guard on your city walls, and make certain the castle is provisioned for a siege."

"What if Numar strikes instead at you and Lord Orvinti?"

"We'll send word." He smiled. "Along with a request for aid."

The young duke merely nodded, grim-faced and earnest. "And you'll have it."

Back in Castle Dantrielle several days later, on the tenth morning of the waning, Tebeo still recalled how his gratitude for Bertin's pledge of support had been tempered by his fear that he was leading the young man and his house to their doom.

Everything now depended on whether Brall had succeeded in convincing Silbron of Bistari and Vistaan of Tounstrel to join them as well. With the duke of Orvinti expected to arrive at his gates within the next few hours, Tebeo could barely keep himself still. He had guards posted on the southern ramparts, watching the road from Tounstrel for any sign of Brall's company, but still he had climbed the tower three times that morning hoping to glimpse the riders himself, shielding his eyes from the sun and straining to spot any sign of Orvinti's blue, white, and green banners.

He was on his way to the tower stairs to check the road yet again, when he heard the gate bells ringing in the city. At first he assumed that these were the midday bells, but when Evanthya appeared in the corridor, her cheeks flushed, and a small smile on her lips, he knew that Brall had arrived, and with him his first minister, Fetnalla ja Prandt. Tebeo had known for some time now that Fetnalla and Evanthya were lovers, and though another duke might have been troubled at the thought of his first minister sharing a bed with a Qirsi from another house, his close friendship with the duke of Orvinti allowed him to be somewhat more lenient.

"They're on the road?" he asked before his first minister could speak. For once he was as eager for the arrival of Brall and his company as she.

"Yes, my lord."

"Have an honor guard sent to greet them. Instruct the soldiers to ride forth from the gates before Brall reaches the city walls. They're to accompany the duke to the east entrance so that he and the minister can enter the castle without crossing through the city. No doubt Numar has spies in the city, perhaps even in the castle, and I'd like them to see as little as possible."

"What of the bells, my lord?"

"They can't be helped. Anyone watching us would think it strange if they didn't ring at the approach of so many riders."

Evanthya nodded. "Yes, my lord." She turned and hurried toward the stairway.

Tebeo returned to his presence chamber to await Brall's arrival. It seemed but a matter of moments before Brall reached the chamber, accompanied by both Fetnalla and Evanthya. Orvinti's duke looked as he always did, hale and tall, with broad, kind features and hair as white as a Qirsi's. His clothes were travel-stained, his face ruddy from the sun and wind. He grinned as he strode across the chamber to grip Tebeo by the shoulders.

"How is it you convinced me to ride from Bistari to Tounstrel?" he asked. "And how is it we agreed to meet here rather than in Orvinti?"

"You miss your castle, my Lord Duke."

"My castle, my bed, my wife. I'm road-weary. We're too old for this nonsense, Tebeo."

"Actually, I found my ride quite invigorating."

Brall frowned. "You're younger than I am."

"Not by much."

"By enough."

Tebeo smiled again, but regarding him more closely, the duke could see that there was more to Brall's complaints than mere jesting. His friend looked tired, and not just physically. It seemed his journeying had taken a toll.

"I know that it's no substitute for your home, Brall, but whatever hospitality Pelgia and I have to offer is yours."

"I'm grateful, my friend, and I hope you'll thank the duchess for me. You and Pelgia have always made me feel welcome here. But I think I'll stay only the one night. I'm ready to be back in Orvinti."

Tebeo indicated a chair with an open hand. "Please sit." He glanced at the ministers. "The two of you as well. We have much to discuss." He turned to his servants. "Food and wine for the duke and his minister. In fact, for all of us. We'll take the midday meal in here."

Both servants bowed and left them.

"You spoke with Silbron and Vistaan?" Tebeo asked, facing Brall once more.

"I did."

"And?"

"Vistaan is with us. He blames all the Solkarans for Vidor's death, though he knows that only Grigor was responsible. He wants no part of Braedon's war, and even if he did, I don't think he'd allow his men to march with the royal army."

"That's good news."

Brall gave a small shrug. "I suppose."

"You have doubts?"

"Tounstrel is the weakest of Aneira's houses to begin with, and I'm not convinced that Vistaan is ready to lead his army into war. He still grieves for his father."

"I'd expect no less."

"Of course. But in many ways he's too much like Vidor for his own good. He's younger than his years and stubborn to the point of foolishness. He's bent on vengeance; it almost seems an obsession. I fear that he'll do more harm than good as our ally in this cause."

"Yet, we need him."

"Yes, we do, even more than you know."

Tebeo felt his stomach tighten. "Silbron?"

Brall shook his head. "He has no desire to oppose the regent."

"Damn!" Tebeo looked away. He had never thought that he would be so avid for civil war, but after his successes in Kett and Noltierre he had come to believe that they could stop Numar's war, that they might even be able to wrest the crown from Solkara if the regent refused to heed their calls for peace. "So it's over, before it's even begun."

"Perhaps not," Brall said. "He won't oppose Numar, but neither will he stand with him against us. Lord Bistari intends to remain above the fray."

"He told you that?"

"Those were his words. I believe he's taken a lesson from the Thorald clan in Eibithar. As the second-strongest house in Aneira, Bistari has the power to tip the balance in this conflict one way or another. By remaining neutral, Silbron leaves the outcome of any civil war very much in doubt."

"You think he seeks to prevent such a war?"

"Maybe. Or perhaps he expects we'll fight anyway, and when we've destroyed each other, Bistari will be left as the realm's preeminent house."

"And the throne will be his."

Brall shrugged a second time.

It made sense. Tebeo found himself surprised that the boy had managed to conceive such a plan on his own. His father, whom Tebeo had considered a good friend, had never been so clever when it came to matters of state.

"Do you think this was his idea?"

"I believe he's been speaking with his mother. Ria was present during many of our discussions, and I saw them speaking in private just after our first audience."

Tebeo shook his head. "This becomes a far more dangerous proposition without Bistari."

"Yes, it does." Brall started to say more, but at that moment the servants returned, bearing platters of food and flagons of wine. It took some time for the food to be arranged, the wine poured. But eventually, after they had begun to eat, the duke faced Tebeo again, a morsel of dark bread in his mouth.

"What of your travels?" he asked.

Tebeo described briefly his conversations with Bertin and Ansis. "They'll stand with us, though neither the army of Kett nor the army of Noltierre is likely to strike fear in the hearts of the Solkarans."

"Perhaps not. But that gives us five houses in all, against only three on the other side."

"Solkara isn't just another house," Tebeo said. "I shouldn't have to tell you that. And after Bistari, Mertesse is the strongest of the dukedoms."

Brall raised a finger. "It was once. But with Rouel dead, and Rowan's army still suffering from its losses at Kentigern, Mertesse is no stronger than Orvinti, or Dantrielle for that matter."

Tebeo wasn't certain that he believed this. It had been nearly a year since the failed siege of Kentigern Tor. The army of Mertesse had to be near full strength again. Perhaps the newer soldiers lacked training, but so large an army could not be dismissed lightly. "I'd feel better if Bistari was with us."

"So would I. But she's not, and I won't allow Silbron's neutrality to force me into an alliance with the empire."

"Did Silbron say if he would be sending men to the royal army?"

Brall shook his head. "I pressed him on the matter, but he told me nothing. To be honest, I'm not certain that he's decided."

"It's a question of some importance. If Numar is only getting men from Mertesse and Rassor, he'll have trouble mustering an army large enough to stand against us. With recruits from Bistari he becomes far more powerful."

"I'm not sure that I agree," Brall said. "Even if Silbron sends men to Solkara, Numar won't have a force large enough to wage war against both Eibithar and us."

"I'm not worried about Eibithar. And Numar won't be either when he realizes that we've lined up the other houses against him. He'll be determined to destroy us—he won't care about anything else."

"You didn't argue thus when last we spoke. You seemed to think that we could avoid civil war entirely, as long as enough of us stood against the royal house."

Tebeo nodded, knowing that his friend was right.

"I guess I'm not as confident of that as I was, particularly in light of Silbron's refusal to join us."

Brall said nothing, though he seemed to consider this for some time. At last, he turned to the ministers, who had kept silent throughout the dukes' discussion.

"What say the two of you?"

Fetnalla looked up from her food. "My lord?"

"Does Bistari's refusal to join our cause render us too weak to stand against the regent?"

The first minister shook her head, her pale eyes straying to Tebeo's face for just an instant. "No, I don't believe it does. Mertesse and Solkara may be powerful, but their combined might is no greater than that of Orvinti, Dantrielle, and Noltierre. And with Tounstrel and Kett joining us, I believe we have the advantage. I don't think the regent will risk a civil war with such a force arrayed against him."

Tebeo was watching his minister, who continued to stare at her cup of wine, as if it were a gleaning stone. She was smaller than Fetnalla, and some might have thought her less graceful than Brall's minister. Tebeo had heard Evanthya compare Fetnalla to a pale heron, and it was an apt description. Evanthya was plainer, not as long of limb, or fair of face. But in the years Evanthya had served Dantrielle, Tebeo had come to realize that she was as courageous as any man in his army, and as intelligent as any noble in the land. "Evanthya?" he asked now.

She pursed her lips briefly. Clearly the duke had placed her in a difficult position, asking her if she agreed with Fetnalla when it seemed plain that she didn't. But in this instance the needs of House Dantrielle outweighed any consideration he might have given her feelings.

"I have to disagree, my lord," she finally said.

Tebeo saw anger flash like sorcerer's fire in Fetnalla's eyes, but he couldn't say if Evanthya noticed.

"If we're to have any hope of standing against the regent," Evanthya went on, "the army we command needs to be far stronger than that of the royal house. It's not enough to lead a force that's merely a match for Numar's. Time and again the Solkarans have shown their willingness to fight when others might have thought better of it. It's one of the reasons their supremacy has lasted so long. Regardless of whether you think them brave or foolhardy, they are ruthless. Unless he knows for certain that he can't prevail, Numar will fight. And even should we manage to win, I fear what such a conflict would do to the realm."

"For one thing, it may end the supremacy you fear so much." Fetnalla was glaring at her. Tebeo had never seen Orvinti's minister look so angry. "By fighting the Solkarans we give Bistari the opportunity she needs to take the crown, and we keep the realm from entering into this alliance with the empire. Surely these are reasons enough to fight."

"I must say, First Minister," Tebeo said, eyeing Evanthya, "I'm surprised to hear you argue as you do now. You were the one who convinced me to begin this process."

"Yes, my lord."

"Now you regret doing so?"

His minister shrugged. "I fear for the realm, my lord. And with Bistari remaining neutral, I fear for your life and that of Lord Orvinti."

He held her gaze for another moment, then nodded. "Very well, Evanthya. Why don't you and Lord Orvinti's first minister leave us for now. I wish to speak with the duke alone."

She stood, as did Fetnalla. "Of course, my lord."

The ministers bowed and left, and Tebeo waved one of the servants over and had the boy refill his goblet.

"It seems that I can say to you much the same thing that I just said to Evanthya."

Brall raised an eyebrow. "I don't understand."

"When I journeyed to Orvinti a turn ago, you were the reluctant one, telling me that it was folly to stand against the Solkarans. Now you're as eager for civil war as Numar is to attack Eibithar. And what's more, you're arguing as Fetnalla does. I thought you didn't trust her."

"I've been riding about the realm for nearly an entire turn, arguing against this war and risking my life and my dukedom so that we might prevail in a conflict with the regent. When last I saw you, I might have been reluctant, but I've given too much to this cause to abandon it now." He looked away, a slight smile tugging at the corners of his mouth. "To be honest, I've found myself imagining Aneira under the rule of House Bistari, or Dantrielle, or even Orvinti, though I never would have thought it possible that I could entertain such ambitions at my age."

"You'd make a fine king, Brall. I've always thought so."

He dismissed the compliment with a vague gesture. "The point is, I've seen in my mind what Aneira could be without the Solkaran Supremacy, and I'm drawn to the possibilities."

"And your first minister?"

"I'm still not certain that I trust her. But in this instance we happen to agree."

"If she is deceiving you then agreeing with her on a matter of such importance could be dangerous."

"So am I to ignore all the counsel she offers? Or worse, am I supposed to listen to her advice and then always do the opposite? It wouldn't take her long to turn that strategy against me."

"No, I don't suppose it would," Tebeo said, grinning. "I just want to be certain that you've considered all the implications of what you're proposing."

"I have," Brall said gravely. "I don't want war with the royal house any more than I want war with Eibithar. And despite what your first minister said, I still hold out some hope that when Numar sees five of his dukes standing against him, he'll relent. But if he doesn't, I believe we can withstand Numar's assault even without Silbron's support, and I think that a civil war is preferable to this alliance with the empire, particularly if we can manage to wrest the crown from Solkara."

Tebeo heaved a sigh and nodded. "Very well."

Brall raised his cup, and Tebeo did the same. "To peace," Orvinti said.

"To peace."

They drank and Brall balanced his goblet on the arm of his chair as he so often did. "What do we do now?" he asked. "Should we send word to the regent of our intention to oppose the war?"

"We won't have to. He's asked for men, and we've refused him. I doubt we'll have to wait long before he brands us as traitors and threatens to lay siege to our castles."

"He can't attack all of us."

"No, he can't. I imagine he'll begin with me."

Brall frowned. "Why with you?"

"Because when he came here last, I made it clear to him that I opposed his war. He has to destroy your house or mine—Kett, Tounstrel, and Noltierre are too small to matter much. And when all else is said and done, he knows that Dantrielle will be the easier castle to take."

Brall's expression had sobered, and there was sympathy in his blue eyes, as if he had only just realized why Tebeo was so averse to a civil war. "My army is yours, Tebeo. You know that."

"I do, my friend, and I thank you. Ean knows, I'm going to need it."

They walked through the corridor in silence, taking the first set of stairs down to the castle ward, and then making their way to the gardens. Fetnalla would rather have gone directly to Evanthya's bedchamber, but she knew her love too well to expect that. They had been on opposite sides of the discussion in her duke's presence chamber, and after their fight in Solkara in the days following the death of King Carden the Third, Fetnalla sensed that Evanthya would be afraid she was angry with her again.

And she was, though not nearly so much as she might have been had she still cared whether or not her duke trusted her. She needed for both dukes to oppose the regent; the Weaver was expecting them to do so, and if by some chance Evanthya's doubts held sway, he would blame Fetnalla, at least in part. But in this instance, her duke agreed with her and would do his best to convince Tebeo regardless of what Evanthya counseled. Fetnalla wished only to forget about wars and alliances for a time, to put aside all this talk of Eandi politics, and be with her love. It had been far too long since last they had lain together; during Evanthya's most recent visit to Orvinti, Fetnalla had been too consumed with her fears of the Weaver and her resentment of Brall's suspicion to give in to her desires.

All that was now in the past. She had cast her lot with the Weaver, and was at peace with that choice. Brall's doubts were an inconvenience, nothing more. They made it a bit more difficult for her to do the Weaver's bidding, but they also reminded her each day of why she had chosen the movement over the courts. Beyond the Qirsi cause, she cared only for Evanthya. And she needed desperately to renew the passion and love they once had shared.

For the time was coming when the Weaver would reveal himself and the Qirsi he commanded would move to crush the Eandi courts. Qirsi who had yet to pledge themselves to his cause would have one last chance to choose: they could serve the Weaver or die with their nobles. Were she forced to make that choice on this day, Evanthya would choose to die with Tebeo. Fetnalla was certain of it. Which meant that in the days remaining until the Weaver's war began, she needed to convince Evanthya that their love was more important than their service to the dukes. It would take some time, perhaps more time than Fetnalla had, but she had to try.

"You're very quiet," she said, as they crossed through the ward.

"No more so than you."

"You fear that I'm angry with you."

"Aren't you? I disagreed with you in front of Brall. Again."

Evanthya glanced at her for but a moment. "I saw the way you looked at me in there. You can't tell me that you weren't furious."

"I don't know about furious. I might have been a bit angry, but only for an instant, only because I feel so strongly that this alliance with the emperor is wrong."

"It seemed like it was more than that."

Fetnalla smiled. "Well, in that case, I'm sorry. You know me, Evanthya. I hate to lose an argument, any argument. I get very passionate when I care about something." She slipped her hand into Evanthya's as she spoke, drawing a smile from the woman and making her cheeks color.

"I can hardly find fault with you for that."

A pair of guards stepped away from the nearest of the castle gates and started walking in their direction. Immediately, Evanthya pulled her hand away. The soldiers didn't appear to notice anything.

"Perhaps we should go somewhere more private to speak."

Evanthya cast a quick look her way. "I'd like that," she whispered. "Maybe later, after the evening meal."

"Must we wait?"

"I think we should. I expect our dukes will call us back to the presence chamber before too long."

"What does it matter if they do? They both know about us."

"Yes, I know. But I'd feel more comfortable if they didn't have to send guards to my bedchamber to find us."

Fetnalla considered arguing the point further, but didn't. Evanthya wasn't going to change her mind, and if this grew into a fight, it might be several turns before they were to have another opportunity to be together.

"All right," Fetnalla said. "What would you say to a walk through the city then? It's been some time since I last came to Dantrielle, and you know how I love the marketplace here."

"That sounds lovely as well, but as I said, I expect our dukes to summon us back to the castle before long. We should be here when they do."

"Why? They sent us away. Why should we concern ourselves with them all the time when they obviously don't give a thought to us?"

Fetnalla regretted the words as soon as she spoke them. Fortunately, however, Evanthya still recalled how Brall mistreated her in the past.

"Is he still so suspicious of you?" she asked, concern in her bright golden eyes. "I had hoped matters might improve. You and he do agree when it comes to opposing the regent."

"Yes, we agree, but that can't undo so many turns of mistrust."

"I know that. But you're not going to regain his trust by defying him either. If we go off to the city, and then they summon us back to my duke's chamber only to find us gone, it will do nothing to improve matters between you and Brall."

She sounded like the worst kind of Qirsi servant, a lackey to the Eandi court who cared more for the noble she served than for her own people. Fetnalla had to bite her tongue to keep from saying as much. She could only imagine how the Weaver would have responded hearing Evanthya speak so.

"You think I'm wrong," Evanthya said, after a lengthy silence.

"I think it's possible to worry too much about offending our dukes, even Brall."

"Maybe. But with the realm on the cusp of civil war, I think it best to err on the side of restraint." The guards had passed, and after glancing about to make certain that no one was watching them, Evanthya took her hand once more. "We'll be together later. I promise."

Fetnalla nodded, made herself smile. She couldn't help thinking, though, that winning Evanthya over to the Weaver's cause would be nearly impossible.

As it happened, the dukes did summon them just before the ringing of the prior's bells. The ministers returned to the presence chamber, where they spoke with their dukes and Dantrielle's master of arms about strategy for the civil war. With Evanthya possessing mists and winds, and Fetnalla being a shaper, both of them would be expected to play important roles in any battles fought against the Solkarans. In the midst of the discussion, Fetnalla realized that she didn't know what the Weaver wanted her to do if Brall called upon her to wield her magic on Orvinti's behalf. She would have to ask when next he walked in her dreams.

Once more, they took their meal in the presence chamber, their conversation continuing well past sunset and nearly to the ringing of the gate close. When finally Tebeo stood and stretched, giving them leave to go, Fetnalla feared that Evanthya would be too tired to do more than go to sleep. To her surprise and pleasure, however, the minister took her hand outside the presence chamber and led her back to her bedchamber.

Once there, they fell into each other's arms, kissing deeply before slowly, gently undressing one another. After that, Fetnalla lost all sense of time. Thoughts of the Weaver and his war faded from her mind, leaving only the cool smoothness of Evanthya's skin, the taste of her lips, the moist warmth she found between her love's legs. The urgency of her own hunger seemed to be matched by Evanthya's as the woman's mouth traveled her body. And when they had sated themselves, their pulses easing, their limbs entangled beneath the candlelight, Fetnalla pulled away, intending to dress and return to her chamber.

"Not yet," Evanthya whispered. "Lie with me for a while."

She hesitated. The Weaver hadn't entered her dreams in some time, and she expected that he would soon, perhaps this night.

Evanthya's fingers wandered gently over her back.

"All right," she said, lying back down. "Just for a while."

It began to rain, slowly at first, then harder. Lightning flashed, and thunder rumbled in the distance.

"A storm in Amon's Turn," Evanthya murmured sleepily. "Just like the day we met. Remember?"

"Of course," she whispered. It seemed like a lifetime ago. They had been so young, so devoted to their dukes and the realms they served. How could she have changed so much, and Evanthya not at all?

She lay in the bed, listening to the rain, and to the rhythm of her love's breathing, which slowed gradually as sleep came to her.

Fetnalla didn't realize that she had fallen asleep as well until she found herself on the Weaver's plain. A cool wind brushed her skin and she remembered that she was naked.

Not now, she thought. *Can't this wait until tomorrow night?*

To which the Weaver's voice replied, "Why should I wait?"

Usually she had to walk a distance to find him, but on this night the Weaver appeared before her immediately, the brilliant light behind him burning her eyes.

"You're not alone, are you?"

She shook her head, crossing her arms over her breasts.

"Dantrielle's minister is with you?"

"Yes, Weaver."

"Are you any closer to turning her?"

She had already felt what he could do to her if she angered him, and so she didn't dare lie. "No, Weaver, not yet."

"You still think it's possible, though."

"I want to believe it. I'm not ready to give up yet."

She saw him nod. "A good answer. Very well. Tell me of your duke and his plans to defy the regent."

"He remains convinced that the war with Eibithar is a bad idea. He fears a civil war, but he believes that with the support of the other houses, he can prevail against the Solkarans."

"Tounstrel and Bistari are with you?"

"No, Weaver. Only Tounstrel. Bistari's new duke refuses to take sides in the matter."

"Ah," the Weaver said, nodding again. "He aspires to the throne."

"That's what the dukes think."

"Did Dantrielle win over Kett and Noltierre?"

"Yes, Weaver. In all, five houses have pledged themselves to stand against the regent."

"Good. Very good. Bistari might have tipped the balance too far. I'm pleased."

She lowered her gaze. Already she had learned what the Weaver expected of her. "Thank you, Weaver. I wanted to ask you, when war comes, shall I wield my power on my duke's behalf?"

"You'll have to. If you refuse, you endanger yourself and the movement. But if your duke is like most Eandi, he knows little of Qirsi magic. You can use your powers on his behalf without using them well. Do you understand?"

"Yes, Weaver."

"Good. I'll leave you now, since you're with the minister."

"Thank you, Weaver."

"Time runs short. You know that. If you don't turn her soon, it will be too late. We'll have no choice but to kill her."

He may as well have reached into her chest and taken hold of her heart.

"Yes, Weaver," she managed, and woke.

The candle flame beside the bed flickered and danced. Evanthya was sitting up, staring at her, a single crease like a scar in the middle of her forehead.

"You were dreaming."

Fetnalla's throat felt dry. "Was I?"

"Yes, and you spoke in your sleep."

She pulled up the bed linens, covering herself. "What did I say?"

"It was hard to make sense of it. But you said something about a Weaver."

"A Weaver." She tried to make herself laugh as she said this, but it came out sounding breathless and desperate to her own ears.

"What was it you were dreaming about?"

"Honestly, Evanthya, I don't remember."

"Was it a vision?"

Fetnalla shook her head. "I'd remember a vision."

Evanthya looked as if she wanted to ask more, but Fetnalla didn't allow her the chance.

"What's the hour?" she demanded, kicking off the linens and swinging herself out of the bed.

"I'm not certain."

She began to dress. "I should return to my chamber."

"Have you had this dream before, Fetnalla?"

"I told you, I don't remember it. How should I know if I've had it before?" She winced at what she heard in her voice. Even in the dim light, she could see the hurt in Evanthya's eyes, the color seeping into her cheeks.

"You seemed frightened," her love said, low and sad. "Whatever you were dreaming seemed to terrify you."

It did. He's going to kill you. Fetnalla stopped buttoning her shirt and sat beside her on the bed. "We all have dreams that scare us, Evanthya. You can't tell me that Shyssir has never brought demons to your sleep."

"Of course, but—"

"It was a dream, that's all." Fetnalla kissed her lightly on the lips. "I promise."

Evanthya gazed at her for several moments, then nodded.

She stood again and finished dressing. "I have to go, but we'll have breakfast together in the morning. All right?"

"All right."

She bent to kiss Evanthya again. "I love you," she whispered.

"And I love you."

Fetnalla turned and let herself out of the chamber. She could feel Evanthya's eyes upon her as she opened and closed the door, but she dared not look back for fear that she'd weep. She could almost feel her love's lips still, warm and soft. But she could only hear the Weaver's voice.

Time runs short. . . .

He hadn't said the one thing she feared most. He didn't have to. She knew it, just as she knew that Ilias would follow Panya into the sky, and a tide once high would soon ebb. When it came time to kill Evanthya, she would have to wield the blade.

Chapter Nine

Kentigern, Eibithar

He was awake before daybreak, driven from his slumber by visions that made him tremble with rage and terror. Aindreas of Kentigern, the tor atop the tor, duke of one of Eibithar's great houses, had been frightened from his bed by wraiths. Again. It almost seemed that his castle was haunted, that the tor had been swallowed by Bian's realm and that shades walked everywhere. Brienne, his beautiful daughter, whose murder had started this spiral down into misery and hatred and, ultimately, betrayal, hovered at his shoulder. The king's man, the soldier of Glyndwr, killed in Aindreas's ducal chambers by Jastanne ja Triln, lurked in corners, silent and grim, his eyes following the duke's every movement, his very presence an accusation. The duke's wife, Ioanna, had fallen back into the dark torpor that first gripped her in the turns following Brienne's murder. She lived still, but as a mere ghost of the woman he once loved.

As always, Aindreas sought shelter in his pursuit of vengeance and his stores of Sanbiri red. But in recent days, he had come to understand that revenge was further from his grasp than it ever had been and that the flagons of wine brought to him by his servants were no longer adequate to ease his mind. Walking through the dimly lit corridors of his fortress with two soldiers in tow, the duke found himself wondering if he wouldn't be better off taking his own life, and joining the specters roaming about his castle. He dismissed the notion immediately, horrified by the workings of his mind, ashamed of his cowardice. But he also took as a measure of how desperate he had grown that such an idea should even occur to him.

Reaching his presence chamber, taking hold of the door handle Aindreas hesitated for just an instant, suddenly aware of the two men behind him. As soon as he opened the door, the smell hit him like a fist, just as he had known it would. He was amazed that the guards didn't notice, so strong was the stench. Blood.

The smell had lingered in the chamber since the murder of the soldier Kearney sent to speak with him. He could still see it all so clearly—the way the soldier fell when the Qirsi woman used her magic to shatter the bone in his leg, the glint of firelight on Jastanne's blade as she raised it to cut open his throat, the man's blood flowing like an ocean tide over the floor of Aindreas's chamber. Jastanne had walked out a moment later, seemingly unaffected by what she had done. And though Aindreas knew that he should stop her, that she deserved to be imprisoned and executed for what she had done, he let her go.

Unwilling to reveal to anyone what truly had happened, Aindreas made it seem that he had killed the man himself, going so far as to pull the man's dagger from its sheath and drop it in the crimson puddle that had formed around his body.

"He insulted me and our house," the duke told Villyd Temsten, his swordmaster, when Villyd arrived in the chamber with several of his soldiers. Aindreas's hands were trembling, and he felt unsteady on his feet, but that served only to make his story more convincing. "When I took offense and ordered him from the castle, he pulled his weapon. I had no choice but to defend myself."

"Of course, my lord," Villyd had said at the time, though his tone left Aindreas wondering if the swordmaster believed him. After making certain that the duke was unhurt he eyed the corpse for several moments, his brow furrowed. When next he spoke, he surprised Aindreas with the direction his thoughts had taken. "Under the circumstances, my lord, we might be best served to keep his death a secret. If the king learns that he's dead, he'll march against us."

"That may be." The duke hesitated. "What would you suggest we do?"

"We should tell the king's other men that he offended you, that he threatened you with his blade in hand. But we'll say that you overpowered him and placed him in your dungeons, and there he'll remain until the king offers a formal apology for the soldier's behavior. That should give us a bit of time to decide . . . how to proceed from here."

"Yes, of course. A fine suggestion, swordmaster."

"That leaves us with the question of what to do with his body."

Aindreas considered this for but a moment. "Is there anyone in the dungeon right now?"

"No, my lord."

"Then we'll put him in the forgetting chamber. Let him molder with the corpses there."

"Yes, my lord."

Villyd ordered his men to dispose of the corpse and clean the blood from the duke's chamber. Then he approached Aindreas again.

"A word, my lord?"

He stepped from the chamber, giving Aindreas little choice but to follow.

"You must understand, my lord," Villyd said, turning to face the duke once more. "I seek only to understand the circumstances of his death. But I have to ask you: what happened to the soldier's leg?"

Aindreas just stared him. "His leg?" he managed at last.

"I couldn't help but notice that his right leg was broken. I'm just wondering how that happened."

"It . . . it must have broken as we struggled. At one point I fell on top of him." He tried to grin, failed. "It isn't that hard to imagine, is it? A man of my size. . . ."

Villyd frowned. Clearly he knew the duke was lying to him. "Yes, my lord." He paused. Then, "Forgive me, my lord. But I heard talk of a woman—"

"Don't, Villyd." The duke rubbed a hand over his face, thirsting for his wine. "Some things are best left unsaid. Kearney's man is dead—I killed him. Nothing else matters. Do you understand?"

"No, my lord. I don't."

At another time, Aindreas might have taken offense. Villyd, though, was not a man given to impertinence, and in this instance he deserved more than Aindreas's lies. How was the duke to explain? He had betrayed his kingdom, his house, his people. He had tied himself to the Qirsi conspiracy, thinking that they might help him strike at Kearney and Javan. He had given his word in writing—in writing!—expecting that he could turn the renegades to his purposes. That, he had believed at the time, was his path to vengeance. Only recently had he come to realize the truth.

Tavis of Curgh hadn't killed his beloved Brienne. It galled him to think it—he hadn't yet found the courage to speak the words aloud. Even alone in his chambers late at night, drunk on Sanbiri red, wrestling with his grief and fury, he hadn't been able to give voice to this horrid truth. Yet he knew it to be so. Brienne was a victim of the conspiracy, and—gods be damned for forcing him to confront this truth as well—so was the boy. The conspiracy had been deceiving them all, making them see enemies in the other courts when in fact the white-hairs were the danger. Others had been saying this to Aindreas for the better part of a year now—Javan of Curgh, Kearney, the strange gleaner whom the duke suspected of having helped Tavis win his freedom. But for so long Aindreas had refused to hear them. He still hadn't found the strength to tell his wife all of this. How could he tell the swordmaster?

"I know you don't," Aindreas said at last. "I'm sorry; truly I am. But I can't tell you any more than I have. I want to make right all I've done, but it's going to take some time."

"Perhaps I can help you, my lord." He sounded so earnest. What had Aindreas done to deserve such fealty?

The duke laid a meaty hand on the man's shoulder. "Thank you, Villyd. But no one can help me. This is something I have to do alone." He glanced back toward the doorway. "See to the cleaning of my presence chamber. Please."

Villyd gave a small bow, still looking displeased. "Yes, my lord."

That had been a half turn ago—nearly all the waning had passed—and still the castle servants had been unable to clean away the reek of the dead man's blood. Aindreas had ordered them back to the floor with their buckets and cloths a dozen times; he had ordered them to use perfumed soaps of the kind used by his wife and her ladies. Nothing worked. Every time he opened the door to his presence chamber, the odor reached him, reminding him of that night, forcing him to envision it all again.

As one might expect, upon being told that their leader had been imprisoned, the other eight riders sent by Kearney demanded to see the man. When Villyd refused, they requested an audience with the duke. Following Aindreas's instructions, the swordmaster denied them this as well, at which point the soldiers broke camp and started back toward the City of

Kings, vowing to inform the king of just how poorly they had been treated since reaching Kentigern's gates. Aindreas had heard nothing from Audun's Castle since.

It was only a matter of time, though. Aindreas had yet to submit to the king's authority as demanded by the soldier. He still owed tribute to the Crown—four turns' worth now. With this last act of defiance he had left no doubt: Kentigern was in rebellion. The Qirsi wanted him to break with the king, to make it plain that Kentigern would fight before it recognized Glyndwr's claim to the throne. And though he had been reluctant to carry his defiance that far, Jastanne, who was one of the leaders of the Qirsi conspiracy, had left him little choice.

As it happened, since that bloody night he hadn't heard anything from the Qirsi, either. Nor was Aindreas surprised by this. They had gotten from him what they wanted. Civil war was inevitable. The realm would be weakened. When Braedon and Aneira attacked, Kearney would be unable to marshal a force strong enough to withstand their assault. Soon, the western half of the Forelands would be engulfed in warfare, and when the white-hairs attacked, Eibithar, Braedon, and Aneira would fall. Wethyrn, Caerisse, Sanbira, and Uulraan would be left standing, but Wethyrn and Caerisse were the weakest of the seven realms, and Uulrann's suzerain had long refused to concern himself with affairs beyond the mountains that bounded his domain. In essence, the warriors of Sanbira's matriarchy would be all that remained of the Eandi armies. It would fall to them to keep the conspiracy from gaining complete dominion over the Forelands. Aindreas didn't believe that Sanbira could hold off the Qirsi by herself for more than a few turns.

He wasn't so vain as to think that the white-hairs wouldn't have succeeded without him. The more he dealt with Jastanne, the more he recognized just how formidable a woman she was. She might be slight as a reed and so young as to make him feel like a wasted old man, but it seemed that she anticipated his every move. She could gauge his moods and fears better than he could himself. He tried to tell himself that her insights were born of magic, that they were little more than a sorcerer's trick, much like the dancing flames he saw in the streets of Kentigern when the Revel came to his city. Yet, even if this was so, it did nothing to diminish their effect. From his first encounter with the woman, she had controlled him, turning to her advantage his grief and his blind certainty that Tavis and Javan were to blame for all that had befallen his house. If all the leaders of the conspiracy were like Jastanne, the Eandi were doomed, and had been from the start. His betrayal merely made matters a bit easier for the renegades.

Yet, knowing this did little to lessen his shame at the ease with which the Qirsi had ensnared him. A thousand times he had made up his mind to seek out Ioanna and confess all, and on each occasion, he hadn't gotten as far as the corridor outside his chamber.

It would kill her, he had told himself. *She would be lost once more to the blackness that gripped her after Brienne's death.* She had taken to her bed again after Aindreas tried to tell her of the woman Kearney held in the prison tower of Audun's Castle, the Qirsi traitor who claimed to have paid gold for Brienne's murder. How far would she fall if he told her of this wicked pact he had forged with the traitors?

He knew, though, that he didn't remain silent out of concern for his wife, at least not entirely. Even had she been strong, her mind whole, he would have kept this from her. He couldn't bear the thought of what she would say to him, what she would call him. And what if his children overheard? How would he explain to Ennis that he had disgraced their house, leaving the boy heir to his infamy? What answer could he possibly find for the tears Affery would shed upon learning of his treason?

Sitting at his writing table, the scent of blood filling his nostrils, Aindreas could think of no way to escape his ignominy, except of course the one he had turned to so many times before.

"Wine!" he bellowed, his voice echoing in the chamber. He glanced behind him at the shuttered window. No light seeped past the edges. It wasn't even dawn, and already he was calling for his beloved Sanbiri red.

"They deserve better than this, Father."

He turned at the sound of the voice, though reluctantly. It wasn't really Brienne. It couldn't be. It wasn't yet Pitch Night, and even if it was, this was no sanctuary. But there she stood, her golden hair shimmering in the lamplight, a look of pity on her lovely face.

"Wine!" he called again, even as he continued to stare at her.

"It's still not too late to end this, to make right all that you've done."

"But it is too late," he said. "Don't you see? There'll soon be civil war, all because of me. Can't you smell the blood?"

"Do something, Father. You must."

Before he could answer, there came a knock at his door. Brienne began to vanish, shaking her head slowly as she faded from view.

Aindreas let out a long, shuddering breath. "That had better be my wine."

The door opened, revealing a frightened boy bearing two flasks of wine. The cellarmaster had learned not to send just one.

"Bring it here, boy," the duke said. "Then be gone."

The servant did as he was told, and for the next hour or two, past the ringing of the dawn bells, Aindreas did little more than sit at his table and drink his wine. After some time, he heard Villyd begin to work the men in the ward below his window, but still the duke didn't leave his chair, though by now both flasks were empty.

Eventually, he must have dozed off, for another knock at his door made him start and overturn his empty goblet.

"Yes! Who is it?"

Ennis poked his head into the chamber, wide-eyed, an impish grin on his round face.

"Can I come in, Father?"

Aindreas stood quickly, stepping around the table to block his son's view of the flagons. But he smiled, pleased to see the boy. "Of course you can." The duke waved the boy into the chamber, crossing to one of the great chairs by his hearth. "Come sit with me," he said, indicating the chair opposite his own with an open hand. Instead, the boy ran to the duke's throne and climbed into it, looking every bit the Little Duke, as Aindreas's soldiers called him.

"Did you sleep well?"

Ennis nodded.

"And have you already eaten?"

"Yes. Mother and Affery have, too."

"Your mother's up and about?" Aindreas asked, hoping he didn't sound too surprised.

Again the lad nodded. "She said she needed to be preparing the castle for the rains."

The duke frowned. "The rains?"

"Yes. Tonight." Ennis regarded his father as if the duke were simple. "It's going to flood tonight, like it does every year."

Aindreas merely stared at the boy. It was the last day of Amon's Turn. Tonight would be Pitch Night after all. He glanced about the chamber, as if expecting to see Brienne once more. How had he managed to lose track of the days? Apparently even Ioanna had known, though she had barely left her bedchamber since the Night of Two Moons.

As the boy said, there would be floods this night all across the Forelands. Atop the tor, of course, none in the castle had cause for concern, and even in the city there was little risk that the rains would do serious damage. But in the surrounding countryside, particularly near Harrier Fen, and in the northern baronies of his dukedom nearest the Heneagh River, many would be forced from their homes until the waters receded. Hundreds from the closer villages would seek refuge in the city this night. No doubt they would be heartened to see their duke and his duchess in the city with them, offering what comfort was theirs to give. He and his wife had gone to the city every year since his investiture as duke. The previous year, Brienne had gone with them. But this year . . . Aindreas wasn't certain that Ioanna was fit to be seen in public by so many, nor did he have it in his heart to be there himself.

"Father?"

He now realized that Ennis had been saying something all this time, though he had no idea what.

"I'm sorry, son. I was thinking of something else. What did you say?"

"I asked you whether the castle has ever flooded."

Aindreas made himself smile. "No. We're up on the tor. Water runs down to the lands below and eventually to the Tarbin. There'll be no flooding here tonight."

Ennis nodded gravely. "That's good. I don't want a flood."

"No, I don't suppose you do."

"Will you and Mother go down to the city again?"

Aindreas looked away. "I'm not certain. We might."

"I think you should."

"You do? Why?"

Ennis shrugged, looking so much older than his nine years. "I think Mother should be out of the castle for a time. I don't think she's left it since . . ." He dropped his gaze. "You know."

He was uncommonly clever, and far wiser than most children several years his senior.

"You're right, she hasn't," the duke said. "And it might well do her some good to walk among her people." *I just don't know if she can do so without humiliating herself.* "I'll think about it, all right?"

"All right."

"Now, don't you have lessons to attend?"

"Not until midmorning bells."

But even as he spoke the words, the bells in the city began to toll. Ennis covered his mouth and laughed, his eyes wide once more.

Aindreas couldn't help but grin. "You'd best be on your way."

"Yes, Father," the boy said, scrambling off the throne and running to the door.

Brienne stood by the doorway, watching her brother leave. Then she turned her gaze accusingly toward the duke.

"You must do something, Father."

Aindreas closed his eyes tightly, refusing to look at her. "You're not real. I know you're not."

"But I can be."

At that his eyes flew open, but the apparition was already

gone. The duke felt dizzy, and he wished that he'd eaten before drinking all that wine.

I can be.

A short time later, Villyd came to the duke's presence chamber, as he did most mornings. Aindreas expected the usual dull report on the day's training, but as soon as the swordmaster entered the chamber it became clear to the duke that this discussion would be different. Villyd looked unusually grim, his stout frame coiled and tense, a troubled expression in his pale blue eyes. He bowed to the duke, but then began to pace rather than standing at attention near the hearth, as he often did.

"Something's troubling you, swordmaster," Aindreas said after a brief silence.

"Aye, my lord," the man said, clearly distracted.

"Do you care to tell me what it is, or shall we just remain here in silence for the rest of the day?"

Villyd halted, meeting the duke's gaze, an embarrassed grin on his face. "Forgive me, my lord. I've only just received the tidings myself. I'm still trying to make sense of them. Seems there's been a good deal of movement along the south bank of the Tarbin."

"The Aneirans have been gathering men there for more than a turn now. It's not that surprising, is it?"

"This is more than just men, my lord. We have reports of carts leaving Mertesse this very morning, of laborers marching from the city as well."

"Do you trust what you're hearing?"

"Normally I would, my lord. These reports come from peddlers we've trusted in the past—several of them, mind you; not just one or two. But with the rains coming tonight, it makes no sense. They have time yet to cross the river, but Pitch Night in Amon's Turn is about as poor a time to begin a siege as I can imagine, especially one that's likely to begin so close to the Tarbin."

"Maybe the peddlers were wrong this time."

"Perhaps," Villyd said, in a way that made it clear he didn't believe this for a moment.

"Do you think they were trying to deceive us?"

The swordmaster nodded, resuming his pacing. "That did occur to me. If they were, if we can't depend on them anymore, it makes it far more difficult to guard against an assault from the south."

No doubt that was the point. Aindreas muttered a curse, then stood and opened the shutters that darkened his window. It was a windy day, cold for so late in Amon's Turn, though clear. He could see no sign of the dark clouds that would cover the sky by nightfall, though there could be no doubt that they would come.

"There will be no attack today," the duke said at last, knowing in his heart that it was so. "But soon, tomorrow perhaps, certainly within the next half turn."

"I agree, my lord."

Aindreas turned to face him, leaving the window unshuttered. "Begin your preparations for a siege, swordmaster. Tell the kitchenmaster and quartermaster that you're to have their complete cooperation, on my orders."

"Yes, my lord."

"How goes your training of the men we've added since the last siege?"

"Well, my lord." The swordmaster smiled faintly.

"They remain a bit raw, do they?"

The man nodded, his expression souring. "A bit, my lord. I intend to work them twice each day until the attack comes. They'll be ready."

"I have no doubt of that. We'll speak again later, Villyd. Let me know if you have any trouble making your preparations."

"Very good, my lord. Thank you." The swordmaster bowed and left the chamber.

Once he was alone, Aindreas fell back into his chair, rubbing his eyes. A siege. He had been expecting it; he was no fool, after all. Nor did he have much doubt as to what the Qirsi would expect of him. He opened his mouth to call for more wine, but then thought better of it, choosing instead to seek out Ioanna. She would be wanting to speak with him.

He found her in the great hall with the prelate, surrounded

by piles of blankets, no doubt intended for the unfortunates who would crowd into the city after sundown.

Aindreas crossed to where she stood and bent to kiss her cheek. She looked in poor health, her cheeks sunken and her skin sallow. Aindreas could only imagine what the city folk would think upon seeing her. But she smiled at the sight of him, and appeared to have regained a good deal of her strength.

"I want to bring them food as well," she said, as Aindreas glanced about at the blankets. "I've already sent word to the kitchenmaster."

"He can give you some," the duke said, sighing and facing her. "Not a lot."

"Whyever not?"

He glanced at the prelate, who had paused in what he was doing. The man would know soon enough. Best to let him hear as well.

"Because there's to be a siege."

Ioanna raised a shaking hand to her mouth. "Ean guard us all! You know this? They're coming already?"

"Not yet, no. But Villyd and I are quite certain. I expect they'll come in the next few days. Certainly before the Night of Two Moons in Elined's Turn."

At least she didn't ask him who would be coming. At that moment he wasn't sure which force would arrive first: Kearney's guard or the army of Mertesse.

"Perhaps I should bring only the blankets then." She looked up at him, looking so frightened. "Or will we need those, too?"

They would, but he hadn't the heart to say so. Planning for this night had done her so much good. "Tomorrow begins Elined's Turn. We shouldn't need the blankets. And I think we can also spare a bit of food. Just not as much as we might in other years."

"All right."

He took her hands, lifting one to his lips. "We'll be all right. The gates will hold."

She nodded.

"We'll ride down to the city at twilight," he said, knowing

that he had to go, that she needed him to. Even as he spoke the words, though, he saw movement behind Ioanna, near the entrance to the hall. Looking past her, he saw Brienne again, watching him, nodding slightly.

"Aindreas? What is it?"

He shook his head, forcing himself to meet his wife's gaze. "It's nothing. I should join Villyd in the ward. He's having trouble with some of the new men. I might be able to help."

"Of course."

The duke kissed her cheek, then hurried off, refusing to look at Brienne, though he could feel her eyes following him.

He found the swordmaster in the castle courtyard, just as he expected, and he spent much of what remained of the day alongside Villyd, working the men. Many of the younger soldiers did need a good deal more training, but they weren't nearly as unskilled as he had feared they might be. He was glad to be out of his chamber, away from his wine and the smell of blood. No doubt his own swordwork needed polishing, though the swordmaster would never presume to say so. It felt good to feel the hilt of a blade in his hand, to work muscles that had been idle for so many turns.

As the day went on, the sky began to cloud over, and by the time Aindreas and Ioanna rode forth from the castle, followed by nearly a hundred men and several carts loaded high with blankets and provisions, the rain had started to fall, driven by a chill wind. Already, the streets of the city were filling with men, women, and children, a good number of them carrying what few possessions they had chosen to save from the rising waters. Most were making their way to the Sanctuary of Bian at the southern end of the city.

As if realizing this, Ioanna abruptly reined her mount to a halt.

"No," she said. "I can't."

"Ioanna?"

"I can't go there!" she said, turning terrified eyes on the duke. "I can't. I don't want to . . . to see . . ."

He saw Brienne again, standing in the rain, watching them,

her golden hair soaked, water running down her cheeks like tears.

And at last he understood.

You're not real, he had told her earlier that very day.

To which she had replied, *I can be.*

Ioanna was sobbing, her entire body convulsing.

"You don't have to," Aindreas said, as gently as he could. *But I do.* He reached out to her, stroking her cheek with the back of his hand. "I'll go. You return to the castle."

"But—"

"It's all right. She'll . . . she'll understand."

Ioanna actually smiled, though an instant later she was sobbing again.

Aindreas waved one of his captains forward. "Take eight of your men, and escort the duchess back to the castle."

"Yes, my lord."

"Go with him, Ioanna. I'll be back before long."

She seemed to hear him, but she did nothing. After several moments Aindreas nodded to the man, who took her reins in hand, turned her mount, and began to lead her back toward the tor. The duke watched her go, then rode back to another captain.

"See these people to the sanctuary. I have . . . matters to discuss with the prioress."

"Yes, my lord."

Aindreas spurred his mount forward. He was shaking now, like a boy awaiting his Fating. But he didn't slow his horse. He had put off this encounter for far too long.

The sanctuary gates were open when he reached them, and hundreds of people had already crowded into the courtyard outside the shrine. Seeing this, Aindreas hesitated.

"Lord Kentigern."

The prioress strode toward him on long legs, her black robe billowing in the wind. She had a hood over her head, but wisps of red and silver hair framed her face.

"Good evening, Prioress. Men from the castle are on their way. They bear food and blankets."

"You have our thanks, my lord."

His eyes flitted toward the shrine. "I had hoped . . ." He swallowed, unable to speak the words.

"I've wondered when you would come to speak with her, my lord. I expected you long ago."

Aindreas glared at her. "You would presume—"

"I presume nothing, my lord. And I serve the god, not you."

"You serve in my realm!"

"The great ones care nothing for realms and titles. You know that as well as I do, my lord."

She was right, of course. The sanctuaries had always existed outside the jurisdiction of the noble courts. When Tavis escaped his dungeon, Aindreas knew that the boy took refuge in the sanctuary. Still, he didn't dare try to take him back by force. Not from here. The cloisters might hold sway in the castles of the Forelands, but only a fool would invite Bian's wrath by violating the Deceiver's sanctuary.

"Do you wish to enter the shrine, my lord?" the prioress asked.

"I . . . I had intended to. But with all these people here, I'm not sure anymore."

"There are always people in the sanctuary on this night, my lord. We shelter them in the novitiate and the clerics' refectory. The shrine is yours, if you so wish it."

Despite the anger he had felt only moments before, he was grateful to her. "I do. Thank you, Mother Prioress."

"Of course, my lord. One of the brothers will see to your mount."

Aindreas swung himself off his horse, but then merely stood there, gazing toward the shrine, heedless of the rain and wind.

"She'll be pleased to see you, my lord. It's been so long since any came to speak with her."

It took him a moment. "Others have come?" he demanded, whirling toward her.

She regarded him placidly, torchlight glittering in her dark eyes. "You know one has."

"Tavis!" he whispered.

"Lord Curgh spoke to her just days after her murder."

"Did you hear them? Do you know what she said to him?"

"The words of the dead are beyond my hearing." She

smiled for just a moment. "Except of course for the words of my dead. I could only hear what Lord Curgh said to your daughter."

"And what was that?"

"It's not my place to say. I will tell you, though, that he spoke to her of his love, of his grief at losing her. I didn't think much of the boy when I met him, but I don't believe that he killed Lady Brienne."

He'd known this already. Yet hearing her say it made his stomach heave. He could only nod.

"Speak to her, my lord. Facing one's dead is never easy, but there is some comfort to be found in the Deceiver's shrine."

"Yes," he said dully. "Thank you, Mother Prioress."

He turned once more, gazing up at the narrow spire atop the great building. Shuddering, he forced himself forward, crossing the courtyard to the shrine's marble stairway. He hesitated at the base of the stairs, but then climbed them and entered the shrine. It was empty of people, just as the prioress had assured him it would be. Tapered candles stood at either end of the altar, and between them a stone bowl and knife for blood offerings. Dozens of candles also flickered along the walls, lighting the shrine and making shadows shift and dance like demons from the Underrealm. Behind the altar, looming over it like storm clouds above the tor, the stained-glass image of the Deceiver glimmered dimly, illuminated from without by torches in the sanctuary's inner courtyard.

Aindreas stepped to the altar, his gaze falling briefly to the knife.

"Hello?" he called, his voice echoing loudly through the shrine.

No answer. Would she refuse to come to him? Had he waited too long to speak with her?

"Brienne?"

"Father!" The reply seemed to come from a great distance, soft as a sigh. Still, the very sound of her voice made him flinch as might the hammering of a siege engine against Kentigern's gates. He took a step back, struggling with an overwhelming urge to run.

Before he could, however, she appeared before him, just on

the other side of the altar. Her form was insubstantial at first, a shimmering pale mist. But it quickly coalesced, his daughter seeming to come to life before his eyes. Her golden hair, her soft grey eyes, glowing as if lit from within. She wore the same sapphire gown he remembered from the night of her death, though it was now unbloodied and whole.

"Brienne," he sobbed, tears coursing down his face.

"Poor Father," she said, a sad smile on her lips. She looked so much like her mother had at the same age.

"Forgive me!" he cried.

"For what, Father?"

"For . . ." He stopped himself. It was so easy to forget that the Brienne he saw in his presence chamber and the corridors of his castle was but a creation of his mind, a false image brought on by grief and guilt. This was the real Brienne, or at least what remained of her. "For not coming sooner," he said at last, silently cursing himself for giving in to weakness and lies, even here, in front of his lost child.

"It's all right. I know how you've mourned me."

He felt as though she had taken hold of his heart. Did she really know? Had she seen all he had done in the name of vengeance? "Your mother wished to come" was all he could think to say. "She's suffered greatly since your . . . since we lost you."

"I understand."

They stood in silence for several moments. Aindreas managed to compose himself, but he couldn't tear his eyes from the wraith. She had been so lovely, so young. And though she looked much as he remembered her, there was something cold and distant in her appearance now. It was as if she had aged centuries without actually being touched by the passage of time. Was this what happened in the Underrealm?

"You have questions for me," she said at last.

He nodded. "So many."

"He didn't do it, Father." There could be no mistaking the rebuke in her voice. "Tavis didn't kill me."

Aindreas so wanted to look away, but her gleaming eyes held his. "I know that now."

"You tortured him."

"Yes."

"You nearly started a civil war."

I might still. "It seemed so clear what had happened."

"I could have told you the truth, had you only come to me and asked."

The duke was crying again. "I know," he whispered.

"He's dead now, the man who killed me."

"What?"

"He's here, in the god's realm. I've seen him."

The god's realm. The Underrealm. Aindreas shivered, his breath catching, as if Bian himself had wrapped an icy hand around his throat.

"How?" he managed to ask.

"Tavis killed him, just as he promised he would."

"Tavis did?"

"Yes. He swore that he would avenge me, and he has. He's suffered enough, Father. He deserved a far better fate."

"So did you," Aindreas said, his voice hardening. He still couldn't bring himself to forgive the boy, though for what he couldn't say. "At least Tavis is alive. At least Javan still has his son."

Brienne stared at him, saying nothing.

"Who was he?" the duke asked after some time, discomfited by her silence. "Who was this man who murdered you?"

"An assassin, hired by the Qirsi. He posed as a servant during the feast that night. But you know all this already, don't you, Father?"

"Not all of it, no."

"Enough. I know what you've done. I gave you the chance to confess all to me just now, but you wouldn't. Now I'm telling you: I know."

She had been testing him, as if he were but a boy. He didn't know whether to be offended or ashamed. He wanted to beg her forgiveness, and also to rail at her for speaking to him so. *You're still my daughter,* he would have liked to say. *You can't possibly know what it's like for a parent to lose a child.* But he couldn't bring himself to respond at all, at least not at first.

"How could you join them, Father? You've made yourself a

traitor. You'll bring disgrace to all who love you—Mother, Affery, Ennis."

"How is it that you know all this?" he asked.

"We can see much from the god's realm. And we speak among ourselves. You sent many Qirsi to the Underrealm before you found those who could help you join their conspiracy. They've told me a great deal."

"Is it . . . Have you suffered much?"

A faint smile touched her face and was gone. "Not much, no."

"Is the god kind to you? Do you walk with the honored dead?"

"He forbids us from speaking of it with the living." For the first time, finally, tears appeared on her cheeks, glistening like dew in the light of early morning. "You needn't worry about me. You should think only of Mother and the others. You have to end this, Father." How many times had he heard her speak those words in his mind? "You can't help the conspiracy anymore."

"It's more complicated than you know."

"Is it? I think you're just frightened of disgracing yourself. I think you're afraid to tell Mother the truth."

"Disgrace is no small thing, Brienne. Shall I leave your brother to rule a dishonored house? Shall I doom Kentigern to centuries of disrepute and irrelevance?"

"If that's what it takes, then yes."

"You don't know what you're saying."

"Yes, Father, I do! You—"

"Enough!"

She winced, her entire body seeming to ripple, like a candle flame that sputters in a sudden gust of wind. For just an instant Aindreas feared that she would leave him.

"I'm sorry," he said quickly. "Please, don't go."

She had lowered her gaze, as she often did when chastised. The assassin's blade might as well have found the duke's heart, so much did it ache as he looked upon her. "You were always headstrong as a child. Your mother said it was because you were so like me, but I think you favored her in every way."

The wraith looked up and smiled, radiant and so alive he wanted nothing more than to hold her in his arms, as he had when she was just a babe.

"There's something I've always wanted to tell you," she said.

"Oh?"

"Do you remember when I was seven, and I went riding and fell off Cirde?"

"Yes, of course. You broke your arm in two places. Your mother was ready to prohibit you from riding again until you were past your Fating."

"But you told her that all riders get thrown, that it would only serve to make me a better horsewoman."

He grinned, his eyes stinging with tears at the memory. "I remember it well."

"I never told you the reason I fell."

"You said that Cirde reared for no reason."

"I lied. I was standing in the saddle."

His eyes widened. "Brienne!"

"I'd seen a rider do it during the Revel, and I wanted to try."

"You're lucky you didn't break your neck. You could have—" He stopped. *You could have been killed,* he was going to say. Was it folly to speak so to a wraith? "It's something I would have done," he muttered instead.

"I know. I was more like you than you think, even then. And I was always proud of that."

Aindreas nodded, unable to speak.

"I'm sorry I angered you, Father. But I don't want my death to be the cause of any more killing, and I certainly don't want it to bring our house to ruin."

"I'm the one who's sorry," he said, his voice breaking. He swallowed, took a long breath. "I'll find a way to undo all that I've done," he told her. "You have my word."

"You'll confess all to Mother?"

"I . . . I'll think about it." But already he was wondering if there might be another way out of this, one that made such a confession unnecessary.

"She loves you, Father. She'll forgive you."

If she survives hearing what I've done. "And you? Can you forgive me?"

She smiled, looking almost shy. "Of course I can."

Aindreas smiled as well. In that single moment nothing else mattered. "Thank you."

The enormous image of Bian behind her flashed for just an instant, the colors in the stained glass vivid and brilliant. Thunder rumbled a few seconds later, making the stone beneath his feet pulse. No doubt it was raining in earnest by now.

"I should return to the castle," he said. "Your mother will want to hear all about you. I'm sorry to have to go."

"It's all right, Father. We can speak again next turn, and every one after that, if you like."

A turn from now his castle would most likely be under siege. Two turns from now he might well be dead. But he just smiled and nodded. "I'd like that very much."

She began to fade from view, slowly, like morning stars disappearing in a brightening sky. "Farewell, Father."

"Goodbye, Brienne," he said, through fresh tears. "I love you."

She said nothing, but he thought he saw her smile one last time before vanishing altogether.

He began to sob once more, standing alone beside the god's altar. He remained there for some time, until he was finally able to compose himself. Then he turned and left the shrine, suddenly eager to be away from the sanctuary and back in his castle, though all that awaited him there was lies and ghosts and the promise of war.

Chapter Ten

Galdasten, Eibithar, Elined's Moon waxing

From so great a distance, even on as clear and bright a day as this one, they might have been merchant ships gathering together on the open sea in some strange waterborne marketplace. Their sails were down, and though Renald, duke of Galdasten, thought he could see sweeps bristling on the sides of the vessels, he couldn't be certain. Or perhaps he didn't wish to be.

They had sailed into view two days before, the first morning of the new waxing. The clouds that had covered the sky on Amon's Pitch Night had still darkened the horizon that morning, and the waters of Falcon Bay were dotted with whitecaps. The vessels had quickly arrayed themselves across the mouth of the bay—a defensive posture. They hadn't moved since. They simply waited there, no doubt for the other cluster of ships to move into position opposite them.

Renald had first noticed this second group of vessels some time ago, and though at so great a distance he could say nothing about them with any confidence, the duke felt reasonably certain that they represented the bulk of the Braedon fleet. From this vantage point in Galdasten Castle, atop the tor that had been the seat of his family's power for centuries, on the ramparts of what his forebears had named the eagle tower, Renald would have a fine view of the coming naval war. And if the weather held, the first battles would begin soon, probably within the next day or two.

Eibithar's fleet had long been a source of great pride for Renald's people. Most of the realm's ships had been built in either Galdasten or Thorald, and though they were not considered quite as swift or sturdy as those constructed in Braedon or Wethyrn, they were as fine as any others in the Forelands. But next to that of the empire, Eibithar's navy appeared pitifully small. Braedon had half again as many ships, and if there was any truth to the tales told by the sailing men who gathered in Galdasten's port, they were captained by some of the finest seamen on Amon's Ocean. "The sun of the empire," it was said, referring to Braedon's flag, which bore a golden sun from which flew great red arrows, "rises and falls on the waters of Amon." There was a reason why the empire had managed to claim as its own most of the important islands off the shores of the Forelands. Her soldiers might not have been any more formidable than those of Aneira or Eibithar, but her fleet had no equal.

Certainly the duke had little doubt that Braedon's navy

would prevail in the battles that were about to be waged within sight of his castle. He just couldn't decide whether to rejoice at this, or to quail.

"It's ironic that they would choose to begin this war in Falcon Bay," the duchess said softly, the ocean wind stirring her dark hair, a hand raised to her brow to shield her eyes from the sun.

Ewan Traylee, Galdasten's swordmaster, glanced at her, a frown on his broad face. "Irony has nothing to do with it, my lady. Braedon's ships will seek to drop anchor off the shores of Galdasten. The cliffs are low here. If they have it in mind to invade the realm, this is the best place to begin their assault."

Elspeth smiled thinly. "Of course, swordmaster."

Renald, who knew precisely what she meant, feared that she might say more. Fortunately, his wife seemed content to mutter the word "idiot" under her breath, and leave it at that.

"We should discuss your plans for the defense of the strand, my lord," Ewan said a moment later, seeming not to have heard. "If the naval battle goes as I fear it might, we'll have to be ready to repel Braedon's invasion sooner rather than later."

Renald kept his eyes on the bay and the ships, refusing to look at either the swordmaster or his wife. He felt queasy, and he wished that both of them would simply leave him alone.

"My lord?"

Elspeth placed her hand in his, something she rarely did, though he knew better than to mistake this for affection. Her skin was hot, as if she had been stricken with a fever.

"Yes, Ewan. We'll speak later today. Perhaps you can come to my chamber at the ringing of the prior's bells."

"Of course, my lord."

She squeezed his hand, so that his signet ring dug painfully into the finger next to it.

"You can go, swordmaster. I'm certain that you have much to do."

"Yes, my lord."

Ewan bowed to Renald and Elspeth in turn, before leaving them alone atop the tower.

She dropped his hand. "You haven't told him," she said, an accusation.

"There's nothing to tell him. I've made no decisions as of yet." The words were brave, but even he could hear the flutter in his voice. *Damn her.*

The duchess actually smiled, sharp white teeth gleaming in the sun. There could be no questioning her beauty. If only he had been wise enough to marry a plainer woman.

"You want me to believe that you've considered riding to war?" She laughed cruelly. "Come now, Renald. You're no warrior. You're afraid of me. You'd never raise your sword against the emperor's army."

How he would have liked to prove her wrong, to strap a blade to his belt, swing himself onto his mount, and lead the Galdasten army into battle. But Elspeth was as brilliant as she was lovely, and she knew him all too well.

"You want to be king, don't you?" she went on. "You want our sons to aspire to more than this dukedom and the worthless thaneships in Lynde and Greyshyre. Both of us do."

He turned his gaze back to the ships. The Revel was in Galdasten City this turn. How strange to think that war could begin amid the music and spectacle of the festival. "It's one thing to side with Aindreas," he said. "It's another thing entirely to sit by idly as the realm is attacked."

"No, it's not! The one leads naturally to the other. Siding with Kentigern has no purpose if you intend to turn around and fight beside Kearney in defense of his kingdom."

"His kingdom is my kingdom! If I allow it to be destroyed—"

She closed her eyes briefly, the way she did when she lost patience with one of their boys. "No one's suggesting that you allow it to be destroyed, Renald. Even now men march toward Galdasten from Curgh, Thorald, and Heneagh, as well as from the City of Kings."

Had she overheard the reports he received from Ewan's scouts? He could almost imagine her standing in the corridor outside his ducal chambers, an ear to his door. He had every right to be angry with her, but he just nodded dully, unable to say anything.

"The realm isn't about to fall, at least not yet. And before it does, you can step in and save it. But for now, your first duty is to the defense of this castle, and the people of Galdasten City.

Rather than marching out to battle with Ewan, you should be readying your fortress for a siege."

"Kearney would see through that in a moment."

"I don't care about Kearney, and neither should you. The question is, what will the people of Galdasten think? Do you believe that they wish to give their sons and husbands over to this king? What will our allies in Eardley and Sussyn think? What will they say in Domnall and Rennach?"

"Some of them may join with Kearney."

"Perhaps. But isn't it just as possible that they'll look to Galdasten before deciding what to do?"

The duke glanced at her. Sunlight shone in her brown eyes, making them appear warm, almost loving. He looked away quickly. It seemed likely that the other houses were doing just what she said: waiting for Galdasten to choose its course so that they might follow. She questioned whether he had courage enough to fight a war. Didn't it require just as much nerve to lead a rebellion?

"What if Ewan won't follow me? What if his men won't?"

"They're not his men, they're yours. And they'll all follow you if you act like a king." She touched his cheek with a warm hand, forcing him to meet her gaze. "The men of this house have no love for Curgh, and though they've had no reason to hate Glyndwr before now, Lady Brienne's death has changed that. If you lead them as you would a rebellion, they may see you as a traitor and defy you. But if you make it clear to them that you fight to restore justice to the realm, that you fight to return Galdasten to its rightful place among the leading houses of Eibithar, they'll follow you anywhere."

He was frightened, and he wanted to tell her so. But such intimacy had been lost to them years ago. Or so he thought.

"When I married you, when you were still thane of Lynde, I saw daring in you, and ambition, and strength." She took both of his hands. "That's why I fell in love with you. Since we've come to Galdasten, since you've become the duke of a house that no longer has any future, I've seen those qualities fade until I feared that they were gone entirely. But this is your chance to find them again, to realize the promise that I glimpsed in you all those years ago. You can have power and wealth." She leaned toward him, kissing him softly on the lips. "You can have me again."

He must have been mad. It had been so long since they had loved one another that Renald wasn't entirely certain it was even possible for them to begin again. Still, even without her love, he knew that he wanted the throne nearly as much as she wanted it for him. He was tired of feeling weak and lost, of sensing her contempt and disdain in every glance she cast his way. But more to the point, he'd had enough of leading an emasculated house. Why should Galdasten suffer so for the act of a madman? Yes, the pestilence had wiped out Kell and his family. But why should their ill fortune doom his house to obscurity and powerlessness for so many generations? Damned be the Rules of Ascension! Damned be Kearney and Javan and all the others who would keep the sons of Galdasten from the Oaken Throne! Let them fall to the emperor's army. When the time came, he would raise his sword and drive the invaders from Eibithar's shores. And when the war was won, he would claim the crown as his own.

"All right," he said, smiling at her.

A look of genuine surprise flitted across her face. "Really?"

"As you say, what was the purpose of siding with Aindreas if not to wrest the crown from Glyndwr?"

"What of Ewan?"

"I'll give him his orders and he'll do as I command. He may not approve, but he's a good soldier. He'll follow my orders."

"Are you certain?"

"Yes."

"And the Qirsi?"

"Pillad? I haven't spoken to him about any of this in nearly two turns. Even if he has an opinion on the matter one way or another, he knows better than to voice it."

"You have someone watching him?"

"There's no need. He may still be first minister in name, but he has no influence anymore. He might as well be counseling another duke."

"Then why not send him away?"

"I will, when all of this is over. Once I have the crown, every Qirsi in Eibithar will want to serve in my court. But for now, sending him away without replacing him will only make me appear weak. And it may embolden those who believe that the conspiracy was behind Brienne's murder."

She raised an eyebrow. "I'm impressed, Renald. Very impressed. Even I hadn't thought of that."

He smiled, knowing that he shouldn't let her see how much her praise pleased him, but unable to help himself.

"Still," she said. "I think you should have someone keeping an eye on the man. He is Qirsi, after all."

"I have other matters to occupy my time, all of them far more pressing than Pillad, but I'll try to remember to say something to Ewan."

She nodded once. "Good. Now go. See to the defense of your castle. If Galdasten falls, all else is lost."

He hesitated a moment, hoping she would kiss him again, ashamed of himself for caring. When she merely turned to look out at the king's fleet, he left her, feeling his cheeks redden.

Fearing that his nerve would fail him before the ringing of the prior's bells, Renald sought out the swordmaster immediately. He found him in the armory, squatting beside a pile of old swords, speaking in low tones with one of his captains.

"I thought we were to speak later, my lord," Ewan said, as both men stood.

The duke nodded to the captain before facing his swordmaster. "Yes, well, I wished to discuss some things with you now."

"Of course, my lord." Ewan looked at the captain. "Have these blades cleaned and oiled. Then do the same with the shields. I want all of these weapons battle-ready by nightfall."

"Yes, swordmaster."

Ewan and the duke left the armory, both of them squinting in the bright sunlight.

"I'm sorry if I angered the duchess today, my lord. I meant no offense."

Renald winced. "Think nothing of it, swordmaster. My wife feels the strain of the coming war, just as we all do."

"Thank you, my lord."

"I want you to make preparations to guard the castle and city in the event of a siege. We won't be meeting the emperor's forces on the strand, nor will we attempt to halt their advance inland."

Ewan gaped at the duke as if Renald had just told him to raze the towers and execute his own men. "But . . . my lord, this is . . . this is lunacy."

Normally he wouldn't have tolerated such a statement, but he could see the man struggling with what he had just said and he thought it best to allow the swordmaster some time to overcome his shock.

"I know that it seems that way, Ewan—"

"The realm is at risk, my lord. The enemy is coming to Galdasten, but he strikes at all of Eibithar."

"Yes, he does. Which is why Kearney and his allies are already converging on Galdasten. But if we simply join the king's forces and surrender ourselves to his authority, we, in effect, accept him as our legitimate sovereign. I'm not prepared to do that."

Renald had expected that the swordmaster would continue to argue the point. To the man's credit, though, he appeared to weigh the duke's words. When at last he spoke, he sounded calmer, as if he had taken to heart what Renald told him.

"What is it you intend to do?" he asked. "Surely you won't allow the empire's forces to conquer Eibithar."

"Of course not. I wish to be king, Ewan. And I expect my son to follow me to the throne. I have every reason to want to preserve the realm. But our first duty must be to Galdasten. I want to keep her strong, and if the king's army is weakened as a result of that, all the better."

"So we allow the king and his allies to bear the brunt of Braedon's assault," the swordmaster said. "And when it seems that he's about to be defeated, we come to his aid, leading Eardley, Domnall, and the other houses."

Renald had to smile. Ewan might have been limited in many ways, but he could be clever at times, and he served the House of Galdasten well. "Precisely, swordmaster. We'll be the ones who save the realm, who atone for Kearney's failure."

"We're playing a dangerous game, my lord. We're risking a

great deal for . . ." He looked away, seemingly unwilling to complete the thought.

"For my ambition?"

"Forgive me, my lord. I shouldn't have spoken thus."

"It's all right, Ewan. What you say is true. I'm risking the safety of the realm in order to put myself on the throne. But what choice do we have? What good does it do to repel the emperor's invasion if we still find ourselves led by a king who invites rebellion and civil war? The realm is threatened from all sides, and I seek a solution that not only defeats our foes, but also strengthens us from within."

"Yes, my lord."

"Are you with me, swordmaster?"

"Of course, my lord."

"I know that you'll follow my orders, but I'm asking you more than that. I want to know if you can put aside your misgivings and fight this war with fervor in the manner I want it fought."

Ewan took a breath, then nodded. "I can, my lord. And I will."

"Thank you, swordmaster. There isn't another man in the Forelands I'd rather have fighting beside me."

Clearly moved, the man bowed deeply. "You honor me, my lord."

"Have riders sent to our allies. Tell them to begin preparations for war immediately, and to march their armies to Domnall. They should try to reach Seamus's castle no later than the tenth day of the waning. That's twenty-one days from now, ample time for them to arm and provision their men, and march to Domnall. They can await word from me there. We need to watch how this war unfolds, and we should allow the king and his allies to commence their assault on Braedon's army."

"The king will have ordered some of our allies to the Tarbin, my lord. The threat from Aneira is nearly as great as that from Braedon."

Renald weighed this briefly. "You may be right. We need to know which houses Kearney sent north, and which he sent south."

"I'd imagine that he ordered Eardley and Domnall north, and Sussyn to the Tarbin. That leaves Rennach."

"I agree. Find out what you can. But the message should still be the same. They're to await my word before marching north from Seamus's castle. Kearney may well have sent them orders to march, but I doubt any of them will. You should also send a rider to Aindreas. Tell him what we have in mind to do, and suggest that he follow a similar course with respect to the Aneiran army."

"Will he follow you, my lord? The others are minor houses, but Kentigern . . ." He shrugged.

"Aindreas is desperate for allies, and he knows better than to think that he has any claim to the throne after all that's happened over the past year. Under the circumstances, he'll have no choice but to join us."

"Yes, my lord." Ewan bowed again before hurrying off to dispatch the messengers.

Renald stood briefly, watching the swordmaster walk away. Then he started back toward his chambers. He had only taken a few steps, however, when he stopped and glanced up at the eagle tower. Elspeth was there, staring down at him, the wind making her hair fly like battle pennons. Their eyes met for just an instant, and the duke thought he saw the merest hint of a smile flit across her features. A moment later she lifted her gaze again, toward Falcon Bay and the warships, leaving Renald to wonder whether she had smiled out of pride in him, or amusement at the ease with which she had bent him to her purposes.

It had all happened as Uestem said it would. Soon after Pillad jal Krenaar's meeting with the merchant in Galdasten City, when the first minister finally agreed to join the Qirsi movement, he found a pouch of gold in his sleeping chamber. He had no idea how it had gotten there; he assumed that it came from the merchant, though he didn't see how Uestem could have slipped into the castle without being seen by the duke's guards.

The pouch contained eighty qinde. Pillad had counted it several times to make certain, unable to believe at first that anyone would see fit to pay him so much. As it turned out, this gold was the least of the surprises awaiting him now that he had agreed to cast his lot with the renegade Qirsi.

That very night, a Weaver came to walk in his dreams. He was tall and broad like some great magical warrior, with wild hair that stood out like a lion's mane against the brilliant white light he conjured to keep Pillad from seeing his face. At first Pillad thought that this was no more than a fanciful vision, a product of his fear and excitement at having been paid for his treachery. But as the Weaver spoke to him of the gold and of Uestem and of the great future awaiting those Qirsi who joined his cause, the minister realized that this was no dream, that in fact this was the leader of the Qirsi movement revealing himself to his newest adherent.

Their conversation was brief. The Weaver seemed to know a good deal about Pillad: where he was born, in which court his father had served, why he had come to Galdasten to serve Renald. As they spoke, he even seemed to sense that Pillad had feelings for Uestem, and his distaste was evident in his voice and the swiftness with which he ended their conversation. As the merchant had promised, the Weaver did give him a small task to perform. Pillad was to learn from Ewan Traylee the precise number of soldiers in the Galdasten army and how they were to be positioned in the event of an attack on the city and castle.

Under most circumstances, he would have had no trouble learning all of this from the swordmaster. But the duke had lost faith in him, which made him suspect in the eyes of the swordmaster as well. It had taken him the better part of the previous waxing to gather the information, and even then the minister could not get more than a rough sense of how the men were to be divided between the defense of the city walls and the defense of the fortress.

Fortunately, the Weaver had commanded him to relate to Uestem what he learned. The Weaver hadn't harmed him during their first encounter, but Pillad was certain that he could, and he didn't wish to dream of the man again any time soon.

He also couldn't deny that he looked forward to his conversations with the merchant. By joining the movement, Pillad had done far more than tie himself to the Qirsi cause. He had, he believed, tied himself to Uestem. He couldn't say what he thought would happen next. Making a traitor of himself had been daring enough. Declaring his affections for a man seemed to be beyond his capabilities. Perhaps he hoped that the merchant would take it upon himself to open his heart first. That would be far easier.

He and Uestem hadn't met since late in Amon's waxing. But this very morning, Pillad had received a cryptic message asking him to come to the White Wave, the Qirsi tavern at which they had spoken many times before. He had known it would be crowded; with the Revel in the city all the taverns were, no matter the time of day. No doubt Uestem thought that they would be safe meeting here precisely because there would be so many people about. No one was likely to notice them.

Sitting now in the tavern, waiting for the merchant to arrive, Pillad reflected with some amazement on how quickly his life had changed. Just a turn or two ago he had been a loyal minister in the House of Galdasten. Now he was part of a great movement that would soon sweep away the Eandi courts and bring a Qirsi ruler to the Forelands. Not long ago he had been alone, friendless. Now he had Uestem. At least, he wanted to believe that he did.

The merchant entered the tavern just as the twilight bells began to toll at the city gates. He stood in the doorway for several moments, scanning the tables for Pillad. Seeing the minister, he strode to the table and sat, his expression grave. He had a lean face and eyes the color of sand on the Galdasten strand. He wasn't particularly tall or powerfully built, but he carried himself with an air of importance. Whether his carriage was rooted in the wealth he had accrued as a merchant, or in the authority he held within the Qirsi movement, Pillad couldn't say. The minister knew only that he envied the man his confidence.

"I'm glad to see you're here already," Uestem said. "We haven't much time."

"Why? Has something happened?"

"Something is on the verge of happening. What can you tell me of your lord's plans for the coming assault?"

Pillad grimaced. "Not a great deal. As I've told you before, he's lost faith in me. He doesn't tell me much anymore."

"And as I've told you, it's time you began to win back his trust. You're of little use to us as an outcast in the duke's court."

He tried to smile. "Yes, but—"

"Tell me what you do know."

Pillad felt his face fall. This wasn't at all the way he had wanted their conversation to go. In fact, it bore almost no resemblance at all to any of their previous encounters, except perhaps the last one, when Uestem had seemed a bit hurried. Perhaps that was the case today, as well.

"Quickly, Pillad. Time runs short."

"From what I observed today, I gather that he has no intention of opposing the emperor's army. I believe he plans to keep his soldiers within the city walls to guard against a siege. No doubt he wants to see Kearney's forces weakened before committing his men to the war."

Uestem nodded. "Good. Did you counsel this approach?"

For just an instant he considered lying to the man. Anything to earn his praise. But he had already admitted having little influence with his duke. Even if he claimed credit for this the merchant wouldn't believe him. More likely the question was a test of sorts.

"No, I didn't. And if I had, he might have done the opposite."

"Yes, I suppose that's possible. It seems the gods are smiling on you, Minister. This is just what we had hoped your duke would do. You need only to keep him on this path."

"I'll try."

Uestem stood, and Pillad cast about for something to say—anything at all—that might keep the merchant with him for another few moments.

"When will we meet again?" he asked, then cringed at what he heard in his own voice.

Uestem glanced about as if fearing that others had heard. "When those we serve command it," he said in a low voice.

"Can't we meet . . . ? Must it always be to speak of these matters?"

The merchant smiled, though Pillad could tell that it was forced. "I think it best that way." He stepped away from the table. "Good day, Pillad."

Pillad opened his mouth to bid the man farewell, but he couldn't even bring himself to say that much. Not that long ago, the day he agreed to join the movement, the man had actually touched his hand. He still remembered the warmth of the merchant's fingers. He could still see the way Uestem smiled at him that day. Had he imagined it all?

He shook his head. It had to be the coming invasion. These were dangerous times for all who would play a role in this war, particularly those who had taken up the Weaver's cause. Uestem couldn't afford to be seen with the duke's first minister. Not with the men and women of the movement so close to realizing their dreams. Pillad saw that now. Once the Eandi courts had been destroyed and the Weaver had taken his place as sovereign of all the Forelands, things would be different.

He waited until Uestem had been gone for some time before standing and leaving the inn himself. Upon stepping into the street, however, Pillad froze. A pair of the duke's soldiers stood a short distance off, watching him from the entrance to a narrow byway. His first thought was to duck back into the tavern, though he knew immediately that this would be folly. No doubt the men had come to the city for some reason that had nothing to do with him. If he acted on his guilt and panic he would only raise their suspicions. Instead, he gathered himself, then walked right over to them.

Both men looked uncomfortable as he drew near. So much so that Pillad was forced to wonder if he had been mistaken a moment before. Perhaps these men were watching him and had just not expected to see him emerge from the inn so soon. He had lost Renald's trust long ago. Would it be so unusual for an Eandi noble to have soldiers following his Qirsi?

"Are you looking for me?" the first minister asked, stopping in front of the men.

"First Minister?" one of the men said, glancing uneasily at his companion.

"Well, you're here. I thought perhaps the duke had sent you to fetch me. Is there news?"

"No, First Minister."

"Then what are you doing here?"

"The duke asked us to keep an eye on you, First Minister," the other man said. "I suspect he fears for your safety. With all this talk of conspiracies and such, I believe he thought a loyal minister would be in some danger. He wanted us to protect you. From a distance, of course, lest we embarrass you."

It had to be a lie, but it was a clever one nevertheless. "Well," Pillad said with false brightness, "I'm most grateful to both of you. I'll feel safer knowing that you're with me."

The man bowed, and his companion hastened to do the same. "We're honored to be of service, First Minister."

Abruptly, Pillad felt his face growing hot. What if Uestem was watching? What if there were others in the Weaver's movement who could see him right now, standing with the duke's men? Would they think that he had betrayed their movement to the duke? Or would they merely understand that Renald had sent these men to spy on him, as if he were some wayward child? Neither possibility appealed to him, though if they thought the latter the price would merely be humiliation. If they came to question his loyalty to the Qirsi cause they wouldn't hesitate to kill him.

The minister found himself scanning the street for other Qirsi, eager now to be away from these men.

"If there's nothing else," he said, his voice tight, "I'll be on my way back to the castle. I think I'll be just fine, thank you. There's no need for you to follow me."

"We have our orders, First Minister."

Damn you, Renald! "Fine, then." He started away from them. "Do what you must."

He started back toward the fortress, walking quickly, aware of the soldiers falling in step a few paces behind him. After going but a short distance, he realized that his hands were hurting. Looking down at them, he saw that he had balled them into fists, his knuckles white as Panya, the skin pulled tight over bone. He couldn't recall ever being this angry before.

He had made his decision to join the conspiracy impetuously. True, Renald had excluded him from his daily audiences, making Pillad feel that he was no longer welcome in the court. But his had not been a calculated choice, nor had it been rooted in hatred of the duke. Indeed, the minister wasn't certain that he could articulate fully why he had cast his lot with the renegade Qirsi. He wanted to be closer to Uestem. He wanted gold. He was hurt by Renald's distrust.

Until now, Pillad had not been driven by a desire to hurt the duke. But this encounter with Renald's soldiers changed everything. He felt violated. He didn't care that the duke's suspicions were warranted. Renald had shamed him; the duke's soldiers were shaming him still. They might have followed at a respectful distance, but no one who saw them would have doubted for even a moment that they were escorting the minister back to the castle.

Pillad had never thought of himself as a vengeful man, but he vowed now that he would strike back at Renald and his court. One way or another, he would see the duke dead. And the promise of that day would do more to compel his service to the movement than all the gold the Weaver could give him.

Chapter Eleven

Dantrielle, Aneira

Rumors chased one another through the streets of Dantrielle like demons on the Night of Bian, whispering darkly to frightened peddlers, driving children back into the relative safety of their homes, leaving men and women to do little more than go about their lives in glum silence while casting wary glances at the great castle in whose shadow they dwelled. Many said that the

Solkaran army already marched toward the city, a thousand strong, with swordsmen and archers in equal number. Others claimed that the host was closer to two thousand, for it included a horde of laborers who had been trained to build siege engines from the trees of the Great Forest. Still others were heard to say that all these men were led by the regent himself, Numar of Renbrere, who had labeled the duke and all his followers as traitors to the realm, and who had sworn that he would not rest until the city and castle had been reduced to rubble.

Tebeo had heard all of these tales, and though his scouts in the north had yet to bring word of the Solkaran army's latest movements, he knew with the certainty of a man facing his own doom that every one of them was true. He had dispatched his fastest riders three days before, on the fifth morning of the waxing, sending one each to Bistari, Orvinti, Kett, Tounstrel, and Noltierre. All carried messages pleading with his fellow dukes to send their armies to his aid.

He had little hope that Silbron of Bistari would offer any reply at all; the young duke, Chago's son, had already declared to Brall his intention to keep Bistari neutral in this struggle. Brall would have only just arrived back in Orvinti from his travels. Like Tebeo, he had spent a good deal of time away from his home, trying to convince the others to join their efforts. It would be a few days at least before he was ready to lead his army southward. But Tebeo hoped and expected that the others would respond swiftly and in force. If they didn't, Dantrielle might not be able to endure the regent's assault for more than half a turn.

Standing atop the tallest of Castle Dantrielle's eight towers with Evanthya and his master of arms, Tebeo tried to banish such thoughts from his mind. The castle of his fathers might not have been as grand as Castle Solkara, nor as powerfully fortified, but still it was not without its defenses. Situated within sight of the confluence of the Rassor and Black Sand rivers, the castle could not easily be attacked from the west or south, or even directly from the north. Any army that attempted to ford the rivers so close to the castle walls would be within range of Tebeo's archers. Numar's assault would have to come from the northeast, and since the castle stood at that end of the city, its red stone walls would bear the brunt of the attack, which was as it should be. These walls were as thick as any in the realm, and the three portcullises that blocked the outer gate had been fashioned centuries ago of iron and the Great Forest's hardiest oak.

Tebeo tried to draw comfort from all of this, and from the banner that flew just above him bearing the red, black, and gold sigil of his house. The Flame in the Night, the fire that endured; a brilliant golden blaze burning above the red towers. The crest dated from the clan wars, when the castle had survived numerous sieges led by the rival families. But Dantrielle's reputation had not been tested for hundreds of years, and neither had the castle walls.

While Tebeo was staring at the banner rising and falling in the wind, Bausef DarLesta, the duke's master of arms, was saying something about the towers and the positioning of Dantrielle's archers. Tebeo had long since lost the thread of whatever point he was trying to make.

"Forgive me, Bausef," he said, interrupting, "but my mind must have wandered. I'm afraid you'll have to begin again."

The master or arms was a capable soldier and, according to some, the finest swordsman in the realm. Certainly he looked the part. He towered over both Evanthya and Tebeo, his long, sinewy limbs making his every movement seem effortless and balanced. Like so many of the men who served under him in Dantrielle's army, he had shaved his head, and with his thick black beard and mustache, his face had a severe look, more like that of a brigand than a swordsman in a noble's court.

He glanced at Evanthya now, frowning slightly at the duke's admission.

"I was saying, my lord, that you should resist the temptation to place all our bowmen on the northern and eastern towers."

"But isn't that where the attack is most likely to come?"

"Yes, my lord," Bausef said, sounding increasingly impatient. "But as I was just saying, it wouldn't surprise me if the regent tried to surprise us by sending part of his force to the south or west. Even if he keeps the Solkaran army together, he may try to have Rassor's men flank us."

Tebeo nodded, seeing the logic in this. The duke considered himself an accomplished statesman, and, though not prone to immodesty, believed that his intellect was as keen as that of any duke in the realm. But he had never been a strategic thinker and had not had cause to train himself in military tactics. For the first time in his life, he found himself wishing that he had.

"Won't he send Rassor's army north, to the Tarbin?" he asked, hoping that he didn't sound too foolish.

"Most of it, yes. But with Solkara menacing Dantrielle, the duke of Rassor has nothing to fear from us or our allies. He can afford to leave only a small contingent of men guarding his castle. Even a few hundred of his soldiers attacking the city walls might prove devastating to our defenses."

"You're right of course. Have two hundred archers positioned on the city walls overlooking the rivers. That should leave us enough to guard the castle, shouldn't it?"

"More than enough. Very good, my lord."

Tebeo turned and crossed the turret so that he could look down on the castle wards. The quartermaster was shouting commands to an army of laborers and soldiers who carried stores to the various towers. Other men gathered weapons—spare swords and shields, axes and pikes, quivers filled with newly made arrows and crossbow bolts. Dantrielle usually seemed a rather quiet castle, almost peaceful. For the last several days, though, it had teemed as if in frenzy, like a nest of ants uncovered by an inquisitive child.

"The provisioning goes well?" Tebeo asked.

This time it was Evanthya who answered. "Yes, my lord. We still have ample stores from the last harvest. The snows were hard, but the growing season was generous. We have food enough to feed the army and the city for two turns."

Two turns. He could hardly fathom fighting a war for two turns, much less withstanding a siege for so long. "That's fine, First Minister," he said. "Thank you."

"Shall we leave you, my lord?" Evanthya asked.

He shrugged, unsure of whether he wished to be alone. "Is there anything else we need to discuss, Bausef?"

"No, my lord. I have men preparing vats of pitch and lime. And we'll have plenty of fire pots for the gates." The armsmaster grinned. "We'll be ready for them, my lord. I promise you that."

Tebeo nodded, struck by the avid gleam in the man's dark eyes. Clearly, Bausef was looking forward to this battle. The duke felt only dread.

"Thank you, Bausef. I have great faith in you and your men."

"They're your men, my lord, and serve you, as do I. We'll fight to the death to preserve this house."

Tebeo didn't know what to say.

"I have but one request, my lord."

"Anything," he said, eager to give this man whatever he could.

"The yellow and red of Aneira should be flying above Dantrielle's banners on all eight towers. You know that the regent will be riding under the colors of the realm, claiming that he fights for Aneira. We have every right to make the same claim, and it will hearten the men to see both banners over our walls."

Tebeo felt privileged to be served by such a man. "See to it immediately, armsmaster."

Bausef bowed. "Yes, my lord."

Tebeo watched the man go, shaking his head slightly. "Would that I could feel so sure of what we were about to do."

"You should," Evanthya said.

"We're going to lose a lot of good men. We may lose the war."

"I don't think so. The loss of life on both sides will be terrible. I've no illusions about that. But I believe the realm will suffer more if the regent prevails and this alliance with the empire continues." Somehow she managed a smile, albeit a sad one. "You're doing what needs to be done, my lord. Don't doubt that."

"And if Brall and the others don't arrive in time?"

"You must have faith that they will."

He walked back to the outer wall, knowing that she was right, feeling unworthy of those who served him.

"It would be better if they reached our walls before the Solkarans."

"They might not," she said evenly. "In which case, our preparations will be tested."

He looked at her briefly. "You speak of these matters with such certainty, First Minister. Have you gleaned anything about this war?"

"No, my lord. Nothing. If I had, I would have told you. Good or bad."

"Of course."

"We have men watching the roads and the rivers, my lord. You should take this opportunity to rest. Once the siege begins there will be precious little time for that."

"What was your impression of Brall and Fetnalla during their recent visit?" he asked, ignoring her counsel for the moment, though he knew it was wise.

She looked away, clearly uncomfortable with the question. "My lord?"

"I know I'm putting you in a difficult spot, Evanthya. No doubt your love for the first minister colors your perceptions of the duke. He's been distrustful of her for some time now, too much so in my view. But this tension between them is about to become far more dangerous than it's ever been. Before it pained us both, but now, with this war, it threatens our very lives."

"Yes, my lord."

"I actually had the impression that their rapport had improved in the interval between this most recent visit and our previous stay in Orvinti. Did you, as well?"

Evanthya shrugged. "Fetnalla still spoke of the duke's suspicions, and she seemed as angry with him as ever. They were in agreement when it came to standing firm against the regent, but I'm not certain that they had reconciled beyond that."

She started to say more, then appeared to reconsider.

"Out with it, First Minister. Please. This is no time for secrets between us."

A gust of wind made her white hair dance about her face, and she brushed it back from her brow. "Fetnalla's resentment runs deep, my lord. She knows that Lord Orvinti was having her watched. She looks for reasons to defy him. Even if the duke were to try to bridge the rift between them, I'm not sure that Fetnalla would welcome his overtures."

"Do you think she'd betray him?"

"I wouldn't have thought it possible half a year ago. But now . . ." She shook her head. "I don't know, my lord."

"This isn't what I wanted to hear, Evanthya."

The minister actually grinned. "When have I ever told you anything simply because I thought you wanted to hear it?"

He tipped his head, acknowledging the point. "Very well. Thank you for your honesty. As I said before, I know that it couldn't have been an easy question to answer."

"Yes, my lord."

He started to walk away, then paused. "What about us?" he asked. "We've had some difficult conversations in recent turns. Should I be concerned about our rapport."

"I can't speak for you, my lord, but for my part, there's no other duke in the realm I'd rather serve."

Tebeo raised an eyebrow. "Given the other dukes in the realm, I'm not certain how to take that."

Evanthya laughed.

"Thank you, First Minister."

"My lord, wait," she said, as he turned to leave.

Tebeo faced her again. Her cheeks had reddened, and it almost seemed to the duke that she wished she had let him go.

"There's something I have to tell you, my lord."

"Oh?"

"I hadn't intended to, but with the regent's army marching on Dantrielle . . ."

I might not have another opportunity. The words hung between them like a storm cloud. "You're scaring me, First Minister."

"Forgive me, my lord. That's not my intent." She lowered her gaze, swallowed. "Several turns ago, before King Carden's death, Fetnalla and I decided the time had come for us to oppose the conspiracy, to do something more than listen for rumors and watch other Qirsi for signs of treachery. I . . . I went to the city, to the Red Boar, and I hired a blade to kill a man in the north whom we suspected was a traitor."

"Demons and fire, Evanthya!"

"I know how it sounds, my lord. But we honestly believed that we were doing the right thing."

"An assassin? You're a minister in a noble house! My house!"

"Yes, my lord."

"Under Aneiran law, you could be executed for this!"

"I know that, my lord. And if you choose to imprison me, I'll understand. But as you said just a moment ago, there shouldn't be any secrets between us."

Tebeo passed a hand over his brow, shaking his head. "An assassin," he said again.

"I'm sorry, my lord."

"Did the man you hired know who you were?"

"I believe he reasoned it out, yes."

"Damn."

"But I think he also knew that I was acting on my own rather than as an agent of House Dantrielle."

He nodded. "I suppose that's something." He regarded her for several moments, noting as he had so many times before how young she looked. In point of fact, she *was* young. For all their power, her people lived shorter lives than did the Eandi, which meant that they sometimes shouldered burdens at a more tender age than was appropriate. "I'm disappointed in you, Evanthya. I've no doubt that you and Fetnalla were doing what you thought was best, but I have to question your methods."

"Yes, my lord."

"I've no intention of imprisoning you—I think you know that—but I trust that in the future you'll fight your battles with the conspiracy in more . . . acceptable ways."

"I will, my lord. You have my word."

They lapsed into silence, the duke grappling with his curiosity. In the end, he was no match for it.

"What happened?"

"My lord?"

"Is the traitor dead?"

"Yes, my lord. I received word from the assassin shortly after our return from the king's funeral."

"Well, I suppose we should be thankful for that."

"Yes, my lord." Another silence. Then, "You should rest, my lord, while you can."

"Perhaps you're right. Thank you, Evanthya."

"Of course, my lord."

Tebeo stepped past her and descended the tower stairs to the corridor on which his chambers were located. He knew better than to try to sleep; even at night, recently, he found that he could do little more than doze off occasionally. Mostly he lay awake, attempting to anticipate Numar's plans and scouring his mind for anything he might have forgotten as he readied his city and castle for civil war.

Rather than returning to his bedchamber, he went in search of Pelgia. He found her in the kitchens, overseeing the kitchenmaster's work.

She smiled at the sight of him, though the strain of these past several days was evident on her face. There were dark circles under her eyes; her cheeks looked leaner than usual, and paler as well. Still, even wan and weary, she was lovely, and he wondered briefly if it would be unseemly for a duke and his wife to take to their bed on the eve of a war.

He walked to where she stood and took her hand, kissing her brow. "Is everything all right?"

She nodded. "Yes. There'll be food enough, anyway."

"Good." He raised her hand to his lips, drawing her gaze. "Walk with me?"

They left the kitchen and walked slowly along the lower corridor, as soldiers hurried past them in either direction.

"Where are the children?" he asked after some time.

"In the cloister. Tas wants to fight, but I've told him that he has to wait another year. And of course Laytsa says that if her brother can raise a sword, she can as well."

Tebeo gave a small laugh, but it gave way instantly to a deep frown. "Everyone is so eager to fight this war. Is there something wrong with me that I'm not?"

"Tas is a year shy of his Fating, Tebeo. And Laytsa's just past her Determining. They don't know any better."

He rubbed a hand over his face. "I realize that. But to hear

Evanthya and Bausef speak of what's coming, you'd think that our victory was assured. I should be able to speak of it the same way."

"You're not a warrior," she said, slipping her arm through his. "You never have been. That's one of the reasons I love you."

"Dantrielle needs a warrior right now." He knew this was true, and it made him feel old and weak. Bausef seemed ready to raise his sword against the entire Solkaran army. And Evanthya was so eager for blood that she had already tried to take on the conspiracy by herself. *I hired a blade . . .*

"No," Pelgia said. "Dantrielle needs a duke, a man with wisdom and compassion and strength. And you possess all those in abundance."

Fearing that he might weep, the duke halted and kissed her deeply, heedless of the men who continued to step past them.

When at last he pulled away, she smiled, though there was a troubled look in her eyes. "You're frightened," she whispered.

"Shouldn't I be?"

"I think you should take to heart the confidence of your first minister and master of arms. If they thought that we were about to be destroyed, they'd tell you to find some path to peace. Your army and your people are strong, my lord. And though you doubt it now, you are as well."

He gazed at her in wonder. "I believe you may be strong enough for us both."

"One doesn't endure four labors and the loss of a babe without finding some strength."

He nodded, stroking her cheek with a finger. "When it begins, I want you in the cloister as well. The tower is farthest from where much of the fighting will be, and it will be well defended. I'll see to that."

"The kitchenmaster will need my help, Tebeo. And so will the healers. A duchess doesn't hide from war."

"Even when her husband commands it?"

She grinned, dark eyes sparkling in the torchlight. "Especially then."

He had to laugh, despite the terror gripping his heart. *If you're hurt or lost to me, I'll kill the regent myself.* "Very well," he said. "But the next time Laytsa defies you, you'll have no sympathy from me."

"And when have I ever had it before?"

He laughed again. She had always been able to make him smile, even in the darkest times.

"I should return to the towers," he said, reluctant to leave her.

"When was the last time you slept?"

He frowned. "You sound like Evanthya."

"You should sleep now, while you can."

He kissed her once more and started away. "If I could sleep I would."

Concern creased her brow, but she nodded, giving his hand a quick squeeze before releasing it.

Suddenly he was anxious to be on the ramparts again, watching for Numar and his army. Instead, Tebeo made his way to the cloister. Having seen Pelgia, he wished to hold his children once more as well. Reaching the entrance to the abbey, however, he heard laughter coming from within: Senaon, his youngest. A moment later he also heard Laytsa. He could almost picture Tas smiling with the others. His oldest boy had always been the quiet one. They were happy, unafraid. Even knowing that the siege was coming—he had spoken of it with them just two days before—they managed to find humor and joy in one another. Who was he to interfere, to bring the shadow of war to their play?

He merely stood near the door, listening to them. After several moments, the prelate emerged from his sanctum. Seeing the duke, he stopped and opened his mouth to speak.

Tebeo raised a finger to his lips and shook his head.

Another peal of laughter echoed through the cloister, and the prelate smiled, walking to where the duke stood.

"They forget the war, my lord," he said, keeping his voice low. "Just as they should."

"Thank you, Father Prelate."

"Of course, my lord. You know they're welcome here as long as you wish them to stay. And should the battle come to these walls, I'll guard them myself." His grin broadened at what he saw on Tebeo's face. "You think it an idle boast. I was quite a swordsman as a youth, and I daresay I can still fight if pressed to do so."

Tebeo had always remained partial to the sanctuaries, even as Pelgia turned increasingly to the cloisters and the New Faith. He liked this prelate, though, and had since the prelacy passed to him nine years ago.

"I have no doubt that you can, Father Prelate. It will ease my mind knowing that our children are under your care."

"You honor me, my lord."

"The cloister has all it needs in the event of a siege?"

"It does, my lord. The duchess has seen to that. She's a most extraordinary woman."

"Indeed, she is. But she's also headstrong and she speaks of helping the healers and the kitchenmaster." He hesitated, but only for an instant. "If the walls are breached—"

"They'll hold, my lord."

"But if they don't, I want you to find her and get her into the cloister."

"You ask a great deal, my lord. I'm not afraid of the Solkarans, but the duchess is another matter."

Tebeo had to smile. The gods had favored his house with so many fine people. "Do your best, Father Prelate. I can't ask more than that."

"You know I will, my lord." He looked like he might say more, but at that moment, bells began to toll throughout the city.

Let it be Brall. But as quickly as the thought entered his mind, he dismissed it. Even if his friend and the Orvinti army had already begun their march they would have to cross two rivers to reach Dantrielle, and that would slow them considerably. Perhaps the duke of Tounstrel had come, or the duke of Noltierre. Most likely, it was the regent with the Solkaran army.

"Ean guard you, my lord," the prelate said. "And may Orlagh guide your blade."

Tebeo turned and hurried toward the tower stairs. "A strange blessing coming from a man of the cloisters," he said over his shoulder.

"At times like these, I believe it best to have as many gods and goddesses on one's side as possible."

An instant later Tebeo was in the tower, taking its stairs two at a time. Once on the wall, he hurried around to where Evanthya and Bausef stood, their eyes fixed on the lands to the north.

Following the line of their gazes, he felt his stomach heave. A grand army was approaching from the northeast, marching under two flags: the yellow and red banner of Aneira, and the red, gold, and black of Solkara. Glancing quickly overhead, the duke saw that Bausef had already managed to have Aneiran banners raised above all eight towers.

As the pealing of the bells continued to reverberate through the castle, ward fires were lit atop the towers, and archers emerged from the stairways, spreading out along the walls as if they had repelled sieges a thousand times before.

"Your men are well prepared, armsmaster."

"Thank you, my lord."

The three of them fell silent, all of them marking the army's progress toward the walls of Dantrielle. It seemed a far larger force than Tebeo had expected, and the duke had to remind himself that Numar would have brought laborers to build his siege engines. Still, in order to make the journey, all of them would have to be able-bodied. And once their axes were done cutting trees, they could be used as weapons.

"I would have thought that they would burn the villages in your countryside," Evanthya said. "But I see no smoke."

"The regent has declared the duke a traitor," Bausef answered before Tebeo could say anything. "He wishes to win the hearts and minds of Dantrielle's subjects. He'll destroy the city and fortress if he can, but he'll do nothing to anger those outside our walls. Unless of course they join the fight on our behalf."

Tebeo heard a voice cry out, and looking at the Solkarans once more, he saw one of the few mounted men raise a hand. Numar. The army halted well beyond the range of Dantrielle's bowmen. A moment later, far sooner than the duke would have thought possible, he heard the faint ringing of steel on wood as they began their assault on the Great Forest.

"It will take them some time to build their engines." The armsmaster's voice was calm, as if he were speaking of the plantings. "Days perhaps, and even when they're ready to start, I'd imagine they'll wait until darkness falls. I don't expect the siege to begin in earnest until tomorrow night, or perhaps the night after that. Tonight, I would expect them to test the defenses of the city walls. That's where our men should be for now."

Tebeo just stared at the regent's army, once again regretting that he hadn't taken more time in his youth to study tactics. "Can you tell if the archminister is with them, First Minister?"

"No, my lord, I can't."

"I would expect that he is. Do you know what powers he possesses?"

"Not with any certainty, my lord. I remember hearing once that he was a shaper and that he also had the magic of mists and winds. But this was little more than rumor. Qirsi rarely reveal what powers they possess, and the archminister and I have never been close."

He knew that she was understating the case quite a bit. As he understood it, the two disliked and distrusted each other.

"We should assume that he has both powers, my lord," said the master of arms. "One shaper against so many bowmen shouldn't be too great a problem, but his mists will make it more difficult for us."

"I've mists and winds as well," Evanthya said. "Perhaps I can raise a gale against his mist."

Tebeo nodded, but said nothing. Already several trees had fallen and other laborers were scrambling over them, cutting away the branches and notching the wood so that the trunks could be used as rams, or in the building of a snare.

"Shall I move some of the men to the city walls, my lord?"

"Yes, Bausef. Make certain they understand, however, that they're not to loose any arrows until they've been fired upon."

"My lord?"

"We're not traitors, armsmaster. The regent brings this war to us, and I will not have Dantrielle spilling the first blood."

"Forgive me for saying so, my lord, but that's madness. This is a siege. If we wait to loose our arrows until the Solkarans have drawn first blood, our archers will be of no use to us. We must fire first. It's our only hope of keeping the regent's soldiers from our gates and our walls."

He was right, of course. Tebeo could see the logic of his point. Yet, still the duke hesitated. "This war is their doing, not ours. The history of this siege should reflect that."

Even as he spoke the words, though, he remembered an old warrior's adage. "Orlagh chooses the hand that will write each battle's tale," it was said. "History is but another spoil of war."

Evanthya gazed at the duke, her expression pained. "I have to agree with Bausef, my lord."

The bells had stopped ringing, and the only sounds Tebeo could hear were made by the banners rising and falling overhead, and the Solkaran axes ravaging his forest.

"My lord?"

Before he could say anything, the bells began to ring again, beginning this time at the eastern end of the city. Tebeo ran along the wall, to the other side of the castle, followed closely by Evanthya and the swordsman. He hadn't yet reached the far tower when he heard a cheer go up from Numar's men. When he gained the tower, he scanned the woods, searching for some sign of what the enemy had seen.

"There!" Evanthya cried, pointing to a gap in the forest, due east of the castle.

Tebeo saw it as well. A second army was approaching the city, this one marching under a green and white banner. Rassor.

It wasn't as large a force as Numar's, but then again, it didn't have to be.

"The siege might begin this night after all," Evanthya muttered.

Bausef faced him, looking far more somber than he had a few moments before. "Your orders, my lord?"

Where was Brall? Where were Ansis and Vistaan and Bertin the Younger?

"See to the city walls, armsmaster," Tebeo said, his mouth so dry he could barely speak. "Tell your men to loose their arrows at the enemy's first approach."

Chapter Twelve

Yserne, Sanbira

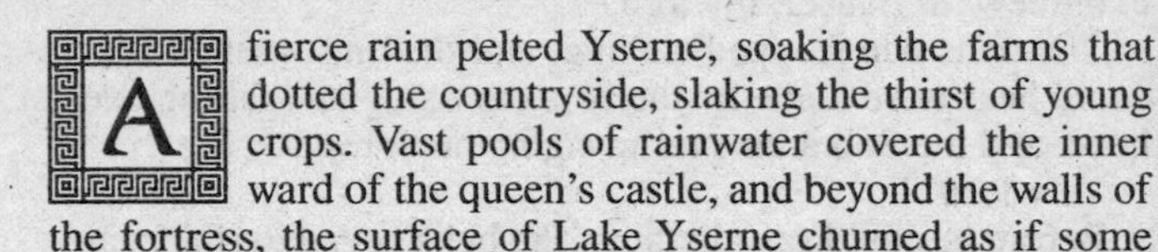

A fierce rain pelted Yserne, soaking the farms that dotted the countryside, slaking the thirst of young crops. Vast pools of rainwater covered the inner ward of the queen's castle, and beyond the walls of the fortress, the surface of Lake Yserne churned as if some fire from Bian's realm heated its waters.

Such storms weren't uncommon in Sanbira during Elined's Turn. As a child, Diani, duchess of Curlinte, had dreaded the moon of the goddess; just the mention of Elined's name called to mind dreary days trapped within the walls of her mother's castle, staring out at the warm rains and the brilliant lightning that arced across the sky on the coast near Curlinte. "Growing rains bring a good harvest," her mother used to say, when Diani complained to her of horseback rides put off by another storm. "It's the growing sun that I fear."

In recent years, as she passed Fating age and began to assume more responsibility for leading the duchy, Diani witnessed for herself the ravages of drought and famine, and came to understand her mother's fondness for the rains. She might even have shared it in some small way. And in the turns since her mother's death, she had realized that the smell of a storm and the gentle rumble of distant thunder would forever remind her of Dalvia, of the rainy days they had shared in Curlinte Castle, speaking of what it meant to rule as duchess.

This storm was different, however. It offered no comforting memories, no solace for the loss of her mother, which still made her chest ache. The rain that fell this day seemed to carry only the dark promise of battle and ominous portents of an uncertain future. Water ran down the castle walls, darkening the red stone so that it seemed to glimmer and flow like blood. Thunder made the walls and floors shudder, as if Orlagh herself, the warrior goddess, were pounding at the earth with her battle hammer.

"Is something wrong, Lady Curlinte?"

Diani turned from the window at the sound of the voice. Edamo, the duke of Brugaosa, was standing beside her, somewhat closer than she would have liked.

"No, Lord Brugaosa. I'm fine."

"You're certain? You looked troubled—one might even go so far as to say, fearful. Is it possible that you know already why the queen has called us here?"

She shook her head, pushing a strand of dark hair back from her brow. "As I said, I'm fine. And I have no idea why the queen wished to speak with us."

A lie, one that came to her easily. The matriarchy was poised on the edge of a blade. It no longer seemed a question of whether Sanbira would go to war, but rather when and against whom. Eibithar might already be at war with Braedon and Aneira; just this morning word of the empire's impending invasion had arrived in the royal city, along with a request from King Kearney that the queen send her army to aid the defense of his realm. Only a few turns before, the Qirsi conspiracy had struck at Sanbira, making an attempt on Diani's life that had been intended to appear the work of Edamo's famed assassins.

This was a time for all subjects of the matriarchy to put aside their hostilities and suspicions, to unite behind their queen and fight as one to protect Sanbira. Yet Diani could not look at Edamo as anything more or less than a rival. She no longer believed that the man's assassins had been responsible for the death of her brother, Cyro, several years before; that too had been a Qirsi deception. But Edamo and his lone ally in the realm, Alao, the duke of Norinde, had resisted the queen's every attempt to prepare the realm for war, fearing that such measures would strengthen House Yserne's hold on power, and Diani saw no reason to show him any more courtesy than he had shown Olesya.

"No idea at all?" the duke said, eyeing her doubtfully. "I find that hard to believe."

"Would you all please be seated?" the queen said from the far end of the room, her handsome face looking lined and wan in the dim light of the oil lamps that burned throughout the chamber.

Diani gave a small smile. "Believe what you will," she told the duke, before leaving him for her seat at the council table.

The other nobles sat as well, Edamo and Alao taking seats as far from the queen as possible, as they always did.

"As you know," Olesya began, after regarding them all briefly, "some time ago I sent a message to the king of Eibithar proposing that our two realms forge an alliance so that we might face the Qirsi threat united. We've waited a long time for Kearney's reply, so long that I had begun to wonder if my message ever reached the City of Kings." She held up a piece of parchment, sealed at the bottom with a swirl of purple and gold wax. "His response has arrived at last."

"You don't look pleased, Your Highness," Edamo said. "I take it he has rejected your overtures."

The queen gave a slight frown. Diani hadn't missed it either. *Your* overtures.

"Actually, Lord Brugaosa, he has accepted our proposal. Indeed, he asks even more of us than we did of him."

"More, Your Highness?" asked Rashel of Trescarri.

"Yes. Apparently the Braedon fleet has been menacing Eibithar's north coast and the Aneirans have been massing along the Tarbin. When he wrote his reply Kearney expected to be at war within half a turn, which would mean that the fighting may have already begun. He asks our help in repelling the invaders, and offers in return his realm's support in our efforts to combat the Qirsi conspiracy."

Edamo glanced around the table before looking at the queen again. "He must know that we'll refuse such a request."

"If so, he knows more than I do." Vasyonne, the duchess of Listaal, had long taken great pleasure in baiting Edamo and Alao. As a close ally of the queen and one of the younger duchesses, she had also gone out of her way to befriend Diani after Dalvia's death, and the two of them often agreed on matters of state. As they did now.

"Surely you can't think that we should go to war with the empire," Edamo said.

"It seems the emperor is bringing war to Eibithar. If he's bold enough to attack there, he may order his fleet to our shores next."

"He wouldn't. We've always enjoyed good relations with the empire. There isn't a realm in the Forelands that buys more of our wine, our gems, or our blades. And Harel himself owns no fewer than forty Sanbiri mounts."

"This isn't about imperial gold!"

"Ah, but it is," Alao said, taking up Edamo's argument. "I value our friendship with Eibithar as much as anyone. But can we afford to make an enemy of the empire, and Aneira as well? Together they're far too formidable a foe, and our people depend upon our trade with both realms." He turned smoothly to the queen. "I must agree with Lord Brugaosa, Your Highness. We have no choice but to deny the king's request for aid."

"As it happens, Lord Norinde, I'm inclined to agree with you."

Diani gaped at her. "But, Your Highness—"

"I know what you're going to say, Lady Curlinte: we need Eibithar as an ally in our fight with the Qirsi. And that may be true. But if we're at war with Braedon and Aneira, we stand no chance against the conspiracy."

The duchess opened her mouth, closed it again. There was little she could say.

"I'll compose a reply," the queen said, her voice low, as if she lamented the soundness of her own point. "Unless anyone can give me a good reason not to."

None of the nobles spoke, though they eyed one another, seeming to hope that someone else would speak. Except of course for the two dukes, who looked far too pleased with themselves.

"What if there's more to this war in the north than just the emperor's greed?"

Everyone looked at the duchess of Macharzo, who merely sat with her hands folded before her, her eyes lowered, and her face so composed that Diani began to wonder if she had been mistaken, if in fact another of the duchesses had spoken. Naditia rarely said anything in council. In the short time Diani had been duchess, she had never known the woman to challenge the word of the queen in even the most oblique way. Indeed, she hardly ever spoke at all, even outside of Olesya's presence chamber. She was a large woman, both broad and tall, with short yellow hair and wide brown eyes. Someone seeing her for the first time might have thought her a warrior, even a commander of fighters. But she could no more have barked orders to an army than she could fly to the top of Olesya's castle.

"What did you say, Lady Macharzo?" the queen asked, appearing as stunned as the rest by the woman's words.

"I asked if there might be more to the empire's invasion than just Harel's greed."

"What do you mean?"

The woman shrugged, looking uncomfortable, as though she wished she'd never spoken at all. "It just seems to me that the conspiracy has managed to make a lot of things happen that might not have happened otherwise."

"Like what?" Alao demanded, making Naditia flinch.

"Like the civil war that nearly tore Eibithar apart," Diani answered for her, drawing a grateful smile from the woman. "Like the recent violence in Aneira. Like the murder of my brother and the attempts on my life."

"We don't know that the conspiracy was responsible for all that. I've heard of no proof linking the Qirsi to anything that's happened in Aneira, and at least half the dukes in Eibithar still blame Tavis of Curgh, and not some Qirsi assassin, for the murder of that girl in Kentigern." Alao's eyes flicked briefly toward Edamo. "And even with your first minister dead, you can't prove yet that the Qirsi killed your brother or tried to kill you."

"You think it more likely that Lord Brugaosa was behind the attacks on my house?"

"Not at all, Lady Curlinte. But as I've said in this chamber before, assuming that the conspiracy is responsible for every dark deed that occurs in Sanbira, or all the Forelands for that matter, is just as dangerous as ignoring the threat entirely. The empire and Aneira have gone to war against Eibithar. Is that really such a surprise?"

"Actually," Edamo said, "now that I give the matter some thought, it is a bit strange."

First Naditia had challenged the queen, and now Edamo was breaking with the duke of Norinde. This was a most extraordinary day. Everyone was looking at the older man, none with more astonishment than Alao.

"Aneira hasn't been this weakened in centuries. The failed siege at Kentigern, the death of Bistari and then Carden, the poisoning of the queen and her council of dukes. This is no time for Aneira to be marshaling its soldiers for war."

"But if the empire proposed an alliance," Alao said, "offering the Aneirans a chance to strike at Eibithar, of course they'd accept."

"Yes, but why would the emperor propose such an alliance now? Wouldn't it be wiser to wait a year or so, to give the regent time to consolidate his authority and allow Mertesse to rebuild its army?"

Diani grinned. "Lord Brugaosa, you should know better than to go looking for wisdom in Curtell."

All of them laughed, easing the tension in the chamber somewhat. But Olesya quickly grew serious once more.

"Am I to understand then, Lord Brugaosa, that you now favor joining forces with the Eibitharians?"

"To be honest, Your Highness, I'm not certain how I feel about it. I don't wish to make an enemy of the emperor." He nodded toward Diani and the duchess of Macharzo. "But I fear that our young friends here may be right. And if the conspiracy wants this war, we might be well served to put a stop to it as swiftly as possible."

"Throwing our army into the fray will only prolong the conflict," Alao said, glowering at Edamo. "If we want it to end quickly we should stay out of it and let them fight."

The queen raised an eyebrow. "I'd like to ask my master of arms about that. I'm not sure what effect our forces would have on this war. But it seems to me a fair question." She turned to one of guards standing near the door. "Have your commander summoned immediately." Then, as if as an afterthought, she added, "And the duke of Curlinte also."

Diani looked up quickly before dropping her gaze to the table, her cheeks coloring. Her father had accompanied her to the royal city when first she came, because at the time she was still recovering from the injuries she suffered during the assassination attempt at the Curlinte coast. Since arriving at Olesya's castle they had fought frequently over the best response to the Qirsi threat and the complicity or innocence of Kreazur jal Sylbe, Curlinte's former first minister. Kreazur died in the streets of Yserne, apparently the victim of assassins he had tried to hire on behalf of the conspiracy, though both Diani and her father now had doubts about this. Diani did not doubt that Sertio had some knowledge of the Braedon army or that he would be able to add much to this discussion; he was master of arms in Curlinte. But she and her father remained at odds, and she feared that his presence here would only serve to remind the other nobles that she was the least experienced of the queen's duchesses.

If Olesya noticed her discomfort, she gave no indication of it, immediately turning her attention back to Edamo. "I believe I speak for all of us, Lord Brugaosa, when I say that I'm . . . surprised by your change of heart."

"Yes, Your Highness."

They all waited, as if expecting an explanation. When it became clear that none was forthcoming, the queen smiled and nodded. "Very well, Lord Brugaosa."

Before she could say more, there was a knock at the door, and at her reply, the master of arms and Diani's father entered the chamber. Both men were soaked and muddied, their color high, their breathing heavy. Ohan Delrasto, the master of arms, had a welt under one of his dark eyes, and Sertio had several on his arms and one vivid red mark at the base of his neck. Both of them were grinning like boys caught in some mischief, though Diani thought that Ohan had to be nearly her father's age.

"Forgive our appearance, Your Highness," said the master of arms, bowing to the queen. "We came as soon as we received your summons."

"Apparently. I take it you were in the ward?"

"Yes, Your Highness. We were . . ." He stopped, licking his lips.

"We were practicing foul weather combat, Your Highness," Sertio said. "Not all wars are fought in sunshine on firm ground."

"Indeed. And your soldiers are still out there, Master Delrasto?"

"They were never out there, Your Highness," Ohan said, grinning again. "Just the two of us."

Sertio added, "We were working on techniques that we intend to teach to our armies, Your Highness."

Even Diani had to laugh. She couldn't help but feel a bit embarrassed for her father, but she was glad to see him enjoying himself. Since her mother's death, Sertio had foundered in his grief, until Diani wondered if he'd ever know happiness again. No doubt this day's mirth would prove fleeting, but the mere fact that he could engage in such swordplay gave her hope. Perhaps the wound on his heart had finally begun to heal itself.

"I would invite you to sit," the queen said, regarding their stained clothing. "But under the circumstances I think it best that you remain standing."

"Of course, Your Highness. How may we serve you?"

The queen picked up the missive from Kearney and read it aloud. By the time she finished, both Sertio and the master of arms had grown deadly serious.

"These are dark tidings, Your Highness," Ohan said, rubbing a hand over his angular face.

"Can Eibithar defend herself?"

He stared at the floor, and after several moments he began to nod slowly. "I should think so. If Aneira was as strong now as she was a year ago, I might say different. The emperor has chosen a weakened ally."

"Does it surprise you that they should attack now?" Edamo asked. "Wouldn't you have expected them to wait?"

"You mean until Aneira could rebuild its northern armies?"

"Precisely."

"Yes, I suppose it does."

"Some of the duchesses have recommended that I grant Kearney's request," the queen said. "They want me to send Sanbiri warriors to fight alongside the men of Eibithar."

Sertio eyed Diani for a moment, as if he knew that she was one of the nobles to whom Olesya referred.

"Are you asking my opinion on the matter, Your Highness?" the master of arms asked.

"Yes, I am."

Ohan took a long breath. "If we send soldiers by sea, we'll need to send most of the fleet. And even then, I don't like our chances against Braedon's ships. Which means we'd have to send them overland, and in order to get them to northern Eibithar in time to do any good, we'd have to send them on horseback."

"We have enough mounts to send a considerable force."

"That's true, Your Highness, but a mounted army is harder to provision. And of course, we'd have to ride through Caerisse or Wethyrn to get there. Their leaders may not look kindly on having our army cross their borders."

The queen waved a hand impatiently. "I'm not concerned about that right now. I'll be with the army, and I trust I can convince a Wethy noble that I'm not interested in conquering his dukedom. What I really want to know is what effect our army is likely to have on the course and duration of this war."

"We'd be prolonging the war, wouldn't we?" Alao broke in.

The master of arms glanced at Sertio, who shrugged.

"I can't be certain, Your Highness. I think with our help the Eibitharians can repel the invasion, but as to how long such a conflict will last, I have no idea. Without our help, Kearney's army might fall quickly, in which case we would be prolonging it. On the other hand, Eibithar might prevail even without our help, which would mean that our soldiers could bring the fighting to a swifter end."

Olesya looked at Sertio. "What do you think, Lord Curlinte?"

"I have little to add to what Master Delrasto has already said."

"Then you also feel that it would have been wiser for the emperor to delay," the duke of Brugaosa asked.

Sertio stared at Edamo, the muscles in his jaw tightening. Even with Kreazur's death and the conspiracy's obvious involvement in the attempts on Diani's life, Sertio still blamed House Brugaosa for Cyro's murder. He and Edamo had not spoken in years, and Diani knew that her father still thirsted for the man's blood.

"Yes, Lord Brugaosa," Sertio said, his voice edged with steel, "I guess I do. Why?"

"Isn't it obvious with everything else that's happened? I believe the Qirsi may be behind this war, just as they were behind the attack on your daughter."

Sertio narrowed his eyes, opening his mouth to reply.

"I'd like to know what the rest of you think," Olesya said, before the duke could speak. "Clearly Lord Norinde opposes any involvement on our part. I believe that Lord Brugaosa now favors sending our soldiers north, as do Lady Curlinte and Lady Listaal." She paused, eyeing the three of them. When they all nodded their agreement, she continued, "What about the rest of you?"

As it turned out, the other duchesses were split evenly, with the older women, Tamyra of Prentarlo and Rashel, opposed, and Ajy of Kinsarta and Naditia in favor.

Olesya made no effort to mask her surprise. "It seems a majority of you wish to honor Kearney's request."

"What about you, Your Highness?" Alao asked. "You were inclined to refuse him a short time ago. Surely your wishes in this matter carry more weight than our own."

"You're right, Lord Norinde. I did intend to refuse. But I find myself swayed by the arguments I've heard here, just as was Lord Brugaosa."

"I fear you're making a grave mistake, Your Highness."

"I share your concerns, Alao. I'm not blind to the dangers.

Which is why I intend to send only five hundred warriors from the royal army. We'll add six hundred from the armies of Brugaosa, Norinde, and Macharzo—two hundred from each of you. That gives us a force of eleven hundred in all."

Vasyonne frowned. It seemed she was eager for this fight. "What about the rest of the houses, Your Highness?"

"It would take nearly half a turn to get messages to the Southern and Eastern houses and then await the arrival of your soldiers. As it is, we're already well into the waxing and Kearney sent his request at the start of the previous waning. I don't wish to delay any longer."

"Then perhaps you should take more soldiers from the three houses you named."

"To send a larger force would be to leave the realm vulnerable to attack."

"Eleven hundred may not be enough," Vasyonne said, shaking her head.

"It will have to be." Olesya faced the master of arms again. "Choose five hundred of your best riders and prepare them for the journey. And inform the quartermaster. Tell him to provision the force as best he can without slowing us down. What he can't provide, we'll gather ourselves as we ride."

"Yes, Your Highness." Ohan bowed, then strode from the chamber.

"Alao, Edamo, Naditia, the three of you should leave at once. Return to your homes, choose two hundred of your finest warriors, and provision them as best you can. We'll meet in Brugaosa as soon as possible and leave for Eibithar from there."

The three nobles stood and bowed to her, even Alao, who still didn't look pleased.

"Your Highness," Vasyonne said, before the others could leave the chamber. "What about the Qirsi? Will your ministers ride with you as well?"

Olesya's eyebrows went up. Clearly she hadn't given any thought to this. Since Kreazur's death there had been little doubt that the conspiracy had indeed come to Sanbira. And as Diani and Sertio grew more convinced of the first minister's innocence, it became clearer to them, and to the queen, that there were still traitors at large, perhaps even in the royal court. The white-hairs had been excluded from the councils and kept under constant watch. The nobles still weren't certain who remained loyal and who did not, and Diani couldn't decide whether it was more dangerous to take suspect ministers into battle or to leave them here, where they could work their mischief in the absence of the queen and several of her duchesses and dukes.

"I think they'll have to come with us," Olesya said after a time. "I don't wish to leave them where they can't be watched." She glanced at Diani. "And other remedies are unacceptable."

After the attempt on her life, Diani had been so wary of her Qirsi that she had had every sorcerer in Castle Curlinte imprisoned. When the queen heard of this, she ordered Diani to release them all, but the duchess still believed it was the best way to ensure that any traitors among the ministers could be controlled.

"Your Highness—" Diani began.

"We're talking about four Qirsi, Lady Curlinte. Abeni, and the first ministers of Norinde, Brugaosa, and Macharzo. And we'll have over a thousand warriors guarding us. It won't be a problem."

The duchess looked away. "Yes, Your Highness."

"Go now," the queen said, looking at the three nobles standing near the doorway. "I'll see you at Castle Brugaosa." The three left, and Olesya turned to the others. "As for the rest of you, you should return to your castles. Be watchful, not only of your Qirsi, but of your borders and shores as well. I believe that Eibithar needs our aid, but I fear for the realm."

Vasyonne stood. "Gods keep you safe, Your Highness."

The others stood as well, all of them invoking the gods before they began to file from the chamber.

"Lady Curlinte, Lord Curlinte," the queen called before Diani and Sertio reached the door. "A word please."

Olesya waited until the last of the duchesses closed the door behind her. "Have you learned anything more about the Qirsi in my court?"

Sertio shook his head. "Still nothing, Your Highness. The traitor—"

"Or traitors," Diani added.

Her father merely glanced at her. "Whoever it may be, this person has been quite clever about hiding his or her treachery. We've neither seen nor heard anything that would indicate that there is a traitor in the court."

"Is it possible that we've been wrong about all this?" Olesya asked. "Perhaps there are no traitors in Yserne."

Clearly the queen wanted to believe this; it was written on her handsome face, in the hopeful look in her dark eyes. But Diani knew better. The conspiracy was everywhere, infesting the land like some pernicious weed, spreading its tendrils through all the houses in the realm, insinuating itself into every court. It would take some time to prove this, perhaps more time than they had. Which was why they had to expose the traitors in the queen's court as quickly as possible. This was where the evil was rooted—she was certain of that, as well. Kill the thing here, and perhaps the tendrils would wither and die.

"The conspiracy is real, Your Highness," Diani told her. "And it's here, in Yserne. Whoever had Kreazur killed was thoroughly familiar with this castle and this city."

Olesya had heard this from her before, but still the words seemed to pain her, bringing a grimace to her lips and leaving her looking bent and frail.

"I'm too old to be fighting two wars at once."

"You're not fighting either of them alone, Your Highness."

The queen forced a smile. "I know that, Diani. Thank you. And thank you, Sertio. I wish you could have learned more, but I know that you did what you could."

"Your Highness," Diani said, sensing that Olesya was about to dismiss them, "I'd like to ride with you to Eibithar."

"Thank you, Diani, but our force will be large enough with the soldiers from the northwest houses, and we really can't delay."

"Forgive me, Your Highness, but you misunderstand. I don't want to lead my army to Eibithar, I merely wish to accompany you myself."

Sertio looked at her sharply, drawing breath to object.

"To what end?" the queen asked, before he could.

"To keep watch on Abeni and the other Qirsi. You'll be occupied with the war, as will Naditia and the others. But since I won't be leading an army, I can give my full attention to the conspiracy." She faltered, but only for an instant. "Besides, this all began with the attack on me. I'd like to see it through to the end."

"This war may be only the beginning, Diani. It may be quite dangerous to allow yourself to be driven by vengeance."

She hadn't said no, at least not yet. Diani pressed her advantage.

"Vengeance has nothing to do with it, Your Highness. You've decided to grant Kearney's request because you see in this war the hand of the conspiracy. We saw it as well in the attempts on my life, and who knows how many times we've failed to see what should have been obvious to us. Our enemies may be all around us, but they won't show themselves until we're most vulnerable. If this war is a Qirsi feint, shouldn't someone be with you, watching for the hidden blade?"

"Why you?" Sertio demanded. "You've never been to war, and as good as you are with steel, you're not accomplished enough to guard the queen's life. You should be in Curlinte, with your people and your army. I'll accompany the queen."

She should have been grateful. He was trying to protect her, as any good father would. But she heard only his challenge, his questioning of her abilities and her judgment.

"No, Father. You can't do this. Whoever goes with the queen must be able to spot the traitor before he or she strikes. And you're just too trusting. What good is steel if it never leaves its sheath?"

His face shaded to crimson, and he leveled a rigid finger at her chest. "Just because—"

"Stop it!" Olesya glared at them both. "I haven't even said yet that I'll allow one of you to accompany me, and already you're fighting over which of you will be riding."

"She has no place in this war, Your Highness. Better you should go without either of us than take her. You can just as easily have one of your men keep watch on the Qirsi."

"I believe you do her a disservice, Sertio. You love her; you fear for her. I understand that." She paused, looking at the duchess. "You must understand that, too, Diani. What he said a moment ago was intended not to diminish you, but to protect you. You may have felt slighted, but until you're a parent yourself, you shouldn't judge your father too harshly."

"Your Highness—"

"Let me finish, Sertio. I know that you want to keep her safe, but she's not a girl anymore. She's a woman, and with Dalvia gone, she is duchess of one of Sanbira's leading houses. The attack at the coast has left you frightened, and rightfully so. But you can't let your life, or Diani's, be ruled by fear. Would you have her lock herself away within the walls of her castle so that no arrows can find her, no traitors can strike at her?"

His cheeks still red, Sertio shook his head and muttered, "Of course not."

"Then let her do this. I think it a fine idea. The two of you have been watching Abeni and the others for some time now; it makes sense that Diani should continue to do so." Diani's father still did not look mollified. "I'll take good care of her, Sertio. You have my word, not only as your queen, but as your friend."

"Yes, Your Highness."

Again they bowed to the queen, before leaving the chamber. Even after they were in the corridor, Sertio said nothing and for a time they walked in silence back toward their chambers on the far end of the inner keep. Only when they reached Diani's door did her father finally look at her, his face like stone.

"You truly think me too trusting?"

"Father—"

"Do you?"

She took a breath. "Sometimes, yes."

"And you believe this weakens me."

"You're a good man, Father, and a strong leader. You have fine qualities, among them your capacity to trust and the loyalty you show your friends. I just believe that some gifts, no matter how bright, have a dark side as well."

"You may be right. And certainly the queen was correct when she said that I wish to keep you safe. But the real reason I don't want you making this journey is that I fear your suspicions will get the better of you. I believe you want to accompany the queen for the same reason you imprisoned all the Qirsi in Curlinte. The attempts on your life have made you so frightened that you can no longer distinguish friend from foe, at least where the white-hairs are concerned. I may trust too willingly, but you see treachery behind every pair of yellow eyes. Tell me, Diani. Which is the darker gift?"

He left her then, and long after the click of his boots on the stone floors had faded to nothing, Diani still stood there, her hand poised on the door handle, her throat so tight she could hardly draw breath.

It took more than the suspicions of a queen and the prejudice of her small-minded nobles to keep Abeni ja Krenta, Sanbira's archminister, from knowing all that happened in Castle Yserne. Though it had been more than a turn since Olesya had trusted her with any important task or confided in her in any meaningful way, there were those in the castle who still did her bidding, because they feared the influence she once had wielded and might someday wield again, or because they feared her magic, or because, like Abeni herself, they served the Weaver's movement. She wasn't without her own resources, her own servants. If it was possible for an Eandi to cast a pale shadow, then that was Abeni. White-skinned, white-haired, she was a counterpart to the queen. Perhaps her power didn't reach as far as Olesya's—yet—but she commanded a force of her own within the walls of this palace.

She herself had seen the messenger arrive, had watched as the castle guards fell over themselves to escort this man to Olesya's chambers. Soon after, she left her chamber to wander the corridors. The Qirsi master who trained her in the use of her magic, as well as in the ways of the Eandi courts, had once said that a person could learn much of what happened in a castle simply by walking through its passages and gardens. "The walls of a castle will whisper secrets to you, if only you listen closely enough," she liked to say. Again and again over the years, Abeni had found this to be true. Just as she did this day. Once in the corridors, she saw several of the other nobles scurrying like mice to the queen's chambers. She overheard two guards speaking of a missive from a king, of war to the north. So she wasn't at all surprised later in the day when another soldier approached her to say that the queen wished to speak with her.

She found Olesya in her presence chamber sitting in the ornate olivewood chair at the end of her council table. The queen appeared composed; if the tidings contained in the messenger's note had shaken her, she showed no sign of it now. It seemed to Abeni a sign of how deep Olesya's mistrust ran; she had never bothered to mask her fears or concerns from the archminister in the past.

Abeni bowed, and the queen indicated a chair at the table with an open hand.

"Please sit, Archminister."

"Thank you, Your Highness. You called for me?"

"I did. You may have heard of a messenger arriving here today."

"Yes, I did, though beyond the fact of his arrival, I've heard nothing."

"He came from Eibithar."

She'd guessed that much, but she allowed surprise to register on her face. "Eibithar?"

"Yes, from Kearney himself. It seems that the Braedon fleet is menacing Eibithar's north coast. At the same time, there's been some movement of Aneiran soldiers along the Tarbin." She paused, eyeing Abeni, as if waiting for some response.

"Kearney fears an attack?" the archminister asked.

"Yes. For all we know, there's already war on the Eibitharian Moorlands."

This was the Weaver's work. The realization came to her so suddenly, with such force, that she knew it had to be true. The last time he walked in her dreams, the Weaver had told her that all their planning was nearly at an end, that the Forelands would soon be theirs. No doubt this war was another attempt—perhaps the culminating one—to weaken the armies of the Eandi courts.

"Kearney has asked me to send warriors to help him meet the emperor's assault. In return, he offers Eibithar's aid in our fight against the conspiracy."

Her expression neutral, her voice even, Abeni said, "He must know that you'll refuse."

"Why do you say that?"

And she knew. The queen would ride to war within the next few days. These were indeed extraordinary times.

"Sanbiri queens have avoided war alliances for centuries. I merely assumed that you would do the same."

"In truth, I had every intention of refusing. But several of the duchesses argued for going to war, as did Edamo."

This time, Abeni's surprise was genuine. "Lord Brugaosa? Arguing in favor of going to war?" It was almost too good to be true. She felt quite certain that this was what the Weaver wanted. The wider the conflict, the better for the movement. Edamo and the others were just the fools the Weaver had hoped they would be.

"I was as shocked as you are. But he made a fine argument for honoring Kearney's request. He believes, as do several of the others, that there's more to this war than there appears."

Abruptly, Abeni felt her confidence leech away. "I don't understand," she said, struggling to keep her voice steady.

Again the queen was watching her, and again Abeni knew what she would say before she said it, though this time she could barely control the pounding of her heart.

"He thinks that the conspiracy has somehow contrived events to bring about this war." She took a breath, her gaze never straying from Abeni's face. "I fear that I must agree with him."

"How could the traitors do such a thing, Your Highness?" Her mouth felt gritty and dry.

"I was hoping that you might be able to tell me."

No doubt the queen had thought to catch her unawares with the accusation, to frighten her into giving herself away. In fact, she gave Abeni just what she needed to overcome her initial dismay at hearing of Edamo's insight.

"I don't know what you mean, Your Highness." But her tone

left little doubt that she did, that she recognized the queen's statement for what it was: an accusation. She could be defensive now, she could be hostile. Olesya had given her just the excuse she needed to close herself off to any more questions.

"I think you know just what I mean. I'm sorry if I've offended you, but I had to ask."

"Did you, Your Highness? For more than a turn now you've been avoiding me, refusing to hear my counsel. And in all that time, while your spies have been watching me—watching all the Qirsi in Castle Yserne—you've found nothing to tie me to the conspiracy." Seeing Olesya pale, she gave a sad smile. "Yes, I know about the soldiers who follow me, and about Lady Curlinte's attempts to prove me a traitor."

"Abeni—"

"I understand why you did it, Your Highness. The betrayal of Curlinte's first minister left all of us shaken. But I'd think that after all this time looking in vain for signs that I'd betrayed the realm, you'd be ready to trust me again."

The queen's eyes strayed to the window. "I'm afraid it's not that easy."

"Why isn't it, Your Highness?" Abeni demanded, surprising herself with the fervor of her question. "What have I done to make you doubt me so?"

She saw Olesya hesitate, so there was something. But after a moment the queen shook her head. "It's nothing, Abeni. You've done nothing." The woman took a breath, then gave a brittle smile. "Indeed, I'd like you to ride with us to Eibithar. I'll be grateful for your counsel, and for the powers you'll wield on our behalf."

"You want me to come with you?" Abeni said, sounding, she knew, like a dullard.

The queen actually smiled. "Yes. Other ministers will be accompanying us as well. I intend to bring five hundred soldiers from the royal army, and another two hundred each from Norinde, Brugaosa, and Macharzo. Alao, Edamo, and Naditia will be riding with us, as will their first ministers."

The first minister of Brugaosa remained loyal to his duke, but Craeffe and Filtem were already with the movement. Having them at hand for the coming battle might prove most fortuitous. Abeni would have liked to have Listaal's first minister there as well. She hadn't turned to the movement yet, but she was close. Craeffe had been working her for nearly a turn, as had Abeni. But she had no cause to complain. Three of the four ministers riding with Sanbira's army belonged to the movement. The Weaver would be pleased.

"You trust us with this?" she asked the queen.

Again, the hesitation. *No,* it seemed to say, *but we want you where we can watch you.* "We'll have to learn to trust again. All of us. And in the meantime, we need you."

It was a more candid answer than she had expected. "All right," she said. "When do we ride?"

"Soon. In the next few days. I'll know more after I've had a chance to speak again with the master of arms and the quartermaster."

"Very good, Your Highness. I'll be ready."

"I know you will, Archminister. Thank you."

Abeni bowed and left her, intending to return to her bedchamber. As she reached it, however, she found Craeffe waiting for her, an avid look in her large bright eyes. Silently, Abeni opened the door to the chamber and they both stepped inside.

"You've heard?" Craeffe asked quietly, once the door was closed and locked.

"Yes." Abeni didn't particularly like the woman, but she knew that the Weaver expected them to work together.

Craeffe gave a cadaverous grin. "Filtem, too." Abeni had wondered before if she and Norinde's first minister might be lovers; seeing how pleased Craeffe looked now, she felt certain of it.

"I know." Abeni could see that the minister expected her to say more, but she could think of nothing to add. There was a queer feeling in her chest—not apprehension, but not eagerness either. She had no name for it.

"This must be it, what we've been waiting for."

Abeni nodded. "I've had the same thought. If so, we're most fortunate to have all three of us together. It almost seems that the gods are smiling on us."

Craeffe's grin widened. "Did you ever doubt that they would?"

Yes, a voice within her replied. *Even now I do.* But Abeni merely made herself smile.

"Something's bothering you. What is it?"

She was always probing, looking for weaknesses she could exploit. Abeni was one of the Weaver's chancellors and Craeffe wished to be. She was nothing if not a creature of her ambitions.

"It's nothing, Craeffe. Go back to your duchess."

"I don't believe you."

Abeni turned away. Regardless of her motives, Craeffe was with her in this movement. She needed to know. "Edamo believes that the movement is behind this war, and he's convinced Olesya of this. They'll be watching us."

Craeffe laughed. "Of course they will. But Edamo is just guessing. He knows nothing for certain."

"He's right."

"Of course he is. It changes nothing. Even forewarned, they're not clever enough to defeat the Weaver." A pause, and then, her voice solicitous and low, "I'm surprised to hear you so filled with doubts, Archminister. Perhaps you question the Weaver's wisdom, or his power?"

Abeni faced her again, a smile fixed on her lips. "Not at all, Craeffe. I just fear that some of his servants may not be worthy of him."

Unruffled, Craeffe raised an eyebrow. "Don't worry, cousin. I'm certain that you'll do the best that you can." She turned on her heel and pulled the door open, not bothering to look at Abeni again. "See you in Brugaosa, Archminister."

Chapter Thirteen

Galdasten, Eibithar

From the tower atop Renald's castle, it seemed a dance of sorts, the slow circling of partners at the outset of some court fourstep. Until the first Braedon ship rammed its prow into the hull of the lead vessel in Eibithar's fleet. After that, there could be no mistaking what was taking shape on the waters of Falcon Bay. For the first time in over a century and a half, Eibithar was at war with the Braedon empire.

Renald was soaked to the skin. A hard rain sliced across the castle ramparts, driven by a cold wind. It should have been warmer—nearly half of Elined's Turn was gone—but it felt more like the harvest than it did the final days of the planting season. Elspeth would have thought him a fool for standing up here in the rain, watching a battle whose outcome had long since been decided. She would have called him weak and worse had she known how he quailed at the very thought of what was happening aboard those ships. As a child, he had heard seamen at the Galdasten quays recounting tales, passed down to them from their grandfathers, of the previous naval wars with Braedon. The Empire Wars, they were called. Braedon had prevailed in those conflicts as well, gaining sovereignty over Enwyl Island in the Gulf of Kreanna. And it had taken the shipbuilders of Galdasten and Thorald more than ten years to rebuild the Eibitharian fleet.

But it wasn't the rammings that stood out in Renald's memory, the descriptions of rending wood and the ghostlike groan of a hull taking on too much water. No, it was the combat that followed the collisions. The boardings and bloody sword battles as the warriors aboard those ships clashed, fighting for control of the vessel that remained seaworthy.

He could still hear the voice of one old sailor—a grizzled old man with leathery brown skin and a misshapen stump where his left arm should have been—asking his companions how many soldiers had been swallowed by the dark waters of the bay during that last war, and laughing at what he saw on Renald's face. Even as a foolish child, easily impressed and more easily frightened, Renald had known that this man could not have fought in the Empire Wars, and later he had come to wonder how much of what those men told him that day had been true, and how much of it had been the blustering yarns of old sailors eager to scare a court boy. Still, watching this new battle in the cold Galdasten rain, Renald thought he could see bodies falling over the sides of the Eibitharian vessel, lost forever to Amon's waters.

The fleets of the two realms had been arrayed against each other for several days, their commanders waiting far longer than Renald had ever guessed they would to begin the war. It almost seemed that both sides were awaiting some sign that they should attack. That sign had finally come this morning, and much to the duke's surprise, it had been the Eibitharian fleet that made the first move. Renald couldn't be certain, but he thought it likely that the rain and wind prompted the attack. On open waters, in calm weather, Eibithar's ships had little chance against Braedon's larger fleet and more skilled seamen. Perhaps the captains of Eibithar's vessels thought that this storm would mitigate the empire's advantages somewhat.

Already it seemed clear to the duke that they had been tragically mistaken. In the span of only a few heartbeats, two more of Eibithar's ships were rammed, and now he was certain that he could see soldiers dressed in the gold and red of Braedon swarming onto the stricken vessels. It would be a slaughter.

"My lord!"

Renald started so violently that he nearly lost his balance.

He hadn't heard Ewan Traylee's approach for the rain and the keening wind. "What is it, swordmaster?"

"Forgive me for disturbing you, my lord, but the duchess is asking after you, and no one knew where you were."

"Well as you can see, I'm right here," he said, staring out at the ships again. "And I've no desire to speak with the duchess just now." It wasn't a tone he would usually have taken with Ewan. Damn this rain. Damn the empire.

"Yes, my lord." The swordmaster looked out at the bay as well. An instant later, his voice rising again, he said, "They've begun!"

"Yes. Just a short time ago."

"It's going poorly."

Renald glanced at the man. Rain plastered his black hair to his brow, and ran down his broad face before being lost in his beard. "Did you doubt that it would?"

"Not really, my lord. But I had hoped . . ." He shrugged, his gaze fixed on the battle.

"Is all ready for a siege?"

"Yes, my lord. We can withstand whatever the emperor's soldiers throw at us."

"Very good, Ewan."

They stood in silence for several moments watching the ships dance. For a time it seemed that Eibithar's vessels might actually be gaining the upper hand. No more Eibitharian ships had been rammed, and in fact they managed to incapacitate two Braedon ships in quick succession. But their success was short-lived, and it soon became clear that the empire's vessels were simply too swift. What had started as a battle was fast turning into a pursuit. Eibithar's ships were no longer looking for openings to attack, but were instead doing all they could to avoid being shattered and boarded.

"Do you think the king sent word to Wethyrn?" Ewan asked after some time.

"He would have been a fool not to. Wethyrn's ships are the only ones in the seven that would stand a chance against the empire's fleet."

"Then perhaps there's hope yet."

"Not unless they arrive today. Now that this battle has begun, it won't last long."

"Yes, my lord."

He should have been pleased. Certainly that was what Elspeth would tell him. Soon Kearney's guard would be routed by the empire's men, and when the army of Galdasten joined the war, turning the tide for Eibithar, the throne would be his. Still, he couldn't help thinking that he had betrayed his forebears, his people, and his kingdom. What if Kearney had been telling the truth? What if the conspiracy was behind the murder of Lady Brienne of Kentigern? What if Tavis of Curgh was not a butcher, but rather a victim of white-hair treachery? Then wasn't Renald himself helping the renegades? Wasn't his refusal to fight the invaders tantamount to treason?

"You say the duchess wishes to speak with me?"

"Yes, my lord."

"Do you know what she wants?"

Ewan grimaced. It took Renald a moment to realize that he was actually grinning. "The duchess rarely tells me anything, my lord." He looked like he might say more, but then he merely shrugged and faced the bay again.

"It's not you, Ewan. She's like that with everyone." *She knows that she's smarter than all of us, and it galls her that she doesn't lead this house.*

"Yes, my lord. Thank you."

Renald's hands had grown numb gripping the stone ramparts. He wanted nothing more than to return to his chambers where he might change into some dry clothes and sit before his hearth. But he couldn't tear his eyes away from the ships.

"I'll keep watch for you, my lord. If something changes, or—" he swallowed, "or if it ends, I'll let you know first thing."

What would his father have said? The lords of Galdasten had long envied the supremacy of the House of Thorald. For more than one hundred years now, there had been no measurable difference between the size of Thorald's army and that of Galdasten, between the riches in Thorald's treasury and those in Galdasten's. Yet, by dint of the Order of Ascension, determined hundreds of years ago, Thorald was the highest ranking house in the land, and Galdasten second. Over the course of Eibithar's history, Thorald kings outnumbered those from Renald's house by nearly three to one. Yet in all that time, no duke of Galdasten had ever led a rebellion against the Rules. True, no duke of Galdasten had ever faced the bleak future that awaited Renald and his sons.

But did that give him just cause to defy the Rules? He could hear Elspeth's reply. *Hasn't Galdasten suffered long enough under Thorald's dominance? Don't the other realms of Eibithar deserve to be freed from a supremacy that has no basis in fact?*

You are weakening the realm to nurture your own ambitions. His father's voice. And once again it was countered in his mind by Elspeth's, just as reasoned, and far more strident. *You do this for our sons, so that they might fulfill their destiny and rule this land.*

"My lord?" Ewan said, interrupting the colloquy in his mind.

"Yes, swordmaster, thank you. I would be grateful for a warm cup of tea and a fire."

"Go, my lord. I'll keep you apprised of all that happens."

Renald nodded, but stood there a moment longer, watching the ships, searching for some shift in the course of the battle, some sign that Eibithar's fleet might still prevail. Seeing none, he finally left the tower, descending the winding stairs to the lower corridor, and making his way from there to his bedchamber. Even the cold stone of the castle passages seemed pleasant after the wind and rain. His chamber was bright and warm, and as comfortable as a child's blanket. He stripped out of his wet clothes and a servant helped him into a dry robe. He was just tying it when he heard a knock at his door. Before he could call a response, Elspeth let herself into the chamber, looking lovely and formidable in a dark violet dress, her brown hair tied back from her face and her eyes glittering with the lamplight.

Her gaze flicked about the chamber, coming to rest briefly on the servant before returning to Renald's face. "I summoned you some time ago. Where have you been?"

He wanted to rail at her for speaking to him so. He should at least have demanded an apology. It was one thing to use such a tone with her duke when they were alone, but to do so in front of others, even a common servant, was unacceptable. But it was all he could do just to say, as if a boy offering excuses to an irate parent, "I was on the tower. The war's started."

Her entire bearing changed. She took a step toward him, eager, a fierce smile on her flawless face. "They've started? You saw them fighting?"

Renald nodded.

"What's happening? Can you tell how the fleet is faring?"

"Not well. They've already lost several ships, and were on the verge of losing more when I left the tower."

She opened her mouth to say something else, then stopped, glaring at the servant. "Leave us!"

The boy nearly jumped to obey, scurrying from the room with a quick backward glance.

"You think it will end quickly?" she asked when the boy was gone, avid and dazzling, her color high.

"I fear it will." He winced at his choice of words, hoping she wouldn't notice.

Little chance of that.

"You fear it will?" she repeated, the smile vanishing.

"I only meant that I wish so many didn't have to die."

"It's war, you fool. Of course they have to die. Eventually you'll have to lead men to kill and be killed. You'll have to raise your sword as well, or fall in battle. You are prepared to do all that, aren't you, Renald?"

"Yes, of course—"

"Because if you're not, you'd best say so now. There still may be time to salvage something from this mess you've created."

"I'm prepared to do whatever I must to take the crown, Elspeth. I've told Ewan to prepare the castle for a siege. Even if I wanted to meet the emperor's army on the strand, it's too late now. I've chosen my path and I'll travel it as far as it will take me."

"Good, Renald. Very good." She began to circle the room,

like a wolf stalking her prey. "What does Ewan think of all this? He can't be happy about it."

"I've told you before: Ewan is a good soldier. He'll do as he's told. I've made it clear to him that I intend to be king, and that he has only to follow me and soon enough he'll be commander of the King's Guard. I'm sure that he laments the loss of life as I do." He paused, eyeing her briefly. "As we all do. But he understands that some sacrifices must be made if we're to rid ourselves of both the invaders from Braedon and the usurpers from Glyndwr and Curgh."

She continued to roam the chamber, passing just behind him, her shoulder brushing his back and her scent, lavender and woodbine, filling him, intoxicating him. He closed his eyes for just an instant, inhaling deeply.

"The usurpers," she said, her voice low. "I like that. Did you think of it yourself?"

"Actually, I did."

"What if the emperor's men besiege the castle? What if it's Kearney who must come to our aid, rather than us to his?"

Renald shook his head. "I don't think that will happen. This is an invasion. A prolonged siege here gains them nothing. Even if they were to prevail—not that they will—but even if they were to, they would only succeed in giving Kearney time to marshal his forces. They need to strike quickly at the heart of the realm. They need to destroy the King's Guard. If they can do that, the houses will fall in turn. At least, that's what the emperor's commanders will think."

"You reasoned this out as well?"

"Yes. Ewan agrees with me," he added quickly, lest she think him overly confident.

But Elspeth smiled at him, a radiant smile, seemingly free of irony or scorn. It had been years since he last saw a smile like this one on her face. She had circled close again. The air around them was redolent. "I agree with you, too." She stopped behind him, slipping her arms beneath his and resting her cheek against his back. "You've been watching Pillad, haven't you?"

"Yes," he whispered. He felt the beginning of an erection

pressing against his robe, and he prayed that she wouldn't notice. "I have men watching all the Qirsi, the first minister in particular. He spends a good deal of time in the city, drinking alone at a tavern there. But he never speaks with anyone, and aside from the ale, he never spends any gold."

She reached a hand inside his robe and began to rub his chest gently. It had been so long since she'd touched him like this. "Still, I wouldn't trust him with anything of importance. Not now, not when we're so close."

Renald closed his eyes. "Of course," he said. In a far corner of his mind he thought, *If I'd known she'd respond like this, I'd have led a rebellion years ago.* He nearly laughed aloud.

A moment later she stepped around to stand before him. Glancing down, seeing the bulge at the front of his robe, she smiled again, though not with her usual cruelty. Still smiling, looking into his eyes once more, she reached down to untie the sash.

"Why are you doing this?" he asked, and then instantly regretted the question.

But she merely gazed at him placidly. "I told you some time ago, Renald, if you were to lead this war as would a king, you could have me again." She reached within his robe and gently took hold of him. "I'm a woman of my word."

She withdrew her hand and began to unfasten the buttons that ran down the length of her dress.

Renald touched her hands with his own, stopping her. "May I?" he asked, something in his voice reminding him once more of a child.

Elspeth's eyes were luminous as she led him to the bed. "Of course."

The White Wave was nearly empty, as it usually was so early in the day. Pillad was already on his third ale, and the darkness that seemed to come with all drink in recent days was already upon him. He no longer bought the ale that was made here in Galdasten, though it was fine enough for most. He preferred the light brew from Thorald, the finest in the land. And since he had gold enough to afford whatever ale he wanted, he didn't think twice about drinking it. True, there might have been some danger in flaunting his newly acquired taste for Thorald's golden. With rumors of the conspiracy running rampant through the realm, and Braedon warships poised off the coast, any Qirsi spending too much of his or her wage was suspect in the eyes of Ean's children. Even his Qirsi masters would not have approved, seeing in his recklessness a threat to their movement, to their very lives.

But Pillad knew better than to be afraid. No one paid any attention to him; nobody cared what he did. His duke had lost faith in him long ago, and because of that, the movement had little use for him anymore. Uestem, the Qirsi merchant who first convinced Pillad to join the Weaver's cause, had scarcely spoken to him since the first minister received his gold. For one brief moment, it had seemed that he was a prize coveted by both sides in this conflict. His loyalty had been a battlefield on which Qirsi and Eandi contended, until he chose to cast his lot with his people, and with the shadowy figure of his dreams who would be the Forelands' first Qirsi king.

It hadn't taken him long to understand that this had been a hollow victory for the Qirsi and a loss without cost for his duke and the Eandi courts. He was worthless. He could provide answers to a few questions that the Weaver's servants deemed important: How would Renald respond to the empire's invasion? How would he allocate his men if Braedon's army laid siege to the city and castle? How long would Galdasten's stores hold out if the siege went on? But beyond these scraps of information, he offered little of importance. He had thought that Uestem cared for him, that they might find in their shared struggle against the courts something more than comradery, something more even, than friendship. He knew now that he had been a fool. All the merchant had wanted was to deliver him to the Weaver. In some small way then, he had been a prize, but knowing this did nothing to heal his wounded pride or ease the pain in his heart.

The ale, though. The ale did both, at least it did after the third or fourth helping. He had gold enough to drink, and time enough to be drunk. And perhaps, if he came to the White Wave each day, and remained here through to the prior's bells, he would see Uestem again. The merchant couldn't avoid this place forever, not if there were others in Galdasten he wished to turn to the Weaver's cause.

He drained his cup and motioned to the serving girl for another, pulling another five qinde piece from the pouch on his belt. The girl glanced briefly at the barkeep, a tall, spear-thin man with eyes the color of sea foam and long white hair that he tied back from his face. The man filled a cup and brought it to the table himself, placing it in front of Pillad before sitting beside him. The first minister noticed that this was Galdasten ale, not the Thorald.

"This isn't what I'm drinking," he said, glaring at the man.

"I think it should be, cousin."

Pillad glanced about the tavern. He was the only one there, other than the barkeep and his servers.

"Why should you care? I'm putting gold in your pocket. It's not as though others are beating down your door to drink your wares."

"It's not my business that concerns me, Minister."

"My point exactly."

The man grinned, though the look in those pale eyes remained deadly serious. "You've a sharp wit, sir, and a good mind. A man as clever as you should know better than to act a fool."

"I beg your pardon!"

Pillad started to stand, but the barkeep laid a firm hand on his forearm, forcing him back into his chair.

"The Eandi are watching all of us right now, particularly you, looking for odd behavior, or extravagance. You're showing them both."

He's with the conspiracy. Pillad felt himself begin to sweat. It hadn't occurred to him that there were others in Galdasten aside from Uestem and himself, though of course it should have. Who better than the owner of the tavern in which Uestem had his discussions and collected prizes for his Weaver?

"You fear for me, cousin?" Pillad asked. But the bluster was gone from his voice.

"I fear for all of us. You don't strike me as the type of man who could endure much on the torturer's table. I suspect that before you died, you'd tell the duke's men all they wanted to know."

Pillad searched for some response. Finding none, he reached for his ale. But the barkeep put his hand over the cup.

"This is the last you'll have today, Minister. And the next time you come to my tavern you'll drink only the Galdasten ale. Two cups, and then you'll be done."

"You can't tell me what to do." His voice quavered, and he cursed himself for being so weak.

"No, I can't, at least not so that anyone else can hear me. But there are others who can. All it takes is a word from me. I think you know who I mean."

It might have been Uestem, or perhaps the Weaver. It didn't matter. In the Eandi world, where Pillad was first minister, this man was nothing. But their status was reversed within the movement. The barkeep held Pillad's life in his hands.

"Yes," he whispered. "I know."

"Good." The barkeep grinned again, and removed his hand from the cup. "Enjoy your ale, cousin."

He stood, but before he could start back toward the bar, someone appeared in the doorway. It was a Qirsi man, one Pillad didn't know. His eyes were wide, and though his hair and clothes were drenched, he didn't seem to care.

"They've started it!" he said. "They're fighting out on the bay!"

Pillad heard fear in his voice, and uncertainty. This man wasn't with the movement, or if he was, he didn't understand how eager the Weaver had been for this war to begin.

The minister and the barkeep shared a look. Then they both followed the man out into the storm.

It was a short walk from the tavern to the Galdasten quays where they could watch the warships struggling to flank each other. A crowd had already gathered, and with the wind blowing cold off Falcon Bay, driving a stinging rain into his eyes, Pillad could barely make out what was happening. It wasn't long, though, before he heard a groan go up from the others, and he knew that the empire's fleet had drawn first blood.

"They haven' a chance agains' those Braedony ships," he heard one man say.

And another added, "There's jus' too many of 'em. If we had the Wethy fleet with us, maybe. But no' like this."

"You'd best be getting back to your duke, cousin," the barkeep said, his voice low, his mouth so close to Pillad's ear that the minister could feel his breath. "If the duke's first minister is seen in Galdasten City as the realm is going to war, it's certain to raise questions."

Pillad nodded and began to back away from the crowd. More people had gathered behind him, and he had to push his way through the throng. The rain and wind helped; with his hair and clothes soaked, and his breath stinking of ale, he hardly looked like the most powerful Qirsi in the dukedom. In just a few moments he was free of the crowd. Leaving the quays, he followed the quickest route through the city and back toward Galdasten Castle. The duke's guards were still following him, watching from byways and narrow lanes, but there wasn't much he could do about that. If he tried to return to the castle by way of some obscure, winding route, it would draw even more attention to the fact that he had been in the city. Best to be seen, to endure the sneers of Renald's guards. All of them knew that the duke no longer confided in him; one didn't have to be a genius to notice that. Perhaps they already knew that he was drinking.

He faltered in midstride, his innards turning to water. Renald's spies might already have seen him ordering the Thorald golden, spending his gold in the White Wave like a drunken noble.

If they knew you were a traitor, they'd have hanged you by now, or they'd be torturing you in the dungeons, demanding the names of others in the movement. He knew it was true, but he found no comfort in the thought. Was it pride to prefer torture and execution to indifference?

A woman bearing a basket of sodden cloth hurried past, staring at him as though he were mad. Pillad realized that he was standing in the middle of the lane by the marketplace, allowing himself to be doused by the rain. Drawing attention to himself yet again.

Did he want to be caught? he wondered, continuing on toward the castle. Was he that desperate to feel that he mattered? And though he understood instantly that he had no desire to be imprisoned or killed, he also knew that he needed to be more than what he had become. It sobered him, as if purging his body of the ale he had downed in the tavern. By the time he reached the north gate of the castle, his mind was clear. One of the guards raised an eyebrow at the sight of him, but the first minister no longer cared. He returned to his chamber, changed his clothes, and went in search of the duke.

The duke's men refused to allow him entry to Renald's chamber, saying something about the duchess being with him. Pillad would have liked to laugh at them—as if the duchess being with the duke were cause for closed doors and hushed voices. She hadn't loved him in years. No doubt she was telling him how he ought to deal with the coming siege and Kearney's pleas for help.

He climbed the nearest of the towers, intending to watch the battle, but upon reaching the ramparts, he saw Ewan Traylee standing at the wall, staring out at the bay. There had been a time when Pillad and the swordmaster got along quite well. They were never truly friends, but in a land where sorcerers and soldiers were often at odds, they had worked together on their duke's behalf, eventually coming to respect one another. Or so the first minister had thought. For when Renald began to question Pillad's loyalty, Ewan stopped speaking to him as well. True, the swordmaster had merely been following the duke's example, but still, it stung.

Pillad turned to go back down the stairway, moving silently lest Ewan should notice him.

"First minister!"

Pillad took a breath, then turned. "Forgive me, swordmaster. I didn't mean to disturb you."

"Not at all. Join me." Ewan faced the bay once more, his expression bleak. "You heard that the fighting had begun?"

"Yes. I was in the city."

Ewan looked over at that.

No sense in lying to the man. Perhaps candor could regain some of the trust he had lost. "I frequent a tavern there. The duke has little use for me anymore, and I prefer to be outside the castle."

The swordmaster nodded, his gaze returning to the warships. "These are difficult times, First Minister. Many of us are frightened. None of us knows who to trust anymore."

"You include yourself in that."

"Yes." The man's grey eyes flicked Pillad's way for just an instant. "I'm sorry. You've done nothing to raise my suspicions, but I have them just the same."

"Because I'm Qirsi."

"Yes. All Qirsi are suspect now. Surely you understand that."

"Of course I do," he said, and meant it. Abruptly, he knew what he would do, what he had to do. The Weaver would be angry with him, as would Uestem. The risk to all of them was great. But he couldn't go on this way. War had come to Galdasten, and even Pillad, who knew little of such things, could see that the Eibitharian fleet was being decimated by Braedon's ships. If he wished to be of use to the Weaver and his movement, he needed to win back Renald's trust. Quickly. He could think of only one way to do so. "I understand perfectly well, swordmaster. That's why I went to speak with the duke just now, but his soldiers wouldn't allow me in to see him."

Ewan looked at him again. "I don't follow, First Minister. Has something happened?"

"I'm afraid it has. I should have come to you sooner. I see that now. I've suspected for some time, but I couldn't prove anything."

"Suspected what?"

"You have to understand, swordmaster, I have no desire to be hated by my people, nor do I wish this man ill. But I can't ignore what's happened."

"First Minister, please!" the swordmaster said, his patience clearly wearing thin. "Tell me what's happened."

Pillad swallowed, as if deeply troubled by what he was about to say. Actually, for the first time in so long, he was enjoying himself. *Let him think twice about speaking to me as if I'm some common Qirsi juggling flames in the Revel or serving drinks in his little tavern.*

"As I said a moment ago," he began, resting his hands on the stone wall, lowering his gaze, "I've spent a good deal of time recently at a tavern in the city. It's called the White Wave, and it's a Qirsi establishment. I've noticed the barkeep there eyeing me strangely at times, as if he wished to speak with me. Today he finally approached me. He asked me why I spent so much time in his tavern, why I wasn't with the duke. I told him to mind his own affairs, but then he told me that he'd heard some saying I'd lost the duke's confidence."

"Did he say who?"

"No. But that's not the worst of it. I tried to deny that this was true, but he wouldn't believe me. 'If the duke still confided in you,' he said, 'you wouldn't be here so often.'" Pillad shook his head. "He has a point, I suppose. This is my own fault. The next thing I know he's offering me gold, telling me that he can help me get back at the duke for his faithlessness."

Ewan's eyes were wide, his face nearly as white as a Qirsi's. "He's with the conspiracy?"

"So it would seem."

"You're certain?"

"As certain as one can be about such things."

The swordmaster pushed away from the castle wall and started toward the stairs, grabbing Pillad by the arm. "We have to tell the duke."

"He won't believe me! He thinks I'm a traitor!"

"You're telling him of a Qirsi renegade. You're offering him a chance to learn a great deal about the conspiracy and its members. If it turns out that you're right, and this man is a traitor, the duke will have no choice but to trust you again."

A chance to learn a great deal . . . "What if the barkeep claims that I'm a renegade as well?"

"Are you?"

"Of course not, but—"

"Then don't worry about it. Torture will make a man say almost anything; the hard part is separating lies from the truth. The dungeonmaster has done this before. He'll learn what he can from your barkeep."

Pillad eyed him briefly, then nodded, wondering if he had made a terrible mistake.

"Come along, First Minister. I'll make certain that the duke sees you."

There were dirty cups everywhere and more than a few spills that needed cleaning, but Mittifar didn't mind, not after a night like this. He would have expected that the war would chase men back to their homes, and if that didn't, then certainly the rain, which continued to deluge the city, swept by winds that seemed more appropriate for the snows than the planting. He had even gone so far as to send his serving girls home early, thinking to save himself the price of their wages. With a war coming, there were bound to be many slow nights in his future.

But while he had thought to stay open for a handful of his regulars, who came in every night no matter what, Mitt soon realized that he had miscalculated badly. By the time the guards on the city walls rang the gate close, the White Wave was packed. Rather than hiding from the war, it seemed that Galdasten's Qirsi wished to take comfort in his tavern, drinking his ale and eating his food. Perhaps they sought refuge from their fears in the company of others. Perhaps they thought to get their fill tonight, before the emperor's soldiers began their siege. Whatever the reason, Mitt spent the entire evening running about the place like a puppy, chasing down orders and drained cups. Escaping the noise and pipeweed smoke for a moment in the alley behind his tavern, he spotted a boy wandering about, picking through refuse. Mitt gave him two silvers and sent the lad to fetch his servers from their homes, but they never came. He was on his own, and though he was exhausted by midnight, and the place was still full, he took some solace in the fact that every qinde left on his tables belonged to him. He paid no wage this night, and he shared no gratuities. He'd be cleaning the tavern until dawn, and would have little chance to sleep if he was to open on time in the morning, but he'd easily clear three hundred qinde tonight.

"It looks like there's been a war in here."

Mitt turned at the sound of the voice, startled. He could have sworn that he had locked the door when the last of his patrons left.

Uestem stood in the doorway, his hooded cloak darkened by the rain. He was smiling, but as always, something seemed to lurk beneath his apparent good cheer. The merchant had brought Mitt into the movement, had paid him his first gold, and for that the barkeep would always be grateful. When at last Qirsi ruled the Forelands, and Mitt received his reward for serving the Weaver's cause, he would have Uestem to thank. But just as the merchant's smile was a mask for something more unsettling, his gifts carried a cost. Over the past year, much to Mitt's dismay, the White Wave had become a center for all the movement's activities here in Galdasten. When Uestem wished to speak with others who served the Weaver, he did so here. He had turned Galdasten's first minister over a cup of Mitt's ale, and so, in a sense, was responsible for the fact that Pillad returned here each day, drinking his Thorald golden and endangering everything for which they had all worked so hard.

"Can I help you with this mess?" the merchant asked, looking around the tavern and then picking his way to where Mitt stood.

"No, thank you. I'm used to it."

"I would have thought this would be a quiet night."

"I thought the same. That's why the girls aren't here."

Uestem looked around again, nodded.

"I hear that you had some trouble with the first minister today."

Mitt had been bending over to wipe up a spill, but he straightened now, his eyes narrowing. "How did you hear about that? There was no one here but me and the g—" He stopped, gave a small bitter laugh, and shook his head. "They're with the movement, too."

"One of them, yes." The merchant raised a hand, as if anticipating Mitt's next question. "I'm not going to tell you which, so don't even ask."

"Can you at least tell me if you turned her before or after she started working for me?"

The smile again. "The First Minister?"

Mitt didn't often back down from a fight. He wasn't particularly strong, nor did he wield the most potent of Qirsi magics, but he could hold his own against most men. Uestem, however, was one of the Weaver's chancellors, which not only meant that he had tremendous influence within the movement, but also that he was a fairly powerful sorcerer. He wasn't a man to be crossed, and both of them knew it.

The barkeep shrugged. "He's been in here a lot recently, drinking several ales at a time. Thorald golden, not the Galdasten swill. I told him today that I thought he should drink less, and be a bit more frugal in his choice of ales, lest someone take notice of all the gold he's spending in my tavern. He didn't like me telling him what to do, but I expect he'll be more careful the next time he's here."

"You did the right thing."

"Thank you."

"But you made him angry, more than you know."

Something in the man's voice . . . It suddenly seemed that the air in his tavern had grown cold. Uestem hadn't moved, but Mitt had to resist an impulse to back away from him. "But surely the Weaver will understand—"

"The Weaver is the least of your troubles, Mitt. Pillad went to the duke and accused you of treason. Even as we speak, Renald's men are gathering in the castle ward, preparing to come here and arrest you."

"I don't believe you. Pillad would have spoken to his duke hours ago. Why would Renald wait until now?"

"I don't really know. Perhaps he feared sending his men into a tavern full of white-hairs, not knowing which of them he could trust and which were with the conspiracy."

Actually it made a great deal of sense. Gods, it was freezing in here. "Doesn't Pillad realize that I'll do to him exactly what he's done to me? If I'm to hang as a traitor, he will as well."

"I'm not certain that Pillad thought this through very carefully, Mitt. He was angry, and he needed to prove his loyalty to the duke. Knowing Pillad as you do, are you surprised that he couldn't see beyond his wounded pride and his fear of Renald?"

The barkeep's stomach heaved. "You won't let them hurt me, will you, Uestem? I've served the Weaver well. I've done everything you've asked of me."

"Yes you have, Mitt."

"Take me onto your ship! I can serve as one of your crew. They'll never think to look for me there."

Uestem gave a sad shake of his head. "I'm afraid that would be too great of a risk. You may be right: they might never look there. But if they did, and if they found you, it would endanger far more than one life. It might destroy the movement. I don't mean to boast, but I'm quite important to the Weaver and his cause. You understand."

Mitt nodded, tried to swallow but couldn't.

"But neither can we allow you to be taken by Renald's men. I don't wish to see you tortured, Mitt."

A different kind of fear gripped his heart. "I wouldn't say anything about you, Uestem. When I said that I'd do that to Pillad, I meant just him. Not you. Certainly not the Weaver."

"I know that. But torture does strange things to people. And to be honest with you, Pillad is valuable to us. He wasn't before, but he's made himself important again." Once more, Uestem smiled, and at the same time he reached out and grabbed the barkeep's hair with a powerful hand. An instant later, his other hand was at Mitt's throat. "I'm sorry. Truly I am."

"Uestem, no!" he sobbed.

"This will be quick. I swear it."

He didn't even have time to struggle. His eyes closed, his heart hammering in his chest, he felt nothing, and heard only the snapping of bone.

Chapter Fourteen

Dantrielle, Aneira

"Behind you, my lord!"

Tebeo spun, his sword arcing downward, intending to cleave his second attacker in half from shoulder to gut. The soldier danced away, avoiding his blade, and the duke allowed his momentum to carry him all the way around so that he faced the other soldier once more.

Let them think on that! he thought with some satisfaction. *I may look like a fat old man, but I've some fight left in me still.*

As if intent on proving him wrong, the man in front of him lunged forward, sword held high, his dagger hand leveling a killing blow at Tebeo's side. The duke wrenched himself down and away from both blades, stumbled and fell heavily on his side. Fortunately, one of Dantrielle's men was there to meet the assault and drive back the Solkaran soldier. It was the second time in the last few moments that Tebeo had needed aid from one of his soldiers just to stay alive.

A small group of Solkarans had caught them unawares, apparently entering the castle through a sally port that had been left unguarded. Bausef DarLesta, his master of arms, had taken several men to secure the entry, leaving Tebeo and perhaps two dozen soldiers to deal with the intruders. It was more than enough men—they outnumbered the Solkarans by nearly two to one—but Tebeo's mistakes had forced the other men of Dantrielle to fight not only for their own lives, but for his as well. He should have found a way to retreat, to allow his soldiers to take care of the enemy and be done with it. But pride held him there.

There had been a time when Tebeo was thought to be one of the finest swordsmen in the realm. Back in the days when Tomaz the Ninth still ruled in Solkara, and Aneiran soldiers raised their steel against one another only in contests of skill, Tebeo had fought in his fair share of battle tournaments. Most considered Vidor of Tounstrel the land's best—certainly he won the lion's share of the competitions, though Tebeo had long thought that Bertin, the old duke of Noltierre, was Vidor's equal—but when the betting began, there were always a few who chose to risk their hard-earned gold on Tebeo, and on more than a few occasions their faith in him had been rewarded.

Those days seemed centuries gone. The duke felt old, sluggish, like a plow horse that's been worked too hard. He could still see the battle in all its intricacies, but too many years and too many castle feasts had taken their toll. He recognized feints, but he couldn't adjust swiftly enough to guard himself against the true attack. He saw openings, weaknesses in the defenses of his opponent, but he couldn't strike quickly enough to exploit them. In a sense, even the strengths that had come to him with advanced age worked against him. He remembered the excitement of old battle tournaments, the surge of strength and alacrity that used to come with it. And he saw much the same thing in the young soldiers he commanded. Warriors had a name for it: battle fury. But Tebeo was too wise to succumb to such emotions, even knowing that they might fuel his fighting and counterbalance some of what he had lost to age. This war was destroying them, weakening the realm when it most needed to be strong, giving aid to Qirsi enemies who needed none.

The second Solkaran soldier advanced on the duke again, his sword and short blade raised. Tebeo scrambled to his feet and readied his steel, his eyes darting to the left and right. All of his men who were close enough to come to his rescue were engaged in combat. He'd have no help with this fight.

The Solkaran, a large, yellow-haired man with small dark eyes and a drooping mustache, gave a harsh grin, seeming to sense this as well. He closed the distance between them with one great stride and leveled a blow at Tebeo's head. Looking for any advantage, Tebeo tried a trick Bertin had once used against him. Just as the man committed to his attack, Tebeo switched his sword to his left hand, turning his stance just enough to throw off the timing of the Solkaran's assault. The big man's sword whistled harmlessly past Tebeo's head. And as it did Tebeo hacked at the man's shoulder with his own blade. The soldier's mail shirt absorbed most of the blow and kept Tebeo's sword from drawing blood, but the Solkaran was staggered and when he faced the duke again, his grin was gone.

He wasted no time beginning his next assault, though he advanced more cautiously this time, and aimed his strike at the center of Tebeo's chest, giving the duke no opportunity to turn a second time. Instead, he was forced to block the man's blade with his own, the force of the blow numbing Tebeo's arm and shoulder. The Solkaran raised his sword to strike again, the grin returning when he saw Tebeo back away. The duke flexed the fingers on his sword hand, trying to get some feeling to return. He took another step back, but came up against the castle wall. Seeing this, perhaps sensing that the end was at hand, the Solkaran launched himself at the duke. Their swords met again and Tebeo's entire body seemed to shudder with the impact. Rather than stepping back to strike at him again, the Solkaran continued to press forward, crushing Tebeo against the stone, pinning the duke's sword beneath his own. Tebeo could feel the man's breath on his face, and even as he tried to free his own dagger, he sensed that the Solkaran was doing the same.

They struggled for several moments, silent save for the rasp of their breathing. And just as Tebeo managed to wrap his fingers around the hilt of his dagger, he saw the man's arm fly free, steel glinting in the sunlight like the wing of a dragonfly. Then the arm angled downward, a blur of steel and mail and flesh, and Tebeo felt a searing pain in his side. His body sagged, though he fought to stay on his feet. The soldier stepped back, raising his sword again, the other hand empty, save for a smear of blood on the crescent between his thumb and forefinger. Tebeo tried to raise his own blade to ward himself, but it was all he could do not to tumble onto his side. The flesh under his right arm was ablaze; he felt himself growing light-headed. He heard someone call out to him from what seemed a great distance, but he couldn't take his eyes off the man standing before him. The Solkaran, with his sword over his head, ready to smite the duke like some warrior god, and a blood stain on his hand that looked oddly like red Ilias early in the waxing.

Tebeo expected to die then. He wondered how the siege would end, whether Bausef and his men would give in to Numar of Solkara, or whether this civil war would continue, perhaps with Brall or one of the others taking up the cause. He thought of Pelgia and their children, and he nearly cried out with his grief at having failed them. All of this in the span of a single heartbeat, as the Solkaran began to bring down his sword for the killing blow.

But then another figure came into view, also a blur, though the duke recognized the colors of his own house, gold, red, and black. This second man crashed into the Solkaran, knocking him off balance, causing the sword to fly from his hand and clatter harmlessly against the wall beside Tebeo's head. The two soldiers fell to the ground and began to struggle. Almost instantly a third man joined them, and then a fourth, both of them wearing the colors of Dantrielle. Still another man rushed to Tebeo's side, crouching beside him, a stricken look on his youthful face.

"I'm all right," the duke muttered, though he knew he wasn't. "Don't kill him."

"My lord?"

"The Solkaran. I don't want him killed."

"But my lord . . ." The man shook his head and gestured at Tebeo's side, forcing the duke to look there. The Solkaran's blade jutted from between his ribs and his surcoat was stained crimson. He closed his eyes and clamped his teeth against a wave of nausea.

"I don't care. I want him alive. We learn nothing if he dies."

"Yes, my lord."

The man shouted something to the others.

Tebeo closed his eyes and leaned his head back against the

stone, and for some time he was aware only of voices shouting around him and the sun on his face.

"The healer's here, my lord."

Tebeo started awake, as if from a deep slumber, though when he opened his eyes he found that he was still in the castle ward, leaning against the castle wall. He glanced around slowly, and saw the Solkaran standing nearby, his arms pinned at his sides by a pair of Tebeo's soldiers. There was a cut over the man's eye, and another on his cheek, but otherwise he appeared unharmed.

"Drink this, my lord."

A Qirsi face loomed before him, pale and bony, yellow eyes like those of a wolf. The healer held out a cup containing a steaming, foul-smelling liquid.

"No," Tebeo said. "Where's Evanthya?"

"The first minister is on her way, my lord. But you must drink this. It will help you rest, and that will allow me to heal your wound."

"I don't know you."

The man frowned. "You should, my lord. I'm Qerban. I've served as a healer in Castle Dantrielle for more than six years."

Tebeo narrowed his eyes. Perhaps there was something familiar about him. "You're still Qirsi."

"Yes, my lord. And you're dying. You're losing far too much blood. If it's poison you're worrying about, you have no need. If I wanted you dead, I'd just let that dagger do its work and be done with it. Now please, my lord. Drink this, and let me help you."

Tebeo nodded, and reached for the cup. But before he could take it in hand, he felt his world pitch and roll, and closing his eyes once more, he fell back into darkness.

When next the duke awoke, he was in his bedchamber. Pelgia sat beside him, holding his hand in hers, worry written in the lines on her face. Her dark eyes were dry, but that was her way.

Evanthya was there as well, looking small and pale. The healer stood beside her, his expression unreadable.

"I take it I'm going to live," the duke said.

Qerban grinned. "It would seem so, my lord."

"Then I have you to thank."

"I'm a healer, my lord," the man said with a shrug. "It's what I do."

"I owe you an apology."

"You were hurt, my lord. You hardly knew what you were saying."

"I knew well enough." His eyes flicked to Evanthya, who had lowered her gaze. "I'm sorry, healer. And I thank you for my life."

"Of course, my lord. There's more of my brew on the table beside your bed. Drink it all, and rest. You should be able to leave your bed in the morning, but no more combat for a few days. I healed the wound, but your body needs time to recover the blood you lost."

Tebeo nodded, saying nothing. Healers were always prescribing more rest than was necessary.

The Qirsi smirked, as if he could read the duke's thoughts. After a moment he bowed and left the chamber.

Pelgia lifted the cup of brew from Tebeo's table and held it out to him. Seeing the face he made, she smiled archly. "You heard him, Tebeo. All of it. And if you argue, I'll have him prepare more."

Reluctantly, the duke took the cup from her and drank, nearly gagging on the stuff. He tried to hand it back to her, but Pelgia merely stared at him until he downed the rest of it. Glancing toward the open window, he saw that it was night. Ward fires still burned atop the castle walls, but he heard nothing unusual.

"What's the time?" he asked.

Evanthya looked up. "It's nearly time for the gate close, my lord."

"I was out that long?"

The first minister nodded.

"What of the Solkaran?"

"He's alive, held in your dungeon."

"I don't want him in the dungeon. Have him moved up into the prison tower."

"Are you certain, my lord? The master of arms insisted that it be the dungeon."

"Bausef put him there because of what the man did to me. To have done less would have been . . . inappropriate. But the man is Aneiran, just as we are. He was ordered by his sovereign to quell a rebellion, and that's what he was trying to do. Our quarrel is with Numar, not with the Solkaran people or their army, nor with the soldiers of any other house for that matter. He may be our prisoner, but he deserves to be treated with some courtesy. I'll question him myself in the morning. Please see to it, First Minister."

Evanthya bowed. "Yes, my lord."

When the minister had gone, Tebeo faced Pelgia again. "Sorry if I gave you a scare."

She gave a small smile, looking lovely in the candlelight. "By the time I'd heard anything, the healer was already quite certain that you'd live. But the children are a bit shaken."

"Well, bring them in. It might do them good to see me."

The duchess shook her head. "In the morning. The healer told you to rest. I intend to make certain that you do as you're told."

"Surely seeing the children—"

"Tomorrow," she said, more firmly this time.

Tebeo grinned. "Yes, my lady."

She patted his hand and stood. "Rest awhile. I'll have some food brought in shortly."

"Where are you going?"

"To tell the children that you're all right. I'll be back soon."

He watched her go, then lay back against his pillow, closing his eyes and savoring the remembered touch of her fingers. His side ached dully and he felt weak, but he had been fortunate this day. Had the Solkaran's dagger found something more vital, or had the man managed to plunge his blade into Tebeo's side a second time, the duke would surely be dead.

This is what becomes of fat old men who fancy themselves warriors. No more fighting for me. That's why Dantrielle has an army.

He felt an unexpected pang of regret at the thought that his days as a swordsman were over, but he knew that this was the right decision. Not only had he risked his own life this day; he had also endangered the men who had been forced to rush to his defense time after time.

After several moments he began to doze off, only to be tugged back awake by a knock at his door. Pelgia.

"Enter," he called sleepily, not even bothering to open his eyes.

He heard the door open and close, and the soft scrape of a boot on stone.

"My lord." A man's voice.

Tebeo opened his eyes and, seeing Bausef standing near the door, sat up too quickly. His head spun.

"Are you all right, my lord? Perhaps I should return later."

"No, armsmaster, I'm fine." He squeezed his eyes shut for a few seconds, then opened them again. The spinning of the chamber seemed to slow somewhat. "What do you want?"

"The first minister told me that you wanted the Solkaran moved to the tower. I wasn't certain that I believed her—I wanted to hear it from you before doing anything."

"You think she'd lie about such a thing?"

"I thought . . . perhaps your injury—"

"Out with it, Bausef. What's on your mind?"

"This man is a danger to you and this castle. He nearly killed you, and he deserves to be punished."

"He needs to be questioned, Bausef."

"I've already seen to that, my lord."

"You've already—" He stopped, comprehension hitting him like a fist. "You tortured him?"

"It was the only way—"

"No, Bausef, it wasn't! I intended to question this man in the morning. He wasn't to be tortured at all."

"That may have been your intention, my lord. But I assure you, if you were determined to get answers from the man, it would have come to torture eventually. Why does it matter, if it was tonight or in the morning?"

"Because I wanted to give him the chance to comply without resorting to pain." Tebeo gazed toward the window shaking his head. "The Solkarans aren't the enemy. Surely you understand that."

"Actually, my lord, I must disagree. Certainly they're not the only enemy; they may not even be the most dangerous. But so long as they lay siege to this castle, we must treat them as a threat to you and your dukedom."

"You think me too soft."

Bausef smiled. "I think you're a good man, and a fine leader," he said, seeming to choose his words with care. "Your lone weakness—if it can be called that—is your aversion to war. You so wish to find a path to peace, that you show your enemies too much kindness."

"You think I'm doing that now."

The armsmaster took a breath. "Yes, I do."

They fell into a lengthy, brooding silence, Bausef still standing near the door, his gaze lowered, the duke in bed, staring at the window once more.

"What did you learn from him?" Tebeo asked at last, feeling that the question signaled a surrender of sorts.

"A good deal, once he started to talk."

Tebeo indicated the chair by his bed with an open hand, and Bausef crossed to it and sat.

"He and his comrades didn't expect to survive their assault. It seems Numar learned of the sally port two days ago and thought to exploit it."

"But to what end? If the men weren't expected to survive, what was the point?"

"The soldier didn't know, but if I had to guess, I'd say the regent is looking for ways to break our spirit. As such attacks continue or even grow more frequent, fear will set in, the people of this city will begin to look for ways to end the siege. They may even turn against you and seek a reconciliation with the royal house."

"It seems a waste of men."

Another smile flitted across the armsmaster's face and was gone. Once more Tebeo found himself thinking that the man saw him as too weak to be an effective leader, at least in times of war. And the duke could only agree.

"Had you been laying siege to another castle, my lord, I would have counseled you to do much the same thing. Today's attack took a toll on the men, and it nearly claimed your life. It was a gamble to be sure, but one that was worth the loss of a few men."

Tebeo said nothing. *Worth the loss.* He could never bring himself to think in such terms. Was he doomed then to fail? Could a leader as softhearted as he ever prevail in a war?

There was another knock, and before Tebeo could call out an answer, the door opened, revealing Pelgia and a servant who carried a platter of food. Seeing Bausef, the duchess frowned, glaring first at the master of arms and then at Tebeo.

"You're supposed to be resting."

"And I am."

She glowered at him.

"We're still under siege, my lady. I can't just sleep the night away while Numar's men threaten my castle and city."

"Do I have to call the healer and have him prepare a sleep tonic?"

"I should be leaving, my lord," Bausef said, standing and bowing first to Tebeo and then to Pelgia.

"Thank you, armsmaster. I found our discussion . . . illuminating."

"Of course, my lord."

Bausef started to leave. But as he reached the threshold of the chamber, the entire castle suddenly quaked, as if some great beast had reached out from the Deceiver's realm to smite Dantrielle's walls with a mighty talon.

The armsmaster whirled to face the duke again. From outside Tebeo's window came shouts of warning and alarm.

"The gate?" Tebeo asked.

Before Bausef could answer, the castle shook a second time.

"I don't think so."

"Then what?"

A soldier appeared in the doorway, breathless and ashen.

"What's happened?" the armsmaster demanded.

"Hurling arms, Commander," the man said. "Two of them."

"But they hadn't any arms built this—" Tebeo stopped,

winced. Now it made sense. There had been more to Numar's wile than even Bausef had guessed. "It was a diversion, to give them time to build the machines and put them in place."

"So it would seem."

For a third time, the walls and floor shivered. More shouts echoed through the castle ward, mingled now with screams of terror and agony.

The duke swung himself out of bed, struggling briefly with another wave of dizziness.

"Tebeo—"

He raised a hand, silencing his wife. "This is no time for me to be resting, Pelgia, no matter what the healer says. My place is on the walls with my men."

She looked like she might argue, but instead she merely nodded, seeming to sense that she would never convince him otherwise.

Bausef and the soldier started down the corridor toward the nearest of the tower stairways. Tebeo followed, though he walked slowly. The pain in his side was much greater now that he was out of bed and moving. The armsmaster glanced back and slowed, but the duke waved him on.

"I'll be along, armsmaster. Go up to the ramparts. There's no sense in both of us going at my pace."

Bausef nodded once before sprinting on.

By the time Tebeo finally reached the top of the stairway, the castle had been hit twice more, and the cries from his men had begun to sound desperate. Stepping into the warm night air, Tebeo immediately saw why. Numar and his men were bombarding the castle with huge stones that had been covered with pitch and set aflame. Judging from the blackened ruins of the ramparts along the north wall, it seemed that their aim had been remarkably true. Several men lay on the stone walkway, some with their skin and clothes burned, others with mangled limbs.

Bausef strode to where Tebeo stood.

"Report."

"They're beyond the range of our archers, my lord. There

appear to be only the two machines, though right now those two are more than enough."

"How many have we lost."

"Eleven dead, my lord. Fourteen others hurt."

"Damn!"

"Look to the skies!" came a shouted warning.

Facing northward, Tebeo saw a bright ball of fire arc into the night, trailing a plume of black smoke. He thought at first that it would strike the top of the wall just beyond the next tower, but as the flaming stone reached its zenith and began to curve downward toward the castle, he realized with much relief that it would fall just short. Still, as it approached the wall, he reached out to brace himself against the stone. An instant later the fiery stone hit, sending a fountain of flame over the wall and making the fortress tremble.

Bausef stared grimly at the small fires burning themselves out on the face of the castle. "We were fortunate that time."

"Is there anything we can do to stop them?"

"Not without aid, my lord. We need Orvinti or Kett or Tounstrel. Anyone. With Rassor guarding Numar's flanks, we have no chance of reaching those siege machines. It would take so many men to fight our way through that we'd have to compromise the safety of the castle."

"What about the first minister? Might she be able to help us?"

"What magics does she possess?"

"I don't know all of them." A lie. But Tebeo knew that many Qirsi did not willingly reveal their powers to others, and he felt that as a courtesy to Evanthya he shouldn't tell the master of arms more than was necessary. "But I do know that she has mists and winds."

"That might be of some use—"

"Look to the skies!" from farther down the wall.

Yet another burning orb leaped into the sky, like some terrible weapon of the goddess of fire, thrown by Eilidh herself. Watching its path, anxiously, the duke quickly realized that this one would not fall short.

Bausef seemed to sense this as well. Before Tebeo could say anything, he shouted to his men, "Off the north wall!"

Without even waiting to see if they followed his command, the armsmaster began to usher the duke back toward the tower stairway. Tebeo followed, though he kept one eye on that arcing flame, marking its progress toward his castle.

Once safely inside the tower entrance, both men turned to watch. "Hold on," Bausef said, eyeing the bright flame and bracing himself against the stone. "This one's going to do some damage."

Indeed. It landed directly on top of the wall, shattering the merlons where it hit, shaking the castle to its foundations, and sending fiery fragments of stone in every direction. Several of the men who had fled only as far as the end of the battlement were struck by pieces. One man's surcoat was aflame. The stone itself, largely intact, remained in its own crater on the wall, still burning and effectively cutting one end of the battlement off from the other. Tebeo heard cheering in the distance. Numar's men.

"Demons and fire," Bausef muttered.

"This can't continue. Summon the first minister."

The master of arms nodded, still staring at the damage. "Yes, my lord. Right away."

Within just a few moments, Evanthya stood before him, her white hair hanging loose to her shoulders and dancing in the wind.

"The master of arms has explained to you?" Tebeo asked.

"Yes, my lord. But as I've told him, I'm not certain that I can be of much use to you."

"Why is that?"

"Pronjed, my lord. Numar's archminister. He has mists and winds as well, and will be able to counter anything I do. If I raise a mist to conceal our men, he'll conjure a wind to sweep it away. And if I call forth a wind to aid our archers or hinder theirs, he'll do just the opposite."

"And none of your other powers can help us?"

"I'm afraid not, my lord. Mine are not the magics of a warrior."

Tebeo actually smiled. It seemed they had this in common.

"I fear, my lord, that the first minister might actually do more harm than good."

"What do you mean?"

"If she raises a mist, and the archminister can indeed defeat it, then we've done nothing except draw Numar's attention to whatever it is we decide to do."

"Look to the skies!"

Another flaming boulder flew up from the north, followed almost instantly by a second. Their conversation stopped and all three of them watched the fires carve their way through the darkness and down toward the castle. Dantrielle's soldiers scrambled to get out of their path, shouting warnings to one another, struggling to carry the wounded from the last impact out of harm's way.

The first of the stones struck the top of the wall, much as the last one had, while the second fell just short, hitting the face of the wall just below the battlements. The entire fortress bucked and shuddered as if it were alive. Flames and shards of stone careened everywhere, clattering off the tower walls and making Evanthya and Tebeo flinch.

Again, the duke heard shouts and taunts from Numar's soldiers.

"We need a plan. Quickly, armsmaster. They're destroying the castle, and it won't be long before one of those missiles finds flesh rather than mere stone."

"As I said, my lord, fighting our way through to the hurling arms is out of the question. But it may be that a small complement of archers can go out through another of the sally ports and get close enough to strike at them."

"Yes, good."

Bausef seemed to hesitate. "I said it may be possible, my lord. I'm not certain that I think it a good idea. We'll be placing these men in great danger, and there's no guarantee that they'll be able to disable the hurling arms."

"Some of them could light their arrows," Evanthya said. "While some try for the soldiers operating the machines, others can try to burn the arms themselves."

"That might work." Still the master of arms did not appear convinced. "I know that it's difficult to watch them harm Castle Dantrielle, my lord. But over the course of its history, this fortress has withstood assaults far worse than this. We may be better off just weathering their attacks. This siege won't be won or lost tonight, and it may be that help is on the way."

"So you think we should do nothing?"

Bausef looked away, perhaps hearing a goad in the question, though Tebeo had intended none. "I'm just telling you that if you're worried about the lives of your men, it may be more of a risk to send them out of the castle than it is to keep them here, even knowing that these attacks will continue."

Tebeo turned to Evanthya. "First Minister?"

"I've nothing to add to what the armsmaster has said, my lord."

The duke stepped out of the tower and gazed northward. The Solkarans were singing now, and he could see two clusters of torchlight, no doubt men working to put the next boulders in the palms of the hurling arms.

As much as he disliked the thought of placing his men in peril, he could not help feeling that there were other costs to this night's assault aside from the injuries and the damage to his castle. Numar's men sang and laughed with the confidence of a victorious army, while his men looked defeated and exhausted. He needed to do something.

"Choose your finest archers, armsmaster, as many as you think appropriate, and send them out. Tell them to loose three rounds of arrows, no more. Even if they do no damage to the machines, they're to return here after that."

"Yes, my lord." Nothing in his voice. Nothing at all.

Tebeo's side ached, a reminder of his shortcomings as a commander.

Whether or not Bausef approved of Tebeo's orders, he moved swiftly to carry them out. The archers left the castle within the hour, using a sally port on the west side of the castle, where the waters of the Black Sand River would mask any noise they made approaching the Solkarans' position.

Bausef had gone with them, leaving Tebeo and Evanthya to watch from the battlements as the battle unfolded. Several more of Numar's flaming missiles had struck the castle, two of them reaching the top of the wall and one of them soaring over the wall to land in the ward below. As of yet, no more of his men had been killed, and as Tebeo inspected the damage, he saw that the master of arms was right. The black scars the assault left on his fortress might have been ugly, but they weren't deep. It was too late to call the men back. Tebeo felt his stomach tightening.

He could do nothing but stare out into the darkness, straining his eyes to catch a glimpse of his soldiers and mark their advance on Numar's men.

"Do you see anything, First Minister?" he asked, for perhaps fifth time.

She shook her head. Then, as if an afterthought, "No, my lord."

They lapsed into silence again. The Solkarans were still singing. *Good,* he thought. *Let them have their songs. It'll be that much easier to catch them unawares.*

Still they waited. Only now did Tebeo think to look up at the moons, to wonder how their light might affect Bausef's plan. It was late in the waxing. Both moons were high overhead, white as bone, red as blood. But a thin haze of cloud now covered the sky, muting their glow somewhat and keeping them from casting much light on the ground. Perhaps the gods were with them.

"There!" the first minister called out, thrusting out an arm to point.

He saw it as well. Several small flames had appeared in the wood; they resembled candles from this distance. Almost immediately they angled skyward, flying toward the hurling arms. The singing stopped abruptly, to be replaced by cries of alarm and then screams of pain. The Solkarans lit more torches and began to converge on Tebeo's archers. A second flurry of arrows flew, and now the duke could see flames on the hurling arms. *Never mind the third volley!* he wanted to shout. *Get away from there!*

But Bausef was a soldier, and soldiers followed orders. The torches advanced, a third round of flaming darts lifted into the night and fell toward the siege machines.

And then the fighting began.

He could hear the ring of steel on steel, the war cries and death shrieks. He even thought he could hear Bausef shouting commands to his men. But he couldn't tear his eyes away from the line of torches flowing like a bright river toward the fighting.

"It'll be a slaughter," Evanthya whispered.

The duke wanted to say something brave, he wanted to reassure her that Bausef would find a way free, that he would rally his men and lead them back to the castle. But there were so many torches, and already the sounds of the battle were starting to fade. The master of arms had spoken of taking only a few men. It wouldn't be much for Numar's army to kill them all.

The hurling arms were ablaze, but already dark shadows were appearing around them to douse the flames.

"Have men posted at all the sally ports," he said, his voice barely carrying over the soft whistle of the wind. "Tell them to watch for survivors, but to be alert for Solkaran attacks."

"Yes, my lord," Evanthya said, her voice like the scrape of steel on stone. She started to leave, then halted. "I would have done the same thing, my lord."

He nodded, still staring out at the torches. But he couldn't find any words to reply.

After a time, he left the battlements, descending the tower stairs to the ward. His men were cleaning away rubble from the tower entrances at the base of the walls. Seeing him, they paused, grim-faced and silent. He sensed no hostility on their part, no reproof. Only a desire to follow his command, to draw strength from his courage. He feared that he had nothing to offer them.

He heard a dull thud as something struck the grass nearby. At the same time, he realized that Numar's men had resumed their singing.

Two of his men walked to where the object had landed and bent to look at it, lowering their torches. Then, both of them jumped back, one of the men crying out like a frightened child. Tebeo hurried to where they stood, hearing another object hit the grass as he did. But already he knew what he would find. He had heard of attacking armies doing such things—in past sieges, it had proved quite effective in breaking the spirit of defending soldiers. Still, he had hoped that Numar was incapable of such cruelty, such ruthlessness. But the man was a Solkaran, and Tebeo should have known better. The duke's stomach heaved and he willed himself not to be sick, even as he tasted bile.

"My lord," one of the soldiers sobbed. "It's . . . I know him."

Tebeo knelt in the grass and stared down at the severed head of one of his men. He, too, recognized the soldier, though he had never learned the man's name. Yet another head hit the grass behind him, and a moment later two more. There had been sixteen archers in all, and, of course, Bausef as well. And so eventually there would be seventeen of them in the courtyard of his castle, grisly reminders of the armsmaster's warning. *It may be more of a risk to send them out of the castle than it is to keep them here.* The words echoed in the duke's mind, like bells calling mourners to funeral rites.

"Clean them up," he said quietly, knowing he ought to say more, but having no words that could possibly have any meaning in the face of this.

He returned to the ramparts, looking out toward the Solkaran army once more. There was a great fire burning near the siege engines—perhaps a pyre for his men. A moment later he saw that something loomed in front of the flames, and he knew that he had been wrong a moment before. There would only be sixteen thrown back into his castle. The seventeenth head, no doubt that of his master of arms, had been impaled upon a pike and raised above the Solkaran camp. A monument to Tebeo's folly.

Chapter Fifteen

Curtell, Braedon, Elined's Moon waning

It had been more than half a turn since Kayiv's death, since Nitara had killed him. In the days since, those who lived in the palace of Emperor Harel the Fourth had spoken of little else. Whispered conjecture about their love affair and Kayiv's ties to the shadowy Qirsi conspiracy drifted among the corridors and bedchambers of the great palace like smoke from a distant fire. And just as the smell of a fire will linger long after the last flame is extinguished, the subtle scent of fear that accompanied these whispers clung to every bed linen, every tapestry, every shred of clothing until the palace reeked of it.

Yet in all this time, and in all these conversations, no one had attempted to cast any doubt on her story. He tried to force himself on me, she had said that day. He loved me still and couldn't bear the thought that I no longer loved him. For how could I love any man who had betrayed the realm? Knife wounds on her shoulder and breast and hand, a bloodied lip, her clothes torn and stained with the minister's blood, she had looked every bit the victim of frustrated passion and rage. None of them thought to question her. Certainly it never occurred to any of them that she would wound herself, that she would draw Kayiv to her with the promise of a kiss, only to drive a hidden dagger into his chest.

Yet she had done all of that and more. Such was the power of her love for the Weaver. And though she knew that they couldn't be together yet, that Dusaan's heart and brilliant mind were intent on his plans for the coming war, she knew as well that someday she would be his queen. He had all but said it in the days following the minister's death. She had only to wait. She had killed for him, and she would be rewarded.

Were it not for her memory of Kayiv's last words to her, murmured as his life's blood flowed over her clothes and his breath against her face slackened, she would have been content merely to wait for their victory.

"I loved you so."

She could hear the words in the keening of the winds that blew down from the Crying Hills, as they always did during the growing turns. She could hear them in the distant rumble of thunder from yet another storm and in the steady rhythm of the rain on the palace roof. They haunted her dreams and seemed to wake her in the morning, like the whispered greeting of a lover.

"I loved you so."

Nitara still wasn't certain why Kayiv had risked so much in the days before his death. Surely he must have known that Dusaan would punish him for his betrayal. She could only guess that perhaps he had thought to win back her love by destroying the high chancellor. If so, he had misjudged her and the depth of her feelings for the Weaver. Without having shared her bed, Dusaan already was more to her than Kayiv had ever been. He was her hope, her dream, her promise of a day when Qirsi would rule the Forelands. No matter what Kayiv might have been to her—no matter what he had desired to be to her again—he could never be all that.

And yet, this very morning she had awakened to the minister's voice again, and without thinking had answered, "I love another now," as if he were still alive, as if she could wound him with the words. "I love the high chancellor."

She nearly laughed at her own foolishness, though her hands trembled as she dressed and her stomach felt too sour to eat any breakfast. Making her way to the high chancellor's chamber for the daily discussion among all of Harel's Qirsi advisors she walked swiftly, as if pursued by Kayiv's wraith. Seeing the Weaver would make her feel better. It always did.

"I loved you so."

She nearly ran the rest of the way, listening to the slap of her feet on the stone floor—anything to drown out the minister's voice. Breathing a sigh of relief when she finally reached Dusaan's ministerial chambers, she took her usual place near the high chancellor and waited for the discussion to begin. Yet, even after Dusaan started speaking, she thought she could hear Kayiv, his voice as soft as a planting breeze.

Nitara tried to occupy her mind with thoughts of Dusaan, of what it would be like to have him love her, to feel him inside her, aflame with desire, wild and rampant. But when she closed her eyes briefly, trying to hold in her thoughts the image of the Weaver above her, moving with her in a cresting rhythm, she found not Dusaan's face, but Kayiv's, the familiar gentle smile on his lips.

She opened her eyes abruptly, shaking herself, as a cat

emerges from a dream. The high chancellor eyed her for just an instant, a frown on his lean, square face. She made herself watch him, drinking him in as she would a dazzling sunrise: his broad shoulders and powerful chest, his glorious mane of white hair, his high cheekbones and gleaming golden eyes. If the gods themselves had ordained that a Qirsi should rule the Forelands—and who was to say that they hadn't?—they would have chosen a man who looked thus to be the first sorcerer king.

She realized that he was glowering at her, and too late she remembered him cautioning her against gazing at him too intently during these audiences.

"Anything you do to draw attention to your feelings for me," he had said, shortly after Kayiv died, "endangers all of our lives, endangers the movement itself."

Nitara looked away, forcing herself to train her mind on what was being said.

"You have no idea why he's summoned you?" Stavel was asking, looking frail and fearful, like an old dog.

Dusaan shook his head. "None. But he hasn't wanted to speak with me in quite some time, so I'll take the mere fact of his summons as a sign that perhaps matters are improving."

"Improving for whom?"

The high chancellor stared at Gorlan, his eyes narrowed. When Kayiv tried to turn the other ministers to his purposes, hoping that they would go together to the emperor and reveal Dusaan's lies, Gorlan had been the most eager. It seemed the minister didn't fear the high chancellor as much as the others did. In fact, in his own way Gorlan was impressive as well. Like Dusaan, he was tall and broad, particularly for a Qirsi. His eyes were the color of old parchment, and he wore his white hair short. Nitara didn't know what powers the minister possessed, but she had no doubt that he wielded at least three, and that one or more of them were among the deeper magics. He looked like a man who had tasted power and desired more.

"Did you have something you wanted to add to our discussion, Minister?" Dusaan asked, after eyeing Gorlan for some time.

Though he stood out among the other Qirsi in Harel's palace, it seemed that Gorlan knew better than to challenge the high chancellor directly. Nitara sensed that he would have liked to say a great many things. But confronted with Dusaan's icy glare, his resolve withered like leaves late in the harvest. Though everyone knew that she had killed Kayiv and appeared to believe that she had done so defending herself from his advances, all knew as well that Kayiv had been plotting against the high chancellor just prior to his death. Fear of Dusaan had never been so great.

"I merely wonder if the emperor intends to take us into his confidence again, High Chancellor." Gorlan lowered his gaze. "It may be that he has some other purpose in mind."

"I suppose that's possible. We'll know soon enough." Dusaan hesitated, glancing at Nitara again. "Still, Minister, you raise an interesting point. It seems that recent events have given the emperor cause to doubt our loyalty, though in truth I can't see why one man's attempted assault on a fellow minister should do so. I won't lie to you: I find myself offended by the emperor's lack of confidence. I've served in his court for nine years, and I feel that I've earned his trust."

"But the conspiracy," Stavel said. "Surely you understand his fear. Nitara told us that Kayiv tried to turn her. And he tried to convince me, as well as some of the others, that you were a traitor to the empire."

Dusaan smiled as if in sympathy. "I understand that the emperor is afraid, that many of us are. But what does it say about him—indeed, about all the Eandi—that their faith in us should be so easily shaken?"

"Is that a question you intend to ask Harel?" Gorlan's face colored, as if he hadn't intended to give voice to the thought.

But the high chancellor just grinned. "An interesting suggestion, Minister. Perhaps I will. My point is this, however. Loyalty and treachery are always spoken of with regard to the Qirsi. We hear of Qirsi traitors, or of ministers who remain loyal to the courts. But isn't it also incumbent upon the Eandi to keep their faith with us? Doesn't our service to the emperor entitle us to something? I know that I would never betray any of you, nor do I believe any of you would knowingly betray me. We share that, perhaps because of the color of our eyes and hair, the fact that all of us know what it is to wield magic."

"So you're saying that the emperor owes fealty to us, just as we do to him?"

"In essence, yes."

Gorlan raised an eyebrow. "An interesting notion, High Chancellor. Do you truly believe that the emperor would agree? Do you think he'd even approve?"

"I don't think he would agree. As to whether he would approve, I can't say that I care. I have little fear that he'll ever know I feel this way."

There was a brief, uncomfortable silence, as the other ministers and chancellors glanced furtively at one another.

"Yes," Dusaan said. "There's another measure of loyalty as well, isn't there? How do we keep faith with each other? Would the emperor approve of all that's said here? Of course not. But I believe that in times like these, we must be able to speak among ourselves with absolute candor, without worrying that one of us might run to the emperor like a tattling child to a parent. I would never reveal any of what you say to me in these discussions without your permission, and I expect the same courtesy."

The words were velvet, but none of them could miss the steel lurking beneath. Yet the high chancellor wasn't done.

"I don't know how far the emperor's distrust will take him. It may be that he hopes to begin our reconciliation today, or he may wish to inform me of his decision to banish all of us from his palace. I honestly don't know. But you have my word that no matter his intentions, I won't break faith with you. If we're to leave Curtell, we'll do so as one, and if we remain, we will all be stronger for having endured this ordeal together."

"Do you really think it will come to that?" Stavel asked.

"I don't know, Chancellor. I hope that it doesn't, but I won't try to mislead you with false assurances."

The old Qirsi nodded, clearly unsettled by the entire conversation.

"And now if you'll all excuse me, I'd like some time to prepare for my audience with the emperor. We'll speak again, tomorrow."

The other Qirsi rose from their seats and began to make their way toward the door, Stavel and many of the older chancellors looking as if they would have liked to ask more questions of Dusaan.

"Minister," the high chancellor called to Gorlan. "I'd like you to remain here for a moment." Then he turned to Nitara. "You as well, Minister."

"Of course, High Chancellor."

Once the rest had gone, Dusaan indicated the two chairs nearest his own with an open hand.

"Please sit."

"I'm sorry if I angered you, High Chancellor," Gorlan said, as if finally realizing just who it was he had thought to challenge a few moments before.

"Think nothing of it, Minister. I didn't ask you to remain in order to wring an apology from you."

"Then why?"

"Tell me what you think of the emperor."

Gorlan's brow creased with puzzlement. After a moment he shrugged. "I think him a fine leader. I'm honored to serve in his court, just as all of us are."

Dusaan gave a small grin. "I see. And you, Nitara?" he asked, facing her.

She sensed what he wanted, and so answered accordingly. "I think him a fat fool who knows as little about statecraft as he does about the Qirsi. I serve him because he is, by dint of his birth, the most powerful and wealthy of Braedon's Eandi. But I have little respect for him or his court."

Gorlan just stared at her, as if unsure that he had heard her correctly.

"Our young friend here knows that she can speak her mind, that I betray no trust."

"So you want to hear the same from me," Gorlan said.

"I want to hear the truth from you."

"All right. I find the emperor a difficult man to serve. His limitations are apparent enough to those who know him, and in the past turn he's compounded these by treating his Qirsi with contempt."

"Yet you were appalled when Kayiv told you that I had lied to the emperor about our counsel regarding the timing of the invasion."

Gorlan looked at Nitara. "So much for trust."

"There were several of you in that discussion, Minister. Any one of your companions could have told me that much."

"Of course," Gorlan said, though clearly he remained convinced that Nitara was the one who had.

"The point remains, however, that you were disturbed by the counsel I gave to Harel."

"Your counsel had nothing to do with it, High Minister, nor did the fact that you lied to the man. What bothered me was your misrepresentation of the rest of us. If you believed that the emperor needed to start the invasion earlier than originally planned, you should have just advised him to do so, without mentioning the rest of us. That you didn't do this tells me you were uncertain of the counsel you offered."

Nitara glanced at the Weaver, expecting that he would be crimson with rage. Instead he was smiling, albeit with a hard look in his brilliant eyes.

"You don't miss much, do you, Minister?"

"No, High Chancellor, I don't."

"What powers do you possess?"

Gorlan's eyes narrowed. "Gleaning, mists and winds, and shaping. Why do you ask?"

Because he doesn't wish you to know that he's a Weaver. As a Weaver, Dusaan could discern the magics of all Qirsi near him. Apparently whatever he hoped to accomplish with this meeting did not include revealing his true powers to the minister.

"Why do you think?" Before Gorlan could answer, Dusaan turned to Nitara again. "Why do you think I asked, Minister?"

She hesitated. "I'm not certain, High Chancellor."

"It's all right. I think you do know, and you can speak freely. I intend to."

She nodded, her hands abruptly trembling. "I think you asked because you want to know what powers Minister Gorlan might bring to the movement."

Gorlan looked from one of them to the other. "The movement?"

"Very good, Nitara."

"The movement," the minister said again, still trying to work it out. "You mean the conspiracy, don't you?"

"A crude term. Certainly it wouldn't have been my choice. Then again, it does sound somewhat menacing, which can be useful."

"You're both with the conspiracy. Kayiv was right."

"Kayiv is dead."

"And is that why?"

"Kayiv was a fool. His death was incidental. He failed to see beyond his dislike of me, to the greater meaning of the movement. He couldn't grasp all that it would mean to our people to overthrow the Eandi courts and rule the Forelands. I don't expect you to make the same mistake. I believe you have far greater vision than he ever did. I hope I'm not mistaken."

"Are you asking me to join? Are you telling me that if I don't, I'll end up dead as well?"

"Let's just concern ourselves with your first question. Yes, I'd like you to join. We're on the verge of victory. The invasion has begun, there's civil war in Aneira, the queen of Sanbira is riding north to Eibithar, and Kearney of Glyndwr rules a land divided against itself. All the major powers of the Forelands will soon be tearing each other apart. And when they're through, the Qirsi will rise up and destroy what's left of them."

Gorlan gave a small, breathless laugh. "You don't lack for confidence."

"No, I don't. When we've won, those Qirsi who fought with us will help to rule the seven realms. Those who remained tethered to their Eandi masters will be executed as traitors to their people. The choice I'm giving you is a gift, one that I may not be extending to all who serve in the palace. You have a chance not only to save your life, but also to share in the glories that await those of us who lead this struggle."

"Why me? Surely there are others who have been here longer, who are more deserving."

This time it was Dusaan's turn to laugh. "In this case, Minister, the length of one's service to the emperor is not necessarily proof of one's worthiness. Still, you ask a valid question. I've chosen you—and in the short time that remains, I may well choose a few others—because I see in you qualities that will be of use to the movement in its final days of preparation, and to our people, as we assume authority over the people of the Forelands. You're not afraid to speak your mind, and when you do, you often make a good deal of sense. Also, your powers are considerable."

Gorlan looked at Nitara, his pale eyes locking on hers. "Why did you join?"

Because I love this man. Because he is like a god living among mortals. "I saw in the movement a way to improve the lives of our people, to ensure that my children, and their children, would grow up knowing that they could find paths to greatness that didn't lead through Eandi courts, or leave them subject to the whims of foolish Eandi nobles."

"But you swore an oath to serve the emperor." Immediately Gorlan held up a hand, shaking his head. "Don't answer. I already know what you'll say."

"What?" Dusaan asked with interest.

"She'll tell me that we have a greater duty to our own people, and that there are many types of betrayal. Those who would put their service to the Eandi above such a movement are guilty of the worst kind of treachery."

The smile returned to the high chancellor's face. "I couldn't have said it better myself. The question is, do you truly believe that, or were you merely anticipating her response?"

"You'll think me a fool for answering this way, but I don't know."

"As I say, I admire your willingness to speak your mind." A smile flitted across the Weaver's face and was gone. "Even when you don't know your mind. You have two days to think on it. After that I'll expect a reply, and believe me when I tell you that I'll know if you're lying to me."

The color drained from Gorlan's face, but his expression didn't change. "You don't worry that I'll go to the emperor with this?"

"No. I think you understand what will happen if you do. Our victory is close, Gorlan. Very close. And if I have to give myself away a bit sooner than I anticipated by killing you, then so be it."

Gorlan looked at Nitara one last time, though she couldn't say for certain what he was thinking. After a moment he stood, nodding to the high chancellor.

"Two days, then," he said, and left.

A short time later, Dusaan made his way to the emperor's hall, leaving Nitara in the corridor looking love-struck and just a bit sad. It was fortunate that he had this audience with Harel; much as he disliked the man, it served as a ready excuse to rid himself of the minister. Dusaan still thought her quite attractive—he had every intention of making her one of his queens when the time came—but he found her need of him stifling. She had killed for him, taking her blade to a man she once had loved, no less. There were few among his most trusted servants who could have done what she had. And she would be rewarded accordingly. But he remained convinced that her desire for him was as dangerous as it was bothersome, and that if he allowed her to lure him to her bed too soon, it might destroy all for which he had been working.

A part of him had hoped that she might be drawn to Gorlan; in many ways the minister reminded Dusaan of Kayiv, and also of a younger incarnation of himself. It seemed that these hopes were in vain.

He couldn't say for certain what he thought Gorlan would decide to do. Faced with such a choice, most men, including those who opposed the movement in their hearts, would join with him and thus save their lives. But the Weaver sensed that this minister was different. In a way this made him that much more eager to have the man as an ally, but it also made what he had done today far more dangerous. If Gorlan concluded that he could not bring himself to join the Qirsi cause, he would go to the emperor. Dusaan was sure of it. There was no greater threat to a movement such as his than a man who didn't fear death.

Reaching the emperor's door, he knocked once and waited for one of the guards within to open the door and announce him to Harel. Instead, the door opened, and two guards joined him in the corridor.

They bowed to him, appearing somewhat uncertain of themselves.

"What is this?" he asked. "I was summoned by the emperor."

"Yes, High Chancellor, we know. But we—" The man stopped, frowning and glancing at his companion.

"By order of His Eminence, Harel the Fourth, Emperor of Braedon, Holder of the Imperial Scepter, Bearer of the Crown of Curtell, we must ask you to remove any arms you may be carrying before entering the imperial hall."

He nearly laughed aloud. As if he needed a dagger to kill the man. He took his blade from its sheath and handed it hilt-first to the guard.

The guard swallowed. "We must also ask that you wear this." He held up a white muslin hood.

Dusaan felt rage surge through him, so suddenly and with such force that it was all he could do not to shatter the man's skull with a thought.

"What possible reason could the emperor have for asking this of me?" he demanded through gritted teeth.

"He knows that you have many powers, High Chancellor. He believes that you'll be less capable of using them against him if you can't see him."

He would have liked to reveal himself then and there. Damned be his plans and his patience. He could kill them all in a matter of moments. With the help of just a few of the other Qirsi, he could control the entire palace within the hour. But he needed more time. Not much, but enough that he could not allow himself the luxury of venting his fury, at least not yet.

"I don't get to see him—" He stopped himself, with a smirk and a shake of his head. "I don't get to speak with him unless I wear this?"

"I'm afraid not, High Chancellor."

"Very well."

As they covered his head, tying the hood loosely at his throat, Dusaan vowed that he would avenge this humiliation, that whatever suffering he had originally intended for Harel would be trebled and more.

When the hood was in place, the two guards led him through the doors and into Harel's hall. A Weaver had powers of perception that went far beyond sight and hearing, though Harel wouldn't have known this, any more than he knew that Dusaan was a Weaver. It was the Eandis' ignorance of Qirsi magic as much as anything that would bring their downfall. Even blind, Dusaan could sense the emperor and the other guards. There were eight of them in all. Two of Harel's wives were there as well, eyeing the high chancellor with curiosity and, he thought, just a touch of amusement.

Laugh all you like, Eandi whores. In the end you'll suffer as well. All of you will.

The guards led him to Harel's throne, one on either side of him, as if he were a prisoner rather than high chancellor. Once there, the two men stepped back to the doorway, leaving Dusaan to kneel before the emperor.

"You may rise, High Chancellor," Harel said, pushing himself from his throne and beginning to circle the chamber.

He hopes to make himself a more challenging target, Dusaan thought with some amusement. As if it would have mattered.

The Weaver stood, facing the throne, though he marked the emperor's path with his mind. After a moment's silence, he gestured at the hood. "You do me a disservice, Your Eminence."

"Forgive me, High Chancellor," Harel said, sounding anything but contrite. "But I feel safer knowing that you can't see me. In light of recent events, you can't blame me for taking certain precautions."

"Have I given you cause to fear me?"

"The death of my minister—what was his name again?"

"Kayiv, Your Eminence."

"Yes. Kayiv's death has given all of us cause to fear. It's one thing for a man to attack a woman as he did. But my guards tell me that she claimed he was a traitor. They say he tried to turn her against me."

It had been Dusaan's idea for Nitara to say these things. He had thought to deflect questions about the circumstances of

Kayiv's death by making a traitor of the man. He had also wanted to raise just the sort of fears Harel was expressing now, believing that the emperor, by his behavior, might drive a few more of the palace Qirsi to Dusaan's cause. He still thought that this might work, but at the very moment he couldn't help but wonder if he had pushed Harel too far.

"I heard that as well, Your Eminence. But to assume that every Qirsi in your palace is a traitor—"

"Is only prudent." Harel halted near one of the windows. "Any one of you might be a part of this conspiracy so I have no choice but to assume that all of you are. If this displeases you, Dusaan, I'd suggest that you learn as quickly as possible who the traitors are and bring them to me." He resumed his pacing. "If I were you, I'd begin with that woman he attacked. She was quick to accuse him once he was dead, but I find it hard to believe that a bed was all they shared."

It was surprisingly clever of the man, trying to pit Qirsi against Qirsi in this matter. "Of course, Your Eminence. I've been searching for other traitors since the day of Kayiv's death, beginning of course with the woman. But I've found no evidence that any of the others have betrayed you."

"Then I'd suggest that you look harder."

"You ask this of me, Your Eminence, and yet you treat me as if I had betrayed you. Does this mean that you have others looking for evidence that I'm with the conspiracy?"

For some time the emperor said nothing, although the Weaver sensed that he had stopped walking again. "I have to check on everyone, Dusaan. Surely you understand that."

Of course I do, you fat fool. But who have you asked to find evidence of my betrayal? If it was merely the palace guards, Dusaan didn't care. They would find nothing, and they would soon be dead or in the palace dungeon. But what if he had found a minister or chancellor to do his spying? What if he had already managed to divide the palace Qirsi?

"Of course I understand, Your Eminence. But I also know that the precautions you've taken today—disarming me, hooding me—are a humiliation. I've served you well for nine years. Don't I deserve better than this?"

"Perhaps. But I expect that today's experience will convince you of how seriously I take this matter, and maybe it will encourage you to find the traitors more quickly."

The high chancellor had to smile. Again, the man had surprised him with his cunning. Could there be more to the emperor than he had realized?

"Is this why you called me here today, Your Eminence? To impress upon me how eager you are to find the renegades?"

"In part, yes. I also wish to ask you about the fee accountings."

For the first time, Dusaan knew a moment of fear. Harel had long entrusted him with the fee accountings for all the realm, and Dusaan had used Braedon's treasury to pay those he turned to his cause. A friend of his, a Qirsi merchant named Tihod jal Brossa, had created a network of couriers who delivered the gold to those who had earned payment through their efforts on behalf of the movement. Without access to Harel's coffers, he would never have gotten this close to the realization of his ambitions. At this point, with success so near, his need for the emperor's gold was not as great as once it had been, but nevertheless, he was loath to lose access to the accountings. And the mere thought of it raised a deeper fear, one that he had managed to keep from his mind so far this day.

"What about them, Your Eminence?" His voice remained even, though he felt sweat running down his temples.

"I've been thinking that perhaps it would be best to let Uriad have control of them until the war is over. Most of the gold we pay out right now goes to the fleet and army anyway, and it seems to make sense that the master of arms should oversee the accountings. That way he can send gold where it's needed without having to bother you."

Dusaan should have expected it. On some level he had. None of what he had done with Harel's gold could ever be traced; he had made certain of that from the very beginning. But once more his rage threatened to overwhelm him. That he should have to debase himself before this man was bad enough. That Dusaan's movement should suffer for Harel's fear and mistrust, however justified they might be, was nearly intolerable.

"As you wish, of course, Your Eminence. But let's not weave mists with our words. You wish to give Uriad control of the fee accountings because you no longer trust me with them. Isn't that so?"

He sensed the emperor's discomfort and knew that he was right.

"Until I know for certain that you can be trusted, wouldn't I be a fool to allow you such open access to my treasury?"

"I see your point, Your Eminence."

"Good. When all this unpleasantness is over, I'm certain that everything will go back to the way it was before."

"I hope you're right, Your Eminence."

"You disagree?"

He regretted his choice of words. No doubt it would have been safer to let the conversation end with the emperor's false hope. But he had spoken and now had little choice but to respond.

"I think that when you make clear your mistrust, you risk driving away those who have served you loyally. I won't lie to you, Your Eminence. There are many among your ministers and chancellors who are offended by the treatment they've received over the past turn."

"And are you as well?"

Dusaan could hear indignation in the emperor's voice, and he knew that he had angered him. Not that he cared anymore. If Harel was intent on taking the fee accountings from him, there was nothing more to be gained by flattering the man or humbling himself. He wasn't about to give the emperor grounds to banish him from the court, but he saw no need to continue offering obeisance at every turn.

"Yes, Your Eminence, I suppose I am."

"Well, that's too bad! I would have thought that you would understand, High Chancellor! You of all people know what kind of man I am! I would never do these things unless I believed the danger was real. And if you can't understand that, then perhaps I don't know you as I thought I did." Dusaan heard the scrape of a shoe on stone, and he could almost see Harel turning his back to the high chancellor in pique. "You can go, High Chancellor. Send word to me when you've found the traitors. Until then, I don't expect to hear from you."

"Yes, Your Eminence." He bowed, though he knew that Harel couldn't see. The guards could, and they would be all too quick to say something if he failed to show the proper respect.

Once more, two men took hold of his arms. They turned him and led him back into the corridor. Once there, they removed the hood from his head.

His face and neck sticky with sweat, Dusaan held out his hand. "My dagger."

"Yes, High Chancellor."

He heard the change in their voices. They had seen how Harel treated him, they had tied a hood over his head. There had been deference in their greeting when he reached the chamber a short time before. It was gone now. Damn the man to Bian's fires.

He sheathed his weapon, then turned smartly on his heel and walked away, saying nothing more to the soldiers.

Nitara was waiting for him in the corridor near his chambers. He sensed her there before she stepped from the shadows, diffident and alluring.

"Can I speak with you, High Chancellor?"

He nodded, though he would have preferred to be alone. She followed him into his chambers, stepping to his window as he closed the door.

"What is it you want? I've told you before, it's dangerous for us to be seen together too often."

"I wanted to make certain that I hadn't angered you today."

"When?"

"During our conversation with Gorlan. I wasn't sure what you wanted me to say, how honest you wanted me to be."

He forced a smile. He was growing increasingly impatient with her weakness, yet he knew that he needed her, particularly now that his source of gold was gone, at least temporarily. He couldn't afford to lose any of his servants just now. "You did just fine. I want him to join our cause and I believe he will, thanks in part to what you said. I'm . . . I'm pleased."

She lowered her gaze. "Thank you, Weaver," she whispered.

"Now, go. I have matters to which I must attend."

"Yes, of course." But still she made no movement toward the door.

"Is there something else?"

Clearly there was. He felt her confusion, the turmoil within her heart. He had no time for this.

"No, Weaver," she said at last. She made a vain attempt at a smile and crossed to the door, hesitating once more as she gripped the handle.

She had been this way since killing Kayiv. It almost seemed that she had still harbored some affection for the man after all. He found himself thinking of Cresenne, of how her seduction of Grinsa jal Arriet had turned to love, rendering her useless to his movement, and then leading her to betray the cause entirely. Brilliant and strong as she was, she had also been terribly young to bear the burdens he had placed upon her. Much like Nitara. Too late, he had come to understand that matters of the heart were more difficult for the younger ones. He would have to take care that this one didn't turn on him as well.

Matters of the heart. He walked to where she still stood, taking her hands in his and forcing her to meet his gaze.

"You've served me well these past several turns. You've done more in so short a time than many have done for me over the course of years. And I'm grateful."

He could feel her trembling as she whispered, "I could do so much more."

"Soon. We can't allow ourselves to be distracted now, when we're so close. But those things that would be distractions before victory will become rewards after. Do you understand?"

She managed a smile. "Yes, Weaver."

"Excellent." He kissed one of her hands, then the other, never taking his eyes off of hers. Her smile deepened and her cheeks shaded to scarlet. "Now go," he said again.

One might have thought that he had commanded her to remove her clothes, so eager was she to obey.

"Yes, Weaver," she said, pulling her hands free and hurrying from his chamber. Once in the corridor, she looked back at him one last time.

"We'll speak again shortly," he assured her, and closed his door.

He listened for the sound of her footsteps retreating down the hallway. Only when he was certain that she had gone did he pull out the fee accountings and begin to pore over them, making certain that there were no entries that would raise the suspicions of Harel's master of arms. It took him the rest of the day to examine all the volumes—there were fourteen in all, and he didn't close the last of them until well after the ringing of the twilight bells—but he was satisfied that they would reveal nothing of his movement to Uriad. A servant came to his door with supper, and the high chancellor ordered the boy to fetch the palace guards.

When the soldiers arrived, he had them remove the volumes from his chamber. They were of no use to him now; they were but reminders of Harel's continued power over him. He didn't want to have to look at them anymore.

"Take them to the master of arms," he commanded. "He's in charge of the fees from now on."

The two soldiers began to carry the volumes off, though they could only carry a few of them at one time. "We'll be back for the rest," one of the men said, straining under the weight of three volumes.

"Yes, fine. Bring two more men with you when you return. I don't want this taking all night."

"Yes, High Chancellor."

The soldiers returned a short time later with two more men, and together they removed what remained of the accountings. Dusaan stood near the window the entire time, staring out at the emerging stars and ignoring the guards. Long after they had gone, he remained there. His meal sat undisturbed on his writing table until some time later, when the servant returned and took it away.

Tihod needed to be informed that there would be no more gold, at least from this source. No doubt some gold remained in the merchant's network, converted from imperial qinde to common currency so that it couldn't be traced back to Dusaan, but not yet disbursed to the Weaver's various underlings. Dusaan needed to know how much was left.

But first he needed to know that Tihod was still alive. He hadn't spoken to his friend in nearly a turn, since the latter half of Amon's waning. At that time Tihod had been on the Wethy Crown, tracking Grinsa, the Weaver who threatened all that Dusaan hoped to accomplish with his movement. Tihod had spoken of killing the man, or at least making the attempt, and though Dusaan had tried to dissuade him, though he had warned the merchant of how dangerous it was for any ordinary Qirsi to pit his powers against those of a Weaver, he had little doubt that Tihod had made the attempt anyway.

As a merchant, and a successful one, Tihod was often a difficult man to find. He conducted business all along the shores of the Forelands, from the Bay of Zahid, in Uulrann, to Sanbira's southern coast and the Sea of Stars. There had been times in the past when Dusaan had reached for Tihod, intending to speak to the man through his dreams, only to discover that the merchant's ship wasn't where he had thought it would be. Since he couldn't cast his mind over all the realms of the Forelands in search of a single man without exhausting even his considerable powers, they often went half a turn or more without speaking.

And perhaps that was the case this time as well. It might have been that Tihod had been forced by business matters to cut short his pursuit of Grinsa, return to his ship, and set sail for another port.

But Dusaan didn't think so. Though he made himself search for the merchant once more, casting his mind eastward over the Strait of Wantrae and along the shores of Eibithar and Wethyrn and Sanbira, he knew that he would fail. If Tihod still lived, the Weaver would have found him by now. Dusaan didn't want to give up what little hope he still grasped, but reason demanded that he do so. Tihod was dead. Grinsa had killed him. That was the only explanation that made any sense.

First this other Weaver had saved Tavis of Curgh from the dungeons of Kentigern, allowing Eibithar to avert a civil war Dusaan had worked for years to ignite. Then Grinsa had taken Cresenne from him, making her fall in love, turning her against the movement. And now he had killed Tihod, Dusaan's most trusted friend, and the only man in the movement he could never replace.

He opened his eyes, breaking off his search for Tihod. "Enough," he said to the darkness in his chamber.

Time after time the gleaner had thwarted him, and Dusaan had allowed it to happen, fearing that he might reveal too much of himself. But the time had come to put an end to this foolishness. Enough, indeed.

Chapter Sixteen

The Moorlands, north of the City of Kings, Eibithar

After their misadventure in the Glyndwr Highlands, they had no more time to waste. Grinsa knew that. No doubt the empire's fleet had begun its assault on the Galdasten shores, and last he and Tavis had heard, the Aneirans were poised to strike at Kentigern. The gleaner felt certain that all of this was the Weaver's doing, that this war was merely a prelude to a far more critical and perilous conflict. He had confided to the Curgh boy several turns ago that he was the only one capable of defeating the leader of the Qirsi conspiracy, and he still believed this to be true. What he had neglected to say to Tavis, what he was loath to admit to himself, was that he didn't know for certain whether he could prevail in a contest of magic against this other Weaver. He knew only that his time was approaching. One way or another, he would learn soon enough. He needed to reach Galdasten as quickly as possible, to keep this burgeoning war from destroying the Forelands, and to convince the leaders of the Eandi armies that their true enemy had yet to show himself.

The wound to his head had healed. He and Tavis had spent only a few nights back in Glyndwr Castle, recovering from their harrowing encounter with the brigands, before riding forth again, intent on reaching the Moorlands. But even that had been too much time. They could no longer afford to stop in the City of Kings, as they had once intended. Still, it had taken nearly all Grinsa's strength of will to ride so near to Audun's Castle without stopping to see Cresenne and his daughter. It would have added only a few leagues to their journey—merely half a day's ride if they pushed their mounts. But he knew that once he reached the castle, once he kissed Cresenne and held Bryntelle in his arms, he would never find it within himself to leave them again. Bryntelle was four turns old now; from what Cresenne had told him it seemed that she was growing quickly, becoming more aware of her surroundings with each passing day. He hadn't spent much time around babies as a Revel gleaner and so knew far less about them than he should have. But he had no doubt that she had changed enormously in just the two turns since he had left her. She was his child, and every day she awoke to a world that didn't include her father. He begrudged every moment he spent away from her.

Tavis had been watching him throughout the day, as if gauging his mood. Grinsa sensed that the boy wanted to say something, but that he feared the gleaner's response. The two of them had been journeying together for nearly a year now, and in that time Grinsa had come to care deeply about the boy. In the beginning, when Tavis still acted the spoiled noble, Grinsa had glimpsed the promise of wisdom and strength that dwelled within the young lord, and had agreed to act as his protector as the two of them attempted to establish Tavis's innocence and learn what they could about the conspiracy. More recently, he had come to view Tavis as a friend.

But he knew that for the boy, their relationship remained more complicated, and in many ways more difficult. Tavis had been exiled from his home, reviled as a butcher throughout the land. Where once he had looked to his father and Hagan MarCullet for guidance, and to Hagan's son, Xaver, for friendship, he now looked to Grinsa for all. To Tavis, the gleaner had become not only his guardian, but also his mentor and his closest friend. And while he was usually willing to speak his mind to Grinsa, it sometimes took him some time to gather the courage to do so.

Grinsa sensed that Tavis was now doing just that, and he didn't push the boy. They rode in silence, as the sun burned a slow arc across a hazy blue sky, and a warm breeze made the tall grasses of the Moorlands bow and dance. Heat rose from Elined's earth, liquid and sinuous, distorting the horizon, creating the illusion of lakes and rivers where none existed. A hawk circled high overhead, crying plaintively, and wild dogs shadowed the two riders at a safe distance.

"We can still go back," Tavis said at last, his voice so low that the words were nearly lost amid the wind and the thudding of their mounts' hooves. He glanced back over his shoulder. "I can still see the castle walls from here. It wouldn't cost us more than a day."

"We can't spare a day," the gleaner said, hearing the weariness in his own voice.

"We'll ride at night, Grinsa. We'll make up the time."

He smiled, though his chest ached "Thank you, Tavis. I'm grateful for the offer. But I can't." The boy started to say more, but Grinsa shook his head. "I can't leave them again. Best to be done with all this so that when I return to them, it's for good."

Tavis nodded. "All right."

It almost seemed that he understood. Perhaps he did.

After a time, the boy said, "I still think we should ride into the night. Kearney and the others have at least eight days on us. I'd like to close the gap a bit."

"Kearney's men are on foot. We draw nearer to them every day that we ride."

"I know. Still . . ." He shrugged.

Tavis had seemed eager for this war since Helke and his confrontation with the assassin. He had told Grinsa some of what happened that stormy day, enough for the gleaner to understand that Cadel had been unarmed when Tavis killed him, and that the young lord felt that he had acquitted himself poorly, even in victory. Though Tavis had denied it, Grinsa believed that he hoped to find some measure of redemption in the coming war, as if heroism on this new battlefield would erase the stain of all that had happened to him since Kentigern. He couldn't say that he shared the boy's eagerness for war, but neither could he deny that he wished to waste as little time as possible on their journey northward.

"Very well," Grinsa said. "We'll continue on past sundown."

Tavis nodded his approval, and they rode on, both of them silent, the young noble seemingly absorbed in his thoughts, Grinsa trying desperately to think of anything other than Cresenne and Bryntelle.

Late in the day, they came to a small village nestled in a gentle crescent of Binthar's Wash. The village didn't amount to very much—a smithy, a wheelwright's shop, and a meager marketplace that, even on its busiest days, could not have accommodated the carts of more than a dozen peddlers. Within sight of the hamlet, there were several farms situated on either side of the wash, and the two riders decided that they would stop to see if they might purchase some food. The stores they had been given by the duke of Glyndwr several days before were running low, and Grinsa didn't want to slow their travels later in the journey in order to search for provisions. Most of the sellers, it seemed, had already packed up their wares for the day, but one man, a white-haired farmer who walked from one end of his cart to the other with a pronounced limp, sold them enough cheese, salted meat, and black bread to last them several days. His prices were somewhat high—Grinsa had the distinct impression that the man had marked Tavis as a noble and had realized that his was the only stall still open—but the time they would save later by buying now was worth the extra gold.

As Tavis and the gleaner rode out of the village, they came across two young boys wrestling in the dirt beside the road. At first Grinsa assumed that the two were playing, but as he and the noble drew nearer to the lads, he realized that their fight was in earnest. They were pummeling one another with their fists, clawing at each other with filthy hands. Grinsa started to yell something at them, but before he could, Tavis was off his mount, lifting one of the boys off of the other and holding them apart.

One of the boys had blood seeping from his nose, though he clearly had gotten the better of the fight. The other had a cracked lip and a nasty scrape on his cheek that was caked with blood and road dust. This second child fought to keep from crying, and the other boy knew it, judging from the smirk he wore.

"What's this all about?" Tavis demanded, sounding very much like an angry parent.

Neither boy answered. The one with the bloodied lip swiped at a tear with the back of his hand.

"You," Tavis said to the other child. "What's your name?"

"Colum," the boy said, insolent and sullen. "Colum Gulstef."

"Why are you fighting, Colum?"

The boy shrugged.

"Do you know who I am?"

"No."

"Have you ever heard of Tavis of Curgh?"

The boy looked up, suddenly fearful. Then he shook his head. "You're just saying that. Tavis of Curgh is in prison, or dead, or something. He's not here."

Tavis ran a finger over his face, tracing his scars. "You see these? I got them in the dungeons of Kentigern, from the duke himself."

Colum's eyes widened. The other boy was staring at Tavis as if the young lord were a wraith or a demon, anything but what he was: a young man, falsely accused, who had fought with all his wits and strength to regain his reputation. Grinsa wasn't certain what Tavis hoped to accomplish by scaring the lads, but he waited and watched.

In the next moment, Colum looked at the gleaner. "Is he telling the truth?"

"Yes. This is Tavis of Curgh. As you can see he's neither dead nor a prisoner."

"Whatever else you might think I am," Tavis said, drawing the boy's gaze once more, "I'm also a noble of the House of

Curgh. And when a noble asks you a question, he expects an answer. Now, one last time, why were you fighting?"

Colum didn't appear entirely convinced, but he did seem to sense that there was more risk in evading the question than in answering it.

"Innis called me a coward," the boy said.

Tavis turned to the other boy. "You're Innis?"

The child swallowed, then nodded.

"Why did you call Colum a coward?"

Innis looked away. "Because he called me a traitor."

"And why did he call you that?"

The second boy said nothing, his gaze still averted.

"Because his father refuses to fight for the king," Colum said. "My father followed King Kearney to war, but Innis's father won't go. He says Kearney isn't the true king and so he refuses to fight. Doesn't that make him a traitor?"

"Does not!" Innis launched himself at Colum, fists and feet flailing.

Tavis pushed him back so forcefully that Innis stumbled and fell, landing on his rear.

Colum gave a small laugh, but Grinsa was watching Tavis, whose face seemed to have turned to stone.

"Go home, Colum," the young lord said, his voice flat.

"But I didn't—"

"Go. You and Innis were friends this morning; you'll be friends tomorrow. Go home and clean yourself up. If your father's gone to war, then your mother has that much more need of you."

The boy lingered a moment longer, eyeing Innis, who still sat in the road. Then he started away. After only a few steps, however, he turned to look at Tavis again. "Are you really Tavis of Curgh?"

"Yes, I am. In another few days I hope to be fighting beside your father in the king's army. It will be my honor to call him a comrade."

Colum just stared, as if he didn't know how to reply. At last he turned and ran, no doubt to tell his mother of his encounter with the strange, scarred man.

Tavis turned to the other boy. "Get up."

He took a step toward the boy and Innis scrabbled away on his hands and feet, never taking his eyes off Tavis's face.

"I said, get up." Tavis drew his blade.

Grinsa started to say something, then stopped himself. A year ago he would have truly feared for the lad's safety, but not anymore. Whatever Tavis had in mind, the gleaner was certain that he wouldn't actually harm Innis.

"My father's not a traitor! And neither am I! I don't care what you and Colum say!"

"All I said was, get up."

The boy stood slowly. His whole body seemed to be trembling.

"Do you know why men like your father question the king's authority?"

Innis shook his head. Watching him, Grinsa wasn't even sure that the boy understood the question.

"Because when I was imprisoned for the murder of Lady Brienne, Kearney believed me innocent. Few others did, but that didn't stop him from—" He stopped himself, smiled briefly. "From helping me. That's all. That's what all this is about. I didn't kill her, and I've just come from Wethyrn, where I killed the man who did." He held up his sword. "With this blade. That's the truth. I swear it to you on Brienne's memory." He narrowed his eyes. "Do you understand?"

Innis hesitated, then shook his head.

"Do you believe that I'm telling you the truth?"

"I think so."

"Well, perhaps that's a start. You should go home, too, Innis. Don't call your friend a coward anymore. And make certain that you clean up that scrape on your face. You don't want to end up with scars like these."

He grinned. Innis didn't.

"Tell your father what I told you, as much of it as you can remember. Maybe that will do some good." He glanced at Grinsa, who offered a sympathetic smile. "Go on," he said, facing the boy again and sheathing his steel.

Innis cast a quick look at the gleaner before he, too, ran off.

"I guess I didn't handle that so well."

"Actually, I thought you did fine."

"They both probably think I'm mad."

"Colum doesn't. He believes you, and from now on, when he thinks of his father, he'll picture the two of you fighting together. There's no harm in that."

Tavis swung himself back onto his mount. "How many men like Innis's father do you think there are in Eibithar?"

"Probably quite a few." They began to ride. "The Rules of Ascension are often revered in Eibithar as a great source of harmony for the realm. Because power is shared, and because the rules provide for almost every contingency when it comes to choosing a new sovereign, most assume that they've prevented civil wars."

"You don't think they have?"

"I don't know—no one does really. But I do believe that they've engendered a great deal of resentment among the major houses. In Aneira, at least until recently, House Solkara has held power, and no one has doubted for even a moment that when one king dies, another will rise from the royal house to replace him. The same can be said of House Yserne and the queens of Sanbira, or of House Enharfe in Caerisse. Here, it's not nearly so simple. There's the expectation that the major houses will share power, and when it doesn't turn out that way, those houses that fail to place a king on the Oaken Throne grow bitter and envious."

"But Glyndwr hasn't claimed a king since the Grand Venture. Surely the other majors can't begrudge the House of Wolves one king in four hundred years."

"They can if it keeps one of their own from wearing the crown. Renald doesn't care that it's Kearney of Glyndwr living in Audun's Castle rather than a Thorald or a Curgh. He knows only that Galdasten has been passed over, and that under the rules his house will have no claim to the throne for another four generations."

"These are Sussyn lands, Grinsa. Or perhaps Domnall's, this far north. It hardly matters—both are minor houses. They have no part in this quarrel. Why should Innis's father hate the king so?"

"I can't say for certain. It may be that he blames you, that he still believes that you killed Brienne and so feels justified in hating this king who protected you. Perhaps he wants no part of this war, and is using Kearney as an excuse not to fight. Or maybe he bears a grudge toward Kearney himself for some reason. But the odd thing is, if your father had ascended to the throne a year ago, as he was supposed to, it's quite likely that Innis's father would be following his commands without question."

"The conspiracy," Tavis said, a pained look on his face.

"Yes. As I've told you before, they knew the realm's weaknesses better than we did ourselves." Grinsa glanced up at the sun, marking its progress toward the western horizon. Storm clouds loomed in the distance, and the gleaner doubted that the fine weather they had enjoyed since leaving Glyndwr would last the night. "Don't be too angry with Innis and his father. They're victims of the Weaver as well, though they don't know it."

The young lord frowned. "I suppose. But I can't help feeling that all of us have made it far too easy for renegades to succeed."

They continued northward, riding well past sundown, eating a light meal in the saddle, and stopping only long enough for their mounts to drink from the wash and eat some of the sweet grasses growing on the Moorlands. As darkness fell, they saw torches burning in distant fields. Tavis pointed them out with some alarm, and for a moment Grinsa wondered if this was some new mischief of the Weaver or his servants.

Then he remembered that Elined's waning had begun, and he guessed that the torches belonged to farmers out walking among their crops. According to the moon legends, if crop seedlings didn't break through the goddess's earth by Pitch Night, the last night of the turn, the harvest was doomed. Judging from the soft green they had seen in field after field as they rode the past few days, Grinsa guessed that the farmers had nothing to fear from omens this year. But it had become tradition in the farming villages of the Forelands for families to walk in the fields during the nights of the goddess's waning.

When their mounts grew too weary to go on, Grinsa and Tavis finally stopped for the night. Lightning flickered in the distance and the low growl of thunder rode a warm wind.

They ate a bit more, then slept amid the grasses, only to be awakened just before dawn by a loud thunderclap and a sudden hard downpour. The storm lasted only a short while, but with its passing the air grew colder, bringing a dawn too dreary and raw for so late in the planting. A stiff wind blew from the north, and a fine, chilling mist fell on the Moorlands. Tavis and the gleaner rode throughout the day, hunched in their riding cloaks, damp and miserable. They would have preferred to ride on into the night once more, but with no light from the moons, they had little choice but to make camp with the last grey light of day. They spoke little, ate quickly, and were soon huddled on their sleeping rolls.

Grinsa couldn't be certain how long he had been sleeping when the dream began. His first thought was that he was on the plain near Eardley where he spoke with Keziah on those nights when he entered her dreams. Except that the sky here was black and starless, the only light a brilliant white sun to the east. Recognition crashed over him like a wave just as he felt the Weaver reaching for his magic. For a moment the two of them grappled for control of the gleaner's power, the Weaver trying to use Grinsa's own shaping power to shatter the gleaner's bones, Grinsa fighting desperately to hold him off. He felt panic rising in his chest, consuming his mind, robbing him of his strength. *This is how he prevails.* The voice was his own, calm, even, the way he might have spoken to Cresenne or Keziah as he explained to them how they could keep the Weaver from harming them. *He uses fear and surprise as weapons, turning your emotions against you. His power can't reach you here. Only yours, which he seeks to wield as he would his own. He only has as much strength as you cede him. Refuse to fear, refuse to give up control, and you defeat him.*

"You can't hurt me," Grinsa said aloud, feeling his initial confusion sluice away, and with it the dread that had touched his heart for one fleeting moment.

"Can't I? I'm in your mind, gleaner. It's but a small matter to take hold of your magic." Brave words, but Grinsa heard frustration in the man's voice.

They continued to struggle, though on that plain of Grinsa's dream, both of them stood utterly still, the Weaver shrouded in shadow against the blinding light, his fists clenched. Again and again he tried to turn Grinsa's magic against him; shaping, fire, healing, even delusion, as if he hoped to fool the gleaner into thinking him a friend. But Grinsa held him at bay, guarding his powers as a king might his gold. After several moments of this, he had an idea. Reaching for his fire magic, he tried to raise a flame that would counter the gleaming white light of the Weaver and allow him to see the man's face. He had done this once before, when he saved Cresenne from the Weaver's assault in Audun's Castle, and had caught a glimpse of his enemy. Golden eyes, a square regal face.

If Grinsa could hold him here longer, he might manage to see the Weaver's face again, and, more important, he might see enough of the plain to recognize it.

The Weaver sensed his danger instantly. Immediately, he stopped struggling for control of Grinsa's other magics and fought with all his might to keep the fire from the gleaner's hand.

"What is it you're hiding, Weaver?" Grinsa asked, a grin springing to his lips. "The plains near Muelry perhaps? Or Ayvencalde Moor?"

Only a turn before, while Tavis was fighting the assassin on the Wethy Crown, Grinsa had been locked in a battle of his own against a Qirsi merchant sent by the Weaver to kill him. The man had died before Grinsa could learn from him all that he wished to know. But the merchant had said something about paying the conspiracy's couriers on behalf of the Weaver, and of the Weaver's fears that any direct payments might be traced back to him. Grinsa had surmised from this that the Weaver was in Braedon, where merchants and lords alike used different currency from that used in the other six realms. Imperial qinde, it was called. What other reason could the Weaver have for channeling his payments through the merchant?

But if the Weaver was shaken by hearing him guess at the plain's location, he gave no outward sign of it.

Instead he laughed, harsh and cruel. "It's too late for that, gleaner. You're still trying to figure out who I am, and where you can find me. In the meantime, I've already won. As we speak, the armies of the Eandi are preparing to fight their foolish wars—some have already begun. Soon they'll have rendered themselves helpless against my offensive. And there's nothing you can do about it."

"You haven't won yet. If you had, you wouldn't be bothering with me, and you wouldn't still be hiding your face."

"I didn't come here because I fear you, or because I have to defeat you before I can win. I came to avenge a friend. That's all."

"The merchant."

At that, for the first time, Grinsa sensed some hesitation on the Weaver's part. "What do you know about him?"

"About Tihod? Quite a bit. He told me much before he died."

"I don't believe you. He wouldn't have told you anything."

"I never gave him the choice. I have mind-bending magic just as you do, remember?"

Again the Weaver tried to seize his magic, the onslaught coming so suddenly that Grinsa nearly failed to ward himself in time.

Immediately on the heels of the man's assault, Grinsa tried to summon a flame, but the Weaver stopped him. After a moment their silent struggle ceased. They were like two armies facing one another across a battle plain, evenly matched, neither of them able to advance against the other. The gleaner knew that the wisest course would be to force himself awake, to end this encounter before the Weaver managed to harm him. Of the two of them, only he was truly in danger. The Weaver had entered his dreams; Grinsa couldn't harm him. The most for which he could hope was an opportunity to learn the Weaver's identity, and valuable though that information might have been, it was hardly worth risking his life. The time was fast approaching when the Weaver would reveal himself for all the Forelands to see. Yet, even knowing all this, Grinsa couldn't bring himself to awake from this dream.

For his part, the Weaver seemed just as intent on prolonging their confrontation, though clearly he still felt he had reason to keep Grinsa from seeing his face or the plain on which they stood. If he had truly come merely to avenge Tihod, he was risking a good deal in the name of vengeance.

It almost seemed that their fascination with each other outweighed any sense of peril they might have felt. For his part, Grinsa had never met another Weaver. All his life, he had been unique, harboring a secret that he could share with but a handful of people. As a Qirsi living among the Eandi he had been a curiosity, eliciting awe and contempt in equal measure from those he met. Children coming to his gleaning tent had feared him as much as they did the judgment of the Qiran. This he shared with other Qirsi. But his powers had set him apart from even his own people. None of those whom he counted among his friends and loved ones had ever known what it was to live as he did. Not Keziah, his sister, who knew him as well as anyone; not Pheba, his wife, who might have understood eventually, had she lived long enough; not Tavis, who had journeyed the Forelands with him for much of the past year; not Cresenne, who loved him and who had felt the wrath of this other Weaver. No one truly knew him. Such was the life of a Weaver.

But he couldn't help but wonder if the same was true of this man standing before him, his face in shadows, his magic like a blade aimed at Grinsa's heart. Didn't it make sense that they should be more alike than not? Wasn't it possible that the leader of the Qirsi conspiracy understood him better than did Keziah or Tavis or Cresenne? In a way, Grinsa and the Weaver had more in common than any two men in the Forelands.

The Weaver seemed to read his thoughts—and why shouldn't he, walking in Grinsa's dreams?

"Yes," he said, his voice low. Grinsa could tell that he was smiling. "We're not all that different, you and I."

"You wish to rule the Forelands. I don't. You send assassins for innocent girls and well-meaning lords; you use your powers to torture and kill; you would gladly plunge all the realms into war in order to feed your ambition. We're nothing alike."

"Of course we are. We're Weavers. We possess powers the likes of which no Eandi can imagine. Indeed, no ordinary Qirsi can fathom what we are. That's what you were thinking a moment ago, isn't it? You sense a bond between us. I sense it as well. It's real, Grinsa. You may hate what I am, but you can't deny that you see yourself in me, just as I see myself in you."

"Even if that's true, what difference does it make?"

"Perhaps none. Perhaps a great deal. Together you and I could destroy the Eandi armies in a matter of hours. These men have never fought against one Weaver, let alone two. We could divide the Forelands between us, create a glorious new world for our people. Tell me, gleaner, do you ever wish for a better life? Do you ever wish that you could reveal the true extent of your powers without fearing execution at the hands of small-minded Eandi nobles?"

Grinsa laughed, but tightened his hold on his magic, expecting another attack at any moment.

"You think my question amusing. But how will you feel if your daughter grows up to be a Weaver, like her father? Will it still seem funny then?"

"If she has to live her life as I have, so be it. I haven't suffered so greatly for being a Weaver. And if you really cared a whit for my daughter, you wouldn't have tried to kill her mother."

"Cresenne betrayed me and she'll be punished for that."

"I find it interesting that in trying to turn me to your cause, you speak only of improving the lives of Weavers. I thought you were doing this for all Qirsi."

"I am!"

"No. You just threatened Cresenne. It seems to me that you care only for those Qirsi who support you and your cause."

"The rest are traitors! All Qirsi who would devote themselves to serving the Eandi deserve death!"

"Is that the kind of ruler you intend to be, Weaver? Will you execute all who question your vision of the world? Do you intend to kill every Eandi in the Forelands, and all the Qirsi who count the Eandi among their friends?"

"If that's what it takes to change the world, then yes, I do."

"And just how are you different from the worst Eandi tyrants of Aneira and Braedon? You're no better than a Solkaran or a Curtell. Your eyes may be yellow, but your blood runs Eandi."

He had known the assault would come if he pushed the

Weaver far enough, and so was able to defend himself with ease, despite the man's fury. As the Weaver hammered at his mind, struggling once more to gain control of Grinsa's shaping power, the gleaner raised his hand and called forth a bright golden flame.

The Weaver's eyes snapped wide and a low growl escaped his throat. Grinsa felt him try to snuff out the flame, but the gleaner held fast to his magic. Beyond the Weaver, across the rocky moorland on which they stood, Grinsa saw the gentle curve of a coastline and the pale glitter of water. And beyond that, more land. He saw an island to the north—Wantrae Island. The body of water had to be the Strait of Wantrae. Which made this plain . . .

"Ayvencalde Moor," he said aloud. "I've never been here, but I know this place."

"I told you, it doesn't matter."

"I beg to differ. You must be the High Chancellor of Braedon. Dusaan jal Kania." He had first heard the name a few turns before, in the City of Kings. After the Weaver tried to kill Cresenne, she told Grinsa of having been a chancellor in the Weaver's movement. Since the emperor of Braedon was the only noble in the Forelands who referred to his Qirsi advisors as chancellors, the gleaner had begun to wonder if the Weaver served in the emperor's court. After his fight with Tihod, his suspicions deepened. Now, seeing the way this man's face shaded to crimson, he was certain. "You say it doesn't matter, Dusaan. Your expression tells me otherwise."

"So you know who I am. How will you explain this to your Eandi allies? Only a Weaver could have learned such a thing. Are you ready to admit to them what you are? Are you ready to die at the hands of your so-called friends?"

"You think them fools. They're not. When they understand that I can defeat you, that I'm their only hope, they'll accept who and what I am."

"You'd let them use you that way? You disgust me."

Grinsa sensed that the Weaver was about to leave him. "I can find you now, Dusaan. The next time we meet, it will be in your dreams. You'd best be ready."

"You can't hurt me, gleaner. And it may be that I can't hurt you. But I can still reach Cresenne, and there's nothing you can do to stop me."

It was only for an instant, a lapse brought on by fear for his love and for his daughter, by his fatigue, and by his belief, wrong though it was, that the Weaver intended to end their conversation. And like a wolf waiting for his prey to show any sign of weakness, Dusaan pounced. Grinsa felt a lancing pain in his temple and then an unbearable pressure on his skull. Fear seized his heart, as if the Weaver himself had reached into his chest and was squeezing his life away. It seemed that his head was being crushed beneath boulders.

Wake up, he heard someone say. Whose voice was that?

Wake up, gleaner. Wake up.

Tavis. Grinsa opened his eyes and felt his world heave and spin. He rolled onto his stomach, pushed himself off the ground and vomited until his gut was empty and his throat was raw.

"You're bleeding," Tavis said, as the gleaner sat back on his knees.

Grinsa raised a hand to his temple. His fingers came away damp and sticky.

"You were dreaming of the Weaver."

"Yes," he said, his voice a hoarse whisper.

"For a long time?"

"A shade too long, it would seem." He closed his eyes tightly for a moment, as if to will away his dizziness. "Do you have any idea of the time?"

"If I had to guess I'd say it was almost dawn."

Grinsa nodded. He felt as if he hadn't slept at all. Now he knew why Keziah complained of their conversations disrupting her sleep.

"Can you heal yourself?" the boy asked. "Or do you want me to dress that for you?"

"I'll take care of it. Thanks."

"Did you learn anything?"

"I know who he is."

Tavis sat up. "What?"

"His name is Dusaan jal Kania. He's the high chancellor of Braedon."

"You're certain?"

He nodded.

"That's just what we've been hoping for!"

"I suppose it could be helpful."

He could barely see the young lord, but he knew that Tavis was frowning. "We've been trying to find out something—anything—about this man since early in the snows. And now you know his name and his title. Why aren't you pleased?"

"You mean aside from the fact that he nearly succeeded in killing me just now?" He winced at what he heard in his own voice. "I'm sorry, Tavis. I'm just not sure that it matters any-more. I don't think he wanted me to see his face again or to learn his name. But once I had, he didn't act overly con-cerned. He thinks he's won already, and after tonight, I fear that he may be right."

"As long as you're still fighting him, he hasn't won."

"He beat me just now. I held my own for a time, but in the end he beat me. And he threatened Cresenne's life again. I'm powerless to protect her. Do you know what that's like?"

"No. I suppose I don't. I mean, I'm powerless to do lots of things, but it must be strange for a Weaver to feel that way."

In spite of everything, Grinsa gave a small laugh. "Yes, it is."

"I don't know what to say, Grinsa. We can still go back to the City of Kings. It's a longer ride now, but we can do it. That way you can protect them both."

The gleaner gazed southward, though he could see nothing for the darkness and the low clouds. He was sorely tempted to ready the horses immediately and ride back to Audun's castle. "I can make the journey alone." He faced Tavis again. "I know how anxious you are to join your father and Hagan and Xaver in the north."

"All right," the boy said. There could be no mistaking the hurt in his voice. "But think about it, gleaner. The Weaver may have threatened Cresenne hoping that you would do just this. You've said yourself that it won't be long until he shows him-self. He's just waiting for the court armies to weaken themselves enough that he'll have nothing to fear from them. What if this is part of his plan as well? What if he doesn't want you there? He can defeat the armies, but he doesn't want to face you as well. And what better way to ensure that he won't have to than to threaten the woman you love."

"I don't think he fears me that much, not after this night."

"You didn't hurt him at all?"

"I couldn't. He entered my dream. I couldn't attack him; I could only hope to keep him from harming me. And I failed at that."

"But you're saying that he had nothing to fear from you."

"Only that I might raise a fire and see his face."

"And you did that."

"Yes."

Tavis opened his arms wide. "Then tonight proves nothing. It would be as if I had entered a battle tournament unarmed and then assumed because I lost that I was a poor swordsman."

Again, Grinsa had to smile. It was crude analogy, but the boy raised a valid point.

"I can't tell you what to do about Cresenne," Tavis went on. "And if you feel that you have to be with her and Bryntelle, I'll understand. But if the Weaver wasn't afraid of you, he wouldn't have entered your dreams, and he wouldn't have said anything about Cresenne. If he merely wanted her dead, he'd kill her and gloat about it afterward. He's trying to confuse you, to give you pause before you reach Galdasten. That's the only explanation that makes any sense."

He knew Tavis was right. The Weaver's strength lay in his ability to sense the weakness in his opponent and turn it to his own advantage. He had done this time and again in his efforts to bring down the courts, and he had done it just now to Grinsa. The pain in his head, the gash on his temple—these were nothing. The true wound had been inflicted on Grinsa's mind. Dusaan had struck at the gleaner's courage, at his resolve, at the love he shared with Cresenne and their daughter. These were the flaws in his armor, the places where the Weaver could draw blood. A paradox, for they were also the sources of Grinsa's strength.

He closed his eyes and again raised a hand to his temple,

drawing upon his magic. After a moment, he felt the skin beginning to heal.

When the pain had subsided, he opened his eyes once more. The sky to the east was starting to brighten. One of the horses nickered and an owl called in the distance.

"I'm ready to ride when you are," Grinsa said.

Tavis merely nodded, and together they broke camp.

Chapter Seventeen

The Moorlands, near Domnall, Eibithar

She rode well back in the column, speaking to no one, her eyes fixed on the path before her, her face a mask of indifference. Keziah and Kearney had agreed that it made more sense for them to ride apart from one another, that if they spent too much time in each other's company it might invite speculation among the soldiers that they had reconciled. More to the point, it might convince the other Qirsi riding with them of the same thing. And since Keziah couldn't be certain that the others weren't traitors allied with the Weaver and his conspiracy, she had to continue behaving as if she, too, was a renegade.

Kearney had assigned a man to her, to keep her safe, but also to make it seem that he still doubted her motives. So she was never truly alone. The soldier rode just behind her, as silent and seemingly withdrawn as she. Kearney knew now of her efforts to join the conspiracy, of her hope that she might learn something of the Weaver that would aid the Eandi courts in their coming battle with the Qirsi movement. But of course he had not shared this with anyone, least of all her guard, who treated her as he might the defeated leader of an invading army, with a cold courtesy that did nothing to hide his contempt for her.

Within only a few days of their departure from Audun's Castle, Keziah had found herself longing for the company of Gershon Trasker. A year ago she would never have imagined that she and Gershon might become friends, but as with so much else, the Weaver and his movement had changed their relationship, forcing them both to see beyond their mutual distrust. Even if the swordmaster had been here, rather than leading the balance of the king's army to Kentigern to fight the Aneirans, he couldn't have spent any more time in her company than could Kearney. But still, she would have drawn comfort just from his presence.

She had no cause to complain. The men around her were all on foot. Only she, the king and his other ministers, and a few of Kearney's captains were on horseback. With the passing of a storm two nights before, the air had turned cool for so late in the planting; high clouds covered the sky over Eibithar's Moorlands, and a soft wind blew across the grasses and hillocks. From all she had learned over the years about Eibithar's history, she knew that armies marching to war often endured terrible hardships. Thus far, they had encountered none of these. Yet, as always seemed to happen to the archminister when she accompanied Kearney and his men, she found herself alone, isolated in a sea of Eandi warriors. She was ashamed of her self-pity, yet she could not help herself.

Late in the morning, just after the last soldiers of the king's army had started up a gentle rise, the column halted abruptly. Keziah looked up, hearing shouts in the distance and feeling her stomach tighten.

She glanced back at her guard. "What is it?"

He shrugged, looking as confused as she felt, his stony belligerence gone at least for the moment.

One of the captains was riding toward them, looking young and slightly afraid. Keziah wondered if Kearney missed Gershon as much as she did.

"What's happening?" she asked as the man approached.

"His Majesty would like you to join him, Archminister. We're nearing the gates of Domnall."

Keziah nodded, kicking at the flanks of Greystar, her mount. Freed suddenly from the tedium of the soldiers' slow pace, the horse practically leaped forward. The archminister sensed that the guard and captain were just behind her, but she didn't look back. As she rode she felt Kearney's men watching her, row after row of them, wary of her, wondering, no doubt, if she would raise her mists on their behalf when the battle was joined, or if, instead, she would betray them. She wanted to stop and yell at them all, to tell them that she remained loyal to Kearney and the realm, to tell them how much she had risked to learn what she could of the Weaver, to make them see how she suffered for the choices she had made. But she merely stared straight ahead, heedless of the burning of her cheeks.

Topping the rise, she found Kearney, utterly still atop his great bay. Following the line of his gaze, Keziah felt fear wrap its hand around her throat. Domnall Castle stood in the distance, her towers rising high above the moor and the low buildings and walls of Domnall City. A single flag flew above the castle's ramparts, bearing the grey, purple, and white sigil of the house. There was no Eibitharian banner, as there should have been, though this was not what made Keziah tremble.

Outside the walls of the city, lining the road on which Kearney and his men were traveling, stood the army of Domnall, a thousand men strong. Before them, in the center of the road, a man waited on horseback, his black and silver hair stirring in the wind. Keziah couldn't be certain from this distance, but she assumed that this was Seamus, duke of Domnall, who long ago had cast his lot with Aindreas of Kentigern in defiance of the Crown.

"Do you think he intends to fight?" Keziah asked.

The king didn't even look at her. "I don't know. If I didn't know better, I'd say that he intends to offer his sword and his men in defense of the realm."

"Isn't that possible?"

Kearney shook his head. "His men are lining the road. If he was offering his aid, they would be positioned in rows for my inspection. He has something else in mind."

"He wouldn't fight us, Your Majesty," said the captain. "It

would be folly even to make the attempt. We outnumber him by more than two to one, our men are better trained, and ours are the better arms. He'd be leading them to a slaughter."

"I agree, Captain. But if he won't fight us, and he won't join us, why is he out here?"

Keziah shifted her gaze back to the lone flag, watching it rise and fall lazily in the wind. "You sent word to Seamus, didn't you, Your Majesty?" She looked at Kearney again. "You ordered his army north, to Galdasten."

"Yes. What of it?"

"The messenger would have arrived here days ago, and yet the duke and his army remain. And he's not flying the colors of the realm."

"You think he's making a show of defying me."

She could hear the pain in his voice. None of the others would have noticed—they didn't know Kearney as she did—but it was there, unmistakable.

"There's no Qirsi with them, Your Majesty," the captain said after a brief silence. "There would be whether they were planning to fight us or join us. I think the archminister may be right."

"I've never known Seamus to be so bold." A sad smile touched the king's lips, then vanished. "He must hate me a great deal."

"They're traitors," the captain said. "Every one of them. We should kill them all."

"We can't." Kearney gave a short, harsh laugh. "Seamus knows we can't. We haven't the time to fight them, and we can't weaken ourselves by trying. It's a coward's gesture."

But Keziah could see from the expression on Kearney's face that it stung nevertheless.

The captain faced him. "So what do we do?"

"We ride past them," the king said. "Captain, I want you to make certain that the men don't respond in any way to Domnall's soldiers. They're going to be taunted, they may be spat upon. They're not to retaliate. Not at all. I want them looking straight ahead, I want them silent, and I want their weapons to remain at their sides. Do you understand?"

The man nodded, though he didn't look at all pleased.

"They're testing us. They want to see if we're disciplined enough to prevail, not only against the empire, not only against the conspiracy, but also against Aindreas and his allies. If we lash out at them, even if it's justified, we weaken ourselves, we weaken the realm." He looked down at Domnall's army once more. "Seamus wants to show that he's not afraid to defy me. Let's show him that we don't care one way or another. Give the order, Captain. Return here when the men are ready."

"Yes, Your Majesty."

The captain rode off, calling to the other commanders.

"He's playing a dangerous game," Kearney said, his voice so low that Keziah had to lean forward just to hear him. "This could get out of hand very quickly."

"Might we be better off leaving the road, putting some distance between our soldiers and his?"

"Probably, but I think you know I can't do that. Seamus is looking for any sign of weakness on my part. I'd be giving him just what he wants."

"Of course, Your Majesty."

He looked at her. "You think I'm wrong."

"No. I'm sure you're right. But I fear for us all. You shouldn't have to consider such things when marching to defend the realm."

The captain returned a short while later to inform the king that the men had been given their orders.

"Then, let's march," the king said.

Keziah hesitated, wondering if she should return to the rear of the column. "Where do you want me, Your Majesty?"

"I think you'd better stay with me, just in case."

They started down the gentle slope, Kearney, his youthful face grim, leading the way.

Seamus remained in the center of the road, a smirk on his thin lips. As they drew nearer to Domnall's army, Keziah could see that the duke's men stood at attention, but with their swords sheathed.

The king seemed to notice this as well. "At least he has

sense enough to keep weapons out of their hands," Kearney murmured. A moment later, he added, his voice still low, "Archminister, I want you to follow my lead. Do what I do, and stay close at hand."

Keziah nodded, her heart hammering at her chest and her mouth dry.

As the road leveled out and the king's army drew ever nearer to Domnall's men, the duke steered his horse off the road, though he halted just beside it, and close to the first of his men.

"At ease!" he called in a clear voice.

Immediately, Domnall's soldiers relaxed their stances and started shouting insults at Kearney's men, calling them cowards and butchers. Keziah glanced back at the soldiers and saw that though they continued to face forward, already the nearest of them were reddening.

"Stop looking back," Kearney said quietly.

She obeyed, but gave a small shake of her head. "This isn't going to work."

"I know. Just follow me."

As he reached Seamus, Kearney steered his mount off the road as well, so that he was positioned just beside the duke. Keziah did the same, taking her place on the other side of Seamus.

"Lord Domnall," the king said, as his men began to file past. "How kind of you to greet my men. You honor us."

Seamus frowned. "That wasn't my intention."

Kearney's sword was in his hand so swiftly that Keziah didn't even see him reach for it. Apparently the duke didn't either. He looked utterly shocked to find the tip of Kearney's blade pressed against the side of his throat.

Immediately Kearney's men halted and a hush fell over the duke's army.

"Continue the march!" the king said, his voice pitched to carry. "Eyes straight ahead!"

After a moment, one of the captains barked a command and the king's soldiers started forward again. Seamus's men, however, kept their silence.

"What did you think to accomplish here, Seamus?" the king asked, speaking softly again. "Surely you didn't think that I'd allow you to mock me and my men in this way."

When the duke said nothing, Kearney pressed harder with his blade, until Keziah wondered how the skin on Seamus's neck didn't break.

"Well?"

"No matter what I'll say, you'll kill me as a traitor."

"If I wanted you to hang, I'd already have cause enough to give the order. I ordered you to Galdasten. Under the laws of the land, your house is already in rebellion."

Seamus said nothing, though the color fled his cheeks. It seemed he hadn't considered this.

"I'm not going to have you executed."

"Then you'll imprison me in my own dungeon."

"I won't do anything to you, Seamus. I have more pressing matters to which to attend. To be honest, you're not worth even this much trouble. But I want an answer. I want to understand this."

The duke eyed him briefly, his mouth set in a thin line, his angular face ashen. "I can speak freely?" he finally said. "Without fear of punishment?"

"You have my word."

"Your word. Very well, Your Majesty. I suppose I have little choice. If you mean to kill me, there's little I can do to stop you, so I might as well speak my mind. I don't believe you deserve to sit on the throne. I have nothing against Glyndwr, nor did I have any reason to distrust you, until you granted asylum to the Curgh boy. But I believe that you and Javan have contrived to take the throne from Aindreas."

"Then you're a fool, Seamus. If Javan had wished to do such a thing, he would have done so in a way that enabled him to keep the crown for himself and his line. Remember, he abdicated, just as Aindreas did."

"He had no choice in the matter. Had he attempted to take the throne after what his son did, it would have led immediately to civil war."

"The boy didn't do anything! We hold in the prison tower

of Audun's Castle a Qirsi woman who admits to hiring the assassin who killed Brienne. Demons and fire, man! Didn't you even bother to read the missive I sent?"

"One more Qirsi deception. They've shown time and again that they can't be trusted, and yet you're so ready to believe this woman who came to your castle. You would seek any evidence, no matter how weak, to justify your faith in the Butcher of Curgh."

Kearney closed his eyes briefly, shaking his head. "Why would she lie about this? The conspiracy wants you and Aindreas and the others to believe in Tavis's guilt. They have no reason to offer proof to the contrary."

"The Qirsi have been lying to us for too long, deluding us with false counsel, striking at us with hidden blades." The duke's eyes flicked toward Keziah. "We can only guess at what their purpose might be. Our only recourse is to stop relying on white-hairs entirely. Nothing they say can be trusted, and that includes this woman in your prison tower. Perhaps she seeks to save herself by telling you what you wish to hear. Or maybe she's been ordered by her leaders to say these things. I don't know. But I will not believe in Tavis's innocence simply because a traitorous Qirsi says that I should."

"Is that why your first minister isn't here, Seamus? Have you lost faith in all your Qirsi?"

"Yes. To be honest, Your Majesty, I'm surprised and disappointed to find that you haven't."

Kearney opened his mouth, then stopped himself, glancing at Keziah with an apology in his green eyes. She knew that he wanted to defend her. "I still don't understand this show of defiance," he said instead. "Why not remain in your castle, and let us march past?"

"That," the duke said, his eyes meeting the king's, "would have been an act of cowardice."

It seemed that Kearney didn't know what to say. For as long as Keziah had known him, he had prided himself on his honor, his refusal to compromise his principles under any circumstance. Though Seamus had committed treason, and then had chosen to flaunt his defiance, there was a certain perverse dignity in this display. At last the king shook his head once more, a bitter smile on his lips. "You're an ass, Seamus," he muttered, and sheathed his sword.

The duke's face reddened, but before he could answer, they heard voices raised in anger at the front of the column.

Kearney leveled a finger at Seamus. "Any blood spilled here is on your head!" Then he kicked at his mount and raced toward the commotion, Keziah and the duke following in his wake.

Near the front of the column, two men were wrestling on the ground, one wearing the colors of the king, the other obviously from Domnall. They had their daggers drawn and the duke's man bore a deep gash on his shoulder. A large group of men, many of them with their swords drawn, had formed a ring around the two combatants. Kearney's captains were shouting for the king's men to stand down, but they had done nothing to separate the two who were fighting, and already other men were pairing off, preparing for combat. It wouldn't take much for the confrontation to escalate into a full battle.

Reaching the ring of soldiers, Kearney didn't hesitate. He swung himself off of his mount, pushed his way through the bystanders, and, drawing his sword, plunged the blade into the earth just beside the men's heads.

The two fighters froze, twisting their necks to stare up at the king. All other conversations stopped.

"Get up!" Kearney said, his tone a match for the ice in his eyes.

Slowly, the two soldiers untangled themselves and stood, both of them looking as sheepish as chastised boys.

"Captain!"

"Yes, Your Majesty?"

"Didn't I tell you that these men were not to respond in any way to the duke's soldiers?"

"You did, Your Majesty."

"And did you convey those orders to the men?"

"Of course I did, Your Majesty."

"Did you think that your captain's commands didn't apply to you?" Kearney asked the soldier.

"No, Your Majesty! But this man called you a milksop and—"

"I don't care what he called me, and neither should you. This man and his duke intend to hide in their castle while we fight to defend the realm." Kearney grinned and looked up at Seamus, who remained on his mount. "Why should it matter to us what any of them say?"

The soldier grinned in return. "Yes, Your Majesty."

"Get these men moving again, Captain. We've wasted enough time here."

Seamus's men were glaring at the king, but none of them said a word, nor did any dare to raise a weapon against him. Still, Keziah wished that Kearney would take to his mount again; he'd be safer in his saddle. The king appeared unconcerned.

"Lord Domnall," he said, allowing his voice to carry. "I hereby declare you and your house to be in rebellion. I'll take no action against you so long as your army remains in the dukedom, but any effort you make to journey beyond your lands will be considered an act of war against the realm and will be met appropriately. With one exception. You may march with us now to meet the invaders at Galdasten. If you do so, all this will be forgotten."

The duke stared at him a moment, then clicked his tongue at his mount and steered the beast away, back toward his castle. He called out to one of his commanders, who began to shout commands at Domnall's soldiers. Soon all of them were following their duke.

Kearney watched them go, his expression as bleak as Keziah had ever seen it, his sword lowered and seemingly forgotten.

"You were right when you called him an ass," she said softly.

"Perhaps. But there'll be others like him. And they may cost us everything." He walked past her, and climbed onto his mount. "I suppose we should ride apart again."

"It's safest if we do."

He nodded, casting one final look at Domnall castle before returning to the front of the column. Keziah turned her mount and started down the road with the last of Kearney's soldiers. A moment later her guard fell in just behind her, still silent, his face like a stone wall. It was all Keziah could do not to rail at the man.

Kearney and his army managed to put several leagues between themselves and Domnall by the time daylight started to fail and they were forced to make camp. As usual, Keziah ate her supper alone, save for the reticent guard. After, she unrolled her sleeping roll and lay down, conscious of the guard doing the same a short distance away. Prior to leaving the City of Kings, Kearney had offered to have his men carry a tent for her, but the archminister refused. If the soldiers had to sleep beneath open skies, she reasoned, so would she. They carried a tent for Wenda, but the high minister was by far the oldest of the king's Qirsi—Keziah didn't begrudge her this small comfort. Indeed, had she realized how bothersome she would find the guard's constant presence, she might have accepted Kearney's offer herself.

The clouds that had covered the skies for the past several days had finally started to break up, and as they drifted overhead, like ice in the northern rivers, she could see an occasional star shining bright in the blackness beyond. The moons offered some light as well, Ilias's red glow blending with Panya's white to give a rose cast to the grasses and boulders of the moor.

When sleep finally came to her, Keziah began to dream, seeing once more the armies of Domnall and Eibithar's king arrayed against each other. This time, however, Kearney could not keep them from fighting and soon Keziah was surrounded by mayhem and carnage. Everywhere she looked, men were dying, their blood flowing from ghastly wounds until it seemed that the entire moor had been stained red. Keziah shouted for them to stop, but they ignored her. She tried to raise a mist, hoping that if they couldn't see one another, they might break off their combat, but her power failed her. Hearing hoofbeats behind her, she turned to see her guard bearing down on her, his blade raised and a fierce grin on his face. She threw up an arm to shield herself and cried out for Kearney, but the soldier was closing the distance between them far too swiftly.

Abruptly, everything went dark, as if the sun had been extinguished. Her footing changed as well, and she nearly stumbled. It took her a moment to realize that she was still dreaming, and another to understand that the Weaver had come to her. Without even thinking, Keziah began to walk, trudging up the incline to where she knew she would find him. The climb was more difficult than she remembered, the hill steeper, the terrain rougher. In the short time she had known the Weaver, she had come to understand that his moods could be measured in such things. This hill was the man's way of telling her that he was displeased. And Keziah knew why.

She was winded and sweating when she reached the summit. Almost the moment she stopped climbing white light flared before her, and the Weaver appeared, framed as always against the harsh radiance so that she couldn't see his features.

"I heard you cry out," he said. "You were dreaming even before I came to you."

"Yes, Weaver."

"Of what?"

Keziah hesitated. She was dazed, her mind addled by the sudden shift to this second, far more dangerous dream. Under any circumstances facing the Weaver terrified her, but to do so without her wits . . .

"Of what?" he demanded again, his voice like iron.

"A battle," she said. "We marched past Domnall today and the duke had his army on the road as a show of defiance. The two armies nearly did battle, and that's what I was dreaming. Only in my dream, one of Kearney's men was trying to kill me."

In this case, she realized only after she had finished, the truth served her purposes quite well, making it seem that she and the king remained at odds.

"You march to Galdasten?"

"Yes, Weaver."

"But Domnall does not."

"No."

"What of the others?"

"We can't be certain yet, but we believe Eardley, Sussyn, Rennach, and Galdasten will also refuse to fight alongside the king."

"Thorald will fight?"

"It seems so. Tobbar's son has allied himself with the king, even though his father refuses to take sides in Kearney's dispute with Kentigern."

"I suppose that can't be helped," the Weaver said, as much to himself as to her. Then the question she had been dreading. "Was Cresenne still alive when you left Audun's Castle?"

She lowered her gaze. "Yes, Weaver."

"Have you made arrangements to have her killed before you return?"

"No, Weaver. I didn't know who to trust with such a task. And I never had the opportunity before we left. Kearney keeps her well guarded. Any time I went to see her—"

Agony. Her chest seemed to be seared by flames. She couldn't breathe; she certainly couldn't speak. She tried to remember what Grinsa had told her, that whenever the Weaver hurt her it was an illusion, a trick of the mind. Her magic and her body were her own. The Weaver might have access to her thoughts, but that was all. She had only to take control of them.

Except that she couldn't. Terror gripped her mind. She could think of nothing but her pain and her desperate need to draw breath.

"You failed me," the Weaver said, his voice low and shockingly cold. "I told you I wanted her dead, that her murder would be a test of your loyalty, and still she lives. Your excuses mean nothing to me; your failure is all that matters."

At that moment she could offer no argument. She had failed him and she would have given anything to be able to beg his forgiveness, to fall at his feet and grovel for mercy. But even this bitter comfort was denied her.

"I sensed your reluctance when I first assigned this task to you. Did you even want to succeed? Or did you think to delay until Kearney marched to war? Was that what happened?"

She shook her head, still fighting for breath. Her vision began to fail her, the figure of the Weaver starting to swim. She wondered how much longer she could remain on her feet.

"I should kill you now, make you an example to all those who would defy my commands. You'd be a message to Kearney as well, lest he think that the movement can be taken lightly."

Keziah dropped to her knees, clutching at her chest.

"Unfortunately, I can't afford to lose even one servant just now, and with your king marching to war you may still prove to be of some value to me."

He released her and she fell onto her side, gasping, greedily sucking sweet air into her lungs, her eyes squeezed shut and her mouth wide. Each breath seemed to soothe the fire in her chest, easing the pain. Her fear lingered, however. The Weaver had only to form the thought and her suffering would begin anew.

"I trust you won't fail me again."

"No, Weaver." She could barely manage to speak the words. "As soon as we return to the City of Kings, I'll take care of the woman. I swear it." And at that very moment, she almost meant it.

"That won't be necessary."

Even prone on the ground in her dreams, afraid for her life and still struggling to shake off the effects of what he had done to her, Keziah had the presence of mind to mute her response to this.

"But I promised you that I'd do it."

"Your promises were worth little in that regard. Now I have little choice but to see to the matter myself. But don't fear, Archminister. I have other tasks for you. One in particular that I believe you'll enjoy. I had been planning to have another do this—an assassin of some renown. It seems now that he's dead, and so I have to turn elsewhere. As it happens, it's just as fine a test of your loyalty to me as Cresenne's murder would have been. It might even be better."

Keziah sensed that he wanted her to ask, that he would be watching her closely to gauge her response. She sat up, then forced herself to her feet.

"What is this task, Weaver?"

"I think you know." She couldn't see his face, but she knew he was smiling. And she did know. Gods help her, she knew exactly what it was, though she couldn't imagine how he expected her do this without being caught and executed herself.

"You want me to kill Kearney."

"Very good, Keziah. Very good indeed."

She didn't bother to conceal her fear and the ache in her heart.

"You still love him, I know. This won't be easy for you. But it must be done. I won't accept failure a second time."

"But how can I possibly—?"

"I don't expect you to do it yet, and I don't want anyone to know it was you. He should die in battle, near Galdasten, if possible."

Of course. What better way to prolong the war and weaken Eibithar than to leave her leaderless in the middle of this conflict? No doubt he hoped that in the wake of Kearney's death Renald, Javan, and Aindreas would all vie for the crown.

"You understand. I sense it."

"Yes, Weaver."

"Good. There may be some hope for you yet."

"Kearney still doesn't trust me entirely. I may not be able to get close enough to him."

"Well, see that you do. You possess both language of beasts and mists and winds. They should serve you quite well in this regard."

"Yes, Weaver," she whispered.

"Perhaps you'll be fortunate and he'll be killed in battle without any help from you. But one way or another, I want him dead."

"It shall be done."

"I expect no less."

She awoke with a start, sitting bolt upright, her chest heaving. Her hair and clothes and sleeping roll were soaked with sweat, and her head spun so violently that she feared she might throw up. Glancing to the side, she saw that her guard was awake, propped up on one arm, eyeing her in the dim light of the moons.

She briefly considered sending the man to Kearney's tent with word that she needed to speak with the king immediately. But in the next moment she dismissed the idea. It would serve only to draw attention to her and it might convince others working for the Weaver that she remained loyal to the king. Certainly she needed to tell Kearney what the Weaver expected her to do, just as she needed to dispatch a message to Cresenne warning her of the Weaver's intent to kill her himself. But she had some time. It would be days before Kearney would lead the men into battle, and Cresenne spent her nights awake, sleeping by day so that she might avoid dreams of the Weaver. Keziah could wait until morning with little risk to either of them.

The archminister lay back down, turning her back to the guard. A gust of wind swept over the Moorlands, scything through her damp clothes and making her shiver. She wasn't fool enough to think that she could get back to sleep, but if she sat up again, or changed clothes, or took a walk, which is what she really longed to do, the guard would follow, watching her, dogging her every step. So Keziah lay there, trembling in the chill air, jerking occasionally as she recalled the Weaver's assault, staring at the swaying grasses.

When at last the dawn broke, the eastern sky glowing gold, she rose and, heedless of the stares of the men around her, changed her clothes. Then she walked to the guard.

"Tell the king his archminister requests a word with him."

She thought he might argue with her, but he seemed to hear something in her tone. He nodded once, then set off across the camp.

When he returned a short while later, one of Kearney's captains was with him.

"I'm to escort you to the king, Archminister."

Keziah nodded. It was a nice touch. It would seem to those watching that Kearney didn't trust her enough to allow her to approach him unguarded. "Very well, Captain. Lead the way."

When they reached Kearney's tent, the captain had the archminister and her guard wait outside while he stepped within and spoke to the king. A moment later he pushed the tent flap aside and motioned for her to enter.

"Thank you, Captain," Kearney said. "Find something to eat. We'll be riding shortly. You, too," he added, looking at the guard.

"Yes, Your Majesty," the captain said.

When both men were gone, Kearney stood, regarding her

with obvious concern. "You don't look well. What's happened?"

"I had a visit from the Weaver last night."

"Are you all right? Did he hurt you?"

"I'm fine," she said, ignoring the second question. "He was angry with me for not killing Cresenne, but he still needs me. Otherwise I'd probably be dead."

"This is madness, Kez! It has to stop!"

"There's no way to stop it except to see it through to the end."

"But—"

"Please," she said, fearing that she might cry at any moment. "Just let me finish. He told me that he intends to kill Cresenne himself. We have to get a message to her, quietly but quickly. She has to know what he plans to do."

"All right. We'll send someone today."

"Thank you." She took a breath, remembering once again the fire that had tortured her the night before. "There's more. He gave me another task, another test of my loyalty to the movement. He wants me to kill you."

Kearney actually smiled. "Is that why you've come?"

She laughed. How could she help it? There were tears in her eyes, but this man had always been able to make her laugh. "I'm to do it during the battle. I won't, of course, but I thought you should know, because he may have others working for him who will make the attempt."

"They won't be alone, Kez. Half the men on that battlefield will be trying to kill me."

"I know. But all the emperor's men are nothing compared to this Weaver and his servants." She swallowed. "I'm afraid for you," she whispered.

Kearney took a step toward her, and, glancing at the tent flap to be certain no one was there, he took her hand. "And I am for you. I suppose somehow we'll have to keep each other safe."

For a moment that stretched to eternity they remained utterly still, their eyes locked. More than anything, Keziah wanted to kiss him; just this once, just so that she could taste his lips again and feel his arms around her. She sensed that he wanted this as well, and she knew that if they unleashed their passion for each other, even if only for one stolen kiss, they would never find the strength to quell it once more.

And so Keziah did the only thing she could, the only thing she dared. Pulling her hand free, she fled the tent.

Chapter Eighteen

Kentigern, Eibithar

For some time now, Aindreas had been preparing the castle and city for a siege, making certain that the quartermaster had all the gold he needed to provision the castle, ordering his swordmaster, Villyd Temsten, to drill the men relentlessly in defensive tactics, and having the prelate and his adherents transform the castle's cloister into a spacious surgeon's chamber. There had been little doubt in his mind that the attack would come, and soon. He hadn't needed his allies in the Qirsi movement to tell him that much. But until this very morning, he hadn't been certain whether the first assault would come from the Aneirans or from the army of Eibithar's king.

Villyd's scouts had been telling him for nearly a turn that the army of Mertesse, just across the river in northern Aneira, was more active than at any time since the siege a year before. And considering all that Aindreas knew of the conspiracy and the recent movements of Braedon's fleet in the waters off northern Eibithar, he fully expected that the renegade Qirsi would do all they could to spark a war along the Tarbin. Why else would they have been pushing him to break with Kearney? United, Eibithar could hold off attacks from both the north and south. Such a war would exact a high price, to be sure, but Aindreas had little doubt that the invaders could be defeated. Divided, however, the realm had a far less certain future.

Aindreas felt certain that had it not been for the presence of Braedon's fleet in the waters off Galdasten, Kearney would already have laid siege to Kentigern Castle. As matters stood, however, the Aneirans were the first to attack the tor. Just after dawn this morning, under cover of a sudden mist no doubt conjured for them by their sorcerers, the soldiers of Mertesse crossed the Tarbin into Eibithar and began building siege engines. Even now, sitting in his presence chamber, drinking his wine, Aindreas could hear the distant beat of axes and hammers on wood and the singing of the Aneiran army. He had stood on the ramparts for a time after Villyd first came to him with word of the mist and the crossing of the river, but the Aneirans remained beyond the reach of Kentigern's archers. There was nothing for any of them to do but watch and wait. A year ago perhaps Aindreas would have stayed with his men. Now all he wished to do was drink his wine and listen in solitude to the sounds of the coming siege.

"Let the Aneirans cross," the Qirsi woman had said. "We want this war."

Yes, but was he to let them have the castle, too? Should he and his men simply lay down their arms, or did his Qirsi masters want him to defend the fortress? In the end Aindreas decided that he didn't care what they expected of him. Kentigern would not fall without a fight. Mertesse could have the rest of the realm for all he cared, but the tor was his. The Tarbin gate, which had failed during the last siege after being weakened by Shurik jal Marcine, his traitorous first minister, had been rebuilt, and though it had not yet been tested in battle, he thought it strong enough to withstand Mertesse's assault. These walls, built and defended by his forebears, would not fail him a second time.

He heard the door creak, and saw Ennis peeking into the chamber. Placing his goblet on the writing table, he rose and stepped around so as to block the cup and flagon from the boy's view.

"Aren't you supposed to be in the cloister?" he asked.

Ennis gave a small shrug. "Father Crasthem says I was in the way."

"Where's your mother?"

"She's in the cloister with the prelate and the surgeon."

This pleased the duke, though it gave him little choice but to let the boy stay. Ioanna continued to show improvement. No matter what happened to him, Ennis and his remaining sister would have their mother to care for them.

"And Affery?" the duke asked, more out of curiosity than any intention to send the boy to her.

"She's helping the kitchenmaster."

"So you've nothing to do."

Ennis shrugged again, looking so much like Aindreas himself that the duke nearly laughed. "I wanted to go up on the walls, but Mother told me I couldn't."

"She was right. It's not safe right now."

"Because of the Aneirans?"

Aindreas sat in a large chair next to his empty hearth, motioning for the boy to climb onto his lap. "Are you frightened?" he asked.

"Not too much. I wouldn't be at all if they hadn't broken the gate the last time."

The boy was clever, a worthy heir to a proud house.

A house you've shamed. You'll leave him nothing but your disgrace.

"You know why they broke the gate last time," Aindreas said, trying to ignore the voice in his mind. "I've explained it to you."

"The Qirsi, you mean. The man who used his magic on the por . . . the por . . ."

"The portcullises. Yes. The gates won't fail this time."

"How do you know that he didn't do it again?"

"Because I have men watching the gates night and day. If the Aneirans want to get into the castle, they'll have to break the portcullises themselves." *Unless they have a shaper with them.* Aindreas shuddered at the thought.

"I heard two of your soldiers talking. They said that the king won't help us. We'll have to beat the Aneirans alone."

Damn them for letting the boy hear such a thing. "You shouldn't be listening to conversations that don't concern you."

"Yes, Father." A pause, and then, "Is it true?"

Aindreas exhaled heavily. "I really don't know what Kearney will do. I suppose it's possible."

Ennis twisted his mouth briefly, as if wishing his father had answered differently. "But we can still win, right?"

"Of course we can." The duke made himself smile. "This castle has stood against the Aneirans for centuries, and if it wasn't for the traitor, it would have held last time, too. We don't need Kearney."

For several moments the boy said nothing, leaning back against Aindreas's chest. Then he tipped his head back to look up at his father's face. "Can I see your dagger again?"

Aindreas grinned, without effort this time. Pulling his blade free, he handed it to the boy, hilt first. "Be careful."

"I know."

He held the dagger reverently, as if it were made of glass, turning it over in his hands, examining the steel with a critical eye and testing its heft in one hand and then the other.

"Why are the Aneirans our enemies?" Ennis asked after some time, still playing with the blade.

"They have been for hundreds of years now. The clans of the north have been fighting the southern families since before the Qirsi Wars and the establishment of the seven realms."

"But why?"

"It started with disputes over land. Now it's mostly about control of the river. The Aneirans used to say that the land between the Tarbin and Kentigern Wood should belong to them."

Ennis looked up again. "You mean they think that the tor is theirs?"

"They used to, yes."

"Is it?"

"No, of course not. It might have belonged to the southern clans once, but when the Forelands were divided into the seven, Eibithar was given all the land south to the river. The Aneirans didn't like it, and they tried to take this land a number of times. But they never succeeded, and every other realm recognized our claim to it."

"But they still think it's theirs."

Aindreas frowned. "Not really. They no longer claim the

land as their own, but they still think of us as their enemy. And I suppose we think of them that way, too. The Tarbin is an important river. During the snows and well into the planting, merchants can sail its waters all the way to the base of the steppe. Eibithar and Aneira share control of the river, and most of the time we trust one another to allow ships from all realms to complete their journeys. But every now and then, we get into fights over who can and can't sail its waters. And occasionally one king or another gets it in his head to imagine what it would be like to control the land on both sides of the river, so that we wouldn't have to share."

Ennis made a face. "That seems dumb."

"Yes, I suppose it does. Kings aren't always as smart as they should be."

"Like Kearney?"

Aindreas looked away. "Kearney's plenty smart." *But the Qirsi are smarter.* "He's a victim of this, too."

"Of what?"

He hadn't intended to speak the words aloud.

"Nothing. Perhaps we should go find your mother. I'd like to see how preparations are going in the Cloister."

"Do we have to?"

The duke hesitated. She'd smell the wine on his breath.

"Not yet. Soon, though."

They sat a while longer, Aindreas gazing toward the window and listening to the hammers and the singing, Ennis intent on the dagger. After a time, the hammering ceased. Aindreas knew what that meant, and so he wasn't surprised by the sharp knock at his door a few moments later.

"Enter," he called.

Ennis had stopped toying with the blade, though he made no move to leave the safety of the duke's lap.

Villyd stepped into the chamber, an avid look in his eyes, as if he were ready to fight the Aneiran army right there. "They're on the move, my lord."

Aindreas nodded. "Very well." He lifted the boy off his lap and turned him around. "You need to go find your mother now. Tell her that the Aneirans are nearing the castle walls."

Ennis gaped at him, wide-eyed and earnest. "Where are you going?"

"Up to the ramparts."

"But you said it wasn't safe."

He cupped the boy's chin in his hand. "It's not safe for a boy, but it's where I belong."

Ennis handed him the dagger, his face as solemn as a prior's.

Aindreas sheathed the blade, then gathered the boy in his arms. "We'll be fine," he whispered. "Take care of your mother and sister for me, all right?"

"Yes, sir."

"Now go." He gave the boy a gentle push toward the door and watched him go. Only when the door had closed behind him did Aindreas stand and turn to the swordmaster.

"Can you tell how many?"

"Not yet, my lord. They're still hiding in the mist. The latest reports we had from the Tarbin put the number near three thousand, most of them from Mertesse, a few from Solkara."

"That's not much of a force."

"The reports were a few days old. They may have more now."

Villyd started to say more, then seemed to stop himself.

"Out with it, swordmaster," the duke said at last. "What's on your mind?"

"It may be nothing, my lord. But we're all aware of the fighting in the north. It seems likely that the emperor and the Aneirans are working together. In which case Mertesse's attack may not be aimed at Kentigern."

"They're preparing siege engines, Villyd. I could hear them building the damned things from my chamber."

"Yes, my lord. But what if the siege is meant only to keep your army occupied, and their true intent is to drive into the heart of the realm?"

Aindreas felt his stomach tightening. "They haven't enough men to try such a thing."

"As I said, my lord, the reports were several days old. They may have more than three thousand by now. And even if they don't, they could commit a thousand soldiers to the siege, leaving two thousand to march inland."

"Two thousand men—"

"Is not many. But when combined with the army of Braedon, it's far more formidable. Certainly it's enough to flank the king's army."

Under most circumstances Aindreas wouldn't have tolerated the interruption, but then again, usually Villyd wouldn't have thought to speak to him so. The swordmaster raised an interesting point. Mertesse had little to gain from another siege, even if it succeeded. But as a diversion from Aneira's larger aims, the siege made a great deal of sense.

The two men left the chamber and began to make their way through the corridors toward the south towers.

"Have you seen any sign that part of their army is trying to slip past us?" the duke asked as they walked.

"No, my lord. But with the sorcerers' mist still covering them, we have no idea how many men are approaching. The rest may already be past us; they may have crossed the Tarbin farther east. Or they may be waiting until the siege is under way and our forces committed to the defense of the city and castle."

Aindreas was barely listening. The more he considered the matter, the more convinced he was that Villyd was right. The siege was secondary; the war in the north would decide Eibithar's fate. The Aneirans had to be stopped here. Aindreas was quite certain, however, that the Qirsi wanted the soldiers of Mertesse to slip past Kentigern. Jastanne would tell him to guard his castle but to make no attempt at stopping the Aneiran advance. *You have doomed your realm, and for nothing—misplaced vengeance and false justice.* He glanced at Villyd, only to find Brienne walking on the far side of the swordmaster, her golden hair shimmering like Panya's Falls at twilight. She stared back at him, her face so grave that it made Aindreas's breath catch in his throat. After a moment, she shook her head, and looked away. She hadn't haunted him since his visit to Bian's Sanctuary, and he had dared hope that she might leave him alone from now on. He should have known better. He had promised her that he would end this alliance with the Qirsi, and he knew that she would hold him to his word.

"What can I do?" he whispered. "There's no way out of this."

"My lord?"

The duke covered his eyes briefly, then looked again. The apparition had vanished.

"Are you all right, my lord?"

Relief and sorrow warred within him. "Yes, I'm fine."

"We were speaking of the Aneirans, my lord. Of the purpose—"

"I know what we were discussing. What would you have me do, swordmaster?"

They entered one of the tower stairways, making their way down to the ward so that they might cross to the castle's outer defenses.

"Send some of your men north, my lord. Send them to Galdasten now, before the siege begins and they can't leave."

Listen to him! Brienne's voice shouted in his mind. *It's not too late to make right again all that you've destroyed!* But while he heard his daughter's voice, it was Jastanne's face that loomed before him, waiflike, yet forbidding. Whatever his uncertainties about the expectations of the conspiracy, he knew how they would respond to any sign that he was breaking his oath to them. Jastanne would expose him as a traitor to the realm, offering as proof the document he had penned for her only a few turns before. There had to be a way out of this, a way to free himself of the conspiracy without disgracing himself and his house. He had no choice but to believe that. But he had yet to find it, and until he did, he could not risk angering the Qirsi.

They entered the south watch tower of the outer wall and started up the stairway to the ramparts. "We haven't enough men to spare, Villyd. It doesn't matter if the Aneirans actually hope to take the tor, or only wish to distract us from their true purpose. Either way, this siege threatens the survival of our house. I'll not weaken our army by chasing phantoms to Galdasten."

"Forgive me for saying so, my lord, but we don't need two thousand men to repel a siege. We can guard the castle and city with half that number."

"The last time I left Kentigern to be guarded by so few, the castle fell."

"That was because of Shurik's treachery, my lord."

"Do you honestly believe that if I had been here, and the men with me, Mertesse would have gained control of the tor, even with the gates weakened?"

The swordmaster could offer but one answer. He looked straight ahead. "No, my lord. Of course not."

They emerged from the stairway into the bright sunshine.

Aindreas held a hand to his brow, shielding his eyes, and looking down on the thick mist that appeared to be crawling up the side of the tor. It wouldn't be long before the Aneirans were at the Tarbin gate. *Let it hold.*

"You don't like being at odds with the Crown, do you, Villyd?"

"No, my lord."

"You think I should have reconciled with Kearney a long time ago. I know that."

"I'm but a warrior, my lord. I know little of court politics."

Aindreas had to grin. "Your reply belies the claim, swordmaster." He waved a hand, as if to dismiss the matter. "It's not important. To be honest, I don't relish being labeled a traitor any more than you do, and I share your concern for the realm. I don't like Kearney and probably I never will, but I have no desire to see Braedon and the Aneirans carving up the kingdom. My first duty, though, is to Kentigern and her people. Until I'm convinced that the tor is safe, I won't send away even a single man. Do I make myself clear?"

"Yes, my lord."

Tearing his gaze from the mist, Aindreas surveyed the castle walls. Already the swordmaster had positioned archers three deep on the top of the wall. They would be ready to loose their arrows as soon as the enemy was within reach.

"You have men preparing fire pots and lime?"

"Yes, my lord. We'll have tar as well. The Aneirans won't have an easy time of it, that's for certain."

Aindreas nodded, surprised by how calm he suddenly felt. "Good." Maybe the gates would hold; maybe they wouldn't. Perhaps the Aneirans were intent on capturing the tor; perhaps, as Villyd suggested, this was all just an elaborate diversion. At least something was finally happening. Yes, the Qirsi still controlled him, and he remained convinced that this siege and the fighting to the north were contrivances of the conspiracy, but once the battles began he'd at least have a chance. The white-hairs couldn't control everything, not amid the turmoil and carnage of war.

A wind began to rise from the south, though the conjured mist clung stubbornly to the side of the tor and the winding road that led from the Tarbin to the castle gate.

"That's a Qirsi wind," Villyd said, eyeing the sky warily. A few pale clouds hung over the city, but they were barely moving. "The Aneirans must think that they're within range of our bowmen."

"Are they?"

The swordmaster looked down on the mist. "Possibly. But we still can't see them."

"How are our stores of long shafts and bolts?"

"We have ample supplies of both, my lord."

"Then let them fly. I want the Aneirans to understand that their Qirsi can't protect them from the soldiers of Kentigern."

At that, the swordmaster faced the duke again, grinning eagerly. "Yes, my lord."

He shouted an order to the archers. Immediately those men with crossbows stepped to the wall and aimed their weapons down at the slope of the tor. Villyd raised his arm, then brought it down sharply. The crossbows snapped loudly in rapid succession, and the bolts whistled as they flew, like trilling birds. A moment later screams of anguish rose from the mist. The first bowmen stepped back, to be replaced at once by archers with longbows. Again the swordmaster's arm rose and fell. Bows thrummed, the long shafts flew, and more cries echoed off the tor and the castle walls.

Aindreas could hear the Aneiran commanders shouting instructions as well, and after a few moments the wind strengthened and shifted so that it blew across the tor. Clearly the attackers wished to make it more difficult for Kentigern's archers to find their mark.

"Continue to loose your arrows, swordmaster," the duke

said. "And call for the tar and fire pots. They're rushing the gate."

The mist had reached the castle entrance and now Aindreas could hear the wheels of the Aneirans' siege engines. There was a pit in the center of the road that had been intended to further impede the approach of snails, rams, and other siege machines. During the last siege, however, the army of Mertesse had filled it in with stones and dirt. In the year since, Aindreas had instructed his men to clear it out once more, but he had been more concerned with the reconstruction of the gate itself, and the pit had been largely neglected. It might slow the Aneirans, but only briefly.

Villyd barked orders, sending men scurrying in every direction. The third line of archers loosed their arrows, and stepped back, making room for the crossbowmen, who had fitted new bolts in their weapons. Soldiers emerged from tower stairways carrying pots of oil and containers of lime, and a short time later, others appeared, with forked poles to fend off the ladders that the Aneirans would use to scale the castle walls. Aindreas was about to call a second time for the tar, when the smell reached him, burning his nostrils. An instant later men appeared in the tower doorways struggling with large vats of the foul stuff.

Villyd shouted again, and the bowmen shifted positions, moving to either side of the Tarbin wall so as to make room for the men with the tar and fire pots.

"All is ready, my lord," the swordmaster said. "We need only wait for the first blow."

"Very well, Villyd. Have the archers continue to fire."

"Yes, my lord."

After but a few seconds the crossbows crackled again, and more howls rent the air. Then one round of longbows. And the other. An otherworldly stillness settled over the tor, broken only by the pulsing of bows, the whistle of arrows, and the shrieks of those dying below the castle ramparts.

Aindreas peered down at the mist again, waiting for the assault on the gate to commence, listening for any indication of what the Aneirans were doing. As he did, he suddenly felt the hairs on his neck stand on end, as if some wraith from Bian's realm had run a ghostly finger down his spine. Unsure as to why he did it, the duke straightened and turned, looking north, toward the shores of the Strait of Wantrae.

Atop a small rise, not far from the city walls, a slight figure sat atop a white mount, seeming to stare back at him. For just a single heartbeat, Aindreas thought it was Brienne, or at least the apparition of his beloved child, haunting him once more. But as he continued to watch the rider, sunlight burst forth from behind a cloud, lighting the figure's hair and face. Both were as white as bleached bone. Jastanne.

"Is something wrong, my lord?"

Aindreas turned so quickly that he nearly lost his balance. "No. I was just—" He shook his head. "It was nothing."

"Of course, my lord."

"Was there something you wanted, Villyd?"

"Yes, my lord. I was wondering if you wanted to send men out to strike at the Aneirans?"

The duke narrowed his eyes, thinking that the swordmaster was trying once more to get him to send part of his army northward. "I thought we had discussed this."

"No, my lord. I mean to strike at them here. We can send a small party of archers out of the east sally port to attack the siege machines as they reach the gate. But we'd need to do it now, while they still have their mists about them. This won't work if the men can be seen."

Aindreas nodded. "Give the order, swordmaster."

"Yes, my lord," Villyd said and hurried away.

The duke turned to look toward the rise again, but Jastanne was gone.

A cry went up from Aindreas's men, and before the duke even had time to turn toward the sound, the castle shuddered, as from a blow. The assault on the gate had begun.

Aindreas strode to Villyd's side and looked down at the side of the tor. The mist was gone, and he could see the ram poised just in front of the gate. Its wooden roof was covered with animal skins, as were the roofs of the snails that still crawled up the road, protecting much of the Aneiran army. The duke heard the Aneirans within the ram shouting in cadence and the castle shook a second time. Yet for all the power of the blow, it seemed that the new gate was holding.

"Fire pots!" Villyd called. "Lime and tar as well! Archers, flaming arrows!"

In another moment, all on the castle walls was frenzy. Ladders rose to the ramparts as if sprouting from the earth, and Aneiran soldiers began to climb them under the cover of volleys from their own archers. Kentigern's men used the forked poles to push the ladders away, sending enemy soldiers tumbling to the ground. Others used torches to light the oil pots, which they then dropped on the ram and snail. Still others poured tar over the edge of the ramparts, drawing wails of pain from below. When a few of the enemy managed to gain the top of the wall, they were immediately beset by swordsmen. Several of the Aneiran bowmen found their mark, killing a number of Aindreas's men, including one soldier only a few fourspans from where the duke stood. Still, most of the casualties in these first moments of the siege were inflicted on the attackers.

"You planned well, swordmaster," the duke said, toppling a ladder himself and ducking beneath a flurry of arrows. The fortress shuddered once more.

"Thank you, my lord." Villyd's tone was a match for his grim expression.

"You're not pleased?"

The man nodded toward the river by way of answer.

Following the direction of the swordmaster's gaze Aindreas saw them as well, though the Aneirans had tried to hide their work within the trees and rushes growing along the Tarbin. Hurling arms. Four of them. They hadn't been completed yet, but from the look of them, it wouldn't be long.

"How can they have built them so quickly?"

"I'd guess that they cut and prepared the timber in Mertesse before crossing the Tarbin, my lord. At least, that's what they did last time."

"Of course."

Another blow to the gate.

"Last time they had only one."

"They only needed one. Shurik had seen to the gates."

"Yes, my lord. I expected two this time, perhaps three. But not four."

"The walls will hold, Villyd. They always have."

"Of course, my lord. But still I fear for the men. No part of the wall will be safe."

"We may have to send out parties through the sally ports after all. Not yet, not until we have an idea of where they intend to place the arms. But you should begin forming several parties of your best archers and swordsmen. Have them ready to go when I give the word."

"Yes, my lord. I'll see to it right away." He sketched a quick bow and returned to the men.

Aindreas looked down at the Aneirans again as yet another jolt from the ram forced him to grip the stone wall. Then he glanced northward, at the rise. There was no sign of the Qirsi woman.

Leaving the walls, the duke descended the stairs again, hurrying back to the inner keep. He had intended to make his way to the cloister, to check on Ioanna and the children. Somehow, however, he ended up back at the door to his presence chamber. Shaking his head, he turned away, again intending to walk to the cloister.

It was the wine that stopped him. He could never admit as much to anyone, certainly not the duchess. A duke shouldn't drink during a siege, not while his men were fighting and dying. But Aindreas knew that the flagon of Sanbiri red was still there on his writing table, just where he had left it.

He rubbed a hand over his face, wanting to walk away, unable to make himself leave.

"Go to them, Father. Mother and Affery and Ennis. They're all waiting for you."

He gave Brienne a sad smile. She was so beautiful, just as her mother once had been. His heart ached at the mere sight of her. "I want to," he said. "Truly I do."

"Then go. Walk away now. Leave the wine."

"It's not as easy as all that. You know the things I've done."

"Yes, Father, I do. And I know as well that it doesn't matter. Go to them, while there's still time."

"I will," he told her, taking hold of the door handle. "Soon. I swear it."

He turned his back to her, knowing that she'd go away. She always did.

"Oh, Father," he heard her sigh as he pushed the door open and stepped into his presence chamber.

Crossing to the table, he grabbed the flagon and filled his goblet.

"I thought there was someone with you."

He spun, spilling wine on his table and on the stone floor.

Jastanne stood before him, an insolent smirk on her youthful face. "I heard you speaking just before you opened the door."

"How did you get in here?"

The smirk broadened into a grin. "Does it really matter?"

He pulled his sword from its sheath. "Yes, it does."

Her golden eyes dropped to the blade for just an instant before locking on his again. All traces of mirth had fled her face. "You realize that I can shatter that sword with a thought. And I can do the same to every bone in your body."

In his rage, he had forgotten that she was a shaper. He longed to kill her, but he didn't dare chance an attempt. He knew all too well what a Qirsi with shaping power could do, be it to the gates of his castle or to his neck. After a moment, he returned the sword to his belt. "I want to know how you got in," he said, though he could do nothing to compel a reply.

To her credit, Jastanne seemed to sense how important this was to him. "I used one of the sally ports. Your guards are more concerned just now with parties of Aneirans than they are with a lone Qirsi."

"How did you know about the sally port?"

"Before you banished all the Qirsi from your castle, we had . . . allies in your court. Our knowledge of Kentigern Castle is extensive." Then, as if to soften the words, she added, "Though no more extensive than our knowledge of the castles in Thorald, Galdasten, even the City of Kings."

"So you can come here unbidden any time you like. You could kill me in my sleep if you wanted to."

The smile sprang to her lips again. "Why would we want to?" When he said nothing, she gave a small shrug. "I suppose we could. As I said, with the siege under way, your guards are intent on the Aneirans. They know me from my previous visits, so even if they saw me, they probably would let me pass. Under other circumstances, that might not be the case."

Aindreas wasn't satisfied by this, but he hadn't the time to pursue the matter further. "Why are you here?" He stopped, eyeing her closely. "Was that you I saw just a short time ago, on the rise north of the castle?"

"Yes, it was. Word of the Aneirans' advance reached the piers a short time ago. I came here to make certain that you know what we want of you."

"I intend to defend my castle."

"Of course you do, Lord Kentigern. We'd expect no less." Something, a catch in the voice. He knew what she'd say next. "But we also expect no more."

"The Aneirans are going to march north, to Galdasten."

Her eyebrows went up. "I'm impressed."

Aindreas looked away, feeling ill. "Actually," he said, not certain why he bothered, "my swordmaster suggested that they would."

"Really? Who'd have thought that an Eandi warrior could be so clever?"

"You want me to let them go."

"Yes. They'll wait until the siege is well under way—I imagine you'll have little choice but to use all your men in the defense of your city and castle. But just in case you have it in mind to stop them, don't."

"You have allies in Mertesse, as well. Or perhaps in Solkara." *Or is it both?* When she didn't answer, he said, "My swordmaster all but begged me to divide my army in order to keep the Aneirans from getting past Kentigern."

"And what did you tell him?"

"That I was most concerned with the defense of the tor, and that I wouldn't take even a single man off the castle walls until I was certain that Aneira's siege had been broken."

"Excellent. Then you have nothing to worry about." But

there was a brittle quality to her voice, as though she sensed that he was wavering.

"We're nearing the end of all this, aren't we?"

"The end of what?" she asked, in a way that made him certain that they were.

"This is what your leaders have been waiting for. This siege, the naval war in Falcon Bay." He forced a smile, despite the pain in his gut. "We're allies, Jastanne. Surely you can tell me this much."

She regarded him briefly, before stepping to the door. "Guard your castle, Lord Kentigern. There may be more to this siege than there appears, but that doesn't mean that the Aneirans are any less earnest in their desire to destroy you. You'd be wise to remain true to your word. Defend your castle, and leave the rest to us." She left him then, her words hanging in the air, pungent as black smoke. And she closed the door so softly that he never heard the latch slip back in place.

Chapter Nineteen

City of Kings, Eibithar

It had taken her some time to adjust to all the changes in her life. Not just bearing a child, watching as her body was transformed to accommodate the tiny life within her, and watching now as she slowly returned to what she remembered as normal. Not just the swelling of her breasts and what seemed to be the doubling of her appetite, as she started to nurse Bryntelle. In order to ensure her survival and that of her daughter, Cresenne ja Terba had altered the rhythm of their existence.

The scars from her last encounter with the Weaver had

faded almost to white. They would always be visible, but they didn't mar her face as once they had. Her hand, which the Weaver had shattered with a mere thought, no longer pained her. She could move the fingers almost as she had before that night, and from what Grinsa had told her, she knew that eventually even this small amount of stiffness would vanish. The Weaver had dealt her other injuries as well, but they too had mended, either on their own or under her beloved gleaner's healing touch. Yet, while the pain the Weaver had caused her was but a memory, and the physical evidence of his attack a shadow of what it once had been, the terror instilled in her by that horrible night remained as raw and crippling as a fresh battle wound.

At Grinsa's urging, she had turned her life topsy-turvy, sleeping by day and keeping herself awake throughout the night. The gleaner had explained that contacting another Qirsi through his or her dreams demanded a great deal of any Weaver, requiring time to prepare beforehand, a tremendous expenditure of magic during the dream itself, and more time to recover afterward. Grinsa believed that the Weaver who led the Qirsi movement was a court Qirsi serving a duke, maybe even a sovereign. And because of the demands placed on such a man by the Eandi noble he served, he would have little opportunity during the day to make a second attempt on her life.

"Sleeping during the day won't keep you safe forever," Grinsa had told her while he was still with her in the City of Kings, "but it will protect you for a time, and perhaps that will be enough."

At the time, Cresenne had wanted desperately to believe him, and in the turns since she had come to accept that he was right. Yet every morning, as the castle began to bustle with activity, and she and her child lay down to rest, she wondered if this would be the day when she closed her eyes for the last time.

She had come to enjoy the solitude of her nights. With the king leading his army to war in the north, and Eibithar's other nobles long since gone, Cresenne and Bryntelle were no longer confined to the chamber in the castle's prison tower. Though they could not leave Audun's Castle, they were free to wander its corridors and courtyards. There were guards on duty at all hours, of course, and they eyed her with manifest distrust. But she saw few people aside from them. Occasionally she sat in one of the wards, staring up at the moons or Morna's stars. Mostly, though, she just walked, singing to Bryntelle, or speaking to her of Grinsa, of her own mother and father, of the world that awaited the girl.

Once, when Cresenne still belonged to the Weaver's movement, she had cursed this world, where the Eandi ruled in all the noble courts, and the success of a Qirsi was measured by how far she advanced in the ministerial ranks or which of the traveling festivals she managed to join. Holding Bryntelle in her arms, however, she found that the world no longer seemed quite so bleak. There was beauty to be found here, and joy, and, yes, love. It wasn't just that she no longer shared the Weaver's desire to change the Forelands. Rather, she feared what might be lost if he and his movement prevailed.

Had she found virtue in the Eandi courts? No, far from it. She had merely come to understand that there was more to the world than nobles and ministers, Qirsi and Eandi.

For her part, Bryntelle seemed perfectly content to listen to her mother's prattle and poor singing. She could stare up at the moons for hours without growing bored or distracted. And on more than one occasion Cresenne had noticed that the child grew especially animated when she heard tales of Grinsa, cooing loudly and giving a wide toothless grin.

On this particular night, they had been forced by rain and a chill wind to remain within the corridors. Cresenne kept to the south end of the castle, away from the queen's tower. Leilia, the queen, apparently had little use for Qirsi and had instructed the guards to keep "the traitor" as far from her as possible. Cresenne was more than happy to comply, having no more wish to encounter the queen than the woman had to cross paths with her.

The midnight bells tolled in the city as she and Bryntelle turned yet another corner onto a torchlit corridor. She had only taken a few steps when she caught sight of the man at the far end of the passageway, lurking near one of the chamber doors. She halted, then took a step back.

He was Qirsi. Cresenne could tell that much. He was tall and so lean that he looked frail. But something about him frightened her. Perhaps it was merely his presence here in the hallway. She saw so few people during the night that any encounter struck her as odd. But more than that, he was one of her people, and she didn't recognize him. A voice in her mind screamed at her to flee. The Weaver had servants throughout the Forelands, including men and women right here in the City of Kings, perhaps even in Audun's Castle. If he couldn't reach her by entering her dreams, he could send any one of them to kill her.

She was in a dark portion of the hallway and she took another step back, hoping that he hadn't seen her, wondering if she could slip back into the corridor she had just left and return to the safety of her chamber. Before Cresenne could take another step, however, Bryntelle let out a small cry. It wasn't loud, but it was enough to draw the attention of the strange man.

He looked up sharply, then strode toward her. Pausing at a torch, he lifted it out of its brace and continued down the corridor, holding the flame high to light his way. Halfway to where she stood, he cast a quick look over his shoulder. Cresenne wondered if he had an accomplice. She thought about running, but with Bryntelle in her arms, she wouldn't have gotten far, and she wasn't certain it was wise to turn her back on the man. Instead she stood her ground. She possessed fire power, and she reached for it now, readying herself for battle, should it come to that.

As the man drew nearer she saw that despite his slight build, he was young, with ghostly pale eyes, a severe, angular face, and close-cropped white hair.

"Stop where you are," she said, when he was still a few strides away from her.

He slowed, looking confused. "What?" He switched the torch to his other hand and reached for something on his belt.

"Stop there!" She held out a hand in warning, clutching Bryntelle to her side with her other arm until the child cried out a second time.

The man halted, raising both hands, as if to show her that he carried no weapon. He still clutched in his hand the object he had taken from his belt, but Cresenne couldn't tell what it was. "All right, I've stopped."

"Who are you?"

"My name is Nurle jal Danteffe. I'm a healer here in the castle."

"What's that in your hand?"

He looked at the object, then held it out to her on an open palm. It was a vial of some sort.

"What is that? Poison?"

"Poison? No. It's a tonic, for the man I was just treating. I thought you were his wife. I sent her away with their child, but I thought perhaps she had returned." He frowned. "Poison?" he said again. "I told you, I'm a healer."

She scrutinized his face. "I don't recognize you."

"Well, I haven't been here very long. I came with the king from Glyndwr."

Glyndwr? Cresenne felt herself begin to relax. He didn't even know who she was, or else he would have realized that she had come to Audun's Castle well after he did. "I suppose that must be why."

Nurle glanced back over his shoulder. "Do you live on this corridor?"

"No, I—" She shook her head. "Our chamber is near the stock house. We were just walking."

"Well, you might want to consider a different corridor. There's a man in the chamber at the far end—one of the older courtiers. He has a fever, and a rash. I fear it may be Caerissan pox." He nodded toward Bryntelle. "It wouldn't be good if the little one got it."

A different kind of fear gripped Cresenne's heart and she looked past the healer, as if expecting the sick man to step out of his chamber and join their conversation. "Yes, of course."

"What's his name?" Nurle asked.

"What? Oh, actually, she's a girl. Her name is Bryntelle."

The man smiled. "My apologies, Bryntelle." He shifted his gaze to Cresenne, the smile lingering. "And yours?"

She looked down at her child, not wanting to answer, but not knowing how to extricate herself from the conversation. In the end she decided that it was best just to tell him and be done with it. "My name is Cresenne."

"Cres—" He faltered, recognition flashing in his eyes. "You're her, aren't you? I should have known. I've heard of the attack on you, and of your wanderings at night." Abruptly his eyes widened. "That's why you thought it was poison! You thought I was . . . I'm sorry I frightened you."

"It's all right."

He took a step forward, then halted again. "May I?"

Cresenne hesitated, then nodded.

The healer came closer, and examined her face. "You've healed well," he said. "The scars are hardly noticeable."

"Thank you," she whispered. "We should probably go."

"I'm sorry. I didn't mean to make you uncomfortable."

"You didn't. I just know . . ." She shook her head. "Most people prefer to avoid us."

He frowned again. "Why?"

She looked at him as if he were simple. "Because of all that I've done. I'm a traitor."

"You were a traitor. It seems to me that you're not anymore."

"You're more generous than most."

He shrugged again, suddenly looking bashful. "Maybe. But I think you're very brave."

She couldn't help but smile. It wasn't the first time a young Qirsi man had been taken with her. "Thank you. Still, I think it's time we were going."

"I guess I should as well." He flashed another grin. "I have to get my sleep at night." He started back toward the ill man's chamber, then stopped himself. "If you see any others heading this way, tell them about the pox. I don't want anyone walking the corridor who doesn't have to be here."

"I will."

He nodded before turning again and walking back to the sick man's chamber.

It wasn't until after Nurle had left her that Cresenne realized she was trembling, her heart pounding. She tried to laugh at her foolishness, but abruptly found that tears were coursing down her cheeks.

"Damn him!" Not Nurle, of course, but the Weaver. There had been a time when Cresenne thought herself fearless, when she had been content to wander the land on her own as a member of the festivals. In the wake of the Weaver's attack, she feared for her life every day, though she never ventured beyond the walls of the strongest fortress in the northern Forelands. Even now, knowing that she had been wrong to distrust the healer, she could not resist the urge to hurry back to her chamber. She tried to tell herself that she did so to feed Bryntelle in privacy, but she knew better, having nursed the child in the courtyards, as well as in empty galleries and corridors. Still, only when she had reached her bedchamber, closed the door, and pushed the bolt home did she feel herself beginning to grow calm again. Soon, she was sitting by the lone, narrow window in her chamber, listening to the rain as Bryntelle suckled at her breast. But just remembering that instant when she first saw Nurle in the corridor was enough to send a shudder through her body.

"I miss your father, little one," she said, her eyes misting.

She passed the rest of the night singing to her daughter within the confines of the tiny room. Only when the sky finally began to brighten to a pale silver grey, did she venture out once more, descending the nearest of the tower stairways to the kitchen, where she ate a small supper. Then she returned to the chamber, locked the door again, and sang Bryntelle to sleep. Reluctantly, Cresenne lay down beside the child, knowing she needed to sleep, but fearing even this. After only a few moments, she rose once more to check the bolt on her door. Satisfied that it was secure she crossed back to her bed and eventually fell asleep.

She found herself on a sunlit plain, grasses dancing in a soft wind that carried a hint of brine.

Grinsa! she had time to think, turning to look for him.

At first she didn't recognize the man who loomed before her so suddenly, wrapping a powerful hand around her throat and lifting her off the ground. Bright golden eyes, hair like a lion's mane, a square, chiseled face. But as soon as he spoke, she knew, hearing her doom in the powerful voice.

"You thought you could escape me!" His eyes were wide, his lips pulled back in a feral grin. "You thought that I wouldn't find you if you slept away the last of your days. You're a fool, and so is Grinsa."

She clawed at his hand, fighting for breath. But his fingers were like steel. In a distant corner of her mind, she marveled that he would let her see his face and this plain. *He has nothing to fear from you anymore. He has no reason to hide himself.*

"I want you to beg me for your life."

She merely stared at him, unable to speak, and unwilling.

He balled his free hand into a fist and hammered it into her cheek. "Beg me!"

Her vision swam, tears stinging her eyes as the pain reached her.

"You think you're brave. You're not. I smell your fear; you stink of it."

He hit her again, and a third time. Pain exploded in her mind, white and hot and merciless. She felt blood on her cheek, but couldn't bring herself to reach up a hand. Her lungs burned for air and her throat ached.

Oh, Grinsa . . .

"He can't help you. He's leagues away, riding to a war he can't win." He narrowed his eyes. "Don't you find that strange? He claims to love you and that child of yours. Certainly he's the only one who can protect you. Yet when you need him most, he's off with his Eandi friends. How very sad."

She was kicking her feet, her eyes feeling as if they might burst from her skull at any moment. Consciousness began to slip away, and Cresenne welcomed the darkness as she would rest after an overlong journey.

"No," the Weaver said, the word seeming to come from a great distance. "I won't let you die yet. Your love can't stop me—I can do with you what I like."

He released her, allowing her to tumble to the ground. Cresenne curled herself into a ball, sobbing and gasping for breath. What was it Grinsa and Keziah had told her?

"I once thought to make you my queen." He gave a bitter laugh. "Now look at you, the whore of another Qirsi, mother of his bastard child."

"She's not a bastard," Cresenne said, her chest still heaving for lack of air, her words coming out as no more than a whisper. "And I'm no whore."

"Aren't you? You took to his bed because I paid you gold to

do so. And then you betrayed me—you betrayed this movement—just to save yourself and your child. If you're not a whore, then I don't know who is."

The Weaver was standing over her, and now he reached down, grabbed her shift, and tore it with one violent motion, so that she lay naked beneath him. He dropped down on top of her, grabbing her breasts viciously and squeezing them until she cried out in pain. Then he forced his knee between her legs. Panic took hold of her and she fought him as best she could, slapping and clawing at his face, clenching her thighs together. He struck her twice, even harder than he had before, leaving her addled and weeping. He forced her legs wide and though she tried to resist, there was nothing she could do. An instant later he plunged into her, tearing her flesh, ripping a scream from her lips.

Again she fought him, but he had a hand on her throat again, and with the other grabbed a handful of her hair. She tried to summon her magic, but she couldn't. It almost seemed that she had lost all her power. She closed her eyes tight and turned her face away, choking back a sob, refusing to give him the satisfaction of hearing her cry. She tried to send her mind away, to think of Bryntelle, of Grinsa, of anything but what he was doing to her. But she couldn't escape the pain, or his hot breath on her neck, or his animal grunts as he drove into her again and again.

After an eternity, marked by the awful rhythm of his movements and the sharp repetition of agony, he finally climaxed with one last racking thrust. He rested for a moment, his full weight bearing down on her, his breath heavy.

"There," he whispered, as if a lover. "Now you're my whore as well."

She turned at that, looking up at his face. And she spat.

The Weaver recoiled, pulling out of her roughly, spittle dripping down his cheek. Seeing him back away emboldened her. Eager now to hurt him, she tried once more to reach for her fire magic. But almost before she could form the thought, he was on her once more, one hand around her neck yet again, and the other, alive with white flame, searing the flesh on her face.

"You'll pay dearly for that!"

Cresenne howled, trying to pull away. But even as she did, a thought came to her, a memory. *He uses your magic against you.* That's what Grinsa had told her, so long ago it might have been another lifetime. Is that what the Weaver had just done? She had thought to summon fire magic, but he did it instead. Then another thought. *He let himself be seen, he brought sunlight to this plain not because he knew he had nothing to fear, but because he didn't want me to know right off that it was him. He was afraid I would resist.*

The Weaver held the flaming hand to her face again. But rather than fight to break free of him, she reached for her power. *Her* power. And this time she found it. The flame sputtered suddenly, then went out.

Cresenne sensed him grasping for the magic again, felt him struggling to reassert his control over her, and she clung to her power with all the strength she had left. He raised a hand to strike her.

"No," she said. Healing magic. That was the other power he had used against her. That was how he had cut her face last time. No doubt that was how he had hurt her tonight, perhaps that was how he had raped her. It didn't matter. The magic was hers, and she would not let him have it again.

"You think that I can't hurt you?" He slapped her across the burned cheek.

Anguish. She felt her certainty crumble. The flame jumped to life in his hand.

"No," she said again. It was her magic. Grinsa had told her so, and she would die believing him if it came to that. The fire died again. "Perhaps you can hurt me," she said. "But you'll not use my magic to do it."

"I don't need your magic." A blade flashed in his hand and he stabbed down at her chest.

She felt the steel pierce her heart, her back arching in agony, despair and horror clawing at her mind. But still she clung to her magic. It was all she had left. If this was to be the end, she would perish fighting him, forcing him to use whatever power he possessed to kill her. But she wouldn't die by her own magic, not if she could help it. And staring at the knife, she saw her skin seal itself around the blade. There was no blood at all.

"He was right," she said breathlessly.

The Weaver roared his rage, pulled his dagger from her, and lifted it to strike again.

But now she knew. It was her power. More to the point, it was her dream. "You'll not kill me today," she said. "You won't kill me at all."

He just stared at her, as if she had transformed herself into a goddess before his eyes.

"You'll die by Grinsa's hand," she said. "There's nothing you can do to save yourself. I'm a gleaner. That's the other magic I possess. And that's the fate I foresee for you."

With that, she forced her eyes open.

Bryntelle was bawling, her face red and damp with tears. Cresenne's own face felt bruised and swollen; her cheek was screaming agony where the Weaver had burned her. And her entire body ached from being brutalized. She was crying as well, and she gathered the baby in her arms, holding her until their sobbing had eased. Diverse emotions warred within her: humiliation at what he had done to her was tempered by pride in how she stood up to him; her relief at finding a way to take control of her magic and escape her dream could not overcome the terror of knowing that the Weaver would find some way to strike at her again. He had tormented and defiled her—who could say if the scars he had left on her mind and body would ever heal?—and yet, by virtue of her survival, she had defeated him. Cresenne lay there holding Bryntelle, weeping, trying to muster the strength and courage to call for a healer. And with tears still in her eyes, she began to laugh. She worried for the soundness of her mind, and yet once she started, she couldn't stop. The child stopped crying and stared at her quizzically.

"I won, Bryntelle. I know it doesn't look like it, but I won."

The baby's expression didn't change, and at last, Cresenne's unnatural mirth began to subside, leaving her spent and teary once more.

She must have fallen asleep again, for she was awakened some time later by knocking at her door. Bryntelle stirred but didn't open her eyes. Careful not to wake her, Cresenne rose, covered herself with a robe, and walked stiffly to the door. She unlocked the bolt and opened the door, finding a guard in the corridor. He held a piece of parchment in his hand, but seeing her, he merely stared, his dark eyes widening.

"I need a healer," she said. Then, remembering her encounter from the night before, she added, "I'd like Nurle. I don't know his whole name. Can you send for him please?"

"Yes," the guard said. "Yes, of course."

He hurried away and Cresenne pushed the door closed before returning to her bed.

In only a few moments, another knock sounded at her door, and at her summons, Nurle entered the chamber. He winced when he saw her and crossed the room quickly to sit beside her on the bed.

"What happened?" he asked.

"The Weaver came for me again last night."

"Your face looks a mess, but I can mend it. Did he hurt you anywhere else?"

She closed her eyes, feeling tears fall again. Had she really been laughing just a short time before?

"There's blood on your bedding."

"Yes. He—" She swallowed, her eyes still shut. "He raped me."

"Demons and fire!" He faltered. "I've never . . . I wouldn't know how—"

"It's all right. I have healing magic. I can see to those wounds myself."

"I'm sorry," he whispered.

She forced her eyes open, made herself look at him. "Don't be. I'm glad you're here."

Nurle managed a smile. "Lie down. Let me start with that burn."

The healer might have been young, but he had a deft touch. Within moments, the scorching pain in her cheek began to ease, as if cool water flowed from the man's hands into the wound. By the time he finished with the burn and turned his attention to her bruises, the fire in her flesh had been doused entirely, leaving only a dull ache that she knew would vanish within a day or two.

"Thank you," she murmured. "That's much better."

Soon, Nurle had healed her bruises as well. He sat back, taking a long breath, his face flushed and covered with a faint sheen of sweat.

"Is there anything more I can do for you?" he asked, sounding weary.

Cresenne shook her head. "I don't think so." She rolled away from him and opened her robe to look at her chest where the Weaver had stabbed at her. The skin was unmarked. "No," she said, with more certainty. "I'm fine."

He nodded grimly. "Then I'll leave you for now. I'll return shortly with a sleeping tonic."

"No!" she said, panic flooding her heart.

"You need rest. I know that you won't sleep during the night, so I want you going back to sleep now, while you can."

I can't sleep at all, she wanted to say, though she knew how ridiculous that would sound. Earlier she had been celebrating her victory over the Weaver. Now, faced with the prospect of meeting him again, she quailed. *I'm a fool.*

"If I sleep, he may come for me again."

A gentle smile touched the healer's lips, reminding her oddly of Grinsa. "So you're never going to sleep again?"

"That's not what I mean."

"All I can tell you, Cresenne, is what I know as a healer. You need rest. You have healing magic, too, so you know that I'm right."

She did. "All right. Nothing too strong, though. A bit of betony perhaps, mixed with just a bit of sweetwort. I have to be able to wake myself. It's bad enough battling the Weaver, but if I'm fighting your tonic as well, he'll kill me."

Nurle frowned, but gave a reluctant nod. "All right. Betony and sweetwort then. I'll return soon."

Once he was gone, and her door closed again, Cresenne removed her robe and began to heal herself, cursing the Weaver repeatedly all the while. When she had finished and put on a new shift, she felt nearly whole again, though more tired than she had been since the earliest days of Bryntelle's life, when sleep had been a precious thing. She sat on the bed once more, and gazed at her daughter until Nurle's knock drew her attention.

When the door opened, however, it was another Qirsi who entered the chamber, one of the older healers, a man she had seen in the castle corridors many times before.

"Where's Nurle?"

"Another patient required his attention," the Qirsi said, closing the door. "A man with Caerissan pox. Nurle told me to prepare this sleeping tonic for you. I believe you wanted betony and sweetwort?"

"Yes, thank you."

He handed her a small cup of hot liquid, taking a moment to examine her face. "Nurle does good work. I'll have to commend him to the master healer."

"Yes, do," she said. She sipped the tonic, making a face at the the overly sweet taste. "How much sweetwort is in this?" she asked.

"Not very much, I assure you. But I added a bit of wild rose to sweeten the tea. I'm told that the queen likes this a good deal. Don't you?"

"Not really."

He reached for the cup. "Would you like me to make a fresh cup for you?"

She shook her head, taking a second sip. "That's all right, thank you."

"Of course. If there's nothing else . . ."

"No, nothing. Again, my thanks."

He tipped his head in reply and left her.

Cresenne finished the tea, then lay down and closed her eyes, falling asleep almost instantly.

The next thing she knew, someone was shaking her, calling her name. She could hear Bryntelle crying, but she couldn't bring herself to open her eyes. Her heart was pounding and she felt hot, as if fevered.

"Cresenne, wake up!"

Somehow she was sitting up. It took her a moment to realize that strong hands were holding her up, gripping her arms. She forced her eyes open. The chamber seemed to pitch and roll; she found it hard to see anything clearly.

"It's Nurle. Can you hear me?"

"Nurle," she said, her voice sounding strange to her own ears. "I don't feel well."

"You're burning with fever. Is it possible that the Weaver did something else to you, something you didn't mention before?"

"The Weaver?"

"Yes. Do you remember the Weaver?"

Her mouth felt dry. She thought of the healer's tonic and gagged. "No. The Weaver didn't do this." She tried to turn toward the small table where she had placed the cup, though she could tell that her head merely lolled to the side. "The sleep tonic."

"Sweetwort and betony wouldn't do this to you."

She shook her head again, felt consciousness slipping away. "The tonic . . . something else in . . ."

"What?" He laid her down gently.

Cresenne closed her eyes once more.

"Demons and fire!" she heard from what seemed a great distance.

Then she was sitting up again, her head falling back.

"Cresenne! Stay awake, Cresenne! Speak to me! Who gave you this tonic?"

"The healer. You sent."

"What healer?"

"The healer. He lives. Here."

"You mean Lenvyd?"

"Yes."

"Impossible! Guard!" he shouted.

Cresenne wanted to ask him what was impossible, but the words wouldn't come.

She heard another voice, and then Nurle again. ". . . the herbmaster! Tell him to bring mustard and bryony, and quickly! She's taken nightshade. And find Lenvyd . . . The healer who was in here earlier today!"

"Bryony," she said, or at least tried to say. "That's poison."

"You've been poisoned," Nurle told her. "The bryony and mustard will purge the poison. That's what we need now."

"Lenvyd?"

"I don't know where he is, but I'll find him. You have my word."

She tried to say more, but couldn't. And a moment later she didn't even remember what she had intended to say. Bryntelle was still crying. Cresenne knew that she needed to do something, but it was all she could do to remain awake. She wasn't even certain that she did that much.

"Drink this," Nurle said suddenly, holding a cup to her lips.

She tried to turn away, but someone held her fast. She flailed with her arms and legs, but it seemed that others took hold of her, forcing the foul liquid into her mouth. She swallowed a bit, sputtered, fought to get away. More was forced into her mouth—she was helpless to stop them. They were killing her and she could do nothing to defend herself.

Her stomach heaved, and she vomited. They forced her to drink once more and again she felt the bile rising in her throat. She clamped her teeth shut, but it was no good. She retched and retched until her throat and stomach ached.

Then, at last, they released her, allowing her to lie back and rest.

When Cresenne woke next, her chamber was dark. Bryntelle was awake, cooing beside her, sounding happy and calm. Somehow they had gotten her to stop crying.

Cresenne tried to sit up, but found that she was too weak.

"Don't move yet. You're not ready." A candle jumped to life next to her bed revealing Nurle, sitting in a chair on the far side of the small chamber. "How do you feel?"

"Terrible. My head hurts, and I don't think I'll ever be hungry again."

A wry smile touched his lips and was gone. "You're fortunate to be alive. For a time there, I thought we were going to lose you."

"I was poisoned?"

He nodded. "Nightshade. Had it not been for one of the guards hearing your daughter cry and trying to wake you, we wouldn't have gotten to you in time."

"Do you know why he did it?"

"Lenvyd, you mean? No, we never got the chance to ask him. It seems that he fled the castle not long after giving you the tonic."

"Send men for him! He couldn't have gotten far."

"We did. They didn't find him."

"But they should still be looking! He might still be . . ." She trailed off, seeing the smile on his face.

"You don't seem to understand, Cresenne. He left here three days ago."

"Three days!" she said, breathless. "I've been . . . ?" She closed her eyes. "Three days."

"Like I said, I thought we were going to lose you."

"But Bryntelle—"

"We found a wet nurse in the city. Bryntelle is fine."

She just stared up at the ceiling, trying to grasp what he had told her. *Three days.* After what seemed a long time, she said, "Thank you," her voice so low that she wondered if he even heard. She lifted Bryntelle onto her chest and held the girl close, silent tears running down her face.

"The master healer wanted me to convey his apologies to you. He feels responsible, having trusted Lenvyd all these years."

"I'm not sure I believe you, Nurle. Why would the king's master healer bother apologizing to a known traitor?"

"Because he's a healer before all else. We're trained to care for those who are ill or wounded, regardless of who they are. To do what Lenvyd did . . ." He shook his head, clearly troubled. "It's not right."

Cresenne couldn't remember having met the master healer. She couldn't even say for certain what he looked like. Probably she meant no more to him than did any other patient. But neither did she mean any less. "Tell the master healer that I'm grateful to him."

"I will."

Bryntelle began to fuss, and Cresenne made herself sit up, enduring a bout of dizziness that turned her stomach.

"You should rest."

"I want to feed her."

The healer must have sensed her resolve. He merely nodded. When she opened her robe he averted his gaze, but he didn't leave as she had feared he might. Soon Bryntelle was suckling greedily. Cresenne closed her eyes and leaned back against the wall.

"He'll head north," she said, after a lengthy silence.

"What?"

"Lenvyd. He'll go to Galdasten. That's where the Weaver will have told him to go. That's where the war will be fought. The Weaver and his allies will need healers, and who knows what other powers Lenvyd possesses." She gave a wan smile. "The Weaver rarely pursues Qirsi who have only one."

"I can ask the captain of the guard to send men northward."

"Don't bother. He won't be found, and he won't make enough of a difference to matter."

Nurle stared at her, seeming uncertain as to whether she meant that the Weaver's victory was already assured. Fortunately, he didn't ask, for she wasn't certain either.

After a few more moments, he stood. "I'll leave you. If you need anything, call for me."

"You don't have to go."

He gave a small laugh. "Actually, I do. I haven't slept in some time."

"Of course. Thank you, Nurle. If not for you, I'd be dead."

"I'm a healer. It's what I do."

He turned to leave. As he did, Cresenne noticed a piece of parchment on the table by her bed. "What's this?"

He stopped, facing her again. "I'd forgotten. It's a message that came for you the day the Weaver . . . the day he hurt you."

Cresenne nodded, remembering the guard who knocked on her door after she had awakened herself. She took it off the table, unfolded it, and began to read. It was from Keziah. And reading the missive, she wasn't sure whether to laugh or cry.

"What does it say?" Nurle asked.

"It's from a friend. She writes to warn me that the Weaver intends to make an attempt on my life."

Chapter Twenty

Kentigern, Eibithar

"Where is my first minister?"

Yaella ja Banvel could hear the duke bellowing for her down at the river, though he stood a full third of the way up the road to Kentigern's western gate. She felt the soldiers nearby watching her, waiting for her to respond, but she pretended that she hadn't heard, continuing to watch the swirl and flow of the Tarbin's dark waters.

She had raised mists for him, and winds as well, risking her life to shield his army from Kentigern's archers. Once the army reached the castle gate, she had thrown fire on the raised drawbridge in order to weaken the thick oak for Rowan's ram. What more could the boy-duke want of her?

She had done much the same for Rowan's father only a year before, when Shurik's magic had done far more to bring down the gates than any power she could offer. And though she had been no less a traitor then, no less contemptuous of the Eandi courts, she had harbored a certain affection for Rouel. The son she hated. Perhaps that was why she hadn't begrudged the use of her magic then as she did now. Maybe that was why she didn't remember feeling so weary during the first siege, why this time she wished only to rest, to close her eyes beside the river and sleep until the war was over.

Or perhaps it was all that had befallen her in the past year. The death of her duke, which saddened her more than she had thought possible. The poisoning in Solkara, which left her weakened and feeling far older than her years. And of course, the murder of Shurik, the one man she had ever loved, which, she remained convinced, had come at the hands of an assassin sent by Grinsa jal Arriet. Too late, she had come to understand that the gods had smiled upon her throughout her life, blessing her with love and power, a strong body and able mind, and even an Eandi lord who was wiser and kinder than most. In the last year, however, perhaps as punishment for her betrayal, or for taking their gifts for granted, the gods had taken it all away.

Yaella felt worn, like a dulled blade. It seemed that she had never recovered entirely from the effects of the oleander placed in her wine by Grigor of Renbrere. The mists and winds she had conjured for Rowan as the army of Mertesse approached Kentigern Tor had taken too much effort. She had barely been able to muster enough fire magic to set the gate ablaze; she doubted that her flame would weaken the oak. Yet her physical suffering was but a trifle compared to the grief that lay on her heart. She still mourned Shurik's death as if it had happened just the day before. Kentigern's former first minister had been her confidant as well as her lover, and she longed for the sound of his voice, the touch of his hands, the caress of his lips. The days they spent together after he sought asylum in Mertesse had been the happiest of her life. Since his death, she had cared for nothing—not the realm, not the Weaver's movement, not even her own survival.

If she could have struck a blow for Shurik, she would have. She had never considered herself a vengeful person, yet she would have given all she had left in this world to see Grinsa dead. But Shurik had suspected the man was a Weaver, and though Yaella had never thought to see the day when two Weavers lived in the Forelands, she had come to believe that he was right. Even as a younger woman, when her magic flowed as easily as the Tarbin, she could not have hoped to best a Weaver. She could hardly expect to do so now. All that was left for her was to follow the Weaver she served and hope that his victory would bring Grinsa's doom.

For now, serving her Weaver meant serving her duke as he made war on the Eibitharians. So when Rowan shouted her name again, steering his mount down the road toward the riverbank, Yaella stood and faced him, smoothing her hair with a thin hand.

"First Minister," he said, halting his horse before her but not bothering to dismount.

"You called for me, my lord?"

"Several times."

"My mind must have been elsewhere, my lord. Forgive me." He was as foolish as his father had been clever, as much a brute as the old duke had been a true noble.

"Well, I need you with me at the gate. Fetch your horse and join me on the road."

"Of course, my lord."

The duke rode back toward Kentigern, and Yaella walked up the bank to where she had tied Pon, her mount. The horse whinnied as she approached and Yaella kissed his nose before untying him and climbing into her saddle. Then she started after her duke, riding slowly and eyeing the castle ramparts far above her.

Soon the road began to bend, curving back on itself as it climbed the tor. She came first to the hurling arms, which were positioned along a portion of the road that offered a clear view of the castle. Rowan's planning for this siege had been uninspired, save for his decision to build the four hurling arms. It was an extravagance, one that had slowed their preparations, as well as their advance across the Tarbin. But defeating a castle as formidable as Kentigern demanded a certain amount of extravagant thinking. For two days now, Rowan's men and those from the regent's army had kept up a constant barrage against the fortress, and while the walls remained whole, they had sustained a good deal of damage. No doubt the bombardment was also taking a toll on the minds of Aindreas's men. Even more than the harm done to the castle walls, that might well prove decisive before the siege was over.

Once past the hurling arms, however, matters began to look far more grim for the Aneiran forces. With every step her mount took, the minister saw increasing numbers of dead and wounded lying beside the lane, most with arrows and quarrels jutting from bloody wounds. Ahead she could see the gate, still burning, but still standing despite repeated blows from the ram. More arrows, some of them afire, rained down on the engine and the men within it. The sharp odor of burning pitch and oil brought tears to her eyes and made her throat hurt.

As far as she could see around the base of the castle, the soldiers of Mertesse and Solkara were raising ladders, trying to scale the walls to the ramparts. But again, dead blanketed the ground, like some grim harvest from the Underrealm, and every few moments another of the ladders would topple back, sending men tumbling to the rocky slopes of the tor.

"I need your mists, Minister!" the duke called from near the ram. "Kentigern's archers are taking too great a toll on my army." He kicked at his horse's flanks and galloped back to her. "How long can you sustain a mist for me?"

"To be honest, my lord, not very long. The approach to the tor taxed me near to my limits, and setting fire to the gate only made matters worse."

"Come now, First Minister. We're at war. All of us are weary. I need you to do this."

"Forgive me for saying so, my lord, but it's not at all the same. A Qirsi's magic can only be stretched so far. This isn't a matter of me being lazy. If I push myself too far beyond my limits, I could render myself entirely powerless. Qirsi have even been known to die from abusing their powers."

Rowan frowned, looking so much like his father that Yaella had to look away.

"I'm not even certain that a mist would be wise at this time," she went on after a moment's pause. "The men need to be able to see, particularly the archers providing cover for those raising the ladders. Shroud them in a mist, and they're liable to kill our own men."

"Then what should I do?" For just a moment, he sounded less like the brash duke she had come to hate over the past year, and more like a young man beyond his depth.

"Concentrate your efforts on the gate, my lord. These are just the outer walls. Even if your men gain the top, they've still the inner walls to climb. Continue to use your hurling arms against the inner keep, but everything depends on defeating this gate. If it fails, the castle will fall. If it doesn't, we have no hope of winning."

He nodded. "Yes, of course. Thank you, First Minister." He actually managed a small smile that again brought to mind the older duke. "I can see why my father valued you so."

She didn't want his praise or his kindness. It was far easier simply to despise him. Still, now that Yaella had heard his uncertainty, she found herself thinking of him as a boy, as Rouel's son, desperate and frightened. *Damn him.* "My lord is too kind."

"Return to the river, First Minister. Rest there and await my commands."

"Yes, my lord."

Yaella turned Pon and started back down the lane. Before she had gotten very far, however, a cry went up from Rowan's men. Twisting around in her saddle, she saw a swarm of flaming arrows arcing high into the sky and descending toward the duke's army, the ram, and the road itself.

"Minister!" the duke shouted.

"I see them, my lord!" she called back, never taking her eyes off the arrows.

Intending to raise a gale, she reached for her power, and despaired at how little was there. She gritted her teeth, drawing on all the magic that remained within her, feeling the effort consume her, like some ravenous beast gnawing at her heart. Yet the wind that she summoned was barely strong enough to stir her hair. And even as she struggled with her weakness, a second volley rose from the castle walls.

"Shields!" the duke called.

The first of the arrows plunged toward them, toward her, the flames snapping in their descent like pennons in a storm. Her wind began to build, though too slowly to do much good. Her head ached and her vision was blurring. She could hear her duke calling to her again, though whether to demand that she do more or to warn her to get away she couldn't say for certain.

An instant later the first volley of darts struck. Several men screamed out, though not as many as Yaella had feared. Flaming shafts pierced the ground all around her, making her mount rear. The minister nearly lost her balance, but she clung to Pon's neck, expecting at any moment to feel an arrow imbed itself in her back.

Get off the road!

Men were shouting everywhere and she couldn't tell if the voice she heard was in her mind or belonged to one of them. Not that it mattered. She kicked at the horse's flanks to steer him off the road. More arrows hit, and judging from the cry that went up from the duke's men, more still were in the air. Two struck in quick succession just in front of her, and again Pon reared. He took the next arrow square in the chest.

The horse screamed as might a wounded soldier, twisting against his reins before crashing down onto his side, and onto Yaella's leg. Her head hit hard, but on the dirt next to the road, rather than on the lane itself. Still, she was dazed, though not so much that she wasn't aware of the crushing pain in her leg, or the smell of Pon's burning flesh. The horse jerked violently, as if trying to get up, but he couldn't seem to move. Yaella had to drag herself out from beneath him as still more arrows struck. Small fires erupted in the brush.

A second arrow buried in Pon's flank and the beast convulsed, then was still. Yaella crawled to where the horse lay and stroked his nose. He was breathing still, in wet gasps, and bloody foam gathered at his mouth. His eyes looked dull, glazed. A sob escaped her and she put a hand to her mouth as tears spilled from her eyes. Was it foolish to shed tears for a horse when all around her men were dying? Did she dishonor her memory of Shurik by weeping for Pon as she had for her love?

"First Minister!" Two soldiers were running to where she knelt. "Are you hurt?" one of them asked.

She nodded. "My leg. I think the bone's broken."

"We'll get you to the healers."

The one who had spoken lifted her off the ground as if she weighed nothing and, accompanied by the other man, who had drawn his sword, they started down the road.

"Goodbye," she whispered, gazing back at Pon and wiping her eyes.

The pain in her leg was manageable, though she was sweating and her limbs were trembling. She was certain the duke would tell her that she was fortunate to be alive at all. She didn't feel that way.

Yet it seemed that her ordeal wasn't yet over. Just as they reached the hurling arms, shouts went up from the nearby brush, to be answered by cries of alarm from the men at the siege engines. A large party of soldiers dressed in the colors of Kentigern burst from among the trees, many of them carrying swords, the rest with bows. Abruptly the minister found herself in the midst of a battle. She had time to consider that the flaming arrows had been but a diversion to allow Aindreas's men to strike at the hurling arms. After that she could think of nothing but the combat that raged on all sides.

Arrows whistled past, making the man carrying her flinch and lower his head. Yaella cowered against his chest, trying to curl herself into a tight ball. That may have been why the arrow that hit her dug into the back of her shoulder rather than her chest. As it was she had never imagined that anything could hurt this much. It almost seemed that the head of the arrow had been made of molten steel, the wound burned so. Agony lanced through her back with every step taken by the soldier who carried her. The man knew she had been hurt, for his companion was already telling her in reassuring tones that the injury didn't look too bad. He might even have slowed his pace to avoid jarring her. Yet each step increased her suffering until she wanted to holler at him to stop and put her down. At last, he did just that, laying her on her side on as gently as he could under the circumstances before both of them rushed to join the battle.

Already, though, it seemed to be too late. Kentigern's archers had killed a number of Aneirans with the first arrows they loosed, and managed to fire off several more volleys before they had to fall back toward the brush. There, guarded by the Eibitharian swordsmen, they brought forth more arrows, the heads of which were wrapped like torches. More quickly than Yaella would have thought possible, they lit the arrows and loosed them at the hurling arms, striking three of the machines and setting them ablaze.

Yaella watched all of this through a haze of pain, gritting her teeth to keep from being ill and blinking her eyes to keep her vision clear. She couldn't move, of course, not with her leg injured and the arrow jutting from her back, and so she could only hope that the fighting wouldn't reach her. Watching the soldiers, she cringed at every arrow that struck true, every sword stroke that bit into mail and flesh, and she muttered a curse as the siege machines began to burn. But she didn't notice the lone Eibitharian swordsman until he was nearly on her. He approached her cautiously, no doubt wary of her magic. She knew, though, that fear wouldn't stay his hand. Qirsi ministers were prized targets in any war, even those who were wounded, even those who were too old and weak to turn the tide of battle.

"Don't come any closer," she said, trying to sound menacing, knowing that she failed.

The man hesitated, but only for a moment. Then he grinned.

Yaella reached for her magic again—fire this time, which was easier to wield than mists and winds. But with her wounds, she felt even weaker than she had by the gates. Sounding the depths of her power, she found the merest residue of what she once had possessed, and she felt shame at what she had become. Still the Eibitharian approached, his sword glinting in the sunlight. Already there was blood on the steel. He had killed this day, and wouldn't hesitate to do so again. Again she reached, and with an effort that tore a cry from her throat, she summoned a flame, trying to direct it at the man's chest.

Instead, she found his arm, setting his sleeve on fire. Still, that was enough to make him halt. He dropped his blade, crying out and flailing at the flames with his other hand. In just a few seconds he had extinguished the fire, but by then one of the Aneiran soldiers had seen him and was sprinting to Yaella's defense. The Eibitharian died before he could reclaim his weapon.

The hurling arms, however, could not be saved. The three that the Eibitharians had managed to set afire were now fully engulfed, frenzied flames crackling and swirling, dark smoke pouring into the midday sky.

Yaella heard more voices and, turning toward the tor, saw more Aneiran soldiers running down the road, reinforcements from the castle gate and walls. Before the men reached the hurling arms, Kentigern's soldiers melted back into the woods and brush, vanishing almost as suddenly as they had appeared. By the time the duke arrived, the fighting had long since ended.

"Damn!" he said, glowering at the raging fires. "How many men did we lose?"

"We're not certain yet, my lord," one of the soldiers answered. "We're making a count now."

"Whatever the number, it's too many. Demons and fire! How did this happen?"

"We had no warning, my lord. They must have snuck around from the north end of the castle."

Rowan nodded, staring at the fires again, clearly struggling to control his ire. "Get started building new ones. I want them ready by sundown tomorrow."

"Yes, my lord."

The duke walked to Yaella and squatted beside her. "You'll live?"

"I expect so, my lord," she managed to say, her voice as thin as parchment.

"Good. I'm going to have some men take you to the healers, again. This time see that you get there."

It was something his father would have said. Yaella couldn't keep the smile from her lips. "Yes, my lord."

He called for the same two men who had carried her this far, to take her the rest of the way to the river. Then, as if an afterthought, he added two more men. Yaella wondered if he would have been so eager to protect her had he truly understood how weak she had grown.

The soldiers conveyed her down to the river without further incident. Rather than finding comfort in the prospect of a healer's soothing touch, however, the minister was horrified by what she saw along the banks of the Tarbin. Everywhere she looked wounded soldiers awaited the Qirsi healers, some of them moaning, others silent, their eyes fixed on the sky and so sunken that they might have been dead already. A few had lost limbs, and most had suffered wounds so bloody that Yaella gagged just to look at them.

The soldiers tried to take her directly into one of the tents, but the minister shook her head. "No. We have to wait. These men were here before me."

"Duke's orders, First Minister," said the one carrying her. "We were to take you to the healers right off."

"But they need help more than I do."

Before he could answer, one of the healers emerged from the tent, a Qirsi woman Yaella recognized from the castle. She was stout for a Qirsi, with short white hair and a round face. Yaella couldn't remember her name.

"What's this about?" the woman demanded, immediately examining Yaella's injuries, gently probing the wound around the arrow shaft with her hands.

"This is the first minister. She—"

"I know who she is, you dolt. Why are you arguing with her?"

"It was my fault," Yaella said, wincing under the woman's touch. "I didn't want him to take me into the tent, not with all these others waiting."

"But the duke wants us to care for you first, is that right?"

"Yes."

"What powers do you possess?"

"What? What does that—"

"What powers? Mists and winds? Fire? Language of beasts? Any of those will help end this siege sooner, and frankly, First Minister, that will save more lives than would any delay in your treatment. So stop wasting my time and let this man put you in my tent."

She could do nothing but nod her agreement and remain silent as the soldier carried her into the tent.

It was warm within, and the air smelled of blood and rot, betony and sweetwort. Again the minister gagged.

"Put her there," the woman said, following them into the tent and pointing at a pallet near the entrance. "Then get out."

The soldier did as he was told and was gone before the minister could thank him.

"Does it hurt much?" the healer asked, kneeling next to her.

"Yes, and my leg is almost as bad."

The woman laid her hands gently on Yaella's leg, frowning. "How did this happen?"

"My horse—" She broke off, fearing that she would cry, knowing that if she did, the woman would think her weak and stupid.

"He fell on you?"

She nodded, her eyes stinging.

"All right. I need a tonic here!" she said, raising her voice for just an instant. "You're going to be fine, but you need to rest, and I don't want you conscious when I set this bone. Do you understand?"

A few moments later a second Qirsi brought a cup of steaming liquid to the healer, who sniffed it once before handing it to Yaella.

"Drink it all," she said. "You'll soon start feeling drowsy. Be sure you're lying on your side. I don't want you falling back on that arrow."

The minister shuddered. "Of course."

Both healers left her and Yaella downed the tonic, despite its sickly sweet taste. As the woman had warned, she began to feel sleepy almost immediately. She lay down on the pallet, positioning herself as comfortably as she could.

She was aware of little after that. She remembered hearing voices, feeling something in her leg akin to pain, though the sensation was fleeting. Later she dreamed of Shurik and the Weaver and another shadowy figure she assumed was Grinsa. But even with the tonic still in her blood, she could tell that none of these visions carried the weight of prophecy, nor did she believe that the Weaver's presence in her dreams was anything more than an illusion.

When Yaella awoke, there were three healers nearby, none of them paying the slightest attention to her. She could tell that it was dark outside, though she had no sense of the time. The tent appeared even more crowded with wounded men than it had when she first entered, and she could hear wails and sobs coming from outside. She pushed herself up on one arm, feeling surprisingly clearheaded.

"What's happened?" she asked.

One of the healers turned, an older man. "You're awake. How do you feel?"

"Much better, thank you."

He nodded, turning back to the soldier whose injuries he had been tending. "Good. It's been a busy night. It seems Kentigern's men attacked the last of the hurling arms and also made a run at our stores. The fighting spread all the way to the river, just east of here. Some thought that they might cross and press on to Mertesse, but at last, our soldiers managed to push them back. Good thing, too. There would have been no way for us to move all of you in time."

"Did they destroy the other hurling arm?"

"Yes," he said, still intent on the soldier. "Word is they nearly burned our provisions, too. But just a short while ago we caught most of the raiding party between the river and the castle. Most of them were killed, a few were captured. Some of the men you hear outside are from Kentigern."

She wanted to ask if the duke had survived the night, but she couldn't bring herself to say the words. She wasn't even certain what answer she wanted to hear. Besides, if Rowan had died, the siege would probably be over. Surely the healer would have included such tidings in his description of the night's events.

Yaella moved her arm cautiously, testing her shoulder. It felt stiff where the arrow had hit, but there was no pain. Her leg still throbbed, however, and when she tried to swing herself off the pallet, making the wood creak, the old healer glanced at her, frowned, and shook his head.

"Wouldn't do that if I were you. You're not ready to be walking about."

"How long until I can?"

"I'm not the one who set the bone. But I heard it was broken in two places—clean breaks, mind you. Two of them, though. That will take a couple of days to heal well enough."

"So I have to remain in here?"

"Didn't say that. We need the space. I'll have someone take you out in the morning. I just don't want you doing it on your own."

Once more, he turned back to the soldier. After a few moments, Yaella lay down again and closed her eyes.

For some time she drifted in and out of sleep, vaguely aware of the comings and goings of healers and wounded men. Eventually she fell into a deeper slumber and began to dream once more. And this time there could be no mistaking the source of her vision.

The Weaver didn't make her walk far, appearing to her, black as pitch against the blinding white, long before she reached the rise he usually forced her to climb.

"You're wounded," he said. There was no concern in his voice, but she sensed that this was more than an idle observation.

"Yes, Weaver. A broken bone in my leg and an arrow in my shoulder."

"You'll be all right?"

"Yes, Weaver. Thank you for asking."

"How goes the siege?"

"Not well. Aindreas's army has destroyed all of my lord's hurling arms and has killed many more of our soldiers than I believe the duke expected."

"Is the siege in danger of being broken?"

"I don't believe so, Weaver. Without the Solkaran soldiers it might have failed already, but with them we have enough men to continue for some time."

"Good. That's good." He seemed to hesitate. For the first time in all her conversations with the man, Yaella sensed on his part a lack of resolve, as if he weren't quite confident in what he intended to say next. When finally he did speak again, he surprised her with the direction of his questioning. "How are you feeling, Yaella?"

"Weaver?"

"I don't refer to your wounds. I sense that they're healing well already. But I sense as well that Shurik's death still weighs heavy on your heart. Isn't that so?"

She lowered her gaze, her throat tightening. "Yes, Weaver."

"Do you still feel as you once did, that I had a hand in his death?"

Fear gripped her heart. "No, Weaver! You told me that you had no part in it and I believe you."

"I'm glad to hear that. I trust then that you blame Grinsa jal Arriet."

She nodded, uncertain still as to where he was going with all this. "Shurik feared that Grinsa would kill him. It seems he was right."

"Yes, it does." A brief silence followed, and then, "How old are you, Yaella?"

"How old?" she repeated, knowing that she sounded dull-witted. "I've just turned thirty-two, Weaver."

"But you feel older, don't you?"

Again, she grew frightened. How much could he sense of her thoughts and feelings? Did he know how her powers had failed her this day? "I . . . I don't know what to say, Weaver."

"It's all right. I'm not angry with you. How could I be? Qirsar has ordained that all of his children will die young, at least when compared with the Eandi. That's the price we pay for the powers he gave us."

"Yes, Weaver."

"I remember you telling me once that your mother died at a young age. You fear that you might as well?"

"I don't know. Yes, I suppose I do."

"It doesn't seem fair, does it? Many have given so much to this movement, and yet some, like Shurik, died before they could see its promise realized. And others may have only a few years to enjoy this new world we're creating."

"We serve you and your movement, Weaver. Even if we don't see this to the end, we share in the glory of what you're doing."

"I'm glad to hear you say that, Yaella." And she sensed that he truly was. She could hear in his words that he was smiling, that the uncertainty she had sensed in him a few moments before had vanished. "I have a task for you. A dangerous task. I can't say for certain that you'll survive, even if you succeed. But you will be doing a great service to the cause we share, and I believe that you'll find peace before you die."

She should have been scared. Perhaps she would be when she woke. But at that moment she wanted only to please him, to do whatever it was he would ask of her.

"Tell me what you want me to do, Weaver."

She saw him nod.

"You serve me well."

They talked for a long time, far longer than they had ever spoken before. He told her much about his plans and about how the movement had taken shape. And though she trembled at what he asked of her, she vowed that she would succeed or die in the attempt.

Yaella woke from her dream of the Weaver to the golden light of early morning and the singing of thrushes outside the healing tent. The pain in her leg had subsided. She felt refreshed, as if she had slept for days and days. Reaching for her power, she sensed that it had replenished itself, that whatever weakness she had felt the day before was but a memory. Seeing that she was awake, one of the healers checked the wound on her back and placed his hands on her leg, probing the bone with his mind. Satisfied that she was healing well, he had two men help her out of the tent to a shady area near the river. There she was placed on another pallet and told to rest.

She watched the swirling waters, shading her eyes against the sun that sparkled off the surface. She had spent much of her life by the Tarbin, marking her years by the rise and fall of its flow. The thought that she would be leaving it soon brought some regret, but it passed quickly.

I have a task for you, he had said.

And she had pledged herself to his service. Death no longer frightened her, not if it had purpose, not if it offered her peace. She would embrace death, and she would strike a blow for her movement.

Chapter Twenty-one

Dantrielle, Aneira

Tebeo had thought that matters couldn't get any worse. After the failure of Bausef's mission to destroy the hurling arms, the bombardment of Castle Dantrielle with the severed heads of his men, and the savage display of the master of arms's head on a pike before the Solkaran camp, the duke was certain that he must have reached some sort of nadir in his conflict with the royal house. Instead that dreadful night had been but the beginning of a downward spiral into an abyss of horror and misery.

The day after Bausef's death, the Solkarans resumed their attacks with the fiery boulders. They were joined in the assault a day later by the men of Rassor, who had constructed their own hurling arm. These missiles did only minimal damage to the castle walls, but they were a fearsome sight, burning brilliantly as they soared high in the air and descended toward the fortress, a long plume of dark smoke trailing behind them. Tebeo's men learned quickly to judge their trajectory and to move to safety before they struck. Still, the besieging armies kept up a withering assault and over time it clearly began to wear on Dantrielle's soldiers.

For three days the attacks continued. Then, abruptly, they ceased. Yet this did nothing to ease the minds of Dantrielle's soldiers or people. Rather, it served only to increase the sense of foreboding that hung over the entire city. It took less than a day for all of them to learn that their fears were justified.

As with the lofting of severed heads into the castle, Tebeo

had heard tales of attacking armies using hurling arms to throw the rotting carcasses of dead animals into a city or castle, thus spreading disease as well as dread. But he had hoped that Aneira's regent would refuse to subject his own people to such terrors, even if those people were in rebellion. Once again, he had misjudged the man, seeing in him more compassion than was there.

Numar began with slaughtered sheep, dead at least two or three days. His hurling arms couldn't be as accurate with the beasts as they had been with the boulders, but they didn't have to be. They needed only to clear the walls. In the heat of Elined's turn, with the remains already decaying, the stench was unbearable. Almost as soon as this newest atrocity began, Tebeo ordered his men to douse the carcasses with oil and set them afire, but even after they carried out his orders, the fetor of rot and burning flesh lingered over all of Dantrielle.

The following day, both the Solkarans and the army of Rassor used dead cattle. Not that it mattered what type of animal dropped into the lanes of the city or the castle wards. Tebeo could hardly step onto the walls of his fortress without feeling his stomach heave. Everywhere he looked, small fires burned, sending foul smoke into the air. He hadn't heard of anyone in his city taking ill because of the animal carcasses, but still his people suffered.

That night, as the soldiers at the hurling arms returned to the flaming stones, interspersing an occasional animal corpse, a party of Solkaran soldiers tried to gain entry to the castle through one of the sally ports. Tebeo still bore a scar on his side from his fight with the last Solkarans to make the attempt. This time, the duke's men were prepared for the attack and drove the party off, killing more than half of them. But even this victory did little to raise the spirits of Tebeo's army.

Yet as much as those within the city and castle suffered for the siege, the duke knew that those who lived in his dukedom beyond the protection of his walls endured far worse. Numar might have been intent on winning the favor of Dantrielle's people, of turning them against their duke, but that wouldn't stop him from plundering the farms and villages in the Dantrielle countryside for food and water. No doubt his men had quartered themselves in the homes of defenseless farmers as they approached the castle, and who knew what else they had done. Soldiers marching to war had been known to make sport of violating their enemies' wives and daughters. With all the horrors Numar's army had visited on them thus far, why should Tebeo expect that these men would be any different? "A war among nobles," it was often said, "bloodied all."

Tebeo had yet to name a new master of arms to replace Bausef. Instead he relied on three of the armsmaster's most trusted captains, and on the eleventh night of the siege, for the first time, two of them raised the prospect of discussing terms of surrender with the regent. The duke and his captains were on the ramparts, watching for the next assault from Numar's men. Tebeo wasn't certain how to respond to their suggestion, but the third captain was appalled.

"You don't really mean that," he said. "The siege isn't going well, but to consider surrender so soon . . ."

"I've never seen the spirit of these men so low. They already feel that we've lost. They have since the master of arms died."

"And," added the second man, "we've inflicted almost no losses on Numar's army."

"Our losses haven't been very high either. We lost the armsmaster's party, but they've had men killed on raids as well. We still outnumber them."

"For how long? I've heard men talk of desertion, and though I don't think many of them are ready to go that far, it will come to that before too long."

"What would you hope to gain through surrender?" Tebeo asked.

The third captain stared at him. "My lord—"

The duke raised a hand, silencing him. "You understand that all four of us would be executed, and most likely my sons as well."

"Yes, my lord," said the first man, looking away. "Forgive me."

"I wasn't trying to silence you, Captain. I really want to know what might be gained. Do you think that the regent would spare the rest of the men?"

"Yes, my lord. He needs soldiers to fight the Eibitharians. He might be so desperate for them that he would even spare the four of us. If you pledge yourself to his cause, you might be able to end all this."

Tebeo gave a grim smile. "That I don't believe. You've seen what he's done, the lengths to which he's gone to break our will. Are these really the actions of a man inclined to such mercy?"

"No, my lord, they're not," the third captain said, glaring at his two comrades, torch fire gleaming in his dark eyes. "You can't surrender, my lord. Not yet. We're still waiting for Orvinti, Kett, and the others. Their arrival might very well break this siege. We should at least wait for them."

"How are our stores?"

Even the third man faltered. "They run low, my lord."

"How low?"

"They may not last to the end of the next waxing."

"They won't," the first man said, sounding so certain that Tebeo found himself questioning the man's loyalty.

The duke nodded. "Well, you've given me much to consider. Since we're not yet done with the waning, I assume we have at least a half turn's provisions left."

"Yes, my lord."

"Good. For now, we'll keep rations as they are. I've no desire to start a panic. We'll speak of this again. For now, return to your posts."

The three men bowed, and the two who advocated surrender moved off, leaving Tebeo alone with the third captain. His name was Gabrys DinTavo. He had come to Dantrielle with Bausef and had long been the armsmaster's favorite among all his captains. That alone made him Bausef's most likely successor in the duke's eyes.

"They'll say that I argued as I did to curry favor with you," the man said, watching the other two captains walk off. "They'll say that I tell you what you want to hear so that you'll choose me as your next master of arms."

"Is that true?"

Gabrys turned sharply. "No, my lord!"

"Then why should you care what they say?"

"I don't suppose I should, my lord."

"I don't want to surrender, Captain. But neither do I wish to see all these men massacred."

"Of course not, my lord."

"If it comes to that choice, you know what I'll do."

He nodded. "Yes, I do."

The duke gazed down at the Solkaran camp, awaiting the next assault. "Bausef thought me too soft to be an effective leader in times of war. I expect you see me much the same way."

The captain started to reply, but Tebeo shook his head. "It's all right. Bausef knew me better than I know myself. I tried to prove him wrong that night when Numar first started to use his hurling arms, and I ended up sending him to his death. Since then I've vowed to follow my instincts rather than be something I'm not. Thus when it comes to questions of warfare, I have no choice but to rely on your counsel, and that of the others."

"I understand, my lord."

"Obviously you don't think I should surrender. So what would you have me do?"

Before Gabrys could answer, the duke heard a light footfall behind him. Turning, he saw Evanthya step out of the tower stairway. She stopped when she saw Tebeo and the captain.

"Forgive me, my lord. I didn't mean to interrupt."

"You're not interrupting, First Minister. Please join us."

He glanced at the captain, only to find the man glowering at Evanthya. It often seemed, particularly in these times, that warriors viewed the Qirsi with even more distrust than did nobles. Bausef had been an exception—he had never struck the duke as having much feeling for Evanthya, or the other ministers, one way or another. But apparently Gabrys did.

"She's served me loyally for many years, Captain. I have as much faith in her and her counsel as I do in any soldier who's ever served me, including the master of arms."

The man's mouth twitched, but he nodded. "Yes, my lord."

"Perhaps I should go," the minister said, her pale skin looking sallow in the glow of the torches and ward fires.

Tebeo shook his head. "There's no need. In fact I was going to call for you. Two of my captains have suggested that I discuss with the regent terms for our surrender. I—"

"Surrender?" she broke in, incredulous. "That's nonsense! It's far too soon to even consider such a thing." She cast a dark look at Gabrys. "If this is typical of the counsel you're receiving from your captains, it may be time to promote some of the other men."

Gabrys grinned, eyeing the minister. "It may be that I've misjudged her, my lord."

"I believe you did. Gabrys agrees with you, First Minister," Tebeo explained. "I was speaking of two other captains."

Her cheeks flushed. "Forgive me, Captain. I spoke rashly."

The man shook his head. "There's nothing to forgive, Minister. It is nonsense to speak of surrender. Had I been one of these other men I would have deserved your contempt and more."

"I have no intention of surrendering," Tebeo said to Evanthya. "I was just asking the captain what I should be doing instead."

"And I'm afraid that I can't offer much by way of reply, my lord," Gabrys said. "The truth is, there's little you can do just now. It's always seemed to me that a siege is far harder on the defending noble than is any other form of combat. Victory for the besieged comes not from aggressive tactics or battlefield genius. Rather, it comes from simple patience. At most times, it's best to do nothing at all. I believe many men find it more difficult to wait than to do something, anything, no matter what it might be."

Tebeo gave a wan smile. "Again, Bausef tried to tell me much the same thing, just before I sent him to attack the hurling arms." He glanced at the first minister, then looked out toward the Solkarans again. "I believe you tried as well, Evanthya. Didn't you?"

"I didn't know what would happen to Master DarLesta's raiding party, my lord. Neither did he. He suggested that we respond to the regent's attacks a certain way, and I agreed. That's all."

"That's a most generous interpretation of what happened, First Minister. I thank you."

"It's the truth, my lord. No more or less. And if you'll forgive me for saying so, I believe it's time you stopped blaming yourself for the master of arms's death."

The duke's hands were resting on the ramparts, and now he gripped the stone until his knuckles whitened. He said nothing, however. Bausef's head was still mounted on a pole high above the Solkaran camp, his sightless eyes seeming to stare directly back at the fortress, the flesh on his face blackened, his slack mouth hanging open, as if he were laughing at some dark jest. The man was a warrior. He had served his duke loyally, following orders regardless of whether or not he agreed with them. He deserved a better fate.

"You both want me to do nothing. Yet the other captains spoke of possible desertions if our prospects for victory don't improve. What do I do to raise the men's spirits?"

"Nothing," said the captain. "They're soldiers. They don't need coddling and they deserve better than false assurances. Let them do their jobs."

"Do you agree with that, too?" he asked the minister.

"I'm not certain. Can the other captains be trusted not to sow discontent among the men?"

Tebeo turned at that. "A good question."

Gabrys cast a disapproving eye at the minister before answering. "The others are fools, my lord. They're not traitors."

Evanthya raked a hand through her white hair. "They don't have to be traitors to stir up trouble. All they need to do is speak openly of surrender, or of how poorly they believe the siege is going. The rest will take care of itself."

"Can they be trusted to be discreet?" the duke asked, afraid that he already knew the answer.

The captain grimaced. "I think I'd best speak with them, just to make certain."

"Please do, Captain. Sooner rather than later."

"Yes, my lord." Gabrys bowed and walked away briskly.

"He seems a good man, don't you think?"

The first minister nodded. "He does, my lord. Do you intend to make him your new master of arms?"

"I think so. When all of this is over."

"Why wait?"

Tebeo looked at her. "You think I should do it now, in the midst of all this?"

"You wanted to know what to do for the men. It seems to me that giving them a new commander would go a long way toward demonstrating that you're not about to surrender. And if your captains are in disagreement over how best to respond to the regent's attacks, it might help to have them answering to a man who shares your resolve to fight on."

"You may be right. I had thought to wait a full turn, out of respect for Bausef, but that may not be possible under these circumstances."

"I believe the master of arms would understand, my lord."

Tebeo smiled again, intending to thank her. He never got the chance.

Men cried out from beyond the castle walls. At the same time, several of Tebeo's men called, "Look to the skies!" as they did each time the Solkarans began an assault with the hurling arms. Yet this time, when Tebeo turned his gaze skyward, he didn't see one of the great fiery boulders or another of the dreaded carcasses. Instead he saw a large cluster of burning arrows blazing across the starlit sky. But it was the direction of their flight that made his heart soar. The arrows weren't headed for the castle, nor had they been loosed from the Solkaran camp; they flew from the east, arcing upward from the shadowed recesses of the Great Forest. And they were aimed at the center of Numar's army.

"It must be Kett!" Evanthya said.

The arrows rained down on the Solkarans, bringing shrieks of pain and frantically shouted orders.

"I agree. Get the captain for me! Quickly, First Minister!"

"Yes, my lord!"

She ran to the tower, leaving him to watch a second volley fly from the wood. He hated this war. He despaired at every lost life, knowing that as the Aneiran armies weakened themselves, the Qirsi movement—the true enemy—grew ever stronger. Yet he could not help but rejoice at the suffering he heard from Numar's men. After all they had done to his people, to his castle, he lusted for vengeance.

"Let them kill the regent," he whispered, shocked by the sentiment, but unable to banish it from his mind, and unwilling to forswear the words.

More arrows soared into the night sky, and now the Solkarans launched their own assault in response.

Tebeo heard footsteps. Evanthya and Gabrys.

"You see them, Captain?"

"I do, my lord. I agree with the first minister. The attack comes from the east; it must be Kett."

"What do we do to help them?"

"My lord, I'm not certain—"

"Surely you don't think that Kett's army can stand alone against the Solkarans. We have to help them in some way, press the advantage they've given us."

"Rassor's army is still out there as well, my lord. If we send out our men, they could be trapped between the regent's force and Rassor's men coming to Numar's aid."

"And if we do nothing, Ansis's men could be destroyed by the combined might of the two houses."

As if prompted by their discussion, another cry went up, this one from east and south of the castle. Tebeo and the captain exchanged a look before all of them began running along the ramparts to the east wall. By the time they could see Rassor's camp the duke's heart was racing, not only with the exertion of getting there, but with elation at what was unfolding before him. Rassor's men were under attack as well, from the south.

"Noltierre?" Evanthya asked, breathless as well.

"Or Tounstrel. Or perhaps both. Right now I don't care."

The minister smiled. "Yes, my lord."

"What say you now, Captain?"

Gabrys gave a small shrug. "That we needn't worry any longer about Kett having to fend off both armies. With Rassor and Solkara both engaged, they can't combine their numbers against either of our allies. Nor can they simply resume their assaults on the castle. We've a respite, my lord. We should take advantage of it and do nothing at all."

More of the flaming barbs flew. Tebeo could hear the ring of steel on steel as the opposing forces met. He had been telling himself repeatedly since the siege began that he was no warrior. Yet he itched to strike at his enemies.

"We'll have our day, my lord," the captain said, as if he could see the battle lust in Tebeo's eyes. "Help has arrived. It's only a matter of time before the siege is broken. But I believe that to attack tonight, before we have a sense of how many men Kett and Tounstrel have brought us, would be a mistake."

Bausef's head leered at him, laughing at his uncertainty.

"Very well, Captain." It felt like a surrender. "But I want you to begin planning with the other captains. We should be prepared to strike tomorrow, at first light."

"My lord—"

Tebeo raised a hand, shaking his head. "I'm not saying that we will, but I want to have that choice. I want to be able to give the order and have it carried out within the hour. Do you understand?"

"Yes, my lord."

The captain left them once more, and the duke turned his attention back to the fighting in the forests surrounding the castle. Already the war cries sounded less strident and those he heard came from a greater distance. He didn't see any arrows flying, nor did he hear as much sword combat. It almost seemed that his friends had sought to harry the armies of Solkara and Rassor just enough to give them pause, and to give the people of Dantrielle that respite of which Gabrys had spoken. Still, Tebeo couldn't help but wonder if Ansis and Vistaan, or whoever it was had come to his defense, expected him to do more.

"I should have considered this," he muttered, thinking back on the time he had spent speaking with his allies prior to the commencement of the siege.

"My lord?"

He had forgotten Evanthya was even there.

"It's nothing, First Minister." He glanced at her, forcing a smile, but she was intent on the shadowed woodlands before them. "What is it? Is something troubling you?"

"No, my lord. I'd just like to know who's out there."

Suddenly he understood. "You think it might be Brall. Do you sense Fetnalla?"

She shook her head, looking wan and very young. "No, my lord. But I don't know for certain that I would. Even a Qirsi's powers don't run that deep."

Tebeo shrugged, trying to conceal his disappointment. "Even if that's not them, they will be here eventually. Brall gave me his word." *And he knows that we can't prevail without them.*

Evanthya said nothing, her pale eyes still fixed on the forest.

"The captain called this a respite," the duke said. "We should use it as such. Get some sleep, First Minister. If you're half as weary as I am, you need it."

"Is that a command, my lord?"

"Yes, it is."

"And is it one you intend to follow as well?"

Tebeo laughed. "I think I'd best. The duchess will have my head if I don't." As soon as the words passed his lips, he winced. After what the Solkarans had done, he would never again feel right using that expression.

Evanthya, though, gave no indication that she had noticed. "Very well, my lord. Until the morning then."

She walked away, continuing to stare at the trees until she reached the tower stairway. After a few moments more on the ramparts, Tebeo descended the stairs as well, and made his way to the cloister, where Pelgia and their children had been spending the nights since the siege began. His family was already asleep, but Pelgia stirred when he sat beside her on her bed.

"Is everything all right?" she whispered, sounding as if she might still be asleep.

He stroked her dark hair. "Yes, everything's fine."

She rolled onto her back and forced her eyes open. "Are you sure?" she asked, more intelligibly this time. "This is the first time I've seen you in here in days."

"Yes, I'm sure. Actually, it seems that Ansis has finally arrived, and at least one of the others."

Pelgia's eyes widened and she sat up. "Really?"

"They attacked both camps before retreating back into the forest. I expect the fighting will be worse for the next few days, but we may be able to break the siege before too long."

She put her arms around him, resting her head on his shoulder. "Gods be praised."

"Careful. You're in Ean's cloister. It might be dangerous to invoke the other gods here."

The duchess laughed, still holding him. "I don't care." She swiped at her eyes and Tebeo realized that she was crying.

He took her by the shoulders and made her look him in the eye. Her cheeks were damp with fresh tears. "Are you all right?"

She dabbed at the tears with her sleeve and nodded. "I'm fine. Or at least as well as I can be. I just want this to be over."

"If I could end it this moment, I would," he said, thinking once more of Bausef and Gabrys, and wondering anew if he had been too quick to defer to the captain's judgment.

He kissed her gently and made himself smile.

"You look so tired," she said.

She lay down again, and he beside her, closing his eyes, hoping that sleep would take him quickly. Instead, he remained awake for a long time, well past the ringing of the midnight bells. Every noise from outside the narrow window made him start, as if he expected Numar to renew his attacks at any moment. Eventually he did fall asleep, but awoke repeatedly, only to fall back into a fitful slumber. At last, when he awoke to the first pale grey gleaming of dawn, he rose, kissed Pelgia's brow, and returned to the walls.

Gabrys was already there—or perhaps he had never slept—speaking with the other captains. They all fell silent as the duke approached, the two who had spoken of surrender lowering their gazes.

"Am I interrupting something?" Tebeo asked.

Gabrys shook his head. "Not at all, my lord. We were discussing the preparations you asked me to make."

"Good. Report."

"We've created eight parties of forty men each. Sixteen archers, twenty-four swordsmen. We have them training right now. They'll use the sally ports to leave and enter the castle, of course, and we'll send them out two parties at a time. That way we'll keep the men fresh, while striking repeatedly at the armies of Solkara and Rassor."

"Excellent, Captain."

"Thank you, my lord." He faltered, but only briefly. "I should add, my lord, that these men will only be effective if the enemy is already engaged with the forces of Kett and Tounstrel. On their own, they won't stand a chance."

"I understand, Captain. Thank you." He glanced at the other two men. "And thank you as well. I'm grateful."

They bowed, muttering, "Yes, my lord," but refusing to meet Tebeo's gaze.

After a brief, awkward silence, Tebeo nodded once. "Very well." He turned to go.

"My lord, a word please," one of the other men said quickly.

"Yes, Captain."

"We owe you an apology, my lord. We shouldn't have been so quick to speak of surrender."

"We shamed ourselves, my lord," the other captain added. "We'd understand if you demoted us and named others captain in our place."

The duke shook his head. "I'm not going to do that. As I've told Gabrys already, I'm not well suited to commanding armies. I'd be a fool to deny myself the services of men who were trusted and valued by my master of arms."

Again they bowed. "Thank you, my lord."

"That said," Tebeo went on, making his choice in that moment, "I have decided to name Captain DinTavo as my new master of arms. I'll announce this formally in the few days, but for now, I want you to consider him your commander and respond to his orders appropriately."

The two men nodded, eyeing Gabrys. "Yes, my lord."

"Congratulations, Commander," Tebeo said, turning to the captain.

If the man was surprised, he hid it well. He merely knelt before the duke and lowered his head. "You honor me, my lord. I'll serve Dantrielle to the best of my abilities."

"Thank you, Gabrys. I know you will. You may rise."

The man hadn't been on his feet for a single heartbeat when the familiar cry sounded from the tower guards.

"Look to the skies!"

Before Tebeo could even turn, soldiers at the far end of the castle shouted the same thing.

Looking up, Gabrys's face blanched. "Demons and fire!"

It wasn't just boulders this time, though two were hurtling toward the castle, one from each of the camps. There were arrows approaching as well. Hundreds of them.

"Shields!" Gabrys hollered.

More shouts, from the wards this time.

"The gates!" said one of the captains.

The master of arms shook his head. "The sally ports." He looked at the duke. "My lord—"

"Go, Gabrys. Do whatever you must to protect the castle."

"Yes, my lord," he said, and ran to the towers, followed closely by the captains.

Tebeo heard cries go up from the camps; it seemed they were under attack as well. In a matter of moments all of Dantrielle had been engulfed in violence, as if a storm had erupted over the castle and city, bringing chaos. Swords and shields clashed, and battle cries rang out, the tumult echoing off the walls. Arrows pelted the castle like rain, and fire descended from the sky, blackening the castle stone and the grass of the wards.

Gabrys and the captains were in the wards by now, shouting orders, with disturbing urgency. Had the Solkarans breached the castle's defenses? Tebeo should have been down in the wards with them, consulting with his new master of arms, giving the commands himself. He should have been fighting alongside his men, despite his shortcomings as a warrior. But still he lingered on the ramparts, straining to see what was happening in the camps beyond the city walls. He could hear war cries coming from the forest, but he could see little through the trees.

Most of those men he did see wore the red and gold of Solkara or the brown and black of Rassor, but the duke also saw soldiers dressed in the colors of Kett and Tounstrel. So it was Ansis and Vistaan. Which meant, perhaps, that Brall and Bertin the Younger were nearby.

Perhaps Numar understood this as well, and this morning's attacks were intended as one final, desperate attempt to take Dantrielle by force. Even as the duke formed the thought, however, his hopes flared and turned to ash.

Abruptly, dark smoke was rising from the Great Forest to both the north and the east, turning the sky to a dirty grey and drifting over the castle like an acrid mist.

"Why would they burn the wood?"

Tebeo nearly jumped out of his skin. Evanthya was beside him, though he hadn't heard her approach.

"First Minister."

"Forgive me, my lord. I didn't mean to startle you."

"It's all right. Have you been here long?"

"No, my lord. I was awakened by the fighting. I thought you'd want me nearby."

"I would, if I knew what to do. The fact is, I don't know why they're burning the forest, unless it's to keep Ansis and Vistaan at bay while they redouble their efforts to take the castle."

More arrows fell on the fortress, forcing them to retreat into the nearest tower. Dantrielle's archers loosed their arrows in return, but already ladders were appearing around the ramparts and Solkaran soldiers were starting to climb. It wouldn't be long before Tebeo's men were fighting to maintain control of the castle walls.

Evanthya said something else to him, but Tebeo was lost in thought, trying to puzzle out all that was happening. By setting these fires, Numar forced Dantrielle's allies to fall back deeper into the wood and away from the castle. But he also risked denying his army and Rassor's a means of escape should the battle for the castle go poorly for them.

"He must believe that he has no choice."

"My lord?"

He looked up, realizing belatedly that he had spoken aloud. "I was thinking of Numar. He'd only risk these fires if he thought that the siege was about to be broken. Otherwise it's simply too dangerous. It may be that the armies of Orvinti and Noltierre are about to join the fight, or he may feel that with the arrival of Tounstrel and Kett, the tide of battle is about to turn against him."

"But if the fires spread, doesn't he trap himself?"

"Only if he fails to take Castle Dantrielle. It seems Numar has staked his life on the success of this siege."

More arrows struck, their tips sparking as they clattered against the stone. An instant later the fortress shook with the impact of yet another boulder from the hurling arms. That Numar would continue to use the hurling arms even as his men scaled the castle walls bespoke a determination that went far beyond desperation. This was no longer about the alliance with Braedon and Dantrielle's loyalty to the Solkaran Supremacy. Somehow this had become far more. It was a blood feud. That was the only way to explain the severed heads, the carcasses, this attack; all of it. Tebeo had defied him, and Numar had made up his mind to crush the duke and his house, no matter the cost. The color had fled Evanthya's cheeks; it seemed that she understood all too well what they faced.

"This is just the beginning then," she said. "He won't stop until he's won."

"Or until he's dead." Tebeo drew his sword. "Follow me, First Minister. Before this is over, we'll need every blade in Dantrielle."

She nodded, and they bounded down the stairway to the wards. Even before they reached the bottom, Tebeo could hear death cries and the clatter of weapons, clear as bells and impossibly close. Thus, he wasn't entirely unprepared when they emerged from the stairs to find the baileys teeming with enemy soldiers. Everywhere he looked men were fighting and dying. At the far end of the ward, Gabrys stood with his back to the stone wall, fighting off two soldiers wearing Rassor's colors.

The duke glanced at Evanthya. "Suggestions?"

The first minister surveyed the scene before them, her jaw set. Then she drew her short blade. "There's nothing to do but fight."

I'm no warrior, he wanted to say. *I never have been.* Yet looking at Evanthya, her white hair hanging to her shoulders, her face as pallid as death, her slender hands gripping her sword, he knew that she wasn't either. Most of the men before them were twice her size. Just as most of them were half his age.

He readied his weapon, and, as an afterthought, pulled his dagger free as well. "Orlagh guide your blade, First Minister."

"And yours, my lord."

"Stay close. Keep your back to mine."

She nodded. And together they waded into the battle.

Chapter Twenty-two

The Great Forest, near Dantrielle, Aneira

ou understand what it is I expect of you," the Weaver said, his voice rising until it rolled like thunder. "You understand that I want you to delay further. Yet you do nothing!"

Fetnalla's entire body shook, as if she were standing naked in a cold rain. She had tried to make him understand, yet the more she explained, the more angry he grew. At this point she had little confidence that she would survive the night.

"How far are you from Dantrielle?" he asked, sounding disgusted.

"Two days' ride, Weaver."

He shook his head. "Two days. That's not enough time."

"I'm sorry if I've failed you, Weaver," she said, trying to mask her frustration by sounding contrite. "I've slowed my duke's advance on the castle as much as I dare. If I do more I fear that I'll raise his suspicions."

A blow to the cheek sent her sprawling onto the ground, though the Weaver hadn't appeared to move.

"I don't give a damn about his suspicions!" he said. "Whether or not you're revealed as a member of this movement is of little consequence to me. I'm concerned now with far weightier matters. If this siege is broken too soon, it may very well lead to the failure of the siege at Kentigern. And if that happens—" The Weaver stopped himself so abruptly that Fetnalla wondered if he had already told her more than he intended. "The success of this movement is all that matters. I had thought you understood that. I'd be disappointed to learn that I was wrong."

"Of course I understand, Weaver. I just—"

A hand covered her mouth, and a second closed around her throat, though thankfully it didn't squeeze too hard.

"It's the woman, isn't it?" he asked, his voice dropping. "The other minister? Answer me honestly, or you'll die right here."

Evanthya. Of course she was part of this. Every day that the siege at Dantrielle went on increased the chances that she might be wounded or killed. But the truth was that Fetnalla feared for herself as much as she did for her love. Perhaps more. She wasn't proud of this, but with the Weaver's hand at her throat, pride was the least of her concerns.

"I do fear for her, Weaver."

His hand relaxed its grip, though he didn't release her. "She's of even less importance to me than you are. Her life was forfeit the moment she agreed to serve her duke. If you could have turned her to our cause, I might have spared her."

"But surely it's not too late!" Fetnalla said without thinking.

"If you haven't turned her by now, you never will."

"But we're together so seldom. If I had another chance—"

He tightened his fist again, this time making it impossible for her to breathe. "See that? You don't understand. There will be no more chances. The two of you can only be together if the regent's siege fails, and I don't want that. I'd rather have Dantrielle fall to the Solkarans, bringing the duke's execution, and, yes, your beloved minister's as well, than have the siege broken. Do I make myself clear?"

She nodded, still unable to speak.

"Good. I must know right now if you can continue to serve me under these circumstances. If you can, you'll live to see the dawn. If you can't, I'll kill you. And believe me when I tell you that no matter your answer, I'll know the truth. So don't lie to me, or your death will be agony."

For the second time he released her, removing the hand from her mouth as well. As before, he didn't appear to move at all.

It was actually an easier question to answer than the Weaver might have thought. When she thought of losing Evanthya, her heart throbbed as though pierced by a blade. But more than anything, she had feared being forced by the Weaver to kill Evanthya herself. On more than one occasion he had warned her that it might come to that before this ended. At least now she knew that it wouldn't be she who struck the fatal blow. Indeed, if the siege went as the Weaver wished, Evanthya need never even know of her betrayal. This was a small consolation to be sure, but it was all she had left.

"Yes, Weaver," she said, trying to keep her voice strong. "I can continue to serve you."

There was a brief silence, during which the minister felt that she was suspended over a yawning abyss.

Then the Weaver said, "I'm pleased to hear it," in a tone that told her he had not expected her to pass his test. "How will you slow your duke's progress toward Dantrielle?"

"I don't know yet, but I'll find a way."

"See that you do."

She opened her eyes to the dim yellow glow of firelight and the breathing and murmurs of a thousand sleeping soldiers. All her encounters with the Weaver left her sweaty and trembling, and this one had been no different. She would have liked to change her clothes, but with so many men sleeping around her, and her duke nearby, she didn't dare. She merely lay still, staring up at the few stars she could see through the canopy of the wood, and trying to ease her racing pulse.

She had never thought that it would come to this. Even when her duke's suspicions were driving her toward the

Weaver and his movement, even when she hoped that the Weaver's first assignment for her would be to kill Brall, she never imagined that she would have to choose between the Qirsi cause and her love for Evanthya.

For several turns, Fetnalla had held out hope of drawing her love into the movement. If only Evanthya could be made to see the future that the Weaver envisioned. If only she could have known what it was like to serve an Eandi noble like Brall. As dukes went, Tebeo was a decent man who had given his first minister little cause to question her loyalty to him. But surely Evanthya could see how Fetnalla suffered. Surely she understood that most other Eandi nobles were brutes and fools, undeserving of the loyalty they demanded from their Qirsi.

Only recently had Fetnalla come to realize that her love was blind to all of this, and that she would never allow herself to be drawn into the movement. Evanthya had too narrow a view of the world. She could never accept that there were different shades to loyalty, that some betrayals could be justified. True, she had been willing to pay gold for Shurik's death. She had, in fact, grown bolder since then, speaking of striking more blows against what she called the conspiracy. But this served only to define the limitations of her thinking. The world, in her mind, consisted of Eandi nobles and Qirsi ministers. She couldn't see any possibilities beyond that. Now, it seemed, her lack of vision would bring her to ruin.

Panic seized Fetnalla, making her stomach heave. "Perhaps there's still a way," she muttered, clenching her teeth against a wave of nausea. "Maybe, I can still convince her." *If she survives the siege.*

She thrust away an image of Evanthya's face, forcing herself to consider instead how she might slow Brall's progress toward Dantrielle. Again. Already she had delayed their departure from Orvinti no less than three times, twice by arguing for an increase in the number of soldiers in Brall's war party. The first time, she had been aided by the arrival of a messenger, who brought word that Rassor's army had joined Numar's in laying siege to Castle Dantrielle. As a result, Brall had agreed to march with an additional two hundred men. The second time she hadn't been nearly so fortunate, but she had managed to convince Traefan Sigrano, Orvinti's master of arms, that another hundred men, archers all, would aid in their efforts to break the siege. With both increases, of course, came greater demands on the quartermaster, which, in turn, prolonged their preparations.

She had then misinformed the weapons makers as to the proportion of archers to swordsmen in the duke's company, so that just before they were finally ready to leave Orvinti, Brall's master of arms discovered that his archers hadn't enough to arrows to fight effectively.

Brall had been livid, of course, but had not known whether to believe the craftsman when he said that Fetnalla misspoke, or his first minister when she swore to him that the weapons maker heard her incorrectly. This did nothing to lessen Brall's suspicions of her, but Fetnalla cared little about that. What mattered was that it added another day and a half to their preparations.

Once they were on the move, however, there wasn't much more Fetnalla could do to slow them. Brall set the pace for the march and expected all in his company to match it, particularly those on horseback. Moreover, he knew of her relationship with Evanthya, and expected that she would be anxious to reach Dantrielle, end the siege, and save Tebeo's minister. Anything Fetnalla did now to impede their progress would make it clear to all concerned that she had betrayed her duke.

Yet, that was precisely what the Weaver expected of her. Simple deception wouldn't work this time. She needed to do more.

It came to her so suddenly, with such force, that she had to resist an urge to jump up and see to it immediately. Instead, she turned over on her sleeping roll, sighing heavily. A few moments later she did so again, and then a third time. At last, as if unable to sleep, she sat up, stretched, and stood. One of the sentries was watching her, but he merely nodded, saying nothing.

Fetnalla began to wander through the trees in the direction

of the horses and the carts that held their provisions, trying to make it appear that she wasn't moving with too much purpose. Still, by the time she drew near the carts, she was trembling again and she cursed her lack of nerve. There were other sentries here, and one of them approached her. Ignoring the pounding of her heart, the minister continued to where her mount was tied, but favored the man with a smile.

"Is everything all right, First Minister?" the sentry asked, eyeing her warily. The duke remained openly distrustful of her; why should his soldiers have treated her differently?

"Yes, fine. I couldn't sleep, so I thought I'd check on Zetya."

She kissed the beast's nose and Zetya nickered in response.

The soldier frowned, as if uncertain of whether to believe her. "We have orders from the duke to keep everyone away from the carts during the night."

"Yes, I know. But surely I'm not doing any harm right here."

His frown deepened. "No, I suppose not. But—"

"I'll just be with her for a few moments more, and you have my word that I won't go near the stores."

He hesitated, then nodded.

Even after the sentry left her, Fetnalla continued to stroke the horse's nose and whisper to her. At the same time though, she reached out with her shaping magic toward the nearest of the carts. The distance wasn't great, but all Qirsi magic worked better when the object on which it was used was close at hand. Shaping magic in particular demanded a certain precision, especially when the point was not to shatter, as one might a blade or arrow, but simply to weaken, as Fetnalla was attempting to do now to the cart's rear wheel. The front wheel actually was closer, but she feared that would be too obvious. A stronger Qirsi than she might have had no trouble with such a task, but by the time she had finished thinning the wood of the rim, her face was covered with a fine sheen of sweat.

She gave Zetya one last kiss, then started back toward her sleeping roll. Glancing toward the soldier, she saw that he was watching her. She raised a hand by way of thanking him and bidding him goodnight, and he did the same.

Reaching her sleeping roll, she lay back down and tried to sleep. But her thoughts kept returning to Evanthya and the siege. Would this delay be the one that sealed her love's fate, or had she done that already with the lies she told in Orvinti? If this newest ploy wasn't enough to keep Brall from breaking the siege, would the Weaver blame her? Would she be the one who died before she and Evanthya could be together again? The rest of the night dragged by, sleepless and unnerving. When dawn broke, the minister was one of the first to rise. A young soldier came by offering her a breakfast of stale bread, cheese, and dried fruit. Fetnalla's stomach felt hard and sour, but she took the meal, fearing that if she didn't it would attract notice.

Soon the entire Orvinti army was on the move once more. Fetnalla rode near the front of the column, not with her duke—Brall wouldn't have allowed that—but close enough so that she could join him as soon as he summoned her. The carts trailed the army, so far back in the column that Fetnalla couldn't hear the rumbling of their wheels. She could do nothing but wait for the shouts and curses she knew would come. She actually hoped that the wheel wouldn't fail until later in the day; the longer it took the less likely suspicions would fall on her. Unfortunately, it seemed that she had weakened the wood too much. Barely an hour after they broke camp, she heard voices raised in anger from the back of the column. A few moments later, a soldier rode by bearing the bad tidings to Brall.

"Demons and fire!" The duke reined his mount to a halt, then turned the animal and started back toward the rear of the army. Passing Fetnalla, he slowed. "You'd best come with me, First Minister. Perhaps your magic can be of some use."

"Of course, my lord."

She fell in behind him and they rode in silence to where the cart sat in the forest lane, tilting toward its rear right wheel, the rim of which had snapped clear through.

Brall swung himself off his mount and rubbed a hand over

his face. "Damn." He glared at the driver. "How did this happen? Did you hit something?"

"No, my lord! The road was clear. The wheel just gave out."

"These are new carts, made just for this march." Brall knelt by the wheel, examining the wood. "I don't see any knots." He hammered his fist against the side of the cart. "I'll have the wheelwright's head when we get back to Orvinti." He stood again, looking at Fetnalla. "Can you fix it?"

"My lord?"

"You have shaping magic, don't you? You can fix wood."

"I can mend some wood, my lord. But I'm not as skilled as some. Shapers are better at . . ." She faltered, feeling her cheeks color. "Our power is more suited to breaking things than putting them together. I can shatter a blade if it's raised against me, but I'm not sure that I could make it whole again." She gestured at the wheel. "The same is true of wood."

"But you can try."

She nodded, dismounting. "Of course, my lord." She knelt beside the cart much as the duke had a moment before. "It will take me some time, and I can't be certain that the wheel will hold. You should have someone work at making a new one while I do this, just in case."

The duke looked away, muttering curses. "We don't have time for this." He appeared to weigh the matter for several moments. Then he stepped to his mount, gesturing for Fetnalla to follow. "Come along, First Minister," he said, climbing into his saddle again.

"But the wheel, my lord."

"You told me yourself you probably can't fix it. We'll leave the cart with a laborer and a party of soldiers. The rest of us will continue on to Dantrielle. We've already lost too much time."

She wanted to argue more. Certainly the Weaver would have expected her to, and would have punished her severely for remaining silent. But no words came to her. She watched the duke ride back to the front of the column. Then, helpless to do more, she swung herself onto Zetya's back and followed.

What was she to do now? She couldn't break another wagon wheel without making her duke suspicious, and she could think of nothing else that she might do to make Brall stop again that wouldn't reveal her as a traitor to Orvinti.

Whether or not you're revealed as a member of this movement is of little consequence to me. The Weaver's words still echoed in her mind, his indifference as blunt as his tone. Yet she couldn't bring herself to do anything too blatant. Her summary execution on this forest road wouldn't help the Weaver's cause any more than had the broken wheel. There had to be a way to serve the Qirsi movement in this matter while still preserving her secret.

She had caught up with her duke, and she fell in behind him now, brooding on the question. So it was that she didn't notice the horse riding past her until its rider addressed the duke. Only then, her attention caught by something in the man's voice, did she look up. It was the sentry from the night before, the man who had spoken to her when she visited with Zetya. When she used her magic on the cart wheel. The sentry was sitting behind the master of arms on Traefan's mount and he spoke in low tones to the duke while the master of arms stared straight ahead.

Brall glanced back at Fetnalla briefly before kicking at his mount and riding on ahead, followed closely by the sentry and master of arms. By the time they slowed again, they were too far away for her to make out any of their conversation. Not that it mattered. She knew precisely what the man would tell Brall, just as she knew that the duke would immediately think the worst of her. That it was true in this instance did little to soften the blow.

This is why I betrayed you, Brall. When you looked at me, you always saw a traitor, even though I served you loyally for years. I only gave you what you deserved.

The sentry and the duke didn't speak for long. After but a few moments the master of arms turned his horse and steered it back toward the rear of the column. Traefan didn't so much as glance in her direction, but the sentry cast a furtive look her way as they rode past, his color high.

"First Minister," Brall called, sounding so very cold. "Would you join me please?"

She spurred her mount forward until she had pulled abreast

of him, her hands and body shaking yet again. What was she that these men should fill her with such dread? How had she become so weak that her life should rest in the hands of this noble and the Weaver? She looked at Brall for but a moment, but that was enough. His broad face was stony and pale, his blue eyes as hard as crystal.

"Would you care to tell me what you were doing by the carts last night?"

She nearly confessed all. Better to be done with all of this than to live constantly with such fear. But cowardice stopped her. Or was it pride?

"The carts, my lord?"

"Don't play games with me, First Minister! That man who just rode past you tells me that you were wandering about the camp last night, and that you were within just a few fourspans of that cart we left behind."

She kept her eyes fixed on the road before her. "It's true that I was awake in the middle of the night—several of the sentries saw me." She glanced at him. "I was making no effort to conceal my movements. I came to see Zetya, I stayed with her a short while, then I returned to where I'd been sleeping and lay down again. I suppose I was near the carts, though it never occurred to me to distinguish one of them from another."

"You want me to believe that you did nothing more than greet your horse?"

"What else do you think I did, my lord?" she asked in return, allowing anger to seep into her voice.

"Isn't it obvious? You're a shaper, and the more I think on it, the more I find myself questioning why the wheel on that cart would simply break, without any warning at all."

"You believe I weakened it somehow."

"Did you?"

"Yes, my lord. I weakened your sword as well, so that the first time you raise it in battle, it will break in two."

"Don't you dare mock me, Fetnalla! You know as well as I that you're perfectly capable of doing such a thing!"

"Do you refer to my magic, my lord, or to my fidelity?"

He faltered.

"You've thought me a traitor for nearly half a year now,

since the duke of Bistari's death. You've searched for any proof you could find to justify your suspicions. And now you've found what you sought. You don't care why I was awake last night, or what I did. You've decided that I betrayed you, and there's nothing I can say to convince you otherwise."

For a long time Brall said nothing. The men at the rear of the company were singing, but otherwise the Orvinti army was as silent as a thousand men could be. "You're right," the duke finally admitted. "It's probably not fair of me, but I do doubt your loyalty. I've come to question the motives of all Qirsi, be they my ministers or my healers. No one has felt the brunt of that mistrust more than you have, First Minister, and for that I apologize. But I can't have you serving me anymore."

She had expected denials, more accusations, or, perhaps, an apology, an admission that he had erred. But Fetnalla never expected this. She merely stared at him, not knowing what to say. She felt tears on her face, but she was too stunned to wipe them away. Strange that this man she had come to hate could still hurt her with such ease.

Giving her a quick look, seeing that she was crying, the duke winced. "You must have known it would come to this, Fetnalla. Certainly I did. For some time now I haven't given your counsel the attention it deserved, and I can't remember the last time we had a civil conversation."

"That's hardly my fault, my lord."

"No, I don't suppose it is. It's the conspiracy and all that they've wrought in these last few turns. Perhaps when we've defeated the renegades, Eandi and Qirsi will be able to trust each other again. But until then . . ." He shook his head.

"Other dukes still trust their ministers. Tebeo still turns to Evanthya for counsel." Why did she continue to argue the point? He was setting her free. Couldn't she serve the Weaver better if she was no longer tied to this fool of a noble?

"Yes, he does, though I've warned him against her."

"He always was wiser than you."

Brall's face reddened and for a moment the minister wondered if he would use this affront as an excuse to punish her, perhaps even execute her. After a few seconds, however, he gave a small, mirthless laugh. "I suppose I deserved that." He eyed her briefly, as if considering something. Then he faced forward again. When next he spoke it was in the officious tone Fetnalla had come to hate over the last several turns. "You may ride with us as far as Dantrielle, First Minister. I know that you'll be anxious to see Evanthya, and we can offer you safe passage into the castle there, provided we succeed in breaking the siege. You're not to ride with me anymore, nor will you be allowed near the carts or provisions. In all other ways, however, you'll remain free to do as you wish. If you decide to leave the army now, I'll understand of course, but I leave that choice to you."

"Thank you, my lord."

"You've earned such consideration," he said, offering no indication that he had noticed the irony in her voice.

They continued to ride together, neither of them speaking, until Fetnalla realized that the duke was awaiting her reply.

"I'll need some time to make my decision," she told him at last.

"Of course. Take until the end of the day if you need to." He slowed his mount, as did Fetnalla. In a few moments a pair of the duke's soldiers had caught up with them. "Accompany the first minister for the remainder of the day," he ordered, looking first at one man and then at the other. "Make certain that she's comfortable. At some point she may wish to speak with me again. Let me know as soon as she does."

"Yes, my lord."

Brall nodded before facing Fetnalla again. "I am sorry, First Minister. Believe what you will about me, but I never wanted matters to come to this."

He kicked at his mount, riding ahead once more, and leaving her with the two soldiers. *I'm to be a prisoner then. Free to do as I wish, he said. But guarded, watched like a thief.* She tried to summon outrage, to replace this ache in her chest with something, anything that might be useful, not only to herself, but also to the Weaver. Yet, it was all she could do to make herself stop crying and ride on in Brall's wake.

She kept a good distance behind the duke for what remained of the day, pausing to rest and eat when he did, and saying nothing to the two men riding with her. They hardly spoke as well, even to one another. Occasionally she could feel one or the other staring at her, but she did her best to ignore them. She had a decision to make. Not the one with which the duke had presented her, but rather one of far greater consequence. The Weaver had been right, though she doubted that even he could have foreseen what would happen this day. It no longer mattered what Brall thought of her. All that mattered now was her service to the movement. And the Weaver had made it clear that if she wished to live long enough to see his plans bear fruit, she would have to keep Brall and his army from reaching Dantrielle too soon.

The question was how to do this. A number of ideas presented themselves to her, but none of them seemed likely to slow the Orvinti army for more than a few hours. Or at least almost none of them.

Surely it needn't come to that, she told herself. Yet the more she pondered the matter, the more convinced she grew. Certainly, she knew what the Weaver would tell her to do, and even as she quailed at the mere thought of it, she recognized the logic.

It's the only way, another voice said within her. The Weaver's voice.

But when she closed her eyes briefly, trying to steady herself with a long breath, it wasn't his dark form she saw, but rather Evanthya's, a disapproving frown on her lovely face.

Brall had given her a gift of sorts, a full day alone with her thoughts, and she used all of it. By the time the sun hung low to the west, its golden light angling sharply through the trees, she knew what she would have to do. Still, she did not give her answer to Brall. He would expect her to struggle with this decision, to wrestle with her hurt feelings and uncertain future. So let him think that she was doing just that.

They made camp just after nightfall, spreading their sleeping rolls within earshot of the Rassor River, in the dappled moonlit shadows of the forest. Still she waited, eating a small dinner by herself before lying down on her sleeping roll to stare up at the stars, as if lost in thought.

It was not until most of the soldiers had already fallen asleep that Fetnalla finally told one of her guards that she wished to speak with the duke. He regarded her doubtfully, but when the other man reminded him of what Brall had said on the road, he stalked off toward the center of the camp, where the duke's tent stood. He returned a short time later, the sour expression on his face making Fetnalla wonder if he had been forced to wake Brall.

"He'll see you," the man said.

Shuddering, hoping that neither man noticed, Fetnalla nodded and followed them across the camp.

Another guard standing by the tent pulled the flap open and motioned her inside. Brall was seated at a table which held a single oil lamp and nothing more. His bedding was disheveled but his eyes looked clear. He hadn't been in bed long.

"It's late," he said. "I expected to have your answer well before now." Any feelings of guilt on his part were gone now, along with the courtesy he had shown her earlier in the day. Good. It would be easier this way.

"My apologies, my lord. It was . . . a difficult decision."

"I'm sure. What do you intend to do?"

"I'll remain with the army as far as Dantrielle, my lord. As you say, I'm eager to see the first minister. And perhaps her duke will have some ideas as to where I might serve next." This last came to her in that very moment. It seemed convincing enough, though she didn't know why she bothered.

Do it. The Weaver's voice again.

"Very well. You understand the conditions under which you may remain with us?"

"Yes, my lord."

"Good." He stood. "Rest well, Fetnalla. We ride at dawn."

A dismissal. Her last. "Yes, my lord," she said. But she didn't move. It had to be done this night. It had to be done now. She knew that. After the early delay, they had covered a good deal of ground today, so much that they might well be within sight of Dantrielle by sundown tomorrow.

"Is there something else?" he asked, impatient, cold.

"Actually, yes." Stalling now. Trying to gather her nerve. "Do you know of others who might need a Qirsi minister?"

She could see how annoyed he was, and for a moment she thought that he would send her away without answering. But it seemed that he did feel some guilt after all. Dragging a hand over his face, he sat again, which was good, very good. He should be sitting.

Do it now! the Weaver screamed in her mind. *This is your chance!*

And Evanthya answered, *Are you mad? Leave him! You don't have to do this!*

One she feared, the other she loved. And most any other night, she would have chosen love. But not now, not when the path of love led inexorably to her own death.

"To be honest, Fetnalla, I know of few nobles who still trust the Qirsi they have. I've heard of none who are actually look—"

He stopped abruptly, interrupted by the muffled crack of bone. His head dropped awkwardly to the side, and he made a queer strangled noise in his throat. But he remained in the chair, his eyes still open.

She should have been terrified. Her hands should have been shaking, her heart pounding like a smith's sledge. But Fetnalla felt more at ease than she could ever remember. Indeed, she felt strangely exhilarated.

She wasn't even frightened when the duke's sentry entered the tent. "My lord, I believe it's time you—" The man halted, staring at the duke, puzzlement and alarm chasing each other across his features. "My lord?" Then to Fetnalla, "What have you—?"

He never had the chance to say more. It took surprisingly little magic to shatter bone, even in one built so powerfully. His neck broken, the man crumpled to the ground, dying nearly as silently as had Brall.

Fetnalla rolled the body to the side of the tent so that it wouldn't be so obvious from the entrance. Then she stepped to the tent flap and peered outside. Her two guards were still there, but otherwise all the soldiers she could see appeared to be sleeping.

"He wants a word with the two of you," she said, gesturing for them to come into the tent.

Of course they did as they were told. They were good Eandi soldiers, and they died as such. One of them, seeing his comrade fall and glimpsing the sentry's body, even managed to work his blade partially free, though he fell before he could raise the alarm.

The Weaver was right. Next to the powers of a Qirsi, the brawn and weapons of Eandi warriors meant nothing. She had never felt so strong, so alive, so proud to be a child of Qirsar.

She stepped out of the tent as if daring the army to stand against her. No one took any notice. Allowing herself a smile, she retrieved her sleeping roll, her saddle, and her other few belongings, then strode to where Zetya was tied. A sentry approached her as she was buckling her saddle into place.

"Where are you going, First Minister?" the man demanded, his hand resting on the hilt of his blade.

She regarded him for but a moment before turning her attention back to her mount. "Didn't you hear? The duke has released me from his service. It seems he doesn't trust me anymore."

"I had heard that. I'd also heard that you were assigned two guards."

"I was. But as you can see, I'm leaving. There's no longer any need to keep watch on me."

She climbed onto Zetya's back.

"Where would you be going in the middle of the night, Minister?"

Fetnalla eyed him again. Would she have to kill this one, too? "Away from here," she said. "I've served this duke since before you were Fated, and in return he accuses me of treason and banishes me from his court. Do you really believe I have any desire to remain in his company?"

The man blinked, clearly unprepared for such a candid response.

"Is there anything else?" she asked.

He shook his head.

Without another word for him, she turned her mount and began to ride off into the wood.

"Where are your guards?" the man called to her.

Fetnalla reined Zetya to a halt and faced him again. "I believe they're with your duke," she said, calm as a planting morning.

The man glanced toward the tent.

Fearing that he might try to stop her, Fetnalla kicked at Zetya's flanks and quickly steered her into the forest. Riding due east, she put some distance between herself and the camp, all the while listening for some indication that the duke and his men had been found. She didn't have to wait long. The first shouts echoed through the trees after only a few moments; it seemed the sentry had gone immediately to find her guards. She knew how fast word of the duke's death would spread through the camp, and while there would be some confusion at first, some uncertainty as to who would lead them and what they should do next, she also knew that it wouldn't take long before Traefan took command and ordered the men to scour the Great Forest for her.

Spurring Zetya to a full gallop, she angled northward, away from the river and deeper into the wood. A few of them would ride after her, but most would be on foot. If she could survive the night, and keep riding until morning, she'd be safe. The Weaver had spoken of battles far to the north, so that was where she would go.

Evanthya, she knew, was forever lost to her. In all likelihood, they would never see each other again, and if they did, Fetnalla would have no choice but to kill her. She wept as she rode, knowing that she was being foolish, that the Weaver would not approve. She had chosen, guided by fear rather than love, driven by the exigencies of her cause rather than by the longing in her heart. Now she would live and die by that choice.

Chapter Twenty-three

Dantrielle, Aneira

That they both survived until nightfall was, in Evanthya's mind, nothing short of miraculous. They fought as if possessed, the duke wielding his sword as the first minister imagined he must have as a far younger man. She had overheard the soldiers speaking in hushed voices of how clumsily he had fought when the siege began, and of how often one or the other of their brethren had been forced to rescue him. And of course, she had seen for herself the wound inflicted on his side by the Solkaran invader.

On this day, however, she saw no sign of the awkward old duke Tebeo himself claimed to have become. Perhaps it was the imminent threat to his castle and family. Perhaps his outrage at all that Numar had done since the siege began finally boiled over into battle lust. Whatever the explanation, Tebeo acquitted himself valiantly. Moreover, his men, seeing how the duke fought, redoubled their efforts on his behalf, driving many of the men of Solkara and Rassor out of the castle and slaughtering those who dared to remain.

For her part, Evanthya benefited from Eandi fears of her people, and their ignorance of Qirsi powers. Her magics—gleaning, mists and winds, language of beasts—did her little good in close combat with larger, stronger warriors. But because the men she fought couldn't be certain that she wouldn't set them ablaze or shatter their bones with shaping power, they approached her warily. Tebeo, who knew precisely what powers she possessed, and who insisted that they remain back-to-back, made certain that she was always facing away from the fiercest fighting. When she was forced into combat, she fought competently. She had learned the rudiments of swordplay long ago—the duke had required this of all his ministers—and what she lacked in strength she made up for in quickness and skill. Nevertheless, she didn't kill a single man, and when forced to parry some of the heavier blows, she nearly fell to the ground. Fortunately, several of Dantrielle's men had positioned themselves around her and the duke, and on those occasions when her life was truly in danger, at least one of them managed to come to her aid.

Dark smoke hung over the castle, stinging Evanthya's eyes and throat. It had shown no sign at all of abating, leading her to believe that the fires still burned in the Great Forest. This was confirmed for her late in the day when one of Dantrielle's captains descended from the castle ramparts to give the duke a report on the fighting atop the walls.

"They keep coming with their ladders, my lord," the man said, as a Qirsi healer mended a gash on his arm. "But they've yet to take any part of the wall."

Tebeo leaned against a stone archway, enjoying a brief respite from the fighting. His face was scarlet and sweat dripped from his cheeks and chin. "Good work, Captain. Please convey my thanks to the men under your command."

"Of course, my lord."

"Have you any sense of how the battle goes beyond our walls?"

"No, my lord. None. We can't see for the smoke and the trees. We hear things occasionally—they're still fighting—but it's hard to say who's got the advantage."

The duke nodded, grim-faced. "Very well, Captain. Return to your men. We'll do our best to hold the gates and ports here."

"Yes, my lord." The man bowed and hurried back to the nearest tower.

Gabrys stood nearby, bleeding from a dozen cuts on his arms, face, and neck, but still looking fresher than Tebeo. "The fires were a desperate measure, my lord. Numar couldn't have attacked us so fiercely and still inflicted many casualties on the armies of Kett and Tounstrel. He simply hasn't enough men."

"You sound very confident, armsmaster."

"I remain convinced that the walls will hold, and that our allies will win through."

Tebeo straightened and examined his blade. "I'd like very much to share your certainty."

The master of arms stepped closer, lowering his voice. "You don't?"

"I know that I should," the duke, his voice dropping as well, "that it's important that I do, not only for myself, but also for the men." He took a long breath. "I'll feel better when Orvinti arrives."

"We can prevail without Orvinti if we have to."

"We shouldn't have to."

Gabrys gave a sad, small smile. "Yes, my lord."

"You don't think he'll come."

"It's not that, my lord," the master of arms said, shifting uncomfortably.

"Then what? Come now, Gabrys, this is no time to be timid."

"Forgive me, my lord. But I fear that you're staking all on the actions of your allies. You're convinced that if they arrive, the siege will be broken, and I sense that you believe their failure to do so dooms us to defeat."

Tebeo opened his mouth, faltered, then frowned. "That's not entirely true," he said, an admission in the words. "But I understand why you might think it is."

"You said a moment ago that we could prevail without Orvinti," Evanthya said, drawing the master of arms's gaze. "How?"

"By continuing to fight as we have been. It may not seem like it, but we've had a good day. The regent has sent raiding party after raiding party, and we've yet to cede any part of the castle. Yes, we've suffered losses, but Rassor and Solkara have lost as many men as we have, perhaps more."

The duke appeared troubled and Evanthya thought she understood why. The master of arms spoke this way with some frequency, measuring Dantrielle's losses against those of the enemy. He was a warrior, no doubt a good one. But Tebeo was not. The loss of life on both sides appalled him. More to the point, he recognized that this war was but a prelude to a much more significant and dangerous conflict. The casualties that Gabrys counted so blithely left them weakened and more deeply divided than ever, just as the leaders of the Qirsi movement wanted.

"You may well be right, armsmaster," the duke said. "But still, I'd like to know what's become of the dukes of Tounstrel and Kett. Can we send out—"

"Look to the skies!"

The three of them spun toward the north wall in time to see another of the great flaming stones crash down the ramparts.

"Damn!" the duke said through clenched teeth.

"I thought the hurling arms had been burned," Gabrys said, sounding more alarmed than he had in some time.

Tebeo nodded, still staring up at the wall. "As did I."

"I'm afraid that may be your answer, my lord. If the Solkarans have managed to repair the arms—"

"Look to the skies!"

Two more burning spheres plummeted toward the castle, one of them hitting the same wall, not far from where the first had landed. The second soared over the wall and landed in the ward, making the ground tremble and splattering flaming pitch in all directions.

Shouts went up from the north and west gates, and an instant later soldiers of Solkara and Rassor swarmed into the castle courtyard.

"Archers!" Gabrys roared, raising his blade and rushing toward the attackers.

Arrows whistled from the walls. Many of the enemy raised shields to guard themselves, but a good number fell anyway, only to be replaced by dozens more storming through the gate.

"What's happened to our defenses?" the duke demanded, readying his sword as well.

"Look to the skies!"

Tebeo looked up once more, his expression more desperate than grim. "He'd kill his own men just to strike harder at me."

Two more boulders smashed down on the ramparts. At the same time, more of Dantrielle's men rushed into the ward from the tower stairways, apparently sent from the walls to meet this newest threat.

"Come with me, First Minister," the duke said, sounding weary as he strode toward the combat. "We'll do this the same way: back-to-back, you facing toward the inner half of the ward."

"Are you certain you're fit to fight, my lord?"

He glanced at her, a hint of anger in his eyes. "What choice do I have?"

"Of course, my lord."

She followed him, wondering how their luck could possibly hold through another fight. Already her arms and shoulders ached from the previous battle and she felt certain that the duke was no better off than she. Still, he didn't hesitate to throw himself into the fray. Evanthya actually had to run to keep up with him, and before she knew it they were surrounded by Solkaran soldiers.

Once more the duke wielded his blade like a man who had been waging war all his life, his steel seeming to dance in the torchlight. The two of them were quickly joined by the master of arms and several of his men and together they formed a phalanx that withstood wave after wave of enemy attacks. Before long, however, Tebeo's breathing began to grow labored, his parries less sure. Evanthya was guarded on both sides by the duke's men; she barely had to fight at all, and when she did, it was only to keep a single man from striking at the duke from behind. But she could do nothing to bolster Tebeo's strength or drive back the men of Solkara and Rassor. She had never envied the powers of other Qirsi, not even Fetnalla, who was a shaper and a healer. But on this night, caught in the tumult of battle, she would have given all that she possessed to break a blade with magic or set afire the flesh and hair of Dantrielle's attackers.

She lost all sense of time, measuring the passage of the

night in screams and the ringing of swords, in the thunder of the flaming stones that crashed down on the ramparts, and in the ever-growing number of dead strewn about the wards of Castle Dantrielle. The minister had little experience with warfare, and immersed in this frenzy she had little sense of what was happening elsewhere in the fortress. But there could be no denying the inexorable retreat of the duke and his men. They gave ground grudgingly, exacting from their foes a dear cost in blood for every backward step. But fall back they did.

It seemed to Evanthya that the regent had to have sent through Dantrielle's gates all of his soldiers save for those few who continued to man the hurling arms. And indeed, in the midst of the fighting, as she glanced over her shoulder to check on Tebeo and the others, she thought she caught sight of Numar himself commanding his men from near the north barbican.

"They're driving us toward the lower ward, my lord," Gabrys said a short while later, his voice strained and tight.

"I know," the duke called back. "If they take the upper ward, we lose the armory, not to mention a good deal of our stores, and the cloister, where I've left my family. If you've an idea for stopping them, this would be a fine time to tell me about it."

"I'm afraid I don't, my lord."

"Can we order the archers to aim at Numar?"

"Most of your archers remain on the walls, my lord. And the regent is keeping himself shielded at the back of the barbican."

"First Minister, is there anything—?"

Before Tebeo could finish, an arrow buried itself in the throat of the man next to him. A instant later, arrows were pelting down on Dantrielle's men. Evanthya raised her shield just in time to stop two darts from striking her in the head.

"To the towers!" Tebeo cried as his men scattered like panicked mice.

Evanthya followed him to the nearest of the tower entrances, peering warily up at the ramparts as she ran. Fighting continued on three of the walls, but one of them was now held by the regent's men. And unlike Dantrielle's archers, who still struggled to keep the Solkarans from climbing onto the ramparts, Numar's men were free to loose their arrows at the soldiers fighting below them in the wards.

"Your castle is falling, Tebeo!" came a voice from the north gate, echoing across the courtyard. "Surrender now, and I'll spare the lives of your warriors. Fight on and you doom them as well as yourself."

"I'll die before I surrender to you, Numar! And the men of Dantrielle will gladly give their lives rather than give in to Solkaran tyranny!" The duke stared across at the regent, his expression belying his brave words. "Do we have any hope of stopping them, armsmaster?" he asked, his voice low.

"Only if our men can retake the west wall, my lord."

"Damn. And we can do nothing to help them?"

"No, my lord. Not without ceding the wards to the regent and his men."

"Then, perhaps I should surrender."

"No, my lord!" Evanthya said, before Gabrys could speak. "You can't!"

"I don't want to either, First Minister, but if it means saving the lives of my men—"

"You don't know that he'll keep his word! Think of the things he's done already! Do you really believe this is a man capable of showing mercy to any who have stood against him?"

"No, I don't. But he has other battles to wage, and he needs soldiers. He can't afford to kill my men if he doesn't have to." Tebeo looked at Gabrys, who was listening intently to their exchange. "Isn't that so, armsmaster?"

"It is, my lord. But still, I agree with the first minister. You shouldn't surrender. Not yet, not while we still have some hope of defeating him."

"Wouldn't it be better to end this folly and spare my army?"

"I can't speak for all of the men, my lord. I've no doubt that there are some out there—a few—who at this moment would trade your life for theirs. But as a warrior, I can tell you that I would rather die for a cause, even a futile one, than live knowing that my friends and my duke had died for nothing."

Tebeo nodded. "All right. Then what in Ean's name do we do now?"

Gabrys surveyed the ward, shaking his head slowly. Once more Numar was shouting orders from the shelter of the barbican, marshaling his men, who now moved about the courtyard with relative freedom. "We need to divert our archers from the ramparts," he said at last. "Some of them at least. We need to counter their advantage."

"Won't your captains on the wall realize that?"

"Their orders are to hold the walls at all cost. They've already lost one. They won't spare a single man if it means endangering the others."

"Unless we tell them to."

"Yes, my lord. But I'm not certain that we should. If we lose the walls, none of the rest matters."

"I can help, my lord."

Both men turned to Evanthya.

"What do you suggest, First Minister?"

"A mist, my lord. It wouldn't have helped before, when we were just fighting hand-to-hand. It might have made matters worse. But now, with the archers above us, it may be our only hope."

"Can you make it hover above us?" Gabrys asked. "So that we can see who we're fighting here on the ground?"

"I believe so."

He looked at Tebeo. "In that case I think it a fine idea."

"Agreed," the duke said. "Weave your mist, Evanthya. Quickly."

"Yes, my lord."

The minister closed her eyes, reaching for her magic. She was weary from her battles, but no more so than the men who would be raising their swords beneath the mist she was conjuring. She ignored her fatigue, losing herself in the flow of power.

Opening her eyes once more, she saw tendrils of pale grey fog rising from the grass before her like thin, ghostly limbs. The mist gathered slowly at first, but then began to build, until it blanketed the ward.

Almost immediately, a wind rose from the north, threatening to sweep away all she had done. Pronjed jal Drenthe, Numar's archminister.

"What's happening?" the duke demanded.

But already Evanthya had summoned a wind of her own, at the same time drawing forth even more mist. Pronjed's gale strengthened, but she matched it. He was stronger than she; probably she would fail before he did. She didn't care. At last she was fighting a battle with a weapon she had mastered, on terrain that felt familiar, even comfortable.

"Evanthya?"

"It's the archminister, my lord. He has mists and winds as well."

"Can you defeat him?"

"I don't have to, my lord. The question is, can he defeat me. I intend to do all I can to resist him."

"How long can you keep the mist above us?"

"I don't know." Power was flowing through her body like melting snow pouring off the Caerissan Steppe, cool and strong. It wouldn't last forever—every Qirsi had his or her limits—but at that moment she felt as though she could keep fighting Pronjed until the first cool breezes of the harvest returned to the Great Forest. "Go and fight them, my lord. I'll hold the mist as long as I must."

She sensed him smiling, though she didn't dare look away from the mist, lest the archminister change the direction of his wind, or attempt some other trickery. "Thank you, Evanthya. The people of Dantrielle will remember what you do here long after you and I are gone."

"Yes, my lord."

A moment later the duke and the master of arms left the shelter of the tower, leading Dantrielle's men back into battle, perhaps for the last time. Evanthya wanted desperately to watch the fighting, to make certain that Tebeo survived, but she kept her gaze fixed on her conjuring. And in the next instant, Pronjed did just what she feared he might. Releasing his wind abruptly, he allowed hers to blow the mist away. She reined in her gale as quickly as she could, still drawing mist from the earth. And the archminister called forth his wind again, from a different direction. She met his gust with her own, only to find that he had switched his yet again. Around and around they went, Pronjed changing the direction of his gale almost continually, feinting in one direction and then turning it full force the opposite way, Evanthya struggling to counter whatever wind he summoned while at the same time maintaining her mist over the entire ward. Before long, the cloud she had created was swirling and seething, like some great storm called forth in anger by Morna herself. But always her mist held.

It seemed to Evanthya that their battle of winds and mist went on for an eternity. Soon she was sweating like an overworked horse. Her limbs shivered as if from cold, and her breath came in great gasps. Not long before, she had felt that her power had no bounds. Now she wondered from one moment to the next if her body would fail. Pronjed had to be growing weary as well, though she couldn't sense any flagging of his magic. If anything, he was pushing her harder than before, his gale becoming something akin to a whirlwind, he changed directions so swiftly.

"How are you bearing up, First Minister?"

The duke. Evanthya could hear the concern in his voice and she could only imagine how she must have looked to him. Still, she didn't so much as glance in his direction, so determined was she to keep watch on her mist.

"I'm doing my best, my lord. How goes the battle?"

"Poorly. We've had to fall back to the towers again."

Her eyes flicked toward him, only for an instant, but that was enough. Like her, he was soaked with sweat. There were bloody gashes on both his arms, as well as on his temple and thigh. Still, he didn't appear broken, not yet.

"You're hurt," she said, staring once more at the roiling cloud.

"Not as badly as some. As I say, we've fallen back to the towers, but we're not ready to cede the ward to them. How much longer can you keep your mists above us?"

"I'm not certain, my lord. Not long, I fear. Pronjed is stronger than I am and he's cunning."

"You've done well, Evanthya," he said, his voice so gentle

she could have wept. "I'm grateful to you. Give us what you can, and we'll fight as long as we're able."

"Yes, my lord," she whispered, feeling a tear on her face.

An instant later, she sensed that he was gone, back to the battle, no doubt. The minister wondered if she'd ever see him alive again.

Grief and rage welled up within her, and she tried to pour them into her magic, that she might overwhelm the archminister with one final surge of power. But she was too weary, and rather than bolstering her strength, her despair seemed to sap it. Perhaps sensing her weakness, Pronjed struck at her conjuring with what must have been all that remained of his power. The mist billowed, like smoke when it's met by a sudden gust. And then it began to dissipate.

Desperate now, Evanthya tried to draw it forth once more, to answer this newest challenge. But she had nothing left. Within moments her mist was gone, and the archminister's wind howled through the castle courtyard, uncontested, triumphant.

Panic gripped her. Eyeing the ramparts, she saw that the enemy now held two of the walls, and she saw as well that their archers were already nocking arrow to bow. It would be a slaughter, the last of this bloody siege.

Even as she continued to look up at the walls, she heard men crying "Look to the skies!" and watched as a flaming stone, the first to be thrown at the castle in some time, dropped toward the ramparts. It was only when she saw the men of Solkara and Rassor scrambling to get away that she realized where the stone would hit. Most of them did manage to escape the fiery impact, but several perished. Perhaps the gods were watching over Dantrielle and its people, Evanthya thought. How else to explain such a mishap?

Only when a second ball of flame arced into view and struck the other wall held by the regent's men did she begin to understand that this was neither good fortune nor a divine act.

More shouts from the ward, more men streaming in through the gates. Seeing the uniforms—green and blue, the colors of Orvinti—Evanthya's heart leaped as she thought it never would again. Fetnalla had come, and with her Brall and his army. There were other uniforms as well. Grey and black for

Tounstrel, blue and silver for Kett, purple and black for Noltierre. In the end, they all had come, just as Tebeo had hoped, just as Brall and Vistaan and Ansis and Bertin the Younger had promised.

It didn't take long for the battle to turn. Against the siege-weary soldiers of Dantrielle, Numar's army held sway. But against the armies of Tebeo's allies, unhurt, hungry for combat after their long marches, the regent's men didn't have a chance. Within what seemed like moments, the men of Solkara and Rassor had been overwhelmed. Many died, many more surrendered, and soon Numar and his archminister stood in the middle of the ward, disarmed, surrounded by hostile swordsmen, each held by two guards, their arms pinned at their sides.

Evanthya strode into the ward to join her duke, who appeared grim despite his sudden, unexpected victory. Pronjed, she was pleased to see, looked every bit as weary as she felt. His narrow, bony face was bathed with sweat, his skin even more pallid than usual. But his pale yellow eyes remained alert, darting about, as if seeking some path to freedom.

For his part, Numar showed no outward sign of being troubled by his defeat. With all that had happened in the past turn, Evanthya found it easy to forget how young the regent was. But standing beside even the younger dukes—Bertin and Vistaan—he seemed a mere lad, only a year or two past his Fating. He wore a sardonic smile on his lips and his brown eyes were fixed on Tebeo, as if he were daring the duke to strike him down.

"Congratulations, Tebeo," the regent said, his head held high. "You and your fellow traitors have managed to win. Because of you, Aneira is weakened. Even now, our armies in the north fight for Kentigern. You've just doomed them to failure. A fine day's work for all of you."

"Kill him now, Tebeo." Ansis drew his blade, stepping forward, so that he stood just before Numar. "Or better yet, let me do it."

"No," Tebeo said, his voice thick. "He'll be imprisoned, along with his archminister and any of his captains who remain alive. The rest of his men are to be released—the wounded will be cared for."

Numar clapped his hands, his smirk deepening as the sound echoed loudly off the walls. "How noble. Do you honestly believe that these little mercies remove the stain of your treason?"

Faster than she had ever seen him move—faster than she had thought possible—her duke swept his sword free and laid it against the regent's face so that its tip was poised at the corner of Numar's eye. The regent's smile vanished, leaving him looking even younger, and deeply frightened.

"I'm not the one who brought this war to Dantrielle," the duke said, his voice low and hard. "Nor am I the one who has weakened the realm by tying us to the emperor and his ambitions. All I've done today is put an end to the Solkara Supremacy, and if you ask me, that should have been done long ago. Now, I've said that I intend to imprison you—you're a noble, the leader of one of Aneira's great houses, and you deserve a certain amount of consideration. But if you dare to call me a traitor again, I'll kill you where you stand. Do I make myself clear?"

The man swallowed. "Yes," he whispered.

Tebeo lowered his blade. "Take them both to the prison tower. I want them in separate chambers."

"My lord," Evanthya said, before the soldiers could lead the two men away. "I recommend that the archminister's watch be doubled and that his hands and ankles be bound with silk rather than irons."

Tebeo frowned. "Explain, First Minister."

"I don't know what powers he possesses, but it wouldn't surprise me to learn that he's a shaper, in which case he can shatter manacles and swords with a thought. He won't be an easy man to hold no matter what we do. But his power will be less effective against silk, and the more men guarding him, the less chance he'll have of disarming all of them."

The duke nodded slowly. "Very well. See to it," he said to one of the guards.

The man bowed. Then he and several other soldiers led the prisoners toward the prison tower.

"I still think he should be executed," Ansis said, his light blue eyes fixed on the regent.

Bertin the Younger nodded. "I tend to agree. Not only does he deserve to die, but he's too dangerous to keep alive."

"I won't make a martyr of him," Tebeo said. "As a prisoner, he's humiliated, diminished. He may be dangerous now, but every day he spends in my prison tower makes him less so." He glanced about the ward, his brow furrowing once more. "I'm certain that Brall would agree with me. Where is he?"

Ansis and Bertin exchanged a look that made Evanthya's stomach turn to stone.

"Come with us for a moment," the duke of Kett said, taking Tebeo gently by the arm, and leading him to a dour, tall soldier who stood a short distance away. It took Evanthya a moment to recognize him as Orvinti's master of arms.

Evanthya watched them talk, saw Tebeo cover his mouth with a hand in a gesture oddly reminiscent of his duchess. A moment later he glanced back her way, wide-eyed, his cheeks devoid of color.

And in that moment it hit her. Fetnalla. She turned a quick circle, frantically searching for her love. There were a few Qirsi in the ward. The ministers of the other dukes, several Qirsi healers. But Fetnalla wasn't there. Her heart was pounding; fear gripped her throat so tightly that she could barely draw breath.

She can't be dead. I'd know if she was dead.

She was crying. She didn't even know why, but she couldn't stop.

At last, unable to stand it any longer, she started walking to where Tebeo still stood talking to the other men. An instant later she was running, unable to reach them fast enough.

As she approached however, Brall's master of arms stepped apart from the dukes and raised his sword, leveling it at her heart.

"Not another step, white-hair!"

Evanthya slowed, her eyes straying to her duke.

"It's all right, Traefan," Tebeo said, laying a hand on the man's arm. "Lower your blade."

"But, Lord Dantrielle—"

"Do as I say, armsmaster. Evanthya has spent the better part of this night fighting to save my castle. She's no traitor."

Clearly Traefan remained unconvinced, but after a moment he lowered his sword. He continued to watch her, though, murder in his eyes.

"Please, my lord," she said, facing Tebeo, her tears still flowing. "Tell me what's happened."

"Brall is dead, Evanthya. That's why it took his men so long to reach us."

"I'm sorry, my lord." She wanted to ask about Fetnalla, but the words stuck in her throat. At last she managed just to speak her love's name. "Fetnalla?"

"The first minister killed the duke," Traefan said, in a voice as bitter as wolfsbane.

Evanthya felt her world buck and shift, as if another boulder had struck the castle. She had expected to hear of Fetnalla's death. Of course she had hoped that her love was all right, that somehow she had escaped Brall's fate, but she had been bracing herself for the worst. The whole land was descending into bedlam and blood. All across the Forelands lovers were learning of such loss. Why should she have been spared? *Fetnalla is dead.* Those were the words she had been dreading, that she had been certain she would hear. But this . . . "That's impossible," she whispered.

"She killed three of his guards as well."

"But she wouldn't—"

"Did your friend possess shaping magic?" the man demanded, his eyes boring into hers.

The question stopped her short, for of course Fetnalla did. Shaping, healing, and gleaning. Fine magics for the minister of a powerful house. Just this night, Evanthya had wished for her love's shaping power. How often had Fetnalla said that she would gladly trade shaping for language of beasts, which was one of Evanthya's magics? They had laughed about it many times, offering to swap powers like merchants in a marketplace comparing wares. In one of their beds. In each other's arms.

Evanthya felt her stomach heave and bit down against the bile.

I will not be sick here, not in front of these men.

"Your silence is answer enough," Traefan said, disgust in his voice. "Their necks were broken. There was no sign they'd been garroted or attacked in any way. Just four broken necks, neat as you please. Explain that. Explain why she fled."

"My lord, you know Fetnalla. She's no murderer." But hadn't Fetnalla pushed her to have Shurik killed? Hadn't she given Evanthya gold to pay the assassin?

"We searched the forest for her all that night," Traefan said, "but we didn't dare delay any longer. She'd already kept us away from Dantrielle long enough."

Evanthya stared at her duke, shaking her head in confusion.

She didn't follow much of what Traefan told her then. There was something about provisions and archers and a broken wheel on one of Orvinti's carts. But she understood enough. Fetnalla had been slowing their march to Dantrielle. If this Eandi warrior was to be believed, she had been doing all she could to keep Brall from breaking Numar's siege. Which meant that she was willing to let Tebeo die in this war. And Evanthya as well.

She wouldn't.

How strangely her love had behaved the last time they were together. How distant she had been, how evasive the night she awoke from some dark terrible dream that had her speaking of Weavers in her sleep.

It's Brall's fault, Evanthya wanted to say. *If all this is true—could it be?—he drove her to it with his mistrust, his accusations.* But she knew better. Traefan spoke of treason, of murder. There could be no justification for that, no matter how poorly her duke might have treated her.

Fetnalla is no traitor.

During the snows, the last time Evanthya and Tebeo journeyed to Orvinti, Fetnalla had given her a pendant, a glimmering sapphire on a finely wrought silver chain. Evanthya wore it still; even now her hand wandered to her chest to feel the pendant beneath her clothes and mail. She had questioned the gift then, wondering how her love could afford to give such a gift when she had given all her gold for Shurik's murder. Fetnalla had grown angry, of course. It seemed recently that they were always angry at one another for something. You sound like Brall, she had said. I've been paid my wage since then. And rather than argue further, Evanthya had accepted this explanation, along with the necklace.

Now, though. . . . What if the gold had come from a different source? It was said that the conspiracy had a good deal of gold, that those who joined it were paid quite well.

"First Minister?"

She stared at the duke, trying to make herself remember what he had been saying to her, trying to focus on his face. It seemed she was in a mist—yet another, on what was becoming a night of mists.

"I'm sorry, my lord. I was . . . I was thinking."

They were alone, or as much alone as two people could hope to be in this castle, with the maimed and dead lying everywhere, with healers moving from wound to wound with swift precision, with conquerors and the conquered coming to grips with an uneasy peace.

"I asked if you thought it possible that Traefan was right about Fetnalla."

No, it couldn't be! Her heart screamed for her to give voice to its denial. But Tebeo deserved better. "I'm not certain what to believe, my lord."

"The rift between them had grown too wide," he said, his voice low, his dark eyes fixed on some distant torch. Evanthya had to remind herself that he had lost his oldest friend and closest ally. "There was a time when I blamed Brall for that . . ." He left the thought unfinished.

"As did I, my lord. I still believe that his suspicions were unjustified. At least at first."

"You think he drove her to it?"

She regarded him briefly, wondering if he was challenging her to make such an accusation, or if he asked the question innocently. Deciding at last that he was as desperate to understand as she, Evanthya nodded. "I think it's possible."

"Then you do believe that she killed him."

"I don't want to believe any of this," she said. "I want to wake up and find that the siege never happened, that Brall and Fetnalla are still alive in Orvinti, bickering like children."

Tebeo said nothing. He merely gazed at her, looking sad and old and so weary that he seemed to be in pain. The truth was that she did believe it, despite the ache in her heart, or perhaps because of it.

"Yes," she finally said, the admission feeling like a betrayal, "I believe it."

"Did she ever speak to you of the conspiracy?"

"Of course she did, my lord. We spoke of it quite often. How could we not? I've told you already . . . what we did. But if you mean, did she ever try to turn me to their cause, the answer is no."

"What would you have done if she had?"

There was a right answer to this. She was certain of it. But she had no idea what it might have been. "I don't know, my lord. I . . . I love her very much." She was crying again, tears pouring from her eyes. "I want to tell you that I would have come to you and told you immediately of her betrayal." She nearly choked on the word. "But I just don't know."

Tebeo actually smiled. He stepped forward and gathered Evanthya in his arms so that she could sob like a babe against his chest. "Thank you," he whispered, "for being honest with me."

After what seemed a long time, Tebeo released her. Evanthya stepped back, wiping tears from her face, embarrassed that she should carry on so in front of her duke. She meant to apologize, but he didn't give her the chance.

"I'm sorry to have to ask this, First Minister, but do you have any idea where Fetnalla might have gone?"

Strange that it hadn't even occurred to her to wonder. "No, my lord, none."

"She must know that we'll be looking for her, and she must know that if we find her, we'll have no choice but to execute her."

The answer came with such force that she knew it had to be true. "She'll go north, my lord."

"How do you know?"

"You've believed for some time now that there was more to this siege and the war with Eibithar than just imperial ambition. And you've believed as well that there was a larger conflict looming, between Eandi and Qirsi. What if the leaders of the conspiracy are waiting for the armies in the north to destroy one another before beginning their own attack?"

"You think she's riding to war?"

"Qirsi warriors and Eandi warriors are quite different, my lord. Fetnalla is a shaper, as well as a healer. Her powers would serve a Qirsi army quite well. So would mine, actually, though you may not believe it. One Qirsi can do quite a bit with mists and winds. Ten working together could overwhelm an entire Eandi army." Another realization, the seed of it planted so long ago by Fetnalla's dream. And abruptly it all made sense. Horrible, terrifying sense. "And," she said, a tremor in her voice, "with a Weaver binding their powers into a single weapon, an army of Qirsi could defeat all the warriors of the Forelands."

His eyes grew wide. "You believe they're led by a Weaver?"

"Fetnalla spoke of one." She blushed. "In her sleep actually, in the throes of a terrible dream. But how else could these Qirsi hope to prevail? In a battle of swords and arrows, they wouldn't have a chance. But with a Weaver leading them, forging together their powers, they would be an imposing force."

"A Weaver," the duke said again, breathless and awed. "I didn't even think such people still walked the Forelands."

"I fear they do, my lord. Or at least one does. I believe Fetnalla has gone to him. If she truly did murder her duke, she'd think nothing of waging war beside a Weaver."

Chapter Twenty-four

The end of Numar's siege did little to lift the black cloud that hung like a curse over Castle Dantrielle. True, the armies of Solkara and Rassor had been defeated, their leaders imprisoned, the soldiers disarmed and banished from the city. But Dantrielle's victory seemed hollow indeed. There were dead and wounded everywhere, many of them in the uniforms of Dantrielle's foes and allies, but most of them wearing the red and black of Tebeo's house. The castle itself had sustained so much damage to its walls, ramparts, and gates that it would be at least a year before all the repairs would be completed. And as if all of this were not enough to temper any celebration that might have greeted Numar's surrender, Brall's death lay heavy on the hearts of Tebeo, his allies, and, by all appearances, even his people, who remembered Orvinti's duke as a reliable friend and formidable leader.

In the days following the breaking of the siege, Evanthya tried as best she could to keep her mind on all that had to be done. Tebeo expected her to see to most of the more mundane tasks facing them—finding room to house the wounded, building great pyres for the dead, beginning work on the castle. With the armies of Kett, Noltierre, Orvinti, and Tounstrel camped just beyond his walls, and with Numar, the duke of Rassor, and their closest advisors imprisoned in the castle towers, the duke had little time for such matters.

Yet, even with all this to occupy her days and nights, the first minister could think only of Fetnalla and what she was accused of having done. At first she had tried to convince herself that Brall's master of arms and his soldiers were wrong about her love, that she herself had been too quick to accept that Fetnalla had betrayed and killed her duke. Fetnalla was no traitor; certainly she was no murderer. Like so many Eandi warriors, Traefan Sograna had little use for Evanthya's people. Given the opportunity to make such accusations against Fetnalla, he would surely have taken it. The conspiracy had made all the Eandi fearful and suspicious. Brall had openly questioned Fetnalla's loyalty for several turns now. How could his own mistrust not sow similar doubts in the minds of those men who served him? The duke's death could have been caused by any number of things. Traefan merely chose to blame Fetnalla.

Except that Evanthya knew this man—not as well as she knew Fetnalla, to be sure, but well enough. As dour and hostile toward most Qirsi as he was, he was also honorable and fair-minded. And while the duke might have died from other causes, how was she to explain the dead soldiers found with him?

More to the point, she no longer felt so confident that she had ever really known her love at all. Perhaps she had early on, when their love was young and bright, shining like a newly forged blade. But more recently, as the world beyond their bedrooms and the castle gardens began to intrude upon their love, bringing word of the conspiracy and rumblings of war and with them the deepening suspicions of their dukes, all that they shared began to tarnish. They fought more, confided in one another less. The last time they were together Fetnalla had been distant, withdrawn, despite the passion of their lovemaking. Evanthya wanted desperately to believe that Fetnalla could never turn away from the life they had shared in the courts, but the more she considered what the men of Orvinti had said of Brall's murder, the more she realized that this life, which still held so much for her, had long since become a prison for her beloved. Brall's mistrust and that of his other advisors had likely left her with few or no friends in Castle Orvinti. In all probability, their love had been the only thing keeping her from joining the conspiracy. It wasn't surprising that it had ceased to be enough.

Walking the ruined ramparts with Gabrys DinTavo, Evanthya brushed a tear from her cheek, hoping that Tebeo's new master of arms wouldn't notice. How many times had she been through all of this? How much longer would the mere thought of Fetnalla reduce her to tears?

"First Minister?"

She looked away, gazing out toward the Great Forest as she dabbed at her tears with the sleeve of her robe. Then she faced the master of arms again and forced a smile.

"Forgive me," she said. "My attention wandered briefly. You were saying?"

He frowned. "Perhaps we should do this another time. As I've told you already, we're making good progress with the gates and lower walls. The ramparts are less important right now, with the danger of a siege removed. The gates are what matter, and they should be fully repaired within half a turn."

Actually, she hadn't heard him say this, either. She needed to clear her mind, to banish Fetnalla from her thoughts, at least for the time being.

"I understand, armsmaster, and I agree with you about the gates. But the duke wanted to hear about all the repairs. So let's continue and get this done, so that we can both see to more important matters."

Gabrys nodded, though his frown lingered. "Well, as you can see, the damage to the ramparts is extensive. I imagine that it will be several turns before they'll even begin to look right again. Repairing the battlements shouldn't be too difficult, but the walkways themselves have been ruined, so . . ."

Walking in silence as the master of arms droned on, Evanthya could imagine what Fetnalla would say. *"How can you stand to listen to him? How can you stand to surround yourself with these Eandi men, all of them so avid for war and power?"* She could see her love's face, her head tipped to the side, an ironic smile on her soft lips, a mischievous gleam in her pale yellow eyes. *"You'd really choose them over me?"*

I didn't choose. You did.

". . . the stonemasons are going to have their hands full for some time to come. If we can prevail upon one of the other dukes to send some of their laborers to Dantrielle, we may be able to complete the repairs sooner, but failing that . . ."

I thought we had decided to oppose the conspiracy. That was why we risked our lives and gave our gold to hire the assassin who killed Shurik. What happened?

"What happened?" A breathless laugh. *"What do you think happened? At the same time that we were hiring that assassin, Brall was already treating me like a traitor. While the Eandi should have been fighting the renegades, they were instead trying to murder one another. Grigor's poison nearly killed me. Don't you remember that? Your precious courts are no place for a Qirsi. The nobles fear us, they mistrust us, they're more than willing to kill a few of us if it means attaining the power they covet so, but they don't care a damn about what happens to us."*

That's not true. You can't judge all of them because of men like Grigor and Brall.

"Can't I?"

". . . You will tell him that, won't you, First Minister?"

Evanthya blinked, searching the man's face. "Yes, of course. We need laborers and stonemasons from the other houses."

"Yes. And it's also imperative that we see to the walkways first. He'll want to repair the battlements—nobles always think the battlements are the most important part of the walls. They're not. As long as my archers have somewhere to stand, they can protect the castle. The battlements are secondary."

She stopped walking, hoping that she might extricate herself from the conversation. "I'll be sure to say as much to the duke, armsmaster. You have my word."

He nodded again, looking doubtful. "I'd be most grateful." He indicated the rest of the wall with an open hand. "Do you wish to see more?"

"I don't think that's necessary. You seem to have matters well in hand."

Gabrys inclined his head, acknowledging the compliment. "Thank you, First Minister."

"Of course. I'm certain that we'll have occasion to speak again soon. The duke will want me to keep him informed of your progress."

"Until next time, then."

She did her best to smile, then hurried away, descending the nearest of the tower stairways and following the shadowed corridors back toward her chamber.

"They don't deserve your loyalty, Evanthya. Surely you see that. They're weak-minded and selfish, and the only thing they can manage to agree on is their hatred of our kind."

That's not true of Tebeo.

"Of course it is. He may have managed to hide it from you up until now. But eventually the mask will slip, and you'll realize that I'm right. And then you'll come after me."

Evanthya halted in midstride, reaching out a hand to steady herself against the stone wall of the passageway.

Go after her.

Thinking of it now, she could hardly believe that she hadn't considered this sooner. True, there had been much to occupy her since the breaking of the siege, and naturally her duke would object. He might even forbid her from going. But that wasn't the reason she hadn't thought of this before. Even knowing that Fetnalla was alive, Evanthya had mourned as if her love had died. Her loss was that complete, that final. Fetnalla had murdered her duke and betrayed the realm. She might as well be dead.

"But I'm not."

No, you're not. And I'm going to find you.

"To what end?"

Her duke would ask the same question. What could she hope to accomplish by going after Fetnalla? Fetnalla would never turn her back on the conspiracy. She had killed for it, and if the renegades were truly led by a Weaver, her punishment for betraying them in turn would be swift and absolute. And even if Evanthya did manage to turn her against the conspiracy, Fetnalla faced certain execution here in Aneira. There was nothing to be gained by pursuing her.

"Yet you will."

Yes.

"Why?"

I don't know. But I have to try.

Evanthya straightened, removing her hand from the wall and taking a long breath. Then she went in search of her duke.

She found him near the north barbican, speaking with the master mason. Seeing her approach, he said something else to the man before walking toward her. "First Minister! I'm glad to see you. I was about to have you summoned."

"Has something happened, my lord?"

He shook his head, looking grim. "No. But I believe the time has come for me to pay a visit to Numar and Grestos. I'd like you with me."

"Yes, my lord."

"I thought we might wish to speak with the archminister as well, but I wanted to ask your opinion before we did."

Her first thought was that Pronjed might know something of Fetnalla's whereabouts. She and her love had long wondered if the archminister was a traitor; Fetnalla and Brall had even speculated that Pronjed was behind the strange death of

King Carden the Third, though this would have meant that the man possessed mind-bending magic, one of the rarest and deepest Qirsi powers.

In the next moment, however, she realized that no matter what the archminister might know, they would find it nearly impossible to pry the truth from him. If he did, in fact, possess delusion magic, he would be able to lie to them without detection.

"I doubt there's much to be gained by speaking with him, my lord."

"You fear him."

"I do. But it's more than that." She faltered. Even a duke as tolerant of Qirsi as Tebeo would be horrified to hear of mind-bending power. It was not a magic most Qirsi discussed freely, for it exemplified all that the nobles of the Forelands feared about her people. It facilitated deception and allowed sorcerers to control the thoughts and actions of unwitting Eandi. "He might tell us a great deal, but determining what to believe and what to dismiss will be next to impossible."

The duke smiled. "Come now, First Minister. I think that between the two of us, we can discern most of his lies."

"No, my lord, we can't. Pronjed may have delusion magic. Brall and Fetnalla both thought so, and I've wondered for some time now."

"Delusion?"

"Mind-bending. Delusion is what we Qirsi call it, because it makes it possible for one Qirsi to lie convincingly to another."

"Ah, yes. I remember now. They thought he had killed Carden."

"Yes, my lord. And I've thought it possible that he used his magic to get information from me when he and the regent came to Dantrielle a few turns back."

His eyes widened slightly. "You never told me that."

"I didn't know for certain, my lord. I still don't. I told you all that I could about the conversation itself, but I was afraid to say more."

Tebeo pressed his lips into a thin line, eyeing her grimly. After a few moments he shook his head. "I don't care what powers the man possesses. I want to speak with him. Brall and Fetnalla also believed he might be with the conspiracy—as I remember it, you did as well. I need to learn what I can from him."

She knew better than to argue the point further. "Yes, my lord."

He started toward the prison tower, walking so swiftly that Evanthya nearly had to run to keep pace. The tower was brightly lit with torches and well guarded; Tebeo had stationed three times the normal number of men there since Numar's capture. The men let Tebeo and Evanthya pass, of course, and four of them began to follow the duke up the stairs.

"No," Tebeo said. "We'll speak with the regent in private."

One of the men, a captain, shook his head. "But, my lord—"

"He's in chains, isn't he?"

"Well, yes, but—"

"Then we have nothing to fear from him." The man's brow remained creased. "I'm armed, Captain," the duke said, putting a hand to the hilt of his blade. "And I'll have the first minister with me."

Not that my powers will do us any good. She kept this thought to herself, and a moment later the captain relented, leaving Tebeo and Evanthya to climb the tower stairs on their own.

The guard outside the regent's chamber unlocked the door for the duke and the first minister, but remained in the corridor when they entered. Numar stood at the far end of the round chamber, shackled to the stone wall, his uniform torn and soiled, his hair, normally the color of wheat, now matted and dark. Yet even amid the filth, a prisoner in his enemy's castle, the regent held himself straight and tall, with the regal bearing of a man who thought himself king.

"Come to gloat, Tebeo?" Numar said, a sardonic smile springing to his lips and then vanishing just as quickly.

"I didn't want this war, Lord Rembrere, and I take no satisfaction in its ending. Too many men were lost on both sides."

"A fine sentiment, Tebeo, but you don't fool me. You and your friends have been hoping for an end to the Solkaran Supremacy for some time now. I can't believe you aren't celebrating its downfall."

The duke glared at him, his eyes glittering like dark crystal in the torch fire. "Believe what you will. I don't give a damn. I've come to inform you that messengers have been dispatched to the other houses informing them of your defeat and imprisonment and asking the other dukes to Dantrielle for a meeting of the council."

"You intend to claim the throne for yourself and your sons."

"Actually, I don't. I'm not certain who will be chosen as the next king. But I know it won't be you or your brother."

"And what about Kalyi? Are you willing to deny her the throne as well? Where is the justice in that, Tebeo? She's but a child. She had nothing to do with this."

The duke shook his head, disbelief and disgust mingling on his round features. "You bastard. You wage war on my house in her name, using your power as regent to tear apart our realm. And you have the gall to blame me for the end of your damned supremacy?"

"You're the one who defied me, Tebeo. You're a traitor, and before this is over, I'll do everything in my power to see that you hang for your betrayal."

The duke smiled, the cruelest, most terrible smile Evanthya had ever seen on his lips. "You'd need the council behind you to do that, Lord Rembrere, and I already have five votes out of nine. Six if you count the new duke of Bistari—surely you can't think that he'll vote with you on anything of substance." He shook his head again. "No, if one of us is going to hang, it will be you. The second Renbrere to hang in less than a year. Poor Henthas is going to be rather lonely."

The regent had paled, though he stood just as tall, his eyes narrowed. "You're weakening us. You know that, don't you? We have an opportunity to destroy Eibithar, to make our kingdom stronger than it's ever been. And you're choosing this moment to end the supremacy. It almost seems that you want us to fail, Tebeo. That won't be lost on the others."

"You weakened us, Numar, not I. You entered into this foolish alliance with the empire—"

"The alliance is the source of our strength!"

"The alliance is a mistake! Eibithar isn't our enemy, at least not the one that matters! Neither is Caerisse, nor Sanbira, nor Wethyrn! The Qirsi renegades are the real threat, and anything that distracts us from fighting them puts all the realm at risk. A wiser leader would have realized this. But you're besotted with the idea of making war on the Eibitharians. And in pursuit of this folly, you've divided our army and set house against house."

"I don't have to listen to this!" The regent turned his head to the side. Evanthya had the feeling that he would have turned his back on them were it not for his shackles. "Leave me! Leave me at once!"

Evanthya thought that her duke would refuse, that he would continue to berate the man. That was what she would have done. But Tebeo merely stared at the regent for a few moments, watching as Numar's jaw clenched and his chest rose and fell. Then he turned and stepped to the door, gesturing for the first minister to do the same. The guard opened the door, allowing them back into the corridor before closing it again and turning the latch key.

Evanthya looked at her duke, who was gazing at the chamber door, as if he could see Numar through the iron. "My lord, do you think he can convince—?"

Tebeo raised a hand, stopping her. He entered the stairwell and the minister followed. Neither of them spoke until they had gone down to the lower corridor.

Grestos, the duke of Rassor, was in the largest of the chambers here, but Tebeo stopped just outside the stairway and faced her. "Now," he said in a low voice, "what were you going to ask?"

"I was just wondering if you thought there was a chance Numar could convince the other dukes that you betrayed the realm."

"No, I don't. Oh, Mertesse and Rassor will go to their graves believing that I did, but the others know better. This is precisely why Brall and I went to such great lengths to build an alliance prior to opposing Numar's war. Noltierre, Tounstrel, Kett, Orvinti—they were all with us. And though Silbron wasn't, no duke of Bistari would ever side with a Solkaran in such a dispute."

"Then what will happen to the regent? Do you really expect that he'll be hanged?"

"I don't know." He rubbed a hand over his face, as if considering the matter. But he said nothing, and after several moments he turned on his heel and strode to the duke of Rassor's door.

Unlike Numar, Grestos was sitting on the stone floor, his back against the wall. One leg was folded beneath him, but the other was stretched out straight, a heavy bandage wrapped around the thigh.

"Lord Rassor," Tebeo said. "I trust your wound is healing well."

Grestos glowered at him from beneath a shock of white hair, his eyes blue and shockingly pale in a tanned, leathery face. "What do you want, Dantrielle? Have you come to put my nose in it?"

Tebeo smiled thinly, though Evanthya thought she first saw a brief flash of anger in his dark eyes. "Numar asked me much the same thing. It seems neither of you thinks very highly of me."

Grestos stared at the floor. "You've been to see Numar, too? Are you here to tell us when we're to be executed?"

"I told the regent what I'll tell you. I've sent messages to the dukes who aren't already here, informing them of Numar's surrender and summoning them to a meeting of the Council of Dukes."

"You intend to bring an end to the supremacy."

"How can I do less?" Tebeo paused, wandering the chamber and eyeing the duke. "I made no mention of you in my messages," he said at last.

Grestos looked up again. "They'll know soon enough that I fought alongside him." But Evanthya thought she saw a flicker of hope in his eyes.

"They don't have to, Grestos. I can prevail upon the dukes who fought with me to say nothing of your involvement."

"Kett would never agree to that."

"He would if I ask it of him."

"Anyway, it doesn't matter. Most of the dukes are here already. We're really only speaking of Rowan and Silbron."

"And Brall's son. He won't have known either."

"How would you keep Henthas quiet? He'll speak against me just out of spite."

"Henthas is disgraced along with his house. No one will care what he has to say."

Rassor's duke shook his head again. "All of this is meaningless. Enough of them know what I've done."

Evanthya watched her duke, unsure as to where he was going with all of this. She had never heard him utter a kind word about Grestos, nor did she think that his allies in this war would be willing to forgive Rassor for casting his lot with the Solkarans.

"You're right," Tebeo said. "They do know, and chances are that the others will learn of it eventually. But knowing is one thing, voting in the council to execute you and censure your house is quite another."

Censure of a house was no small matter. As described in the laws governing Aneira's Council of Dukes, censure included confiscation of lands, vast increases in royal fees, and suspension of council voting privileges. Even if Grestos was executed, his sons might be forced to pay for their father's error for years to come.

"What's all this about, Tebeo? What is it you want from me?"

"I want the Solkaran Supremacy ended, once and for all."

"You have that already. You've defeated Numar's army—"

"Only half of it."

"More than half, from what he told me. The point is, you've beaten him, and you already have enough votes in the council."

Tebeo halted in front of the man and squatted down to look him in the eye. "I want more than that. I want the vote to be so overwhelming as to give Henthas no hope of reclaiming the throne. If the council vote breaks six to three, he'll consider that he might still have strength enough to strike at the new king. I want him isolated and weak."

"You should be talking to Rowan. Mertesse is far stronger than Rassor."

"Rowan's house may be strong, but he's not a bold man. He won't stand alone with Henthas, knowing how the Jackal is hated throughout the realm. If you join with the rest of us in the council, Rowan will follow, and the Solkaran Supremacy will truly be broken."

Grestos grinned, though the look in his eyes remained hard. "You covet the crown for yourself."

Tebeo straightened and stepped to the chamber's narrow window. "Again, you echo the regent. The fact is, I don't wish to be king." Glancing back and seeing the doubt on Rassor's face, Tebeo smiled. "I don't claim that I've never wanted the crown, but I'm too old for it now. Besides, I don't have a mind for politics, and I'm not warrior enough to lead the realm into battle."

"Then who?"

For the first time since entering the chamber, Evanthya saw her duke hesitate, as if unsure of himself.

"I'll find out soon enough, Tebeo."

"First I want your word that you'll side with us in the council."

Grestos shrugged. "What choice do I have?"

"You could betray us. Pledge yourself to us now and support Henthas when the time comes."

The man bristled. "I would never do such a thing! When a Rassor gives an oath, he honors it! That's been true of every man who has ever ruled my house, and it's true of me! You may consider me an enemy, Tebeo. I have no doubt that you dislike me. But I fought beside Numar because I had sworn to do so. You're the one who withdrew your support from the supremacy, you and Kett and the others. I have always been true to my word, and I will be now."

"Then you'll oppose Henthas?"

"I've never liked the man. I certainly have no desire to see him as king or regent."

"And if we choose to spare Numar's life?"

"I'll oppose him as well. I swear it."

Evanthya sensed no deception in his words. She couldn't be certain of course—her powers didn't run that deep—but she believed that he would honor his oath. Tebeo seemed to think so as well, judging from the look of relief on his face.

"Thank you, Grestos. In return, I'll make certain that your life is spared and your house is subject to no formal punishment."

"Does that mean that I can leave your prison?"

"I'll need to inform the others first, particularly Ansis, but yes, I'll release you."

Grestos raised an eyebrow. "Will I have to wait until Kett agrees to this? If so, I could be in here for years."

"I didn't say he had to approve. I just want to tell him first."

Rassor seemed skeptical.

"You'll be free within a day. I promise."

Grestos still didn't appear convinced, but he nodded. "So, who will be your new king?"

"I can't be sure, of course. Not until I've discussed it with the rest of the council. But I expect it will be Silbron."

"The boy?"

"He's nearly a year past his Fating and Brall told me that losing his father has tempered him, made him mature beyond his years. He's young still, but Silbron is no boy. And he has Ria with him. The duchess is every bit as clever as Chago was, and knows a good deal about Aneira's other houses."

"All that may be true, but I have to wonder if the other houses will follow such a young king."

"He's a thoughtful man, and he commands the strongest army in Aneira. Indeed, he's that much stronger for having kept his house out of this war."

"Won't that make him suspect in the eyes of Kett and the rest?"

"I doubt it. He's a Bistari. No one doubts that he hates the Solkarans. And by remaining neutral, he's made himself more acceptable to Mertesse."

Grestos gave a small shrug. "Very well, Tebeo. I've given you my word. If Silbron's your choice then so be it. He'll have my vote in the council."

Tebeo nodded and crossed to the door. "Thank you, Lord Rassor."

"I think you're mistaken about one thing, though," Grestos said, drawing Tebeo's gaze once more. "You have more skill with politics than you think. If you can truly manage to convince Kett to agree to all this, you'd make a fine king indeed."

Tebeo grinned and left the chamber, with Evanthya following close behind. This time, she knew enough to say nothing until they were in the stairway, and even then she kept her voice to a whisper.

"Silbron, my lord? Are you certain?"

"There is no one else, First Minister. If Brall still lived, he'd be my first choice. But his death leaves Silbron and me, and having led the rebellion against House Solkara, I can't take the throne for Dantrielle without making it seem that all I've done was driven by ambition. That's not how I wish to be remembered."

Evanthya had to smile. This was why she continued to serve her duke. Any Qirsi who dared say that all Eandi nobles were alike had only to listen to Tebeo of Dantrielle to be proven wrong. "Yes, my lord," she said.

The sound of tolling bells reached them in the stairway, echoing softly.

"Is that the prior's bell already?" the duke asked.

"It is, my lord." Perhaps he would postpone his conversation with Pronjed until the next day. Perhaps, given a bit more time, he would think better of speaking with the archminister at all. Would that he were so easily dissuaded.

"We'd better hurry then," her duke said. "I dine with the other dukes this evening, and first I want to meet with Numar's minister."

The prison was nothing. Stone and iron. He could shatter both with a mere thought, and would when the time came. They had bound his wrists and ankles with silk, fearing that he would shatter iron manacles, but he would find a way to free himself from these bonds as well. Nor did he concern himself with the guards who stood beyond the chamber door. With his mind-bending magic he could turn the Eandi brutes to his purposes whenever he chose. For those who proved less pliable, he still had his shaping power, which worked just as well on bone as it did on rock and steel. The army that awaited him beyond the tower presented a somewhat more formidable challenge, but Pronjed felt certain that he could find his way past a thousand men if he had to.

And he did have to. The Weaver had ordered him north, to Eibithar, where fighting between Kearney's army and the soldiers of the empire had already begun, and where, quite soon, the Weaver intended to commence his own war.

"The time is at hand, Pronjed," the man had said to him, looming in his dreams like a god, or a demon, black as pitch against the brilliant white sun that was always at his back. "All for which we have worked is about to come to fruition. All past failures will be forgiven. Even the breaking of your siege will soon mean nothing. Meet me on the Eibithar Moorlands, give your power to me to wield as a weapon, and I shall give in return the future of which we've spoken so many times."

There had been nothing for him to say, except, "Yes, Weaver."

He had, of course, been planning to escape even before the Weaver came to him. At first he intended to shatter the walls of his prison the night he was captured, but Dantrielle's duke, uncertain as to what powers he possessed, had posted eight archers in the corridor outside his chamber, too many even for a man of Pronjed's considerable powers to defeat. Over the past several days, however, as the archminister gave no indication that he was a threat to the castle or its duke, the number of guards outside his chamber had been reduced. This morning, the last of the archers had been removed. He had only to wait until nightfall.

Pronjed still wasn't certain how he would reach the Moorlands in time to join the Weaver's battle. His horse had been taken by Tebeo's men, and though he would do what was necessary to win his own freedom, he didn't know if he could risk a visit to the stables before he fled the castle. But the Weaver wouldn't tolerate excuses, and Pronjed, spurred on by the promise of wealth and power should the Weaver's plan succeed, had worked too hard on behalf of the movement to be absent at its culmination. Somehow, he would make his way to Eibithar and fight alongside the Weaver. He would share in the Qirsi victory, and when the Weaver swept away the Eandi courts and began to reward his most faithful servants, Pronjed would be among the new nobility.

Not long after the ringing of the prior's bell, he heard footsteps on the stairs leading to his corridor. He assumed at first that this was merely a guard bringing what passed for his evening meal a bit earlier than usual. Only when he heard a woman speaking in hushed tones did he understand that the duke had come, and with him his lovely first minister.

Pronjed stood and faced the door, holding himself as proudly as he could under the circumstances. He would not allow them to think that he had been broken, no matter how much it might aid his escape.

He heard Tebeo order the guards to open the door. A moment later the lock turned loudly and the door swung open.

Tebeo had never looked like the duke of a major house. He was fat and short, with a face that was far too pleasant to be imposing. Still, the minister knew that he possessed a keen mind, and in the past half turn, as he withstood Numar's assault, he had more than proved his mettle.

His first minister was the perfect complement to the duke. Pale where he was dark, lithe where he was round, reserved where he was affable. Yet Pronjed also knew her to be formidable in her own way. He had clashed with the woman on more than one occasion and had no doubts as to her loyalty to the duke and the realm.

"Archminister," the duke said, eyeing him, a tight smile on his face.

He's afraid. She's warned him against you. "My lord Dantrielle. To what do I owe this courtesy?"

"Curiosity, I suppose," Tebeo answered, surprising Pronjed with his candor. "I have certain questions, and I know better than to expect honest answers from the regent."

"You expect that I'll be more forthcoming?"

"I hope that you will."

"And what can I expect in return?"

"Clemency. Perhaps, eventually, your release from this prison."

Pronjed glanced at the first minister, who was watching him with obvious interest. "I'll tell you what I can, my lord."

Tebeo began to pace in front of him, his hands clasped tightly behind his back. "How many men did Numar send north to the Tarbin?"

"About a thousand. He expected the army of Mertesse to make up the rest of the force. The rest of his men he divided between guarding Solkara and attacking you."

"Has he been in contact with the duke of Bistari?"

"Bistari?" Pronjed said, with a small breathless laugh. "Surely you jest, my lord."

"No, but never mind the question."

The archminister narrowed his eyes, wondering why Tebeo would ask about Bistari's young duke. Had they been alone, he would have used mind-bending magic to force the duke to explain himself, but with Evanthya watching, he didn't dare.

Tebeo paced in silence for a moment. Then, "Tell me, Archminister, what do you know of the Qirsi conspiracy?"

"Not much, my lord. Probably no more than you do. I know what it's reputed to have done. The murders in Eibithar, the assassination of Lord Bistari. There are rumors of an attempt on the life of Curlinte's duchess in Sanbira, though of course we can't be certain if this is true."

"What about the death of our own king?"

Perhaps he should have been prepared for this. But Pronjed couldn't entirely keep his voice from catching as he said, "My lord?"

"The duke of Orvinti and his first minister have wondered if Carden might have been murdered."

"His Majesty took his own life, my lord. I saw his body, and I can tell you that the evidence of this was unmistakable."

"We'd heard as much," Evanthya said. "Fetnalla wondered if someone might have used mind-bending magic to make the king kill himself."

Pronjed glanced at Tebeo's first minister. "This is the first time I've heard anyone suggest such a thing."

"Do you possess this magic, Archminister?"

Pronjed held Evanthya's gaze for another moment before forcing himself to face the duke again. "No, my lord, I don't." He could have used his power to make the lie more convincing; delusion worked on Eandi and Qirsi alike. But Evanthya would have been expecting this, and delusion magic, when used against a Qirsi, only worked on the unsuspecting.

"You heard of Lord Orvinti's death?"

"I've heard rumors of it, my lord." Again he chanced a look at the first minister, but suddenly she was avoiding his gaze. It seemed the rumors were true: Fetnalla had killed Brall.

"Lord Orvinti's first minister vanished after Brall was killed. I'm wondering if you have any idea of where she might have gone."

She went north, just as I will. "No, my lord, none."

Tebeo nodded again. "I thought as much." He looked as if he might say more, but instead he stopped his pacing and glanced quickly about the chamber. "I take it you're comfortable enough, Archminister. You're being fed, you have enough blankets for the nights?"

Pronjed gave a thin smile. "Of course, my lord. For a prison, this is quite comfortable." He held up his hands, showing Tebeo the silk cords wrapped around his wrists. "That said, I'd have freer movement with normal manacles."

"Those were my idea," Evanthya said. "I seem to remember that you have shaping power. In which case, chains wouldn't do much good, would they?"

"No, I don't suppose they would."

"We'll speak again, Archminister," Tebeo said, as one of the guards unlocked the door. He stepped into the corridor and paused, as if waiting for Evanthya.

"I'll be along in a moment, my lord," she said, stepping closer to Tebeo and lowering her voice. "I have a few more questions to ask the archminister, and I suspect he'll be more forthcoming if he and I are alone."

Tebeo frowned, but after a moment he nodded and left the corridor. The guard closed the door once more.

Evanthya crossed to where Pronjed stood. "You intend to escape, don't you?" she whispered.

"I don't know what you mean."

"Of course you do. It's just a matter of time. You're a shaper, you have delusion magic. It should be relatively easy."

He started to deny it again, but she raised a finger to his lips, stopping him.

"Don't say anything. I don't care if you get away. You have no reason to harm my duke or me, and every reason to head northward as quickly as possible."

His heart was pounding. How could she know all of this?

"What do you want?" he asked.

"I want Fetnalla. You must know that she and I were lovers."

He'd had an inkling of this.

"I want to find her. She's joined your conspiracy and she's gone north to find the Weaver."

"I don't know what you're talking about." It sounded hollow, forced. For several turns now he had been lying to Numar and Henthas, Kalyi and Chofya. For years before that, he had lied to his king. He felt as comfortable with deception as he did with the truth. But somehow this woman had seen into his mind, as if she were a Weaver and he a simple festival Qirsi.

"I won't help you escape, but neither will I alert my duke to the danger. In return, you're to leave here directly without harming anyone." She hesitated, her eyes locked on his. "And if by some chance you sense that you're being followed, you're to do nothing about it."

"What's to stop me from killing you once we're away from Dantrielle?"

"Nothing, if you can catch me. But if you can't, and I make it all the way north to your Weaver, I'll make certain that he learns you allowed yourself to be followed. I can't imagine he'd be pleased."

"I can't do this."

"I just want her back, Pronjed. I don't give a damn about the rest. Not anymore. I just want Fetnalla. And even if I did want to stop your conspiracy, I couldn't. I'd be one Qirsi against an army, against a Weaver."

He shook his head, opened his mouth, then closed it again. He'd almost said, *He'll kill me.* But he stopped himself in time. What if this were a trick, an attempt on her part to make him admit that there was in fact a Weaver?

Except that she didn't seem to be lying. Did she have delusion magic as well? Was that how she had learned that he did?

"He'll never know," she whispered. "Just ride north, and don't look back."

She gazed up at him for another moment, her eyes as golden and bright as a setting sun. Then she turned away and left him.

Chapter Twenty-five

Kentigern, Eibithar, Adriel's Moon waxing

The smells of the siege had become as familiar to him as the scent of Ioanna's perfume, as ordinary as the aroma of freshly baked bread rising from the kitchens. Burning tar and oil, boiled sweetwort and betony, gangrene and blood, sweat and fear. There were sounds as well—death cries, the moaning of the wounded, the distant singing of the Aneiran soldiers—and, of course, so many horrors to see. But the smells were what stuck in Aindreas's mind. Long after the siege ended, either with the fall of his castle or the defeat of his enemy, the duke would remember breathing in this air that blanketed Kentigern, redolent with the stench of war.

After the successes his men enjoyed during the first day or two of the siege, Aindreas had begun to think that he might break the siege with ease. And though he had known that his Qirsi allies would not be pleased by this, he had secretly rejoiced at the possibility, seeing in the Aneirans' failure a setback for the conspiracy as well. If the armies of Mertesse and Solkara could not maintain their siege, they certainly couldn't send any men northward to join the fighting near Galdasten. There was nothing he could do to atone for his crime. He had allied himself with the renegade white-hairs; he was a traitor. But perhaps, merely by fighting to protect his house, he could thwart the Qirsi's plans and thus undo some of what he had wrought.

But after losing so many men, and seeing their hurling arms burned beyond use, the Aneiran army rallied. Redoubling their assault on the gates and walls, they broke through the drawbridge at the Tarbin gate and turned their rams against the portcullises. During the second night of the siege, hours after the ringing of the midnight bells, a large group of Solkaran soldiers gained the top of the outer wall and held it into the morning before being overrun by Aindreas's men. They did no lasting damage to the castle and Kentigern's losses were not great, but the duke could see that his men were shaken by the incursion. Up until the previous year, Kentigern Castle had enjoyed a centuries-old reputation as one of the most unassailable fortresses in the Forelands. The near success of Mertesse's siege the year before was a black mark on the castle's history, but one that could be explained away by Shurik's betrayal. Now, however, as the Aneirans began to exact a toll on the defenders, Aindreas sensed that doubt was growing in the minds of his men.

By the end of the eighth day, the Aneirans had managed to build four new hurling arms. As soon as all four were functioning, the men of Mertesse and Solkara began their assault on the castle battlements, heaving great stones, pots of burning oil, and dead animal carcasses at the walls. Aindreas sent out a raiding party, hoping to destroy these siege engines as he had the last, but the Aneirans were watching for this, and Kentigern's men, suffering heavy losses, were driven back.

The following morning, the first of the Tarbin gate portcullises fell, and though three more remained, this further eroded the confidence of the duke's men. His bowmen, using the archer chambers built into the walls of the gate, and the murder holes built into the ceiling, kept up a withering assault on the attackers. But the enemy's rams still offered the Aneirans some protection, enough to allow them to begin their attack on the next portcullis.

By nightfall, the wood and iron were groaning. Aindreas

knew that it wouldn't be long before the second portcullis was defeated as well. The men stationed on his battlements had been forced to seek shelter within the towers, emerging only long enough to loose their arrows and quarrels before being chased back inside by the bombardment from Aneira's hurling arms. The only saving grace was that with the arms constantly striking at the walls, the enemy soldiers could not risk raising ladders to climb to the ramparts.

Aindreas could do little but watch the siege unfold from his chamber. He would have preferred to fight; despite his girth, he remained a formidable presence on the battlefield, powerful, yet quick with a blade. But this type of war demanded patience, a virtue he had always lacked. Sitting at his desk, the smell of smoke stinging his nostrils, it was all he could do to keep from drowning himself in Sanbiri red.

Early the next morning, as the duke finished a small breakfast, Villyd Temsten, his swordmaster, came to his chamber, face grim, eyes smoldering. He had a bandage on his forearm and an untreated gash above his left eye, but these only served to make him appear even more fearsome than usual.

"What news, swordmaster?" the duke asked, rising from his chair and stepping around his writing table.

"Little has changed, my lord. The second portcullis still stands, though it won't last the day. Our archers have had some success from the ramparts, but they're still being chased back to the towers by Rowan's hurling arms."

"How are our stores?"

Villyd's mouth twisted sourly for a moment. "Shrinking, my lord. Slowly, to be sure, but we can't hold out indefinitely."

"Neither can they."

"Actually, Mertesse is near enough that they can reprovision more readily than we can."

Aindreas frowned. "Is this why you've come? To tell me that our stores are running low?"

"No, my lord. There's something else. I think you should come see for yourself."

"What is it?"

"Please, my lord. Come with me."

Aindreas took a long breath, then indicated the door with

an open hand and followed Villyd into the corridor. The swordmaster led him from the inner keep to the nearest of the towers on the outer wall. They climbed to the battlements, then strode to the northeast corner of the castle.

"Look," he said, pointing toward the farmland beyond the city walls.

The duke had known while still in his chamber what it was Villyd intended to show him. Still, he couldn't keep from muttering a curse.

A long column of Aneiran soldiers was marching north toward Kentigern Wood, some in the black and gold of Mertesse, many in the red and gold of Solkarą. They had set fire to two of the nearer farmhouses and were in the process of setting ablaze a field of grain.

"Bastards," the duke said, staring down at them, feeling helpless and foolish.

They'll wait until the siege is well under way, Jastanne had said, with the prescience one would expect from a Qirsi. *In all likelihood you'll have little choice but to use all your men in the defense of your city and castle. But just in case you have it in mind to stop them, don't.*

He could hear her voice, so calm and sure of herself. He would have liked to scream her name, and he found himself glancing due north, to the rise on which he had seen her the day the siege began. No one was there now.

"We should stop them, my lord. We should protect the people in your dukedom, and we should keep them from reaching the Moorlands."

"We can't," Aindreas said, his voice thick.

"But, my lord—"

"We can't!" The words echoed off the fortress walls, drawing the stares of his men. "It's what they want us to do," he went on, more quietly this time. "That's why they're burning the houses and crops, to draw us into the open." He knew this was so, just as he knew that if he divided his army his castle would be at risk. Just as he knew that Villyd was right, that he should have been willing to risk Kentigern to save Eibithar.

"What are your orders, my lord?" the swordmaster asked,

his voice so flat, it made Aindreas's throat constrict just to hear it.

"We'll go after the hurling arms again. If we can destroy them, we might be able to break the siege. Rowan has fewer men now."

"Yes, my lord."

Villyd turned and walked away, his shoulders hunched and his head low. Protocol demanded that he await permission from Aindreas before leaving, but the duke hadn't the heart to call him back.

"People are dying, father."

Aindreas turned to see Brienne standing beside him, her golden hair rising and falling in the warm wind.

"They're dying because of you. And because of you, the kingdom is in peril of being overrun."

"What am I supposed to do?"

"Tell them the truth."

"I'll be hanged, and Ennis will be left to rule a shamed house."

"Yes. But still, you have to."

He turned away from her, searching the rise once more for Jastanne, fearing that he might see her.

"Our best hope now lies with the Qirsi. As long as they prevail, we'll be fine."

"The Qirsi killed me. You know they did, and yet you continue to help them."

Tears stung his eyes and he squeezed them shut rather than look at her, rather than allow any of his men to see him weep.

"You should be ashamed," he heard her whisper.

You're a ghost. You're not real.

When at last he opened his eyes, she was gone. Several of his soldiers were eyeing him, some with open curiosity, others more discreetly, though with apprehensive looks on their faces.

In the next instant, the castle shook, and their attention was drawn once more to the Aneirans and their ram, which was hammering again at the Tarbin gate. A moment later, several of the men shouted warnings, pointing toward the sky. Mertesse's soldiers had returned to the hurling arms as well. One of the great stones crashed harmlessly against the outer wall, and another passed over the ramparts and landed in the castle's outer ward. But two clay oil pots found their mark, shattering on the walkways atop the wall and splattering flaming oil in all directions. Several men dropped to the stone, rolling frantically back and forth, trying to put out the fires on their uniforms and hair. Aindreas rushed to help them, batting at the blazes with his hands, tearing off his cape and throwing it over one man whose clothes were fully engulfed.

When the flames had finally been put out and healers summoned, an uninjured soldier approached the duke.

"You must leave the walls, my lord. They're certain to attack again, and you could be killed."

Aindreas glared at the man, ready to tell him to mind his own affairs. But he knew the soldier was right. He was no good to the army dead. Indeed, his death might well hasten the castle's fall.

"Fine," he said. "Where's the swordmaster?"

"I don't know, my lord."

He glanced toward Kentigern Wood once more. Smoke continued to rise from farmhouses and fields, and the column of Solkaran soldiers was still in view, farther from the castle, but near enough to be overtaken by an army on foot.

They'll tell the world what you've done. Think of Ennis and Affery. Think of Ioanna.

Aindreas entered the nearest tower, descended the stairway to the outer ward, and crossed the courtyard to where Villyd stood, speaking with three of his captains.

"My lord," the swordmaster said, seeing him approach. The captains fell silent.

Aindreas had intended to pursue the Solkarans. He had been ready to confess all to Villyd, to explain what would happen when the Qirsi learned that he had stopped the Aneirans' march northward. But faced with the prospect of doing so, seeing the way the captains looked at him, the duke couldn't bring himself to speak the words.

"Was there something you wanted, my lord?"

"Yes. Yes, I—I want you to send out raiding parties against those hurling arms immediately. They're striking at the battlements again, and I want it to stop."

"Yes, my lord. We were just discussing that. We had thought to send twice the number of men this time, half through the south sally port, half through the west. Perhaps if we flank them, they'll have a more difficult time driving back the assault."

"Very good, swordmaster. That sounds like a fine plan." His hands were trembling. What he would have given for some wine.

"Very well, my lord. We'll prepare the raiding parties immediately."

Aindreas nodded. "Good. I'll be in my chamber."

He hurried away, certain that Villyd and the others were staring after him, but too eager to be back in his chamber to care.

Brienne was waiting for him in the corridor outside his door, but he ignored her, reaching for the door handle with his eyes fixed on the stone floor.

"Father."

He opened the door.

"Father!"

He chanced a glance at the girl, then blinked and looked again. It was Affery, not Brienne. She was frowning at him, looking more peeved than hurt.

"I'm sorry, Affery. I . . . I'm sorry." He walked over to her and pulled her close in a quick embrace. "What is it you need?"

"Mother was asking for you. We felt the castle shake and I think she was afraid."

He brushed a strand of hair from her face. She'd be beautiful, too, just as her sister and mother had been. "How is she?"

Affery shrugged. "Not too bad. She sings with us, which she hasn't done in a long time. And she's been eating. I know that you worry when she doesn't."

Clever child, like her brother. She'd make a fine duchess someday.

Who will marry a girl from a disgraced house?

"Tell her not to worry. The Aneirans are using their hurling arms again, but we're sending out men to destroy them. Can you remember all that?"

"Yes, but she'll want to hear it from you."

"I know. I'll come to the cloister later."

"When?"

"This evening. I'll try to be there for dinner. Tell her that."

Affery nodded, looking terribly sad. "Yes, Father."

Aindreas knew that he should say more. Perhaps he should have gone with her immediately back to the cloister, but all he could think about was his wine and the Qirsi and what a mess he had made of everything.

"That's a good girl," he said, kissing the top of her head.

She gave a half smile before walking back down the corridor toward the cloister. Aindreas watched her go, waiting until she had turned the corner before entering his chamber, bolting the door, and pouring himself a cup of Sanbiri red.

By the time the prior's bell sounded in the city, Aindreas had gone through two flagons of wine and was well on his way to finishing a third. He wasn't drunk—he had consumed so much wine in the year since Brienne's death that he wasn't certain he was capable of getting drunk anymore—but he had grown sleepy. Sitting by his window, his goblet in his hand, he nearly dozed off, but was pulled awake again by a knock at his door.

His first thought was that it must be Jastanne, and he kept silent, hoping that she would leave him. But then he heard Villyd calling for him.

The duke stood, feeling a bit unsteady on his feet, and crossed to the door. He unlocked it and pulled it open, but then retreated to his writing table, not wanting the swordmaster to smell wine on his breath.

"Report," he said, sitting once more. "You sent out the raiding parties?"

"Yes, my lord."

"And?"

As if in answer, the castle shuddered, and cries went up from the ramparts.

"Our men managed to destroy one of them, my lord, but they were driven back before they could do more."

"How many did we lose?"

"Fourteen, my lord. And eight others wounded."

"Demons and fire." The fortress shook again. "Do we dare try again?"

"We can, my lord, but I doubt we'll be any more successful."

"What if we tried at night? Give the men flints to light their arrows so they wouldn't need to carry torches."

"That might—" Villyd stopped, eyes narrowing.

Aindreas heard it as well. More cries from the walls, though these were different from those that had come before. "What is it?"

"I don't know, my lord."

The duke stood and together they strode to the closest tower and climbed the stairs to the battlements. Kentigern's men were gathered at the eastern end of the outer wall, and several of them were pointing toward the lower edge of the wood. For a moment, hurrying toward the east end of the walkway, he wondered if the Solkarans had returned, but they would have had no reason to do so.

Reaching the wall, looking down where his men were pointing, the duke felt his stomach heave. A tremendous column of soldiers was approaching the tor—at least three thousand men. Some marched under the green and white banner of Labruinn, others under the tawny and black of Tremain. Even from a distance, the duke recognized the sigils on their banners. But his eyes were drawn to the lead group, all of them dressed in purple and gold, all of them marching under the flag of the realm. These were Kearney's men, the King's Guard.

"They've come to save us!" one of the soldiers shouted, drawing cheers from the others.

Aindreas wanted to believe this, but he had defied the king at every turn, refusing to pay his ducal fees, ignoring Kearney's demand that he journey to the City of Kings. He had even allowed Jastanne to murder Kearney's emissary in his chamber. Had he been king, he wouldn't have sent his army to aid such a duke. He would have sent it to destroy him.

* * *

Gershon had pushed his men hard since leaving the City of Kings, and to their credit, the dukes of Tremain and Labruinn had done the same with their soldiers, matching the King's Guard league for league even though neither house was known for its military prowess. Lathrop, the duke of Tremain, who was a good deal older than Gershon and Caius, had been particularly impressive. He was a heavy man, and he looked too soft to command an army, much less travel with one covering nearly thirty leagues in but five days. Yet this was just what he had done. Caius, one of the realm's younger dukes, had actually journeyed twenty leagues farther than had Gershon, crossing both the Thorald River and Binthar's Wash before joining the swordmaster outside the walls of the royal city.

Gershon had long dismissed Eibithar's minor houses as being of little consequence when it came to matters of state or war. The Rules of Ascension gave the minors only a small role in the selection of new kings, and all military men knew that the strength of the realm came from its major houses—Thorald and Galdasten, Curgh, Kentigern, and Glyndwr. But marching with these two men and their soldiers, watching how Caius and Lathrop shouldered the burdens of leadership, the swordmaster found himself wondering if the distance between the houses might not be nearly so great as he had thought.

He had also feared that one or the other of the two men might challenge his leadership of the army. True they ruled minor houses, while Gershon was the king's man, but they were both noble born, educated in the courts, wealthy. The swordmaster was none of these things. Yet from the beginning, both men deferred to him, willingly placing their armies under his command, and following his instructions without question. Even more improbably, the swordmaster and Caius quickly developed an easy friendship. The duke was at least ten years Gershon's junior, but despite their different ages and upbringings, it seemed they had a good deal in common. Like

Gershon, the duke was a quiet man. He had studied combat under his father, long renowned as one of the realm's finest swordsmen, and had obviously taken an interest in all matters related to warfare. Each day, as they rode at the front of the armies, the duke peppered Gershon with questions about swordplay, military tactics, and weaponry. At first Gershon had thought that the young duke was merely making conversation, but his lines of questioning quickly revealed a thorough understanding of the subtleties of all matters related to battle. Labruinn's swordmaster, who was even younger than his duke, rode with them as well, listening intently to their discussion, and occasionally asking questions of his own.

Sulwen would have teased Gershon mercilessly about their conversations. "You're like little boys playing at war and ogling fancy blades," she would have said. "How can you not find it tiresome talking about the same thing day after day?"

The fact was, Gershon didn't find it the least bit tiresome. The march from the royal city to Tremain, which the swordmaster had expected to be endless, went by all too quickly. After spending the last several turns consumed by talk of war and the conspiracy and the archminister's attempt to draw the Weaver's attention, Gershon could not help but enjoy himself, even as he marched toward battle.

After reaching Tremain and adding Lathrop's army to their force, Gershon and the duke of Labruinn grew more sober. And with every league they covered, drawing ever nearer to Kentigern Tor, the swordmaster's apprehension grew. His scouts had informed him of the siege and its progress; from all they had told him it seemed that the Aneirans were exacting a toll, but that Kentigern Castle was not in imminent danger of falling to the enemy. They couldn't tell him, however—they had no way of knowing—how Aindreas and his men would receive them. Would he and the dukes reach the tor only to find themselves under attack from both Kentigern and the Aneirans?

Lathrop, it seemed, harbored similar fears. "Forgive me for asking, swordmaster," he said, as they rode in the shade of Kentigern Wood, less than a full day's ride from the castle. "But are you and His Majesty certain that Aindreas will accept aid from the King's Guard, or, for that matter, from the armies of His Majesty's allies?"

"He's fighting the Aneirans, Lord Tremain," Caius answered before Gershon could say anything. "Of course he'll accept our aid." He glanced at Gershon. "Don't you agree?"

"I wish I did."

"But all the realm is at risk. Surely Aindreas can see that as clearly as we can."

Lathrop gave a small shrug. "I don't know if Aindreas cares about the realm anymore. He'll do all he can to save the tor, but if it comes to keeping the Aneiran army from advancing beyond Kentigern, I doubt very much that he'll try to stop them."

"Then why should we bother with him at all?" Caius demanded. He passed a hand over his yellow beard, rage in his dark eyes. "I hope you won't think me disrespectful for saying so, Sir Trasker, but I wonder sometimes if our king isn't too kindhearted for his own good."

"We're not here to defend Aindreas," Gershon said. "We've come to keep the Aneirans from taking Kentigern and striking deeper into the heart of Eibithar."

Caius said nothing, his lips pressed thin, but after a moment he nodded.

Not long after, they began to smell smoke. They were getting close. An uneasy silence fell over the army, the dense wood muffling the sound of the soldiers' steps and the jangling of their swords. Gershon would never have thought that over three thousand men could make so little noise.

Even after they first smelled the fires, which the swordmaster assumed had to be burning at Kentigern, it was several hours more before Gershon and his army emerged from Kentigern Wood.

"Damn," Gershon muttered gazing toward the tor. Smoke rose from Kentigern Castle, which he had expected. No doubt the Aneirans had used hurling arms to assail the fortress with burning oil and fiery projectiles. However, he hadn't thought to see the smoldering remains of farmhouses and crop fields.

"Do you think Kentigern has fallen already?" Caius asked.

Gershon shook his head, staring up at the castle. They were a long way off, but he could see banners of blue, silver, and white flying atop the castle's towers. "No, Aindreas still holds the tor."

Lathrop glanced at the swordmaster. "Has he made a pact with the Aneirans, then? Did he let them pass?"

Gershon was wondering this as well. But even as he opened his mouth to answer, he saw a flaming ball rise from the south side of the tor and arc across the sky toward the battlements.

"It seems they're still under attack."

"Then what happened to those farmhouses?"

"I don't know," Gershon said. "But that can wait. His Majesty sent us to break the siege, and that's what we're going to do."

At the swordmaster's signal, the army started forward again, advancing on the tor.

"When we reach the city walls, we'll turn to the south and follow them to the Aneiran camp. I want your archers ready as quickly as possible."

"Shall we divide the army?" Lathrop asked. "Half of us could cut toward the river and flank them if they try to withdraw."

Gershon shook his head. "No. I want them to withdraw. Our force is a good deal larger than theirs. I'm hoping that when they see this, they'll retreat across the Tarbin without much of a fight. Our aim should be to lose as few men as possible, so that we'll be near full strength when we join the king on the Moorlands."

"And if Aindreas turns his bowmen on us?"

The swordmaster glanced at Lathrop. "I'm hoping he won't."

The duke nodded. If he thought Gershon a fool, he had the good grace not to say so.

They soon reached the city walls, and encountering no resistance from the men of Kentigern, they turned southward, advancing on the Aneiran army. It even seemed to Gershon that he heard cheers from the castle, though he wasn't certain, and he wasn't about to place any faith in Kentigern's goodwill. As they drew nearer to the Aneirans, the captains brought the archers forward, instructing them to be ready to loose their arrows as soon as they were within range of the enemy camp.

Before the bowmen could fire, however, cries reached them from the castle and Gershon shouted a warning to his men. The Aneirans had turned one of their hurling arms so that it faced his army, and they had launched a huge vat of flaming oil in his direction. Men scattered in all directions. Gershon and the dukes spurred their mounts trying to escape the fiery mass plummeting toward them.

By sheer good fortune, much of the oil fell short of the king's army, and most of Gershon's men were able to avoid the rest. A few soldiers fell, writhing in the flames, but losses were minor.

"Archers!" the swordmaster called. "Quickly! Before they can ready another attack!"

The bowmen surged forward, arrows nocked, and when they were close enough, they fired. Screams rose from the Aneiran side.

"Again!"

The bowmen let loose with a second volley.

"Swordsmen!" Gershon called. "Attack!"

With a deafening cry and the ringing of three thousand blades, his army rushed the Aneiran lines. And raising his own blade, the swordmaster kicked at his horse's flanks, plunging into the fray with his men.

He saw flames jump to life in the distance, and for a moment Gershon feared that the soldiers of Mertesse would manage to send another mass of flaming oil at his army. But his warriors closed the distance too quickly. In only a few seconds they had crashed into the Aneiran army, the ground seeming to tremble with the impact. It appeared briefly that the enemy would hold their ground, but Gershon's force was simply too vast. The men of Mertesse began to give way, slowly at first, then more quickly. When a large raiding party emerged from the castle and swept down the tor in their direction, the Aneirans broke formation and fled toward the river. Those who remained, including the soldiers manning the hurling arms, were overrun. Many of the rest perished under a hail of arrows and crossbow bolts.

Kentigern's men let loose with a cheer that threatened to

topple the fortress, and Gershon's soldiers shouted triumphantly in response. For that moment, at least, it was easy to forget that the realm still tottered on the cusp of civil war.

Then the moment passed and a tense stillness descended on the armies.

"Where's your duke?" Gershon called to the nearest of Aindreas's soldiers. "Is he still alive?"

"Yes, my lord. He's in the castle."

Gershon didn't bother to tell the man that he wasn't anybody's lord. In this instance, it behooved him to have Kentigern's soldiers think him more than he really was. He looked at Lathrop and Caius, both of whom had come through the battle unscathed. They nodded in return. "Take us to him," he said, facing the soldier once more.

"Yes, my lord."

Aindreas's man started up the road, along with at least a dozen of his comrades. Gershon and the dukes followed warily, accompanied by a small contingent of the king's soldiers.

Another cheer went up behind them and Gershon turned to look. The hurling arms had been set ablaze. It was hard to distinguish Kentigern's men from his own, but it seemed that they had done this together.

"Should one of us go back?" Caius asked quietly.

Gershon shook his head. "No. Let them have their fun. Who knows when they'll have cause to celebrate again?"

They continued up the road, finally reaching what once had been the famed Tarbin gate. The drawbridge lay in charred pieces by the side of the lane, and two of the portcullises had been destroyed, the iron twisted into grotesque shapes, the wood splintered and blackened by fire. The third portcullis had been damaged as well, though it still stood. The fourth had not been touched.

The soldiers led them through the wicket gate and into the first of the castle wards. Aindreas awaited them there.

It had been nearly a year since Gershon had last seen the duke. The turns had taken their toll on the man. He was still huge; indeed, if anything, he looked heavier than he had at Kearney's investiture. But his eyes were sunken, his skin blotchy, unnaturally flushed in some places, ghostly pale in others. It seemed to the swordmaster that the duke was being consumed from within, as if his grief and hatred had loosed a demon in his heart.

The duke didn't move as Gershon and the others approached. His sword was sheathed on his belt, and his feet were firmly planted in the grass, as though he were daring his guests to step past him.

"Trasker," Aindreas said, his voice taut. He eyed the dukes. "Tremain, Labruinn."

Gershon gave a small bow, though a part of him felt that the man didn't even deserve that much. "Lord Kentigern."

"Have you come to take my castle?"

"Had it been up to me, I would have. But Kearney sent me to drive back the Aneirans and to offer what aid we could. Are you in need of provisions, healers, arms?"

Aindreas narrowed his eyes, his gaze shifting from Gershon to Caius to Lathrop and back to the swordmaster. "Kearney told you to do all that?"

"He did."

A man approached the duke, his face bloodied, his uniform torn and stained. He was powerfully built, like the duke of Labruinn, but shorter of stature. It took Gershon a moment to recognize him as Villyd Temsten, Aindreas's swordmaster. He whispered something to the duke, who eyed him briefly before nodding and dismissing him with a wave of his hand. Villyd hesitated, then walked away.

Aindreas raked a hand through his red hair, his pale eyes fixed on the ground before him, as if he were deep in thought.

Watching him, Gershon began to feel uneasy. He glanced about the ward, as if expecting to see Kentigern's soldiers closing on them, but he saw only a few men lingering near the gates to the inner keep. "Lord Kent—"

"I have something to tell you."

"By all means."

"A large contingent of the Aneiran force that had been laying siege to my castle marched northward this morning."

"The farmhouses," Gershon whispered.

Aindreas looked up at that, meeting the swordmaster's gaze. "Yes. They burned the farmhouses and fields as they went."

"How many men?"

"Well over a thousand, most of them from Solkara. I believe they were headed toward Galdasten."

Gershon nodded. Of course they were. A thousand men wasn't many, but with enough bowmen, they could inflict heavy losses on Kearney's army from the south as the king battled the men from Braedon to the north.

"There was nothing I could do to stop them," the duke said, seeming to misinterpret Gershon's silence. "They sought to draw me out of the castle with the fires they set, but I couldn't risk compromising the safety of the tor. You understand."

"I do, my lord. But we need to go after them. They're already nearly a full day's march ahead of us." He turned to Lathrop and Caius. "My lords, please ready your men, and inform my captains of what's happened. We march within the hour."

Both men nodded. "Of course, swordmaster," Lathrop said.

Facing Aindreas once more, Gershon said, "Thank you, Lord Kentigern. I'm sorry that we can't do more for you, but my first duty is to the king."

"I want to go with you."

Gershon stared at the man. Lathrop and Caius, who were nearly to the gate, had stopped and were eyeing him as well.

"But after all the damage that your castle sustained—"

"Mertesse is in retreat. He's lost too many men, and he no longer has the Solkarans by his side. I'll leave a few hundred men here to guard the tor, but he won't attack again, at least not soon."

"My lord—"

"Kearney thinks me a traitor." He faltered, looking to the side for just an instant, almost as if he had spotted something out of the corner of his eye. "I want to win back his trust," he said at last. "You can't tell me that several hundred more men wouldn't help your cause."

"Of course they would, my lord." He took a breath, then pressed on, knowing that he was about to put his life and that of his companions at risk. "But I don't know if I trust you to ride with us. You've made no secret of your hatred for the king, and you've done nothing in the turns leading up to this war to indicate that you care a whit for the welfare of this realm. I fear that if you march with us, you may betray us."

Aindreas's face shaded to scarlet, but rather than flying into a rage, he merely shook his head. "I won't. Everything you say about me is true. But this siege has . . . has opened my eyes. And so has your arrival here. I'm in debt to the king, and to you, even more than you know. I'd be grateful for the opportunity to repay that debt." His eyes darted to the side, once more, and he licked his lips. "I swear to you on the memory of my daughter, Brienne, that I will not betray you or defy the king again."

Unsure of what to do, Gershon looked over at Lathrop and Caius. Labruinn held himself still, but after a moment the duke of Tremain gave a single nod.

"Very well, Lord Kentigern. Ready your men. They'll be marching under the king's banner, and so will be under my command. Are you prepared to follow my orders?"

"I am, swordmaster."

Gershon nodded. He still wasn't certain that he was doing the right thing; he dearly wished that the king were here. But something in Kentigern's manner convinced him that the man wouldn't betray them. After a moment he turned and followed Caius and Lathrop out of the castle and back down the road toward the king's army.

"I don't trust him," Caius said quietly.

Gershon glanced back at Aindreas, who was watching them walk away. "Neither do I, Lord Labruinn. But he swore on the memory of his daughter. He wouldn't have done so lightly."

"So we're placing our faith in a ghost?"

"No," Lathrop said. "We're placing our faith in a father's love. And I, for one, feel quite confident that our trust will be rewarded."

Yaella was by the river when the siege failed. She had heard shouting and screams, and had watched as the blazing pots of oil flew from the hurling arms, but she had merely assumed that the duke of Kentigern had sent out another raiding party. Only when the cries of Aneira's men turned desperate did she begin to understand that another army had come to break the siege.

Soon men were streaming down the road toward the Tarbin, many of them falling as arrows and bolts pelted down upon them. She heard her duke shouting orders, urging his men to stand and fight, but the soldiers would not listen, and soon Rowan gave up. She saw him at the rear of his army, fleeing as well.

And she knew that the time had come.

All around her was bedlam—panicked men, horses straining against their reins, healers and their wounded desperate to cross the river before the men of Eibithar descended upon them. It was perfect.

A small part of her grieved at the thought of leaving Mertesse. She had served in Rouel's court for nine years, and had been with Rowan for another. A decade. Not much to an Eandi, but nearly a third of her life. She had possessions in her chamber in Castle Mertesse that she would never see again. Gold she had earned in the Weaver's service, clothes and baubles she had accumulated over the years, gifts Shurik had given to her. She regretted having to give these up, particularly the gifts from her beloved. She knew as well that she would have some need of gold in the coming days.

But if she returned to Mertesse she would never find another opportunity to slip away. On the other hand, if she left now, amid the tumult of the retreat, no one would miss her for hours, not even the duke. Eventually they would conclude that she had been killed in the Eibitharian assault, or had drowned as she tried to cross the river. Certainly they wouldn't bother searching for her, at least not for long. She would become a walking wraith.

Those had been the Weaver's words. A walking wraith. "No one will know you," he had said, the night he entered her dreams and spoke to her of his movement, and of her special place in his plans. "No one will think to stop you. You'll be able to go anywhere you choose, anywhere I tell you."

"Yes, Weaver," she had said.

He had told her to go east. There lay glory and revenge and peace; all that she sought.

"Yes, Weaver."

And so, as the Eandi soldiers ran toward the river, followed by their duke, pursued by the enemy, Yaella ja Banvel, first minister to House Mertesse, slipped into the brush by the north bank of the Tarbin and crept slowly away. At one point she thought she heard Rowan calling for her, but by then she had put some distance between herself and the army's camp. She knew that he would never find her. Still, she stayed low, keeping herself hidden, always in motion, always putting more distance between herself and the life she had known for so long.

Only when night fell, bringing darkness and safety, did she stand and begin to walk. She would have preferred to ride, but her mount had been taken from her by one of Kentigern's bowmen. She was truly alone. There was nothing for her here anymore.

She kept her eyes fixed on the eastern sky, where the moons were climbing into the night. White Panya and red Ilias, guiding her. Eastward, toward glory.

Chapter Twenty-six

Solkara, Aneira

The sun shone bright in a hazy sky of pale blue, warming the grasses of Castle Solkara's vast courtyard and making the garden blooms of borage and gilly flower, columbine and sweetbriar, woodbine, iris, and lavender glow like Qirsi fire in the hands of festival sorcerers. A gentle wind blew off the Kett and across the castle walls, carrying the smell of fish from the river piers, and rustling the leaves of poplars and willows growing along its banks.

All her life, Chofya had loved the slow, hot days of the growing turns. While others complained of the heat, she basked in it, thinking back to her youth in the hills south of Noltierre, where the sun baked the clay and the brush and the skin of small children to a fine golden brown. Here in Aneira's royal city, where the waters of the river and the shadows of the Great Forest cooled the air, it never grew warm enough to suit her taste. But still, she welcomed these mornings in the garden. Later she would take Kalyi to the marketplace—there were always so many peddlers in Solkara this time of year.

It was easy to forget that there was war, that less than forty leagues to the south, Aneirans were killing Aneirans for no reason that Chofya could see. Oh, she understood well enough Numar's pretense for marching south; she simply saw no sense in it. Never mind that Dantrielle's defiance in the face of this foolish war to the north was entirely justified. Even had she not agreed with Tebeo and his allies, she would have seen Numar's siege as a wasteful, spiteful gesture, one that served only to weaken the throne as well as the realm. Chofya wasn't vain enough to believe that the years she spent as Carden's queen were enough to teach her all the finer points of statecraft. Carden himself hadn't mastered them; how was she to do so? But in her capacity as lady of the castle and hostess to all sorts of feasts, ceremonies, and councils, she had observed a great deal. Presiding over the realm, she had decided long ago, was not that different from running a castle. In both endeavors, one needed authority enough to maintain order, but also a modicum of flexibility, a willingness and capacity to cope with the unexpected. In the same way, she had come to believe that dealing with a wayward duke was not all that different from teaching discipline to a contrary child. Anger and violence served only to stiffen the resolve of the one who needed to be mollified;

only patience and reason would produce the desired result. She had raised a daughter nearly to womanhood. She knew she was right.

But in all her years as queen she had also learned that men knew little of patience and even less of reason. And they had no interest in taking counsel from a woman, unless she happened to be Qirsi. Before leaving for Dantrielle, Numar had refused to grant her an audience, no doubt knowing that she would speak against his alliance with the empire and the siege he was planning. Chofya then went to her daughter, knowing that the regent could not refuse to hear his queen, only to discover that Numar had already convinced Kalyi of the wisdom of both the alliance and the siege.

Realizing that there was nothing she could do to save Aneira from the folly and vanity of its regent, Chofya stopped trying. The realm had survived for nearly nine centuries, weathering civil wars, rebellions, ill-advised wars with its neighbors, and countless other tragedies. It would survive Numar.

Still, she did not ignore the war entirely. Nearly every day Henthas received messages from Numar describing the progress of the siege, and though the duke was under no obligation to share any of what the regent told him with Chofya, he had no choice but to share the messages with Kalyi. And since the queen remained terrified of her uncle the duke—with good reason—she always had Chofya accompany her to Henthas's chamber. Naturally there was some delay between Numar's writing of the messages and their arrival in Solkara—usually three or four days—but there was an immediacy to Numar's account of events on the battlefield that was quite compelling. Though Chofya wished to maintain her indifference to the course of the siege, she soon realized that she looked forward to the daily audiences with Henthas. It didn't matter that she hated the duke, or that, with his dark blue eyes, fine features, and muscular frame, he bore a disturbing resemblance to her late husband. She found the descriptions of the siege exciting, almost as if she were hearing of some ancient battle from Aneira's glorious past, rather than of Numar's foolish war. On those few occasions when no message arrived, she was deeply disappointed, even more so than was Kalyi.

Still, fascinated as she was by the regent's reports, and versed as she was in the subtleties of Aneiran statecraft, it took a conversation with Kalyi, still two years shy of her Determining, to make Chofya understand fully how dangerous this siege was for her and her child.

They had returned to their chambers from yet another audience with the duke. The prior's bells had just tolled in the city and they had an hour or so to wait before the evening meal. Kalyi seemed to have sensed long ago that Chofya did not approve of the siege or much else that Numar had done in her name. Outside of Henthas's chamber, the two of them had not spoken of the conflict in some time. But on this day, the news from Dantrielle had not been good, at least not for House Solkara. Chofya liked Tebeo and Brall and still remembered how they had stood with her when Grigor, Carden's ruthless brother, had tried to wrest the crown from her daughter. Listening to Henthas read Numar's accounts, she often found herself silently cheering Dantrielle's successes and the regent's failures.

According to the message that arrived that day, the last of the waxing, Numar's scouts had seen men approaching Castle Dantrielle from the north, south, and east—no doubt the armies of Orvinti, Tounstrel, and Kett. Tebeo's defenses were beginning to fail, Numar wrote, but there was no way of knowing if the castle would fall before Dantrielle's allies arrived.

Kalyi had said nothing as they walked through the corridors back to their chamber. She looked pale, her lips pressed tight. With her dark hair and eyes, she favored Chofya, but like her father, she carried her worries where all could see them.

"What if the siege fails?" she asked abruptly, once they were back in their quarters. "What if Uncle Numar can't take Castle Dantrielle after all?"

Chofya sat on their bed and beckoned Kalyi to her side. "If the siege fails, your uncle will have to fight his war against Eibithar without the soldiers of Dantrielle, Orvinti, and the rest. He'll still have his alliance with the emperor of Braedon, but he won't bring quite so strong an army to it."

Actually, this was essentially what Chofya had expected from the start would happen. She thought the siege was destined to fail; Castle Dantrielle was as strong as it was beautiful, and Numar had already sent part of his army north. Though Rassor had joined him, the regent's force remained too small to defeat Tebeo and his allies. Their only hope had been a quick and decisive victory. Clearly that hadn't happened. None of this surprised her, which might have been why she never considered the possibility raised by Kalyi's next question.

"What if Uncle Numar is killed?"

She didn't care for the man at all. When it came to choosing a regent for Kalyi, she had preferred him to either Grigor or Henthas, but she knew better than to think him kind or to believe that he had taken on the responsibilities of being regent out of concern for his niece. He was clever and ambitious and nearly as dangerous as the other two. So why did she tremble so at the mere thought of his death?

"He won't be," she said, knowing how foolish she sounded.

"What if he's struck by an arrow or killed by one of Dantrielle's swordsmen? What if Pronjed kills him?"

"What? Why would Pronjed kill Numar?"

"He killed Father. At least that's what Uncle Numar thinks."

"Damn him!" Chofya muttered, drawing a shocked stare from Kalyi. Why would Numar tell the girl such a thing? She had thought that they were past this nonsense. For several turns Kalyi had been trying to learn what she could about her father's death, as if there had been any doubt but that he had taken his own life, as if such an endeavor were appropriate for a ten-year-old girl. Numar should have kept his crazed theories to himself.

"Your father took his own life, Kalyi," she said wearily, bracing herself for the all-too-familiar argument. "I've told you that before."

Kalyi shook her head, the golden circlet she wore as a crown flying from her hair, but at least she wasn't crying.

"That's just how Pronjed made it seem. He used magic to make father kill himself. Uncle Numar said it's called mind . . . turning, or something like that."

It seemed to Chofya that someone was kneeling on her chest, making it difficult for her to draw breath. She had heard tales of Qirsi who could control the thoughts of others, though she had placed little stock in such stories. Certainly she had never thought that she would know such a man. "Mind-bending?" she whispered.

"Yes! That's it! That's how he killed Father!"

"Mind-bending magic is very rare. We don't know that Pronjed—"

"Yes, we do. I . . ." She lowered her eyes. "I overheard a conversation, a long time ago. Pronjed used that magic on the master of arms."

"Kalyi!" she said, trying to sound stern. "You listened?"

The girl nodded, her eyes still fixed on the floor. "Yes."

Chofya should have been cross with her; it was unseemly for any young girl to listen in on a conversation between adults, but it was particularly so when that girl was queen. Still, Chofya's eagerness to know what her daughter had heard was a match for any anger she might have felt. Perhaps more than a match.

"Tell me what you heard," she said, as if admitting defeat.

Kalyi looked up, smiling. The conversation she described made little sense in terms of military matters; clearly the girl had not understood much of what she heard. But when Kalyi told her how Pronjed had instructed the master of arms to give certain advice to the regent, when she said that the archminister told Tradden what he was to remember of their conversation, she had little choice but to believe that Pronjed possessed mind-bending power.

"Why would he have killed Carden?" she asked, speaking more to herself than to Kalyi.

"Uncle Numar thinks he's a traitor. He may be part of the conspiracy."

Chofya nodded. If all of this were true, that would be the only explanation that made any sense. Was it possible then that this alliance with Braedon was part of the Qirsi plot? Was the siege as well? Pronjed had come to her recently, hoping that she would help him push the regent toward the alliance. He said at the time that he sought to strengthen the realm so that when Kalyi came to power Aneira would have nothing to fear from its enemies. Had that been a lie? If he possessed this power, and had truly sought to enlist her as an ally, why didn't he try to control her thoughts as he had Tradden's?

"None of this makes any sense, Kalyi," she said, trying to convince herself. "Even if he was with the conspiracy, I'm not certain that he had any reason to kill your father. And not long ago he came to me hoping I would help him with something. When I refused, he simply accepted it and never raised the matter with me again. If he had this power surely he would have used it against me."

"He tried to use it on Uncle Numar. Uncle is sure of it."

Could the regent have been lying about all of this, trying to turn Kalyi against the archminister? Or had Pronjed decided that Chofya wasn't important enough to risk using his powers against her?

Ultimately, none of this was as important as Kalyi's initial question. The young queen seemed to realize this as well.

"Just because he doesn't have that power, doesn't meant that he won't try to kill Uncle Numar," Kalyi said. "They don't like each other."

That much Chofya knew already. "No, they don't," she admitted. Not that the regent needed Pronjed thirsting for his blood. There would be thousands of soldiers wearing the uniforms of Dantrielle, Tounstrel, Orvinti, and Kett, just as avid for his death as any Qirsi, loyal or not.

"If Uncle Numar dies, will Uncle Henthas become my regent?"

She could see the fear in Kalyi's eyes, and knew that it was mirrored in her own. "Not if I can help it. The other dukes don't trust him. They wouldn't—"

It came to her so suddenly that she actually shuddered. What an idiot she had been, dismissing Numar's siege as if it were foolishness and nothing more. Pronjed had asked her to help him, and obviously she hadn't been willing to do that. Rather, she should have insisted that Numar call off his attack on Dantrielle, or at the very least, send Henthas in his stead. The realm needed its regent. Kalyi needed him, but more to the point, Solkara needed him.

If Numar was killed or captured, his army overwhelmed by Dantrielle and its allies, it would mark the end of the Solkaran Supremacy. Chofya didn't care much for power, at least not anymore. Even if she had, it hardly would have mattered. With Carden dead, she was nothing. They called her the queen mother, but it was a title without authority. Had it not been for Kalyi, she wouldn't have cared at all for House Solkara and its damned supremacy. She still thought of Noltierre as her home, and would gladly have taken Kalyi there to live out their days in peace. But for better or worse, Kalyi was Solkaran, the sole heir to Carden the Third. If Numar died, she would have to look to the Council of Dukes to protect her daughter from Henthas. And if the supremacy fell that recourse would be denied her as well. Leadership of House Solkara would cease to be a concern of the other houses. She and she alone would be all that stood between the Jackal and her daughter. For Henthas would always see Kalyi as a threat to his ambitions, no matter how limited they might be. As Carden's child, she had a legitimate claim to the family seat, one that might convince soldiers in the Solkaran army to side with her in any dispute that arose between them. Kalyi could renounce all claims to leadership of the house, and the two of them could return to Cestaar's Hills. But that might not appease the man. There was nothing to stop her from going back on her word, he would say. Until she was dead, he would always see her as a rival.

"They wouldn't what, Mother?"

Chofya shook her head. "What?"

"You were speaking of the other dukes. You were telling me that they wouldn't do something, but then you just stopped."

"I'm sorry, child. I was just going to say that the dukes wouldn't allow Henthas to become regent. They'd find someone else to help you rule the realm."

"Then why do you look so scared?"

Clever child. She was so young, and yet it seemed that the

world around her was demanding that she grow up before her time. Who was Chofya to fight such a powerful tide? "Because if by some chance Numar is defeated and Solkara loses the crown, the Council of Dukes will be powerless to help us."

"Do you think that could happen?"

"I don't—" She pressed her lips thin. That was the trouble with sharing hard truths with a child so young. How did one go back to lies after doing so? "Yes, I'm afraid I do."

"Then we should speak with the captains."

Clever indeed. "Why, love?"

"Because if Numar is gone, and the dukes can't help us, we'll need to have the army on our side."

Chofya had to smile. She was Carden's child through and through, and though Chofya had stopped loving her husband long before his death, she took pride in seeing his strength in the girl. "They might not side with us, Kalyi. Most soldiers won't willingly follow a woman, much less a young girl."

"I'm queen," she said, as if the matter were so easily settled. "I'm Father's heir. They'll help me."

If it were put to the men that way, they just might. "I'll speak with them tonight," Chofya said.

"I want to go with you."

"No, Kalyi."

"But—"

Chofya raised a finger to the girl's lips. "I know that you're wise beyond your years. But the soldiers still see you as a child. If you go with me, they won't take us seriously; we could do ourselves more harm that good." She leaned forward and kissed Kalyi's forehead. "Trust me with this."

Kalyi twisted her mouth, looking unhappy. But after a moment she gave a small nod. "I hope Numar wins," she said. "Then we won't have to worry about any of this."

Long after Chofya and her brat left his chamber Henthas continued to read through Numar's message—the passages he hadn't shared with them, as well as those he had.

"It's but a matter of time before we're surrounded," his brother had written. "We will make one last effort to take the

castle, sparing nothing in our assault, but I feel certain that w
will fail."

Henthas saw no benefit in reading this to the girl or he
mother, for it led directly to the heart of Numar's missive.

> If the supremacy can be preserved—and I'm not sure that it can—it falls to you, brother, to lead it. The five hundred men who remain with you in Solkara will not be enough, and though I expect Dantrielle will let the soldiers under my command go free after he has disarmed them, they will not be enough either. Your best hope, I believe, lies with the men I've sent north, to Kentigern. If they can be called back before they march on to the Eibitharian Moorlands, they can preserve House Solkara's hold on the crown. If not, you will have nothing left but the dukedom.
>
> There is probably nothing I can say that will convince you to spare the girl. I believe that she may still prove useful to you, even if you are relegated to being duke of a fallen house. But if you truly wish to be duke yourself and to pass leadership of House Solkara on to any sons you may beget, you will have to kill her. Beware of Chofya, for she's clever and respected by the realm's other dukes. And beware Pronjed. I'm convinced that he is a traitor who possesses mind-bending magic.
>
> I don't expect that we will meet again, Henthas. I know that we have had our differences in the past, but we are both sons of Tomaz the Ninth. Keep our house strong.

Numar went on to write that he would attempt to send anothe
message the following day, to inform Henthas of how his fina
offensive had gone, but the duke knew that the letter he held i
his hand was the last he would receive from his younge
brother. Numar might not have been the fool they all though
he was, but neither was he a master of military planning. I

Tebeo and his allies had him surrounded, he'd be dead within a matter of days.

More to the point, like the older brothers Renbrere, and even like their father, who truly had been a genius, Numar had always been obsessed with the supremacy. He had killed Grigor so that he might lead it. He had as much as given his life defending it. And even now, with one foot in Bian's realm, he was trying to tell Henthas how he ought to preserve it. Well, Henthas had no intention of doing anything of the sort.

So long as he fought to hold the throne, the other dukes would do all they could to destroy his armies and kill him. If he relinquished the crown, however, if he allowed this damned supremacy to die at long last, they would leave him alone. They might even let him keep the dukedom. Yes, they hated him. Perhaps they feared him still, though Numar and Grigor and Carden had all succeeded in diminishing House Solkara so that it no longer struck terror in the hearts of those who would oppose it, as it had when Tomaz ruled. But if he was just another duke they would believe him harmless, or at least less dangerous than Carden and Grigor had been.

Henthas tossed Numar's message aside. As far as he was concerned, the supremacy was over, and good riddance to it. The question that confronted him now was what to do about the girl-queen. Regardless of the fate of the supremacy, she would still be the nominal leader of House Solkara. Of course, a child could no more lead the house as duchess than she could rule the realm, and so the need for a regency would remain, and he would be the logical choice to take Numar's place in that role. Chofya would oppose him, but where else could she turn? She herself had no claim to authority, and with all his brothers dead there was no one else.

But did he want to be regent, or did he prefer to kill Kalyi now? It didn't take him more than a moment to understand that his choices were as limited as Chofya's. He would move against the girl eventually, but for now he could not. A good many of Solkara's soldiers remained loyal to her, seeing her as Carden's true heir. A few chafed at the idea of seeing their house led by a girl, but not enough yet to challenge her authority. If he killed her, they would turn on him. He needed first to win their trust, to convince them that in both temperament and ability, he was closer than anyone to their lost king. That would take some time.

Pleased with himself for working all this out so quickly, the duke left his chambers for the great hall, where his supper would soon be served. There was a woman who was to meet him there, one of Chofya's ladies, as it happened, and he didn't wish to keep her waiting too long.

Just as Henthas had expected, there was no message from Numar the following day. Shortly before the ringing of the prior's bells, Chofya and Kalyi arrived at his quarters, eager for word of the siege.

"I'm afraid I've heard nothing," he told them, standing in the doorway, blocking their entry to his chamber.

Chofya's expression didn't change—clearly she had expected this—but Kalyi looked disappointed, and just a bit scared.

She looked up at her mother. "Do you think—?"

Chofya laid a hand on her shoulder, silencing her. "Thank you, my lord duke," she said. "We won't disturb you any further."

"Actually, my lady, I wish a word with you." He nodded to one of the guards positioned outside his chamber. "If Her Highness would be so kind as to remain out here, this will only take a moment."

Once again Kalyi looked at her mother. This time there could be no mistaking the fear in her eyes.

"It's all right. Stay with the soldiers. I'll be just inside."

The girl nodded, and Henthas backed away from the doorway, allowing Chofya to enter.

"What is it you want?" she asked, once he had closed the door. She sounded impatient, but he felt certain that the chill in her voice was intended to mask her own apprehension.

"Just to talk, my lady." He faced her and smiled.

She eyed him briefly, then crossed to the window, crossing her arms over her chest as if cold. She really was quite lovely.

Black hair, black eyes, olive skin. There could be no mistaking her for a woman of Solkara, but she was beautiful nevertheless. Carden had done well for himself, despite his many limitations.

"What could we possibly need to discuss?"

"Come now, Chofya. You're an intelligent woman. You weren't at all surprised to learn that I'd received no message today. Numar is on the verge of being defeated. If he's not yet captured or dead, he will be soon. The supremacy is over and your daughter, who will soon be just duchess, will be needing a new regent."

She turned to face him. "And you think I'd trust you with that?"

Henthas grinned. "Let's pretend for a moment that you have other choices. Solkara will have just lost its hold on the throne, it will be led, at least in name, by a child, and a girl at that. What's to keep Bistari, or Orvinti, or one of the other houses from taking our lands?"

"The other houses wouldn't do that."

"Wouldn't they? They've hated us for centuries."

"Yes, well, the men of your family have seen to that, haven't they?"

"Indeed, none more so than your husband."

Chofya started to say something, then stopped herself, appearing to think better of it.

"The point, my lady, is that Kalyi might be well served to have me standing beside her." He gave a thin smile. "You hate me, and you're afraid of me. So are the other dukes. Isn't it possible that the fear I instill might prove a boon to the ambitions you harbor for your daughter?"

"You'll turn against her eventually, when it suits your purposes. Just as Grigor would have, just as Numar was going to."

His eyebrows went up. "You don't miss much, do you?"

"Not where my daughter is concerned."

"You're right, I may turn against her. I can't now, but there may come a time when I can, and I may well take that opportunity. But for now, we need each other. The fact of the matter is, you have no other choices. If you give the regency to someone from another house, the army may turn against you. And if I move against Kalyi now, they'll turn against me."

She stared at him, her eyes narrowed, as if she were trying to discern from his appearance whether he could be trusted.

"I've surprised you."

"You are unusually direct, my lord. I hadn't expected that from a Renbrere."

"My brothers are all lost, my lady. The supremacy of my forebears is gone. I haven't the heart for more games. The survival of our house is at stake, and I'll do nothing to weaken us further."

"Very well, my lord. Allow me to think on it for a day or two. We'll speak again."

It was probably as much as he could ask for just now. "Of course, my lady. In the meantime, if I hear anything new from Dantrielle, I'll let you know."

She inclined her head slightly. "Thank you, my lord." She crossed to the door, opened it, and stepped into the corridor. He saw Kalyi rush to her side, looking deeply relieved, as if she had expected Henthas to kill her mother right there in his chamber. A moment later, one of the guards closed the door again, leaving the duke to contemplate what had passed between them.

Chofya had lived in the Solkaran court long enough to know how desperate he was. If he couldn't be duke, and she refused to give him the regency, he'd have nothing left except the marquessate. No doubt she'd use this knowledge to try to control him, to make him agree to conditions another man would reject out of hand. He'd make a show of resisting her efforts to rein him in, but in the end he'd agree to whatever stipulations she proposed. He'd bide his time, allowing her to believe that she had succeeded in tethering him, letting her grow comfortable until her vigilance slackened. Then he'd deal with them both.

Numar had warned him of Pronjed, but Henthas doubted that he'd ever see the archminister again. If Numar had been captured, so had the Qirsi. And if by some chance Pronjed did manage to escape, and Numar was correct in thinking him a traitor, he wouldn't bother returning to a disgraced house, far removed from Aneira's new royal city, wherever that was going to be. He'd join his fellow renegades in striking at the Eandi courts. Again, Henthas didn't know where they might strike first, nor did he care. It wouldn't be Solkara—a year ago maybe, but not anymore. That was fine with the duke. For now, Henthas cared only about his own survival. The conspiracy might threaten him eventually, and when they did, he would make certain that he was ready. But today, here in this castle, he was more concerned with a ten-year-old girl and her resourceful mother.

He didn't see Kalyi or Chofya that night at dinner, nor did he see the queen mother for the next two days. It almost seemed that she was avoiding him. No new messages arrived from Numar, but on the third morning, a messenger arrived wearing the colors of Dantrielle. Henthas, who had been informed of the man's approach to the city, ordered the guards to escort the man to his chamber, but the messenger refused to enter the castle, demanding instead that the duke and queen be summoned to the castle gate. Descending the tower stairs and making his way across the courtyard to the outer gate, Henthas knew just what this meant. A messenger didn't make such demands of members of a royal house.

Somehow, Chofya and the girl were already at the gate when he arrived, though he had wasted no time in following the soldier from his own chamber. He gave the woman a puzzled look, but she barely glanced at him before facing the messenger again.

"You may begin now," she said. Kalyi stood in front of her, and Chofya had placed her hands on the girl's shoulders. She almost appeared to be using her body to shield the queen from Henthas.

"I've been sent by Tebeo, duke of Dantrielle, to inform you that Numar of Renbrere has failed in his attempt to take Castle Dantrielle and has been imprisoned for crimes against the realm. The duke of Dantrielle along with the dukes of Kett, Rassor, Tounstrel, and Noltierre have met in council and voted to end the Solkaran Supremacy. They have yet—"

"Wait a moment," Henthas broke in. "Did you say Rassor?"

"Yes, my lord. The duke of Rassor."

"That's impossible. Rassor fought with Numar. You mean Orvinti."

"Lord Orvinti is dead, my lord." The man held out a scroll tied with satin ribbons or red, gold, and black. "You may read this for yourself."

Henthas grabbed it from him, pulled off the ribbons, and unrolled the parchment, scanning the message quickly. It matched what the man had said almost word for word, and was signed by the five dukes he had mentioned, including Grestos.

"Traitorous bastard!" he muttered, crumpling the parchment in his fist.

"Did the message say anything else?" Chofya asked. "Did it . . . did it offer any instructions for us?"

"No, my lady. Nothing of that sort."

She pressed her lips thin. Clearly she had been hoping for some indication that they wanted Kalyi to be made duchess. Perhaps she even hoped they would demand that Henthas be imprisoned, or sent back to Dantrielle to be punished with his brother.

"Well, you must be weary from your journey," she said to the man a moment later, recovering as would a queen. "We can feed you and tend to your mount before you begin the ride back to Dantrielle."

"Thank you, my lady, but I was instructed not to enter your castle."

Chofya frowned. "What?"

"They don't trust us, my lady," Henthas said, eyeing the man, watching for his response. "Or more to the point, they don't trust me. Isn't that so, Dantrielle?"

"I merely know what I was told, my lord."

"Fine. Begone then. If they wish to make an outcast of House Solkara, then so be it."

"No!" Chofya said, glaring at him. "We will not become the bane of every house in this realm. Tell the other dukes that when the time comes to choose a new king, we would like very much to be party to the council."

"You will tell them no such thing!"

"You do not speak for this house, Henthas! Kalyi was queen and is now duchess! And if you aren't prepared to recognize her authority then I'll assume the role of regent myself!"

"Don't presume to challenge me, Chofya. I'll crush you, just as Numar should have done, and Grigor before him." He turned on his heal and started back through the gate.

As Henthas walked away, he heard Chofya tell the rider to deliver her message to his duke, but he didn't care. By the time Tebeo received word of their confrontation, the matter would be settled, once and for all.

Before he had managed to cross the courtyard, someone called to him. Turning, he saw one of the younger captains approach. He couldn't remember the man's name. He knew only that for a man this young to be here, rather than with one of the two forces Numar had sent to war, he couldn't be much of a soldier.

"What do you want?" he demanded.

"Your pardon, my lord, but I couldn't help hearing what you and the lady was just saying."

"Yes, what of it?"

"Well, I wanted you to know that not all the men is with her."

"What?"

"Some of us is siding with you."

"What are you—?" He stared at the man a moment, his mind racing to catch up with the implications of what this fool was telling him. "Are you saying that Chofya's been talking to the captains, trying to turn the army against me?"

"Yes, my lord. But not all of us is ready to join her."

The whore! He'd kill her, and the brat, too.

"What do you want us to do, my lord? Just say the word, and we's with you."

"How many?"

"My lord?"

"How many of the soldiers are with me?"

" 'Bout a hundred, my lord."

"One hundred? That's all?"

The soldier flinched. "Well . . . well, by the time we thought to do anything, she had got to most of the men."

Henthas shook his head. A hundred men. And if the others were anything like this one, he didn't stand a chance. Best to handle this on his own. After, he'd deal with the ones she had turned. "Tell them to be ready," he said. "Tell them to watch for my signal."

"What signal will that be, my lord?"

"They'll know it when they see it. In the meantime, see if you can persuade any of the others to join me. Quietly."

"Yes, my lord."

Henthas spun away from the man, striding back to his chamber, his hands trembling with rage, his heart pounding like that of an overworked mount. He should have expected this. For several turns he had been warning Numar against taking Carden's woman too lightly. Now it seemed that he had done just that. All the time he had been lying to her, lulling her, he thought, into a false sense of trust, she had been doing the same to him, with far more success.

Well, no more. Court games such as this had long been Numar's strength, and Grigor's before him. Henthas was a different sort of animal, and it was time he began acting as such.

Once in his chamber, he closed and locked the door behind him. He would allow himself no distractions until he had decided on a course of action. There were several ways to do this; he just had to decide which of them conveyed the proper message to those men who had joined with the queen mother. It didn't take him long to realize that his choices were actually quite limited. This was one instance when the brutality for which he and Grigor had long been reviled would serve him best. He had only to wait.

He took his meal in his chamber, sitting by his window, waiting for nightfall. When at last the sky darkened, the duke stood, strapped on his sword, and left his chamber, making his way through the corridors to the sleeping quarters of Chofya and Kalyi.

Two men stood watch outside their door, both of them tall and muscular. Neither of them was young—most of the young men had marched with Numar or had gone north to join Mertesse—but neither were they as old as some of those who now guarded the castle.

Seeing Henthas approach, they straightened, their hands falling quickly to the hilt of their blades, though neither man drew his weapon.

"Can we be of service, my lord?"

"I wish to see the queen."

The men glanced at one another. "I'm sorry, my lord. The duchess's mother left instructions you weren't to be allowed in."

The *duchess's* mother . . . Chofya had already claimed the family seat for her daughter. "Did she?" he said, itching to draw his blade. "Did she also mention that I don't recognize the child's claim to the duchy? When I awoke this morning, I was duke of Solkara, and I have no reason to believe that I'm any less than that now."

"The duchess awoke as queen, my lord, which gives her as much claim to the duchy as anyone."

This was ridiculous. He was a nobleman, and he wasn't about to debate matters of state with this fool of a soldier.

"Whatever I am," he said, forcing a smile, "I'm a man of this court. And I'm ordering you to step aside and allow me to speak with my niece."

"I'm sorry, my lord. I can't do that."

Henthas had known it would come to this. In a way, he had looked forward to it, seeing in it a chance to enhance his already formidable reputation. Killing the child and her mother did little in that regard. Fighting his way past two of Chofya's guards would do a good deal.

"You force me to do this," he said, drawing his sword. "I fight for my house and my castle."

He was a swordsman, perhaps not Carden's equal, or even Grigor's, but a skilled fighter nevertheless, taught by Tomaz himself. These men might have been well trained, but they hadn't a chance.

The first of the soldiers fell quickly—so concerned was he with the duke's sword that he didn't see the dagger in Henthas's left hand until it was too late. To his credit, the second man didn't flee. Indeed, he fought quite well, parrying deftly with his sword hand and using a torch that he grabbed with his free hand to keep the duke's smaller blade at bay.

For several moments they circled in the dark corridor, trading feints and sudden thrusts, neither man gaining any advantage. It soon became clear to Henthas, however, that the soldier, while adept, was unimaginative. All his attacks were the same—straightforward, powerful, but leveled at the duke's chest and head. So when he began his next assault, Henthas dropped to one knee, slashing at the man's leg with his dirk. When the soldier fell to his knees, dropping the torch, Henthas stood, and with a mighty sweep of his sword, hacked off his head.

"Let them speak of that come morning," he muttered.

He was winded, sweat running down his temples, but he felt good. It had been too long since he raised his blade in battle. He had missed this.

The chamber was locked, of course. But one of the guards carried a ring of keys on his belt. In a matter of moments, Henthas had found the correct one and unlocked the door.

"You should have made me regent, Chofya," he said, pushing it open. "That was the only way your child was going to live past her Fating."

Her mother had been telling her for much of the day how safe they would be, how Henthas would not be able to reach them with so many of the castle guards on their side. But that had done little to allay Kalyi's fears. It had seemed that her mother was trying to convince herself as much as she was Kalyi. Adults always did that—offering the most reassurances when they were least certain of what they were saying.

Kalyi was frightened all day, and didn't begin to feel safe until her mother agreed to take their evening meal in their bedchamber. Once they were in their quarters for the night, the door locked, the two guards positioned outside in the corridor, she finally started to believe that her uncle couldn't reach them.

Then she heard the voices. They had finished eating. Her mother was knitting by the light of one of the oil lamps, while Kalyi sat on her bed, copying the numbers her tutor had given her in the morning. Kalyi recognized her uncle's voice immediately, as did her mother, judging by the way she dropped her needles into her lap, her eyes fixed on the door.

For several moments they just listened, trying to make out what was said. Kalyi was shaking so badly that her bed creaked. Then she heard the ring of steel and she actually cried out.

Her mother pushed herself out of her chair and hurried to Kalyi's side, putting her arms around the girl's shoulders.

"Hush, child," she whispered.

"What are we going to do? He's going to kill us."

Chofya shook her head, but before she could say anything, they heard someone fall. A moment later they heard steel ringing again. The fight was continuing. One of the soldiers was dead.

Her mother stood and walked quickly to the wardrobe. For a few seconds she rummaged through her belongings, her back blocking Kalyi's view. Then she straightened and turned. She held a sword in one hand and a small dagger in the other. It took Kalyi a moment to realize that both weapons had belonged to her father.

"I was keeping these for you," her mother explained, crossing back to the bed. "I guess we need them sooner than I had thought." She handed Kalyi the dagger, keeping the sword for herself.

Kalyi glanced at the dagger. Its hilt was made of silver, the blade of glimmering clear crystal. It looked almost new. A sudden memory. "Is this the knife he used to . . . to—"

"Yes. Don't worry about that now. If you can get past him, into the corridor, do. Run as fast you can and get help."

"What if I can't?"

"Just try."

"Should we put out the lamps? He won't be able to see us."

Her mother considered this for a moment, then shook her head. "The corridor is darker than the chamber. He'll be able to see before we will."

They heard a man cry out, and then a second strangled noise that was cut off abruptly. A moment later, they heard the jangling of keys and all too soon, the clicking of the door lock.

"You should have made me regent, Chofya. That was the only way your child was going to live past her Fating."

He stood in the doorway, his sword, stained crimson, glinting in the glow of the lamps, his face shining and flushed. He grinned at them both, wiping the back of his hand across his brow. He held a dagger in that hand, and there was blood on that blade, too.

"Your Highness," he said, nodding at Kalyi.

"Get out, Henthas," her mother said. "Leave us alone."

He stepped farther into the chamber, closing the door behind him and turning the lock once more. "You've turned the army against me, Chofya. You shouldn't have done that."

He lunged at her, swinging his sword so suddenly, with such savagery, that Kalyi screamed.

Chofya jumped back out of reach.

"You can have the dukedom. Just let Kalyi go."

"It's too late for that. I gave you that chance the other day, and you turned on me, *you whore*!" With these last words he leaped at her again, slashing with his sword, forcing her to parry with hers. She staggered under the force of his blow, and he stabbed at her with his dagger. Once more she avoided his steel, stumbling as she fled from him.

Kalyi ran to the window and started screaming for help.

"Stop that!" he shouted.

"Kalyi!"

Turning at the sound of her mother's voice, the girl saw Henthas rushing at her, his sword raised to strike. She ducked away, running to her bed, rolling over it, and cowering on the far side.

He advanced on her, but had only taken a step or two when Chofya charged at him, shouting his name.

Henthas turned quickly, both of his blades flashing. Kalyi had never seen anyone move with such speed, such ease. Her mother reeled away from him again, but this time, as she did, she clutched at her chest, just below her shoulder. An instant later, a dark stain appeared on her white gown and began to spread, like fire across parchment.

"Mother!"

Before Chofya could speak, Henthas was on her again, hammering at her with his blade, forcing her back and then to her knees.

Kalyi rushed out from behind her bed, brandishing her dagger. Before she reached him, though, Henthas looked back at her, pointing his dagger at her face, all the while keeping Chofya pinned to the floor with his sword.

"Stop right there, girl, or I'll kill your dear mother. You wouldn't want that, would you?"

There was a knock at the door.

"Your Highness?" came a voice from the corridor.

"Not a word!" Henthas warned, his voice dropping to a harsh whisper. "Or your mother dies."

"I'm dead anyway," Chofya said. And then, she shouted, "Help us! The duke is trying to kill us!"

"Damn you!" He pulled back his sword and plunged it into her. At the last moment Chofya hacked at his blade with her own so that his thrust missed her heart. Still, it lanced deep into her side, tearing a gasp from her lips and staining her gown with another gush of blood.

Someone began to pound at the door, the wood moaning but not giving way.

"By the time they break that door, you'll both be dead."

"They'll kill you anyway," Chofya said through clenched teeth.

"I'll take that chance."

The next blow would kill her. Kalyi knew it, just as she knew that he'd turn his steel on her next. She grabbed her mother's knitting needles and threw them. They hit Henthas in the arm and clattered harmlessly to the floor.

He looked back at her and laughed, then faced Chofya again, raising his sword.

She grabbed for something again, and this time she found the oil lamp. She threw it as hard as she could, striking him in the back. The glass shattered, the oil soaked his shirt and burst into flame.

Henthas roared and spun toward her, dropping his weapons to flail with both hands at the flames. And rather than retreating from him, Kalyi ran forward, gripping her father's dagger in her fist and pounding the crystal blade—the same blade that had taken her father's life—into her uncle's chest.

Henthas stopped in midstride, his face contorting, his entire body swaying, like some great oak in a harvest storm. Then he toppled forward, falling toward Kalyi as if he meant to crush her beneath his weight.

She scrambled out of the way, sobbing now, wanting only to be away from him. But he merely hit the floor and lay still, the flames still blackening his shirt and flesh.

In the next moment the door crashed open. Several men rushed into the chamber. A few of them bent to attend to Kalyi's mother. Others hurried to smother the fire. One man crossed to Kalyi and knelt before her.

"Are you all right, Your Highness?"

She nodded, crying too hard to speak.

"Did you kill him?"

Again she nodded.

The soldier shook his head, looking at her with awe and admiration. "People will sing of this day. Of you, Your Highness. They may yet keep you as their queen."

Kalyi just stared at him. That was the last thing she wanted.

Chapter Twenty-seven

The Moorlands, Eibithar

Tavis and Grinsa finally met up with the king's company ten leagues north of Domnall. Kearney and his men had made camp on the moors here two days before, awaiting the arrival of the dukes of Curgh and Heneagh, who were to lead their armies to this place before the three forces continued northward toward Galdasten. According to reports from Eibithar's north shore, the Braedon army had made land within the last half turn and after facing little resistance from the army of Galdasten, had marched southward into the heart of the realm.

Javan of Curgh and Welfyl of Heneagh had arrived this very morning, Tavis's father leading a force of just under two thousand men, nearly the entire Curgh army, and Welfyl commanding a force of almost fifteen hundred. Combined with Kearney's warriors, they made a formidable army. The Moorlands appeared to teem with men, their armor and blades gleaming beneath a hazy white sky. Kearney rode among his warriors, his head uncovered, the silver, red, and black baldric of his fathers strapped to his back. Grinsa had to admit that he looked every bit the soldier-king. Unfortunately, the king continued to act the part as well.

Since returning from the Wethy Crown, where Tavis finally avenged Brienne's murder, Grinsa had been determined to prevent this war between the empire and Eibithar. After leaving Glyndwr a second time, the wound to his head healed, he and Tavis had ridden north at a punishing pace. If he could only reach the king before the fighting started, he had thought, he could find a way to dissuade Kearney from making war on the empire's army. Yes, Eibithar had been attacked, and yes, these men of Braedon were an invading force. But Kearney knew of the Weaver. He had seen what the man could do, how brutal he could be in pursuit of his ambitions. Surely so wise a leader would understand that anything he did to weaken the Eandi armies would aid the Weaver's cause.

But though Kearney had welcomed Tavis and the gleaner to his force, inviting them to ride with him at the head of his army, he would not listen when Grinsa argued for peace.

"My realm is under attack, gleaner," he had said more than once. "Harel started this war, not I. But war he will have."

Still Grinsa argued, until Kearney finally told his guards that the gleaner was to be kept at a distance. It wouldn't be long until men of both realms were killing one another, every sword stroke and loosed arrow weakening the courts, making the Weaver's victory that much more certain. Grinsa felt helpless to stop it, and he despaired at what it would mean for the coming war—not this one, between the Eandi armies, but the real conflict, between the renegade Qirsi and all the realms of the Forelands.

The memory of his last encounter with Dusaan jal Kania still preyed on Grinsa's mind, robbing him of his confidence, weakening his resolve. How many times had he told Tavis that he was the only man in the Forelands who could defeat the Weaver? Hadn't he said much the same thing to Kearney during the snows, when he revealed to the king that he, too, was a Weaver? Hadn't he told Keziah and Cresenne that they had the power to drive the Weaver from their dreams, that they had only to take control of their magic and the man couldn't hurt them? And yet, when Dusaan entered his dreams hadn't Grinsa allowed the man to best him, to turn the gleaner's own power to his purposes? If Tavis hadn't called to him, waking him from his slumber, Grinsa would have died, his skull crushed by his own shaping power.

Not so long ago he had wondered if he might be betraying his people by fighting the Weaver's movement. He had imagined himself being remembered as the Carthach of his time, the Qirsi who fought beside Eandi nobles, destroying his people's best hope of escaping the prejudice that still burdened their entire race. But wasn't it just as likely that he wouldn't be remembered at all? If Dusaan could defeat him with such ease once, what was to stop him from doing so again on the battle plains of Galdasten?

He realized now that he had raced northward and argued with the king as he did to keep the Eandi armies from destroying themselves, not because he needed their aid in fighting the Qirsi renegades, but rather because he wanted to keep them strong, so that they could take up the battle when he failed.

He didn't dare give voice to his doubts. Tavis still had faith in Grinsa's ability to defeat the Weaver, and had shown little patience for the gleaner's self-doubt. Keziah was finally taking to heart his insistence that she could guard herself from the Weaver's attacks, should it become necessary.

And despite the king's impatience with his arguments for peace, Kearney had made it clear that he still expected Grinsa to lead their fight against the Qirsi. How could he tell any of them that he expected Dusaan to prevail in their battle, that he didn't even believe the Weaver would have much difficulty killing him?

The gleaner had wrestled with these fears for so long that he was starting to lose patience with himself. Perhaps Tavis was justified in showing him so little sympathy the few times Grinsa did broach the subject. Tavis rode to war having no more assurance than did Grinsa that he would survive. So did the king and his dukes, Keziah, Fotir, and the other ministers. So, too, did every soldier in the King's Guard and the ducal armies. As a Weaver, Grinsa rarely had to fear for his life. Tavis had known such fears nearly every day since Brienne's death. Yet the boy thought of himself as a coward and looked to Grinsa as if he were some sort of hero. Perhaps the time had come for the gleaner to emulate the young lord. He wouldn't have considered such a thing a year ago, but today he saw much to admire in Lord Tavis of Curgh.

"Why are you looking at me that way?" the boy asked.

They were readying their mounts. With the arrival of Javan and Welfyl, Kearney had issued orders for the armies to march at midday. Tavis had spent much of the morning with Xaver MarCullet, his pledged liege man and closest friend, and the companionship seemed to have done him much good. Grinsa and the boy had been living off the land for many turns now, and Tavis's face had become tanned in the sun of the planting season, his hair a lighter shade of brown. His dark scars still showed—they always would—but they seemed to stand out less than once they had, particularly when he smiled.

"I find myself wishing that I had your courage, Tavis," the gleaner told him.

A frown creased the young lord's brow, then was replaced almost immediately by a self-conscious grin. "My courage?" he repeated, turning his attention back to his mount. "You must be confusing me with your horse."

The gleaner laughed. "Not at all. You think too poorly of yourself."

"You're the one wishing for my bravery, gleaner. If either of us needs a better opinion of himself, it's you."

Grinsa shook his head, his smile lingering. "Forget I mentioned it."

They stood in silence for a few moments.

"You're thinking about the Weaver again, aren't you?"

I certainly wish I had your insight. "Yes," Grinsa admitted. "I have been all morning."

"That's good," Tavis said, surprising him. "You should be. You should spend every waking hour thinking about how you're going to defeat him, imagining how your war might go, anticipating his tactics. Hagan always used to say that a strong mind and a shrewd battle plan were the most powerful weapons any swordsman could carry into battle. I find it hard to believe that this is any less true for sorcerers."

"Hagan MarCullet is a wise man. Unfortunately, that's hardly the direction my thoughts have taken."

"You're frightened."

Grinsa looked at him. "Yes."

"I think that's probably a good thing, too." Seeing the expression on the gleaner's face, the young lord said, "I'm serious, Grinsa. I was terrified before my fight with the assassin. Both fights, really," he added with a quick smile. "And I'm sure that helped me survive. Fear makes us wary, it makes us think. If you weren't afraid riding to this war, I'd be worried for all of us."

For some time Grinsa said nothing, until eventually Tavis glanced his way.

"Maybe I'm wrong," the boy said. "Probably I am. I was lucky to live through my second encounter with Cadel. It's possible I was too scared. Or just too weak."

"I don't think you're wrong, Tavis. I'm just thinking that maybe I should be wishing for your wisdom, rather than your courage."

"I think you should stop wishing at all, and just accept your strengths and your limitations for what they are." Tavis cast a quick look at the gleaner, smiling once more. "I learned that from you."

"And here I thought you weren't even listening."

When they had finished readying their horses, Tavis climbed into his saddle.

"Do you mind if we ride with my father? I'd like more time with Xaver."

Actually, Grinsa had also been looking forward to riding with the men of Curgh. Keziah rode at the rear of Kearney's army, still trying to convince all who saw her that she had fallen out of favor with the king. It would have been inappropriate for Grinsa to ride with her. Instead, he wished to speak with Fotir jal Salene, Javan's first minister. First, though, there was something else he needed to do.

"That's fine," said. "But before we ride, I want to reach for Cresenne. It's been some time now."

Tavis nodded. "Of course. Catch up with us when you can."

The young lord rode off toward the banners of his house, leaving Grinsa alone, or as close to alone as a man could be amid six thousand Eandi soldiers. Still, he led his mount even farther from the warriors, stopping by the banks of a small stream that flowed past the army camp. There, he sat on the grasses beside the glimmering waters, closed his eyes, and sent his mind southward toward the City of Kings. He quickly found Cresenne and stepped into her dreams, summoning the familiar vision of the plain near Eardley.

An instant later, she stood before him, though some distance away. He sensed immediately that she was warding herself, expecting at any moment to be attacked.

"Cresenne?"

"Grinsa!" She ran to him, throwing her arms around him and pressing her face to his chest, her body racked by sobs.

"What's happened?" he asked, his throat so tight he could barely breathe. When she didn't answer, he tried to look at her face. "Cresenne?"

"Just hold me."

"Let me see you."

"Not yet."

He found that he was shaking, though whether from apprehension at what she might tell him, or rage at the Weaver for whatever new atrocity the man had committed, he couldn't say for certain. At last, unable to wait any longer, he put his hands on her shoulders and gently forced her to take a step back.

One side of her face bore a newly healed burn and he could see the faint remnants of several bruises. Whoever had tended her wounds had done so with great skill and care. Yet even the touch of healing magic couldn't hide the gauntness of her cheeks, or the unhealthy sallow color of her skin, which made her old scars appear more stark than Grinsa remembered from the last time he walked in her dreams.

I should never have left you. I should be by your side now.

"Tell me what happened," the gleaner said, struggling to keep from being overwhelmed by his grief.

"I was poisoned."

Grinsa frowned. "Poisoned?" That was the last thing he had expected her to say.

"Yes. One of the castle's healers gave me a tonic that had nightshade in it."

"A Qirsi healer?"

She nodded. "A man named Lenvyd jal Qosten."

The name meant nothing to him. "Have they questioned him? Do they know what else he's done for the Weaver?"

"He got away. By the time the master healer learned what had happened, Lenvyd had long since fled."

He stroked her cheek with the back of his hand, feeling a tear roll down his face. "How bad was it?"

Cresenne shrugged, looking away. "I was unconscious for three days."

"Three days!" he whispered, pulling her to him again. "Damn him!"

They stood that way for some time until at last, Cresenne stepped back, her face damp with fresh tears.

"Is Bryntelle all right?"

She nodded, smiling faintly. "Yes, she's fine. She's beautiful. I wish you could see her."

"So do I. I'm so sorry I'm not there with you. I'm so sorry I let this—"

She held a finger to his lips, shaking her head. "Don't. None of this is your doing."

"Wait," Grinsa said narrowing his eyes. How could it have taken him so long to realize what she had told him? He felt addled, as if he were the one dreaming. "You said a healer did this to you. Why did you need a healer?" He examined her wounds a second time. "Did he also heal that burn and the bruises?"

She averted her gaze. "No. That was another healer."

"The Weaver attacked you again?"

Cresenne nodded, crying once more.

"He burned you?"

"Yes," she said, so softly it might have been the wind.

"And he hit you?"

"Please don't ask me anymore, Grinsa."

"He tortured you, didn't he?"

"He did nothing to me that I couldn't heal."

"That *you* couldn't heal . . ." He swallowed, feeling ill. "Cresenne, did he—"

She closed her eyes, shaking her head. "Please don't," she whispered.

I'm going to kill him. He didn't say it aloud, knowing how fatuous it would sound, how much like the empty, vengeful oath of a man consumed with his own vanity. But those were the words that repeated themselves again and again in his mind. *I'm going to kill him.*

Once again, he took her in his arms, his hands shaking with fury and bloodlust.

"He called me your whore," she said quietly. "And then he said he was going to make me his whore, too."

"But you're alive."

She looked at him, pride in her pale eyes. "Yes. I finally grasped what you'd been trying to tell me about taking control of my own magic. I couldn't do it in time to . . . to stop him. But I managed to wake myself before he could kill me."

Grinsa smiled. "That's very nearly more than I did."

"What?" she said, frowning.

"It's not important. What matters is, you defeated him."

"Hardly."

"You did, Cresenne. He wants you dead. Whatever else he

took from you, he couldn't kill you. And that means that you won."

"I saw him strike at me with a dagger. I felt the blade in my heart. But when I looked at the wound, the skin healed itself."

"You see?" the gleaner said, so proud of her that he thought he might weep. "He must have been horrified."

"He was."

Grinsa kissed her brow. "You've nothing to fear from him anymore. He may send others to kill you, men like the healer. But you can sleep in peace."

"I've tried. I can't."

"But—"

"I know that I should be able to. As you say, if I can drive him from my dreams, I have no reason to fear him. I could even go back to sleeping at night again. I'm still afraid, though. I think of . . . of what he did to me, of how close Bryntelle came to losing me forever, and it's all I can do to close my eyes at midmorning."

"It'll take some time, Cresenne. But eventually you'll find peace."

"Not until he's dead. You have to kill him, Grinsa. I know that you want to—more than ever, no doubt, having heard all of this. And I'm telling you, that's what you have to do. For me, for Bryntelle, for Keziah. I don't know how I ever could have been so blind as to follow him, to do all those terrible things on his behalf. But I realize now that the Forelands won't be safe until he's dead."

"The Forelands will be safe," he said. "You have my word." He kissed her softly on the lips. "You should sleep. And when you wake, you need to eat something. You look so thin."

Cresenne twisted her mouth sourly. "I haven't been able to eat since I was poisoned."

"You have to. Bryntelle needs you to be strong."

"I know. I'll try."

He gazed at her, brushing a strand of hair from her face. Even drawn and weary she remained beautiful.

"What is it?" she asked.

"Nothing. I love you."

"And I you. Are you well? Have you recovered from your fall in the highlands?"

"Yes, I'm fine."

"Where are you?"

"On the Moorlands, north of Domnall. We're with Kearney."

She nodded, crossing her arms, as if suddenly cold. "Has the Braedon army landed yet?"

"Yes. They march toward us even as we speak."

"Gods keep you safe."

"And you." He kissed her one last time, then opened his eyes to the hazy brightness of the moors.

Taking a long, shuddering breath, he stood and started leading his mount back to where the armies were gathering in formation. He should have been relieved. Despite being brutalized, despite the fact that she had very nearly died, Cresenne had found the strength to defend herself from the Weaver's attacks. But any comfort he drew from this was overmastered by his lingering fears and his remorse. If only he hadn't left her. . . .

"How is she?" Tavis asked, when Grinsa found him.

The gleaner shrugged. "Considering all she's been through, she's doing well." Seeing the puzzlement on the young lord's face, he explained, "The Weaver attacked her again, and then she was poisoned by one of the healers in Audun's Castle."

"Demons and fire! She survived all that?"

"I find it hard to believe, too."

"Is Bryntelle all right?"

Grinsa smiled. "Yes, thank you. She's fine."

"Gods be praised for that."

"Indeed."

The gleaner glanced southward, grappling with a sudden urge to ride back to the City of Kings.

"You can do more for her by fighting this war than you ever could in Audun's Castle."

He looked at the boy, nodded. "I know. So does she."

A short time later, the armies resumed their march toward Galdasten. Tavis and Xaver rode just ahead of him, speaking in quiet voices and laughing occasionally. Fotir rode beside him, but Grinsa couldn't bring himself to start a conversation, and the minister seemed content to ride in silence.

During what remained of the day, the armies marched without rest past villages and farms. And at every cluster of homes, every lone farmhouse that rose from the earth, people came out to stare at the warriors, with their shining weapons and dull grey coats of mail. Some of the children cheered, no doubt thinking it all a grand game. But their parents just watched, apprehensive and silent.

Sitting atop his mount at the head of such a vast force, Grinsa couldn't help but wonder if the people he saw knew of the storm that menaced their land. Surely they had heard of the threats from Braedon and Aneira, but did they understand the greater danger they faced? A part of him wanted to stop and warn them of this Weaver, this Dusaan jal Kania, who was poised to make himself sovereign over all the Forelands. Everyone in the seven realms needed to know, Eandi and Qirsi alike.

But if Kearney wouldn't listen to him, why should these simple folk?

"We both have our wars to fight, gleaner," the king had told him the night before. "Mine is with the empire. Yours is with the Weaver. I'll offer you whatever aid I can, and I'll ask no less of you. But both wars must be fought and won, or else Eibithar is doomed."

At the time, hearing Kearney speak so, Grinsa had grown angry and stalked off. Perhaps the king was right, though. The gleaner had claimed this war as his own long ago. He might have been brazen and foolish to do so, but that changed nothing.

The time for self-doubt had passed. He knew that at last, thanks to Cresenne and Tavis. Would he have liked to be stronger? Would he have taken comfort in some divine assurance that he would prevail against this foe? Of course. What warrior didn't wish for such things on the eve of battle? Somewhere to the north, Dusaan might well have been wishing for them as well.

"If the Weaver wasn't afraid of you," Tavis had said that

night half a turn ago, when Dusaan attacked him, "he wouldn't have entered your dreams."

Grinsa had doubted this at the time, but now he saw that he had no choice but to believe it. For all of Dusaan's confidence, the Weaver had to harbor doubts of his own. There could be no certainty in this coming conflict, no assurances for anyone, not even for the high chancellor. How could it be otherwise?

This was to be a war between Weavers. In all its long history, the Forelands had never witnessed such a thing.

Here's a sneak peek at

Weavers of War

by DAVID B. COE

The concluding volume of

Winds of the Forelands

Turn the page for a preview

She awoke to the sound of swifts chattering as they soared past the narrow window of her chamber. Bryntelle still slept in her cradle, her arms stretched over her head, her mouth making suckling movements. Cresenne sat up, taking a long breath and running both hands through her hair. Grinsa deserved better from her. He carried the burdens of every man and woman of the Forelands on his shoulders, and all she could think to do was tell him what he already knew: that in order to be whole again she needed for him to destroy the Weaver.

Her wounds had healed, and in recent days she had finally begun to eat again, slowly regaining her strength after the poisoning that almost killed her. But the Weaver had left her with other scars that remained beyond a healer's touch. True, she had managed to fight Dusaan off and then to end that horrific dream before he could take her life, but the memory of the rape clung to her bed, her hair, her body—the stench of his breath, hot and damp against her neck. She could still feel him driving himself into her again and again, tearing her flesh, his weight bearing down on her until she wondered if she could even draw breath. She could hear him calling her "whore." It had only been a dream, she tried to tell herself, an illusion he had conjured by using her own magic against her. But did that lessen the humiliation or deepen it? It had been a violation in so many ways and on so many levels. Did his invasion of her mind make what he seemed to have done to her body any less real?

She feared that she might never again be able to bear

Grinsa's touch. The Weaver had poisoned all of her dreams, even those in which her love spoke to her. Grinsa's merest kiss when he walked in her sleep, his most gentle caress, made her feel once more the savagery of Dusaan's assault. Cresenne wanted desperately to believe that it was the dreams that did this, that once she and Grinsa were together again, and he could hold her in his arms without touching her mind, everything would be all right. But she had no way of knowing this for certain, and doubt lay heavy on her heart.

Grinsa would have told her to sleep more. The sun would be up for several hours yet, and since she still didn't dare sleep at night, for fear of another attack from the Weaver, she wouldn't have another opportunity to rest for quite some time. But she was awake now, and she knew herself well enough to know that she could lie on her bed from now until dusk, and she wouldn't get back to sleep. Instead, she stared out the window and waited for Bryntelle to wake, knowing that the baby would be hungry when she did.

She didn't have long to wait. After nursing Bryntelle and changing her wet swaddling, Cresenne took her daughter in her arms and left their small chamber to wander the grounds of Audun's Castle. It was a rare treat for them to be out of doors during the daylight hours; Cresenne savored the warm touch of the sun on her skin, and the mild breeze that stirred her hair. Bryntelle seemed to enjoy the day as well. She squinted up at the sun repeatedly and squealed happily at the sight of clove-pink and irises blooming brightly in the gardens.

One of the advantages of wandering the castle at night was that Cresenne rarely found herself in the company of others. She had no desire to make conversation with ladies in the queen's court, and she dreaded being recognized as the "Qirsi traitor." Nurle, the young healer who saw her through the poisoning, occasionally joined her after tending to patients during the course of the night, but mostly she and Bryntelle kept to themselves. On this day, however, there were several people walking the castle grounds, and though Cresenne was loath to return to her chamber, she dreaded the thought of being among other people, particularly since everyone she saw was Eandi.

Hesitating, yet eager to find some way to enjoy this day without having to endure the stares of all these people, Cresenne ducked into a small courtyard off one of the main paths that meandered through the garden.

She knew immediately that she had erred. Cresenne had seen Leilia of Glyndwr, Eibithar's queen, only once before, but she recognized the woman immediately. The queen was seated on a small marble bench in the middle of the courtyard. Sunlight angled across her face, making her skin look pale and thick. Her black hair was tied up in a tight bun, and the dress she wore appeared so tight around the bust that Cresenne found it hard to imagine that she could be comfortable. Several of the queen's ladies stood around her, chatting amiably, and four guards stood at attention nearby.

Cresennne had every intention of leaving the courtyard, but at that moment Bryntelle let out a small cry, drawing the stares of every person there. The guards turned toward her, glowering, and the ladies regarded her with frowns and pursed lips.

"Forgive me," she muttered, not entirely certain that they could even hear her. "I didn't know there was anyone here." She curtsied quickly and started to leave.

"You there! Wait a moment!"

Cresenne turned back to them. Leilia was eyeing her with obvious interest, though there was no warmth in her expression.

"Yes, Your Highness," Cresenne said, curtsying again.

For a moment she wondered if the queen expected her to approach, but then Leilia stood, and as the guards rushed to her side the queen began to walk toward her. Leilia paused, regarded them with obvious disdain, and waved a hand, seeming to dismiss them. One of the men said something to her in a low voice, but she merely glared at him until he bowed and backed away. Then she started toward Cresenne again.

Bryntelle had begun to make a good deal of noise—she wasn't crying, fortunately, nor did she seem particularly unhappy. But she certainly was being loud. Leilia glanced at the babe as she drew near, but only for a moment. Mostly, she kept her dark eyes fixed on Cresenne.

"They tell me that you're the renegade," the queen said, stopping just in front of Cresenne, and gesturing vaguely at the soldiers behind her. "The one who had Brienne killed. Is this true?"

Cresenne stared at the ground before her, her cheeks burning. A thousand replies sprang to her lips, any one of which would have earned her a summary hanging. In the end, she merely muttered, "Yes, Your Highness."

"They also warn me that you might make an attempt on my life. Is that your intent?"

"No, Your Highness."

"Good. Walk with me."

Leilia stepped out of the courtyard, and turned toward the north corner of the gardens, leaving Cresenne little choice but to follow. Emerging from the courtyard, she found Leilia waiting for her a few strides away, an arch look on her face.

"Well?" the queen said. "Aren't you coming?"

"Yes, of course, Your Highness. Forgive me."

But even after Cresenne reached her, the queen didn't resume her walking, at least not immediately. Instead, she regarded Cresenne's face critically, as if examining a new piece of art. It took Cresenne but a second to realize that Leilia was staring at her scars. She had to resist an urge to stomp off.

"You've healed well."

"Thank you, Your Highness."

"I can see why some think you pretty."

"Do they, Your Highness?"

Leilia began to walk again, sniffing loudly. "Come now, my dear. Let's not be coy. I'm certain that you've had no shortage of men in your life. Certainly, Eandi men seem fascinated by your kind."

Something in the way the queen said this caught her ear. As she hurried to keep up with the woman, Cresenne remembered that during her many conversations with Keziah ja Dafydd, Eibithar's archminister, she had found herself speculating about Keziah's relationships with both Grinsa and

Kearney, the king. On several occasions she had wondered if one of the men might have been Keziah's lover. The same thought came to her now. Leilia sounded very much the wounded wife, though clearly she had no cause to be jealous of Cresenne.

"Silenced you, have I?" the queen said, glancing at her sidelong.

"Have I given offense in some way, Your Highness? Is that why you wished to speak with me?"

That, of all things, brought a smile to Leilia's lips, though it was fleeting. "No. You haven't given offense. I've been . . . curious about you."

"I see."

"Do you?"

"I've been a curiosity since I arrived here, Your Highness."

"Yes, I'm sure you have. Is that why you spend your days in your chamber and your nights wandering the castle corridors?"

She thought the queen a strange women. Her directness was both disconcerting and refreshing, and while Cresenne thought it best to keep her replies circumspect, she sensed that Leilia would not have taken offense had she chosen to be more candid.

"Actually, Your Highness, I sleep during the day to avoid the Weaver who attacks me in my dreams."

"I'd heard that, but I wondered if there were other reasons as well."

Cresenne said nothing.

"The child doesn't seem to mind?"

"She's hardly known any other way to live."

Leilia nodded, and they walked in silence for several moments, Cresenne gazing at a bed of brilliant ruby peonies.

"Tell me of the child's father," the queen said abruptly.

Cresenne made herself smile, sensing that their conversation had taken a perilous turn. "Her father, Your Highness?"

"Yes. This tall Qirsi who's been the subject of so much talk throughout the castle."

"I didn't know that people were speaking of him."

"Shouldn't they? He's little more than a Revel gleaner, yet

he was Tavis of Curgh's lone confidant over the last year, and my husband thinks highly enough of him to include him in councils of war. Doesn't that strike you as odd?"

"Grinsa is a wise man, Your Highness, as I'm sure Lord Tavis will attest. I've no doubt that he'll serve the king well."

"I'm not questioning his worth, my dear. I'm merely asking you to tell me more about him. And I sense your reluctance."

"I'm not—"

"Don't dissemble with me." Leilia glanced at her again, as if gauging Cresennne's reaction. "Is he a traitor? Is that it? Have you both contrived this elaborate farce to gain Kearney's trust?"

"No, Your Highness! I swear it! Grinsa's no traitor!"

Again, the queen smiled. "I believe you. You love him very much."

Cresenne nodded, afraid to speak. She had come close to losing him so many times, all of them her own fault. She had betrayed him, sent assassins for him, and nearly driven him away with her stubborn, foolish devotion to the Weaver and his movement. And she knew that she might lose him still. Or he her. Who could say whether he would survive the fighting between the Eandi armies, much less his inevitable encounter with Dusaan? Who knew how many more of the Weaver's servants had been sent to kill her?

"You fear for him."

"I fear for all of us, Your Highness. I've seen how wicked this Weaver is, though I was blind to it for too long."

"Kearney will find a way to prevail." The corners of her mouth twitched. "He always does." When Cresenne didn't respond, the queen looked at her again. "War is hardest on the women, you know. It's always been so, though men will deny it. Remaining behind, awaiting the outcome, fearing that the next messenger will bear word that your husband or lover or brother has fallen." She gazed up at the sky, as if to judge the time. "I envy the women of Sanbira, who fight their own battles alongside the men. Their way strikes me as being far more just."

"Yes, Your Highness."

"You're humoring me." She wore a smirk on her fleshy face.

"No, Your Highness! I was just—"

"It's all right, my dear. I suppose I deserve it. I find it easy to complain here, safe behind Audun's walls. But given the opportunity to ride to war, I'm not at all certain that I would." She frowned. "Does that make me a coward?"

"I believe it makes you honest, Your Highness."

About the Author

DAVID B. COE, the author of seven epic fantasy novels, won the Crawford Award for Best First Fantasy for *Children of Amarid* and *The Outlanders,* the first two books of his LonTobyn trilogy. His Winds of the Forelands series, which includes *Rules of Ascension, Seeds of Betrayal,* and *Bonds of Vengeance,* will conclude with *Weavers of War*. He lives with his wife and their two daughters on the Cumberland Plateau in Tennessee.